6

FULL-LENGTH PLAYS

VOLUME TWO

by
Edward Crosby Wells

CONTENTS

To Ronald L. Perkins
for the journey of a lifetime.

BY THE AUTHOR

PLAYS (Full Length)
3 Guys in Drag Selling Their Stuff
A Baker's Dozen (short play collection)
Desert Devils
Flowers Out Of Season
In The Venus Arms
Poet's Wake
Streets of Old New York (Musical)
Tales of Darkest Suburbia
The Moon Away
The Proctologist's Daughter
Thor's Day
Wait A Minute!
West Texas MassacrePLAYS (30 to 60 minutes)
20th Century Sketches
Empire (40-minutes)
Slow Boat to China (30-minutes)
Tough Cookies (60-minutes)

PLAYS (under 30-minutes)
21 Today (monologue)
Civil Unionized
Cornered
Dick and Jane Meet Barry Manilow
Harry the Chair
Leaving Tampa
Missing Baggage
Next
Pedaling to Paradise
Pink Gin for the Blues (monologue)
Road Kill
Samson and Delilah
Sisters of Little Mercy
Slow Boat to China
Vampyre Holiday

Whiskers

COLLECTIONS
A Baker's Dozen
19 One-Acts, Monologs & Short Plays
6 Full-Length Plays, Volume ONE
6 Full-Length Plays, Volume TWO

SCREENPLAY
Road Kill

6 FULL-LENGTH PLAYS
VOLUME TWO

Edward Crosby Wells

THE PLAYWRIGHT ON THE PLAYS

After writing a brief autobiography that led to the writing of my first play, *In the Venus Arms,* I find it difficult writing another forward without repeating what was written in volume one of this collection. When and where and the time I was born seems inconsequential and a waste of precious time in the reading and in the writing. I spare you that.

The first play in this volume was a commission to write an updated adaptation of the 1857 drama, *The Poor of New York,* by Dion Boucicault. *The Poor of New York* (produced subsequently under many titles, including *The Poor of Liverpool* and *The Poor of London*) was first staged in New York City, and subsequently in London (1857), and Liverpool (1864). It was actually an adaptation of Eugène Nus and Édouard Brisebarre's *Les Pauvres de Paris* (Paris, 1856). Wow. That's quite a bit of history. When I got my hands on it, more than 150 years later, the original drama morphed into a boo-and-cheer sing-along musical-melodrama set in the 1890s. Sure to please all ages, this play is about greed, murder, revenge, thievery, them-that-have and them-that-don't, showgirls, good girls and bad girls, burning buildings, villains and heroes—all the ingredients for good wholesome fun for the entire family! *Streets*....was a fun play to work on. Though the dialog was all there in the original script to begin with, I used it merely as a skeletal outline for this loosely based update—with apologies to Eugène Nus, Édouard Brisebarre. and Dion Boucicault if I have strayed too far from their original intent. Although I do not think I have. *Streets of Old New York, a musical melodrama* premiered in 2004 at the Iridium Jazz Club, Broadway and 51st St. in New York City.

While spending Memorial day in Georgetown, Colorado I saw a sign in someone's front yard on our way to a bar-b-que picnic in the park. That sign read, "the last yard sale." What a nifty title for a skit or short play. That night I began work on it. At twenty minutes of running-time I stopped. It was fabulously performed by 3 women in a retirement home in Denver, Colorado. In time it grew to about 40 minutes—just short of a decent one-act. After sharing it with Frank Calo, a producer/director in NYC, he decided to produce it if I could get it up to a full-length play. So, after several months of development, the play soon grew to nearly 2 hours. After further development it was produced by Spotlight On Productions and premiered as *3 Guys In Drag Selling Their Stuff* at the Raw Space Theatre in NYC on January 20, 2000.under the direction of Frank Calo. This crazy comedy about 3 guys in drag having a yard sale has had 40 plus productions worldwide as of this writing. It is not my favorite play, but certainly my most successful.

The 3rd play in this collection is an intense 90 minute thriller titled *Thor's Day*. Philip Winter, a middle-aged insurance salesman, brings home a gorgeous young man, Buck Rose, for an afternoon tryst. Their encounter is fraught with pleasure and danger as the clock ticks down to an explosive and unexpected climax. Perhaps possessed with supernatural powers, Buck takes Philip on a breathtaking, life-altering journey into the unexplored territory of his long-suppressed and hidden desires. *"Intelligent, erotic, powerful, provocative and terrifying, this thriller is sure to keep an audience on the edge of its seat,"* raved one NYC critic. *Thor's Day* was first presented by Tony Award winning The Glines at the Trilogy Theatre, 341 W. 44th St., New York City, April 30, 1997, under the direction of Steven E. Thornburg. *Thor's Day* eventually made its way to downtown Manhattan and ran at the Wings Theatre Company on Christopher Street.

Wait A Minute! is a fun-packed collection of 30 witty, smart, laugh-out-loud skits—and all with twists and surprise endings. The skits range from 1 to 5 minutes each to create a full evening's entertainment. I wrote these skits as exercises while waiting for my Muse to come with a great idea for a new full-length play. Eventually, I had written enough of these fun exercises to create *Wait A Minute!* Hey, if you don't like the skit you're watching, wait a minute and there will be another.

Tales from Darkest Suburbia is black comedy constructed in six interconnected tales—each complete in themselves—that explore the typical quirks associated with American Suburbia: murder, adultery, blackmail, kidnapping, cutthroat art critics, devious financial advisors, cannibalism, back-stabbing divas, flesh eating perfume, Tallulah Bankhead and the nature of reality. This play premiered at the Riverfront Playhouse in Aurora, IL where it opened on March 20, 2009 under the direction of Shawn Dooley. When the play made it's way to Europe, David Muncaster of "Amateur Stage Magazine" in the U.K. wrote: *"Tales from Darkest Suburbia is a remarkable achievement. Although each story works very well on its own and could be presented independently as a short play; as a complete piece it comes together very well, is most satisfying and very funny."*

The final play in this collection is *Poet's Wake.* At the time of this writing, it is yet to be produced. The play is set at the wake of a Poet Laureate. Mourners come and go, delivering monologues. We learn, through the mourners, about the life of the poet and about the mourners themselves. Some define us by the people in our lives. The life of the celebrity after death is too often defined by those who are left behind—enemies, friends, competitors, lovers, critics and academics; some have axes to grind; some speak out of ignorance. Although each may believe they are telling the truth, it is the teller's truth—truth is subjective. The artist's work is too often overshadowed by the tales and the writings of the survivors. In the end we must discover, uncover or simply choose to decide the truth for and/or of ourselves. The truth of others and the truth of oneself is, perhaps, merely a matter of perception. I love this play!

Please note that all plays are in the order in which they were originally written.

ECW 2020

STREETS OF
OLD NEW YORK

(A musical melodrama)

THE SCENES

ACT ONE:

Scene 1 — The bank office of Gideon Bloodgood.

Scene 2 — Twenty years later. A bench in a park.

Scene 3 — Exterior of Bloodgood's Bank, Nassau Street

Scene 4 — Olio.

Scene 5 — The humble dining room of the Fairweather family.

Scene 6 — Olio.

Scene 7 — The drawing room of the Bloodgood home.

ACT TWO:

Scene 1 — Olio.

Scene 2 — The drawing room of the Bloodgood home.

Scene 3 — Outside the Astor mansion on 5th Avenue.

Scene 4 — Adjoining attic rooms in a tenement on Cross Street in the slums of Five Points.

Scene 5 — The Fairweather's old cottage in Brooklyn Heights.

Scene 6 — Outside the Cross Street tenement house.

Scene 7 — Olio

Scene 8 — The drawing room of the Bloodgood home.

"A musical melodrama set in the late 19th century, Streets of Old New York is a piece of old fashioned "throw popcorn at the villain" type of entertainment. The audience more than enjoyed this play; they howled with laughter! The music was all of the period and surprisingly stands the test of time. Mr. Wells wrote a gem of a piece that takes you back to the old Penelope Pitstop on the train track days and yet still writes in a way that anybody from the 21st century can enjoy and understand. A smart producer should pick this piece up for an extended Broadway run. It could bring back fun and innocence to Broadway as well as have a long life in community theatres and the school circuit."
—NYC STAGE PAGES, July 2004

Streets of Old New York, produced by Spotlight On and Arthur Pomposello, premiered at Iridium Jazz Club, 1650 Broadway, NYC on April 24, 2004 with the following cast:

DUF: Chuck Bunting
BLOODGOOD: Ken Bachtold
BADGER: J. Dolan Byrnes
CAPTAIN FAIRWEATHER: Nathanael Reimer
MARK LIVINGSTONE: Patrick O'Hare
MR. PUFFY: Knox Bundy
PAUL FAIRWEATHER: Nathanael Reimer
MRS. FAIRWEATHER: Teresa Fischer
ALIDA BLOODGOOD: Nicole Cicchella
LUCY FAIRWEATHER: Cameron Peterson
Director: Frank Calo
Musical Director: Martin St. Lawrence

SONGS*

"Sidewalks of New York" (ACT I, Scene 1 — ENTIRE CAST)
"Some Sweet Day" (ACT 1, Scene 1 — BLOODGOOD & BADGER)
"The Fountain in the Park" (ACT I, Scene 2 — ENSEMBLE)
"The Bowery" (ACT I, Scene 2 — ENSEMBLE)
"Meet Me Tonight in Dreamland" (ACT I, Scene 4 — LUCY FAIRWEATHER)
"Streets of Cairo" (ACT I, Scene 6 — ALIDA)
"The Man Who Broke the Bank at Monte Carlo" (ACT I, Scene 7 — BLOODGOOD)
"Give My Regards to Broadway" (ACT II, Scene 1 — ENTIRE CAST)
"Let Me Call You Sweetheart" (ACT II, Scene 2 — LIVINGSTONE & LUCY)
"Hello, Ma Baby" (ACT II, Scene 3 — BADGER)
"After the Ball is Over" (ACT II, Scene 3 — MRS. FAIRWEATHER)
"After the Ball is Over" (Reprise) (ACT II, Scene 3 — PAUL)
"You're a Grand Old Flag" (ACT II, Scene 5 — ENSEMBLE)
"Let Me Call You Sweetheart" (Reprise) (ACT II, Scene 5 — LIVINGSTONE & LUCY)
"Ta-ra-ra Boom-de-ay" (ACT II, Scene 7 — ALIDA)
"America the Beautiful, Medley" (ACT II, Scene 8 — ENTIRE CAST)

IMPORTANT NOTE: The songs included in this text are, as of the date of this writing, in public domain.* Therefore, neither royalties nor permission is needed to perform them in the sing-along portions of this play. Sheet music is easily obtained. Since music and/or lyrics copyrights can be re-established, it is strongly advised that the producing agent perform follow-up research. Should any copyrights be re-established and infringed upon, the playwright will not be held liable.

DRAMATIST PERSONAE (in order of appearance)
6M/3W (optional townspeople)

DUF: A beggar in the streets of New York. He is dressed in rags, a high hat, and gloves with the fingers missing. He describes the setting, the time and the place—and leads the audience in sing-along. He has the ability to stop the action of the play and freeze it into a tableau. He is also expected to perform a limited amount of ad lib while prompting the audience into hissing and booing, etc.

BLOODGOOD: A banker. Evil through and through.

BADGER: A bank clerk, gone astray.

CAPTAIN FAIRWEATHER: An ancient mariner. To be doubled by the actor playing Paul Fairweather.

MARK LIVINGSTONE: A young hero, fallen on hard times.

MR. PUFFY: A Baker, short of dough.

PAUL FAIRWEATHER: Tenant of Mr. Puffy. He lives on the second floor with his mother and sister.

MRS. FAIRWEATHER: Mother of Paul and Lucy.

ALIDA BLOODGOOD: Gideon's social-climbing daughter. She is a VAP (Villainess American Princess).

LUCY FAIRWEATHER: The ingénue. Mark Livingstone's love-interest.

THE TIME: Act One, Scene 1 takes place in the late 1870's. The remainder of the play takes place in the 1890s.

THE SETTING: Can be as simple as a backdrop depicting the late 19th century skyline of New York City. Also an area for projecting the lyrics to the songs would be a nice touch; however, printing the lyrics in the programs or on flyers to hand out to the audience would suffice.

6 FULL-LENGTH PLAYS
VOLUME TWO

Edward Crosby Wells

ACT ONE — *Scene 1*
The bank office of Gideon Bloodgood.

DUF: Welcome to the streets of old New York. Our play is set near the end of the 19th Century. A time when there were villains to hiss and boo at and heroes and heroines to cheer for. A time when there were songs to sing, and everybody sang them. Tonight, we invite you to join in our revelry by hissing and booing, throwing popcorn and peanuts, but most of all, to sing along with us!

(ENTIRE CAST fills the stage and EXTRAS if any.)

DUF: *(Con't)* Are you ready? I said, are you ready? Then, let's warm up those vocal cords.

(ALL: *(Sing.)* SIDEWALKS OF NEW YORK
Lyrics: James W. Blake and Charles E. Lawlor
Music: James W. Blake and Charles E. Lawlor)

East Side, West Side, all around the town
The kids sang "ring around rosie", "London Bridge is falling down"
Boys and girls together, me and Mamie O'Rourke
We tripped the light fantastic on the sidewalks of New York

East Side, West Side, all around the town
Sweet Mamie grew up and bough herself a sweet little Alice-blue gown
All the fellas dug her, you should have heard them squark
When I escorted Mamie round the sidewalks of New York

East Side, West Side, riding through the parks
We started swinging at Jilly's then we split to P.J.Clark's
On to Chuck's Composite, then a drink at The Stork

We won't get home until morning 'cause we're going to take a walk
On the sidewalks of New York

(ALL exit except DUF.)

DUF: They call me Duf. I was raised by pirates, until I escaped the Black Barnacle—a ship of thieves and cutthroats sailing under the jolly roger. I washed ashore down where the Hudson spills into the mighty Atlantic. I was a mere scalawag of a tadpole. I came to Five Points and begged for my daily bread and I've been a beggar ever since. I knows my name is Duf 'cause it's printed right here. *(Holding out medal that hangs on a chain around his neck.)* D-U-F, Duf, that's m' name—Duf the beggar. *(Pause to survey the audience.)* Now, what would a melodrama be without a villain? Meet our villain. As mean a villain as you ever want to meet!

(GIDEON BLOODGOOD enters and takes his position onstage. DUF holds out his hand in BLOODGOOD's direction.)

DUF: *(Con't.)* Please, sir, can you spare poor ol' Duf the beggar a penny or two? *(No response.)* Thought not. *(A beat.)* This is Gideon Bloodgood. But his blood is bad, very bad, as you will soon find out. He owns the Bloodgood Bank of New York. He is in his office and you are about to witness his unholy treachery as he performs his dastardly deeds.

BLOODGOOD: *(Unfreezes. Reads from sheet of paper and then suddenly crumples it within his mean and angry hands.)* As I expected! Every stock is down, and my last effort to retrieve my fortune has plunged me into utter ruin. The Bloodgood Bank is officially bankrupt. But, the money's in my pocket and in my pocket it stays. *Ha, ha, ha.*

DUF: This would be a good time to boo. *(Leads the audience into booing.)* Boo-o-o . . .

BADGER: *(Enters.)* Mr. Bloodgood, sir.

BLOODGOOD: Can you not see that I am busy, Badger?

BADGER: Sir, the building committee of St. Peter's new church has come for the donation you promised them. They'd like a thousand dollars.

BLOODGOOD: Tell them to come back tomorrow and lock the doors! It is past banking hours.

(BADGER exits.)

BLOODGOOD: *(Con't.)* Tomorrow my daughter and I will be safe on board a ship bound for Liverpool. My dear little girl, my beautiful Alida will be safe from the troubles and wants of the poor out there on the streets of New York.

BADGER: *(Enters.)* The committee people will return tomorrow, sir.

BLOODGOOD: Don't you ever knock?

BADGER: Knock, sir?

DUF: Oh, excuse me. *Knock, knock!*

BLOODGOOD: Who's there?

BADGER: It's me, your head clerk.

BLOODGOOD: Why are you still shilly-shallying around after business hours?

BADGER: I've discovered a few problems with your accounting.

BLOODGOOD: My accounting?

BADGER: The books. They are cooked, sir—like a goose on Christmas.

BLOODGOOD: My goose?

BADGER: *Yup.* Your goose is cooked, sir!

BLOODGOOD: Have you told anybody about this, Badger?

BADGER: Not a soul. But, I have taken the liberty of leaving a letter to be opened just in case I should go missing . . . or something. For more than two years I have carefully watched your business transactions.   When you thought me idle, my hands were everywhere . . . in your books, in your safe, in your vaults, in places I won't even mention. If you doubt me question me about your operations for the last three months.

BLOODGOOD: This is treachery! You are despicable!

BADGER: Thank you, sir. Good to know, sir. By the way, there is an old seafaring gentleman in the lobby waiting for a receipt to be written in your hand for a deposit in the sum of one hundred thousand dollars. His name is Captain Fairweather. He is in the India Trade.

BLOODGOOD: One hundred thousand dollars! *One hundred thousand dollars! Aside.)* With that kind of money I could save the bank and my reputation as well.

BADGER: It is his life's savings and he would like to deposit it before leaving his family over in Brooklyn while he sails for India. He's says he's got a weak ticker, so he'd like to leave his money with us, just in case something happens—if you get my meaning.

BLOODGOOD: Indeed I do. Show the old salt in, Badger.

(BADGER exits.)

BLOODGOOD: *(Con't. Aside.)* This may yet prove a fortuitous Friday the 13th.

(BADGER and FAIRWEATHER enter.)

BADGER: Mr. Bloodgood, this is Captain Fairweather.

BLOODGOOD: *(Jumps towards FAIRWEATHER, shouting.)* Aye, aye, Captain!

CAPTAIN FAIRWEATHER: *(A weak and old sailor.)* Oh! My heart! You startled me, sir. I need to catch my breath. I've a weak, old heart, I have.

BLOODGOOD: Of course you do. Badger here should have warned me.

BADGER: But, I did . . .

BLOODGOOD: *(Cutting BADGER off.)* A good first mate is hard to find, aye?

CAPTAIN FAIRWEATHER: You don't know the half of it, sir.

BLOODGOOD: Perhaps, but the portion I do know causes me to lose many a good night's sleep.

BADGER: *(Aside.)* There is nary a good night's sleep for the wicked.

CAPTAIN FAIRWEATHER: Tomorrow I sail for China. Today I bethought me of your bank. Your name stands beyond suspicion. I would like to deposit one hundred thousand dollars—all the money I have in this world. I can sleep nightly with the happy assurance that whatever happens to me, my dearest ones will be well provided for.

BADGER: *(To the CAPTAIN.)* You may pull your nightcap over your ears and sleep like a baby. *(Aside.)* While Bloodgood pulls the wool over his eyes.

BLOODGOOD: Mr. Badger, would you be so kind as to go about your chores while the good captain and I finish up a bit of business. *(BADGER frowns and exits.)* Now, where were we? Ah, yes. You were about to hand over—make a deposit—of one hundred thousand dollars for safekeeping.

CAPTAIN FAIRWEATHER: Indeed, sir. This money is for the future of my beautiful children, Paul and Lucy. *(Hands over the money.)* I shall require a receipt, sir.

BLOODGOOD: *(Shouting.)* Of course, of course!

CAPTAIN FAIRWEATHER: *(Grabbing his heart.)* You frighten me, sir. Loud and unexpected noises bring me closer to my Creator.

BLOODGOOD: *(Loudly.)* Really? *(Softly.)* I mean, really? Ah, the bosom of the Lord is a comforting place, is it not?

CAPTAIN FAIRWEATHER: Aye, it is, sir.

BLOODGOOD: It certainly is. *(Writing receipt.)* "New York, Friday the 13th of . . . *(Shouts in the CAPTAIN's ear.)* Comfortable?

CAPTAIN FAIRWEATHER: *(Startled.)* Aye-aye. Quite.

BLOODGOOD: Good, good. Where was I?

CAPTAIN FAIRWEATHER: Friday the 13th.

BLOODGOOD: *(Continues writing.)* Indeed. 1878. Received, on special deposit, from—

CAPTAIN FAIRWEATHER: Captain Fairweather, of the good ship Danny Boy, of New York—named after me poor dead son, bless his heart.

BLOODGOOD: Captain Fairweather, of the good ship Danny Boy, of . . . *(Shouting into the CAPTAIN's ear.)* One hundred thousand dollars!

CAPTAIN FAIRWEATHER: *(In pain.)* My heart, sir, my heart . . .

BLOODGOOD: Yes, You have a good heart, sir!

CAPTAIN FAIRWEATHER: No, no . . . my heart is . . . is . . .

BLOODGOOD: *(Still shouting.)* . . . is as big as all Creation! Now I shall stamp your receipt! *(Rubber-stamping the receipt loudly.)* Wait!

CAPTAIN FAIRWEATHER: *(About to pass out.)* What?

BLOODGOOD: I forgot. *(Jumping up and down.)* I forgot to sign it! *(Signs it and puts it into the CAPTAIN's hand.)* THERE! YOUR RECEIPT, SIR! *(Jumping up and down a few more times, attempting to give the CAPTAIN a heart attack. Shortly, the CAPTAIN looks up, startled, and then he keels over, dead. The receipt falls to the floor and BLOODGOOD pockets the money.*

DUF: *(Aside,) Knock, knock.*

(Enter BADGER.)

BLOODGOOD: Had your ear to the door, did you?

BADGER: Of course. Surely, you would expect nothing less.

BLOODGOOD: We had a little mishap.

BADGER: So I see.

BLOODGOOD: Is he . . .?

BADGER: Purple, sir?

BLOODGOOD: No, no, is he . . . you know . . .?

BADGER: Blue about the lips with eyes about to pop?

BLOODGOOD: No, no, is he . . . oh, c'mon, man! Is he or isn't he?

BADGER: I'd say he isn't. He was, but he ain't no more.

BLOODGOOD: You mean, he is dead?

BADGER: *Yup.* They don't get no deader. Apoplexy, I'd say. The cause is natural, over-excitement and sudden emotion. Speaking of sudden emotion, your daughter, Miss Alida is in the carriage at the door, screaming to be admitted. She has torn her nurse's face in a fearful manner. Quite a bloody mess actually. Children! They are the devils in disguise, aren't they? Mark my words, that little Alida will be your undoing. And by the way, sir, I will require a sizable payoff to remain mum, if you know what I mean.

BLOODGOOD: Precisely. You yearn for joy and sweeter days.

BADGER: I hear it is summer year-round in California. But, it takes a great deal of money to get there, my dear Gideon.

BLOODGOOD: You shall have all you deserve, my dear Badger.

BLOODGOOD (sings SOME SWEET DAY)
Words by Edward L. Park
Music by William Howard Doane

We shall reach the summer land,
Some sweet day, by and by,
We shall press the golden strand,
Some sweet day, by and by;
O the loved ones watching there,
By the tree of life so fair,
Till we come their joy to share,
Some sweet day, by and by.

BADGER & BLOODGOOD (Sing.):
By and by some sweet day,
We shall meet our lov'd ones gone,
Some sweet day by and by.

BADGER: *(Sings.)*
At the crystal river's brink,
Some sweet day, by and by,
We shall find each broken link,
Some sweet day, by and by;
Then the star that fading here,
Left our hearts and homes so dear,
We shall see more bright and clear,
Some sweet day, by and by.

BOTH:
By and by some sweet day,
We shall meet our lov'd ones gone,
Some sweet day by and by.

BLOODGOOD:
O these parting scenes will end,

Some sweet day by and by;

BADGER:
We shall gather friend with friend,
Some sweet day, by and by;

BLOODGOOD:
There before our Father's throne,
When the mist and clouds have flown,

BADGER:
We shall know as we are known,
Some sweet day by and by.

BOTH: By and by some sweet day,
We shall meet our lov'd ones gone,
Some sweet day by and by.

(Singing ends.)

BLOODGOOD: My dear Mr. Badger, if you come back at nightfall and help me get rid of this body, I will see you are paid more than enough to remain mum—permanently.

BADGER: Very good, sir. (Notices receipt on floor and quickly recovers it. Aside.) Ha! Here is the receipt! Signed by Bloodgood himself. As a general rule never destroy a receipt—there is no knowing when it may prove useful. California, here I come. *Tableau.*

LIGHTING FADES to Black.

END ACT ONE — *Scene 1*

ACT ONE — *Scene 2*

A bench in a park. There is a fountain nearby. Twenty years later.

The entire cast strolls through the park while lazily whistling "The Fountain in the Park." The men wear dapper high hats and the women sport busy floral and feathered hats and carry parasols. Perhaps, a couple dances round a May Pole. DUF enters.

DUF: *(To audience.)* It is now 1898—twenty years after the tragic death of Captain Fairweather. It is May Day here in the park. There is a chill in the morning air.

(The entire cast begins singing and DUF prompts the audience to do likewise.)

THE FOUNTAIN IN THE PARK
Words and Music by Ed Haley

VERSE 1: While strolling in the park one day,
All in the merry month of May,
A roguish pair of eyes they took me by surprise,
In a moment my poor heart they stole away!
Oh a sunny smile was all she gave to me
And of course we were as happy as could be.

(Instrumental phrase.)

So neatly I raised my hat
And made a polite remark.
I never shall forget that lovely afternoon,
When I met her at the fountain in the park.

(Dance interlude.)

VERSE 2: We linger'd there beneath the trees,

Her voice was like the fragrant breeze.
We talked of happy love until the stars above
When her loving "yes" she gave my heart to please.
A smile was all she gave to me
Of course we were as happy as could be.

(Instrumental phrase. Repeat.)

(DUF and ALL except LIVINGSTONE exit.)

LIVINGSTONE: *(To audience.)* Nine o'clock. For the last hour I have been hovering 'round —trying to sell my overcoat to some enterprising merchant. Three months ago I was the fashionable Mark Livingstone. Today I am a ruined man from investments in stocks gone bust. I am reduced to breakfast off this coat. *(Feels in his pocket.)* What do I feel? A gold dollar—undiscovered in the imprudence of other days! (Withdraws his hand.) No. 'Tis but a five-cent piece!

PUFFY: *(Enters, carrying a pail.)* Past nine o'clock. I am late this morning.

LIVINGSTONE: I say, good man, what a delicious aroma permeates the air. What are you carrying in that pail?

PUFFY: Sweet potatoes, delicious, piping hot, sweet potatoes— five penny a potato, sir.

LIVINGSTONE: Indeed! *(Aside.)* If the Union Club saw me now, but hunger cries aloud.

PUFFY: Why, bless me, if it ain't Mr. Paul Livingstone!

LIVINGSTONE: *(Aside.)* The devil! He knows me. I dare not eat a morsel.

PUFFY: I'm Puffy, sir—the baker. Served you and your good father afore you.

LIVINGSTONE: Oh, Puffy! Good to see you. *(Aside.)* I wonder if I owe him anything.

PUFFY: Down in the world now, sir, like so many of us nowadays. Me and the wee wifey had our bakery in Broadway—where you and your good father used to come. When the economy took a turn downward, we rented in the Bowery, set up house in the bakery and let out the rooms overhead.

LIVINGSTONE: So you are poor now, are you?

PUFFY: I ain't ashamed to say so, sir. I got no pride to support. There's my lodgers—a widow and her two grown children—poor as mice they are, but proud, sir. They was grand folks once; you can see that by how they try to hide it. Mrs. Fairweather's a

——

LIVINGSTONE: Fairweather—the widow of the sea captain Fairweather?

PUFFY: That be her. Do you know my lodgers?

LIVINGSTONE: Three months ago they lived in Brooklyn—had a lovely cottage in the Heights. Paul had a clerkship in the Navy Yard.

PUFFY: Quite right, but when the economy went south, the government paid off a number of employees, and Mr. Paul was discharged.

LIVINGSTONE: They are reduced to poverty and I did not know it. *(Aside.)* Since my ruin I have avoided them. *(To PUFFY.)* And Lucy—I mean Miss Fairweather—?

PUFFY: She works at a milliner's in Broadway—such a sweet child.

(Enter PAUL and MRS. FAIRWEATHER, dressed in black.)

LIVINGSTONE: Oh! *(He quickly walks away, leaving his coat on the park bench. Aside.)* I wonder if they know me. *(Exits.)*

MRS. FAIRWEATHER: *Ah,* Mr. Puffy.

PUFFY: *Ah,* my second floor—Mrs. Fairweather, Paul—good morning. I hope no misfortune has happened; you seem to be dressed in mourning.

MRS FAIRWEATHER: This is the anniversary of my poor husband's death. This day, twenty years ago, he was taken away from us. We keep this day sacred to his memory.

PAUL: It was a fatal day for us. When my father left home he had one hundred thousand dollars. When he was found lying dead on the sidewalk, he was robbed of all.

MRS. FAIRWEATHER: Oh, woe. Woe, woe, woe. And now we are friendless.

PUFFY: Friends—that reminds me—where is Mr. Livingstone? There be his coat.

PAUL: Mr. Livingstone?

PUFFY: We were talking of you just afore you came. He seems to have slipped away.

LIVINGSTONE: *(Enters.)* I think I left my coat. Paul, is that you?

PAUL: Good morning, sir.

MRS. FAIRWEATHER: Morning, Mr. Livingstone.

LIVINGSTONE: "Sir?" "Mr. Livingstone?" Have I offended you?

PAUL: We could not expect you to descend to visit us in our poor lodging.

MRS. FAIRWEATHER: We cannot afford the pleasure of your society.

LIVINGSTONE: Let me assure you that I was ignorant of your misfortunes. And, if I had not called, it was because . . . because . . . *(Aside.)* What shall I say? *(Aloud.)* I have been absent from the city. May I ask how is your sister?

PAUL: My sister Lucy is now employed in a millinery store in Broadway. She sees you pass the door every day.

LIVINGSTONE: *(Aside.)* I must confess my ruin, or appear a contemptible scoundrel.

PAUL: Livingstone, I cannot conceal my feelings. I'm a blunt New York boy, and I've something of the old sailor's blood. Sir, you have behaved badly to my sister Lucy.

LIVINGSTONE: For many months I was a daily visitor at your house. I loved your sister.

PAUL: You asked me for Lucy's hand and I gave it, because I loved you as a brother—not because you were rich.

LIVINGSTONE: *(Aside.)* To retrieve my fortunes so that I might marry I speculated in stock and lost all I possessed.

PAUL: The next day I lost my clerkship, we were reduced to poverty, and you disappeared.

LIVINGSTONE: I can't stand it. I will confess all. Let me sacrifice every feeling but Lucy's love and your esteem—

MRS. FAIRWEATHER: Beware, Mr. Livingstone, how you seek to renew our acquaintance. Recollect my daughter earns a pittance behind a counter, I take in work and Paul now seeks for the poorest means of earning an honest crust of bread.

LIVINGSTONE: And what would you say if I were no better off than yourselves?

PUFFY: You, who own a square mile of New York, no better off than ourselves?

(Enter BLOODGOOD.)

LIVINGSTONE: Mr. Bloodgood!

BLOODGOOD: Ah, Livingstone, do you not call to see us? You know our address. My daughter, Alida, would be delighted. By the way, I have some notes of yours at the bank that come due today. Ten thousand dollars, I think.

PAUL: Mr. Bloodgood, pardon me—I was about to call on you to solicit employment.

BLOODGOOD: I'm full, sir. In fact, I've been thinking of cutting staff and reducing salaries. Everybody is doing it nowadays. Let twenty workers do the work of forty and pay them half as much. *(Recognizing PUFFY.)* Ah, Mr. Puffy, that note of yours—

PUFFY: Oh, Lord! *(Aside.)* It is the note Mrs. Fairweather gave me for her rent.

BLOODGOOD: My patience is worn out.

PUFFY: It's all right, sir.

BLOODGOOD: *(Threatening.)* Take care it is. *(Exits.)*

LIVINGSTONE: Paul, will you believe me? My feelings are the same towards you—nay, more tender, more sincere than ever—but there are circumstances I cannot explain. Let me visit you—let me return to the place that I once held in your hearts.

PUFFY: 219 Division Street. Dinner is at half past one. Come today, sir—please, sir.

PAUL: We cannot refuse you.

MRS. FAIRWEATHER: I will go to Lucy's store and let her know. *(Exits.)*

PAUL: And now to hunt for work, to go from office to office pleading for employment, to be met always with the same answer, "we are full" or "we are discharging hands." Livingstone, my friend, I begin to envy the common laborer who has no fears, no care, beyond his food and shelter. I am beginning to lose my pity for the poor.

LIVINGSTONE: The poor? Do you know them? Do you see them? *(To audience.)* The poor man is the clerk with a family, forced to maintain a decent suit of clothes, paid for out of the hunger of his children. *(A crowd begins to gather and listen.)* The poor man is the artist who is obliged to pledge the tools of his trade to buy medicine for his sick wife. The poor man is one who struggles daily, working harder and longer hours, only to dig himself into an early grave. The poor are those who work all their lives and realize so little in return.

(PUFFY and the crowd that has gathered "Bravo" and cheer. DUF enters and oversees the following sing-along.)

THE BOWERY
From The Show "A Trip To Chinatown"
Words by Charles H. Hoyt & Music by Percy Gaunt (1892)

VERSE 1: Oh! the night that I struck New York,
I went out for a quiet walk.
Folks who are on to the city say,
Better by far that I took Broadway.
But I was out to enjoy the sights,
There was the Bow'ry a blaze with lights;
I had one of the devil's own nights,
I'll never go there any more!

CHORUS: The Bow'ry, the Bow'ry!
They say such things,
And they do strange things
On the Bow'ry!
The Bow'ry!
I'll never go there any more!

VERSE 2: I had walked but a block or two,
When up came a fellow and me he knew;
Then a policeman came walking by
Chased him away, and I ask'd him, "Why?"
"Wasn't he pulling your leg?" said he;
Said I: "He never laid hands on me!"
"Get off the Bow'ry, you, yep!" said he.
I'll never go there any more!

(CHORUS.)

VERSE 3: Then I went into an auction store,
I never saw any thieves before.
First he sold me a pair of socks,
Then said he, "How much for the box?"
Someone said "two dollars!", I said "three!"
He emptied the box and he gave it to me,

"I told you the box, not the socks," said he.
I'll never go there any more!

(CHORUS.)

VERSE 4: I went into a concert hall,
I didn't have a good time at all.
Just the minute that I sat down
Girls began singing "New Goon in Town."
I got up mad, and I spoke out free,
"Somebody put that man out," said she;
A man called a bouncer attended to me,
I'll never go there any more!

(CHORUS)

VERSE 5: I went into a barber shop,
He talk'd till I thought he'd never stop.
I: "Cut it short", he misunderstood,
Clipp'd down my hair just as close as he could.
He shaved with a razor that scratched like a pin,
Took off my whiskers and most of my chin.
That was the worst scrape I ever got in,
I'll never go there any more!

(CHORUS)

VERSE 6: I struck a place that they called a "dive,"
I was in luck to get out alive.
When the policeman had heard my woes,
Saw my black eyes and my battered nose;
"You've been held up!" said the copper, "Fly!"
"No, sir, but I've been knock'd down!" said I;
Then he laughed, tho' I couldn't see why,
I'll never go there any more!

(CHORUS)

(Tableau.)

LIGHTING FADES to BLACK

END ACT ONE—Scene 2

ACT ONE—*Scene 3*
Exterior of Bloodgood's Bank, Nassau Street.

DUF: Just a two-minute walk from the park, we find ourselves on Nassau Street where stands The Bloodgood Bank of New York. The scene is the sidewalk outside that great modern edifice of garish architecture. 'Tis a shame that money and good taste are wasted on the rich. A penny—a penny for poor ol' Duf — *(Exits.)*

BLOODGOOD: *(Enters, looking at papers.)* Four per cent a month—ha! If the economy continues on its current course, I shall double my fortune! Twenty years ago this very month—ay, this very day—I stood in yonder bank, a ruined man. Shall I never forget that night—when my accomplice and I carried out the body of the old sailor and laid it there? *(Pointing down the street.)* I never pass the spot without a shudder. But his money— oh, his glorious money—became the foundation of my new fortune. *(Enter ALIDA.)* Alida, my dear child, what brings you to this part of the city?

ALIDA: Oh, daddy, daddy, daddy. I want two thousand dollars.

BLOODGOOD: My dearest child, I gave you five hundred last week.

ALIDA: Pooh! Pig pooh and bear pooh! What's five hundred to you, the richest banker in all of New York?

BLOODGOOD: But, child, you must learn—

ALIDA: I've learned all I need to learn, daddy! Now, get me the money! I must have it! I must, I must!

BLOODGOOD: But—

ALIDA: Don't stand there lallygagging. Go get the money. I must have it.

BLOODGOOD: Well, my sweet darling, if you must you must.

ALIDA: Yes, I must. I really, really must.

BLOODGOOD: Will you step in?

ALIDA: Not I. I'm not going into your dirty bank. I've seen all your clerks, old and ugly—they will offend my delicate senses and give me a headache, no doubt.

BLOODGOOD: I'll go fetch it. *(Exits into bank.)*

ALIDA: *(To audience.)* This is positively the last time I will submit to his extortion. *(Opens a letter and reads.)* "My adored Alida, I am the most wretched of men. Last night I lost two thousand dollars while gambling—it must be paid before twelve o'clock. My queen, my angel, invent some excuse to get this money from your father and meet me at the usual place at half past eleven. There, shall I can press my warm, wet lips to your superb eyes, and twine my soft, royal hands in your magnificent hair. *Adios carissima!* THE DUKE OF CALCAVELLA." *(Folds letter.)*

BLOODGOOD: *(Re-enters, followed by PUFFY.)* I tell you, sir, it must be paid. I have given you plenty of time.

PUFFY: You gave me the time necessary for you to obtain a court order.

BLOODGOOD: Alida, my love, here is your money. *(Gives her notes. She takes them.)* And now, will you do me a favor?

ALIDA: Oh, must I?

BLOODGOOD: Do not be seen about so much, in public, with that foreign Duke. I do not like him.

ALIDA: But, I do. Goodbye, darling daddy. *(She exits.)*

BLOODGOOD: How grand she looks! That girl possesses my whole heart.

PUFFY: Reserve a little for me, sir. This here note, it was give to me by my second floor tenants in payment of rent. It's as good as gold, sir—when they are able to pay it.

BLOODGOOD: Mr. Puffy, you are the worst kind of man, you are a weak honest fool.

PUFFY: Lord, love you, sir! If you was to see my tenants—the kindest, purest second floor as ever drew God's breath. I told them that this note was all right—for if they know'd I was put about, I believe they'd sell the clothes off their backs to pay it.

BLOODGOOD: *(Aside.)* This fellow is a nincompoop. But, I see if I levy execution the note will be paid. *(To PUFFY.)* Very good, Mr. Puffy, I will see about it.

PUFFY: You will? I knew it! I knew you would, sir.

BLOODGOOD: Very good. *(Aside.)* I'll put an execution on his house at once! A bakery with rooms to let! How delightful! *(Aloud.)* Good day, sir. *(Exits.)*

PUFFY: *(Watching him exit. Wistfully.)* A good day—for some.

(PUFFY stands alone as the LIGHTING slowly FADES to black.)

END ACT ONE—*Scene 3*

6 FULL-LENGTH PLAYS
VOLUME TWO

Edward Crosby Wells

ACT ONE—Scene 4:
An Olio.

DUF: Ladies and gentlemen, the Union Square Music Hall proudly presents the belle of New York—that sweet songbird with the golden voice—Miss Lucy Fairweather!

A tight spotlight captures a dreamy LUCY FAIRWEATHER. The stage is completely dark around her. LUCY sings the verses and DUF oversees getting the audience to sing the Chorus.

MEET ME TO-NIGHT IN DREAMLAND
Words by Leo Friedman, Music by Beth Slater Whitson

VERSE 1: Dreaming of you, that's all I do,
Night and day for you I'm pining.
And in your eyes, blue as the skies
I can see the love-light softly shining;
Because you love me there it seems,
Pray meet me in the land of dreams.

CHORUS: Meet me to-night in Dreamland, under the silv'ry moon.
Meet me tonight in Dreamland, where love's sweet roses bloom;
Come with the love-light gleaming, in your dear eyes of blue,
Meet me in Dreamland Sweet, dreamy Dreamland,
There let my dreams come true.

VERSE 2: Sighing all day when you're away,
Longing for you dear, you only;
In blissful dreams, sweet-heart it seems
One is never sad and never lonely.
And if you'll come with me to stay,We'll live in Dreamland night and day.

CHORUS: Meet me to-night in Dreamland, under the silv'ry
moon.
Meet me tonight in Dreamland, where love's sweet roses bloom;
Come with the love-light gleaming, in your dear eyes of blue,
Meet me in Dreamland Sweet, dreamy Dreamland,
There let my dreams come true.

LIGHTING FADES to black.

END ACT TWO—Scene 4

ACT ONE—*Scene 5*
The humble dining room of the Fairweather family.

MRS. FAIRWEATHER: *(Setting the dining room table.)* Did I hear you singing, Lucy?

LUCY: *(In the same position she was at the end of the last scene.)* I may have been, mother. I was just trying on my new dress. Do you think it makes me look pretty?

MRS. FAIRWEATHER: Oh, you are so beautiful, child, you make the dress look pretty.

LUCY: My dear, dear mother—you are so kind to me.

MRS. FAIRWEATHER: Lucy, my darling, I do believe the thought of seeing Mark Livingstone has revived your smile. *(Pause.)* Is your work over, Lucy, already? Are you through for the day?

LUCY: For this day and always, mother. What we expected has arrived. This dress is all I shall receive from Madame Victorine —payment in full. I am discharged.

MRS. FAIRWEATHER: Bless us and save us. More misfortunes.

DUF: Knock-knock.

PUFFY: *(Enters with arms full)* 'tis only Puffy. Knowing you had company; the missus made you a pigeon pie. Um, ooh, mutton kidneys in it. And, a lovely chicken and a couple loaves of bread hot from the oven, and sweet potatoes baked to perfection.

MRS. FAIRWEATHER: My dear Mr. Puffy, really—such an expense—

PUFFY: Expense? Think nothing of it. Why, those pigeons was just goin' to waste. I shot 'em myself—pigeon droppings all over the front stoop and the sidewalk for customers to slip and slide on while running and trying to keep their pumpernickel covered. Terrible thing—pigeon droppings. Then the rooster was running 'round—always raisin' hereafter early in the morning—a nuisance it was. *(Notices LUCY nearby.)* Ah, Miss Lucy, may I comment on how well you are looking?

LUCY: Thank you, Mr. Puffy.

MRS. FAIRWEATHER: Mr. Puffy, I don't know how we will ever repay you. My beloved Lucy was let go from Madam Victorine's today.

PUFFY: Things will get better. Never lose hope, ma'am.

MRS. FAIRWEATHER: Bless you and yours, Mr. Puffy. I owe you too much already, but you must bestow on us no more out of your own poverty.

(Enter PAUL and LIVINGSTONE.)

PAUL: Allow me to take your coat, Paul. *(Takes coat.)*

LIVINGSTONE: Thank you.

PUFFY: Now, I must be off. I'll just leave you fine folks to your lovely dinner. *(Exits.)*

LIVINGSTON: How like the old times, eh, Lucy?

MRS. FAIRWEATHER: *(Aside to PAUL.)* Well, Paul, have you obtained employment?

PAUL: No, but Livingstone is rich—he must have influence.

MRS. FAIRWEATHER: Bless us and save us! I fear the worst is not yet come.

PAUL: Nonsense, mother, cheer up! Is there anything you have concealed from me?

MRS. FAIRWEATHER: No, nothing you need to know. *(Aside.)* If he only knew that for five weeks we have been subsisting on the charity of the poor—Mr. and Mrs. Puffy.

LIVINGSTONE: Look at all this magnificent food!

(PUFFY enters. He is shaken and trembling.)

MRS. FAIRWEATHER: Why, Mr. Puffy, you look as though you've seen a ghost.

PUFFY: The Deputy Sheriff, he came at the suit of Gideon Bloodgood against Susan Fairweather and Jonas Puffy. The amount of debt is one hundred and fifty dollars.

LUCY: Mother!

PUFFY: He's waiting downstairs. He wants the money immediately.

MRS. FAIRWEATHER: Bless us and save us!

PAUL: Oh, dear Livingstone, if you could—

LIVINGSTONE: *(After a pause.)* I cannot help you. Alas, I am penniless, broken.

Tableau.

LIGHTING slowly FADES to black.

END ACT ONE—*Scene 5*

6 FULL-LENGTH PLAYS
VOLUME TWO

Edward Crosby Wells

ACT ONE—*Scene 6:*
An Olio. A darkened stage.

DUF: And now, to help alleviate the sadness of our last scene, we present Miss Alida Bloodgood doing her conspicuous act of self-absorption.

(A tight key light breaks the darkness to reveal ALIDA BLOODGOOD. ALIDA sings the verses and prompt the audience to sing the Chorus.)

STREETS OF CAIRO
Words and some Music by James Thornton,
Original tune Composer unknown.
Additional words by the playwright.

VERSE 1: I will sing you a song, and it won't be very long,
'Bout a maiden sweet, and she never would do wrong,
Ev'ryone said she was pretty, she was alone in the city,
All alone, oh, what a pity, poor little maid.

CHORUS 1: She never saw the streets of Cairo,
On the Midway she had never strayed,
She never saw the kutchy, kutchy,
Poor little New York maid.

VERSE 2: She went out one night, did this innocent divine,
With a nice young man, who invited her to dine,
Now he's sorry that he met her, and he never will forget her,
In the future he'll know better, poor little maid.

CHORUS 2: She never saw the streets of Cairo,
On the Midway she had never strayed,
She never saw the kutchy, kutchy,
Poor little New York maid.

VERSE 3: She was engaged, as a picture for to pose,
To appear each night, in abbreviated clothes,
All the dudes were in a flurry, for to catch her they did hurry,
One who caught her now is sorry, poor little maid.

CHORUS 3: She was much fairer far than Trilby,
Lots of more men sorry will be,
If they don't try to keep away from this
Poor little New York maid.

LIGHTING FADES to BLACK.

END ACT ONE—Scene 6

ACT ONE—*Scene 7*

The drawing room of the Bloodgood home.

(BLOODGOOD is seen writing at a table, while ALIDA is reading a newspaper. BOTH remain frozen until after DUF speaks.)

DUF: Ah, domestic tranquility—at home with the Bloodgoods. There is no Mrs. Bloodgood. Annabelle Bloodgood died of complications from little Alida's clawing her way out into the world. Feel free to hiss and boo at your pleasure. *(Exit.)*

BLOODGOOD: What are you reading?

ALIDA: The New York Herald. Shall I read aloud?

BLOODGOOD: Do.

ALIDA: *(Reads.)* "Wall Street is a perch on which a row of human vultures sit. Amongst these birds of prey, the most vulturous is perhaps Gideon Bloodgood." *(To BLOODGOOD.)* Isn't that nice, daddy? They've mentioned you in The Herald. *(Reads.)* "Bloodgood made his fortune in the lottery business. He then dabbled in the slave trade—long after the Emancipation. Last week he made fifty thousand dollars speculating in flour, which raised the price of bread four cents a loaf. Now there are thousands starving in the hovels of New York." Daddy, dearest! Are you not rich?

BLOODGOOD: Why do you ask?

ALIDA: Because people say that riches are worshipped in high society—yet, I am refused admission into the best families whose intimacy I have sought.

BLOODGOOD: Refused admission! Is not Fifth Avenue open to you?

ALIDA: Pooh on Fifth Avenue! Why do we not visit those families whose names demand respect—the Livingstones, the Astors, the Vanderbilts, the Van Renssalaers?

BLOODGOOD: Is not the Duke of Calcavella at your feet?

ALIDA: The Duke de Calcavella is an adventurer who escorts me to my box at the opera so that he may attend free. I am not speaking of love—but of marriage.

BLOODGOOD: Marriage?

ALIDA: Yes, marriage into New York society, which has shut its doors to me. It is from amongst these families that I have resolved to choose a husband.

BLOODGOOD: *(Rising.)* Alida, my dearest, I have but one treasure and that is you. You may have my fortune—take it, but leave me a tiny portion of your affection.

ALIDA: Oh, daddy! Pooh! Pig pooh and bear pooh! You talk as if I were still a child. Surely, you don't wish me to marry the Duke de Calcavella?

BLOODGOOD: A *roué*, a gambler? Heaven forbid.

ALIDA: Besides, they say he has a wife in Italy.

BLOODGOOD: Then I shall forbid him entry into this house. His reputation will compromise yours.

ALIDA: Pish-posh. I care not for my reputation.

DUF: Knock-knock!

BLOODGOOD: I wonder who that could be.

DUF: Wonder no more, sir. It is Mr. Mark Livingstone.

ALIDA: Livingstone! This is the first time that name has been announced in this house.

DUF: He comes on business.

ALIDA: Well! Show him in at once!

LIVINGSTONE: *(Entering.)* Mr. Bloodgood, Miss Bloodgood— *(Bows.)* I am most fortunate to find you at home.

ALIDA: Shall I leave you alone to your business with my father?

LIVINGSTONE: Not at all, Miss Bloodgood, my business can be said in three words.

BLOODSTONE: Indeed?

LIVINGSTONE: I am ruined.

ALIDA: Ruined?

LIVINGSTONE: My father was in a position to leave me a handsome fortune. I spent it—extravagantly—foolishly. My mother heard that my name was pledged for a large amount— Mr. Bloodgood held my paper—so, she sold out all her fortune without my knowledge, and rescued my credit from dishonor.

BLOODGOOD: Allow me to observe, I think she acted honorably, but foolishly.

LIVINGSTONE: She shared my father's principles on these matters. *(To ALIDA.)* Finding I was such good pay, your father lent me a further sum with which I speculated in stocks to recover my mother's loss. I lost everything—again—and now I am ruined.

BLOODGOOD: Mr. Livingstone, if you had applied to me a few days earlier I might have been able to be of assistance, but at the moment it is quite impossible.

LIVINGSTONE: *(Aside.)* Impossible—the usual expression! I am familiar with it! *(To BLOODGOOD.)* I regret exceedingly that I did not fall into ruin on that more fortunate moment to which you allude—a thousand pardons for my untimely demand. *(He exits.)*

BLOODGOOD: What impudence!

ALIDA: *(At table.)* Father, come here. I am writing a letter that I wish you to sign.

BLOODGOOD: To whom?

ALIDA: To Mr. Livingstone. Here, read it. *(Hands it to him.)*

BLOODGOOD: *(Reads.)* "My dear sir, give yourself no further anxiety about your debt to me. I will see that your debts are paid —and if the loan of ten thousand dollars will serve you, I beg to hold that amount at your service to be repaid at your convenience. Yours truly—" *(Throwing down letter.)* I will sign nothing of the kind.

ALIDA: Pish-posh. Daddy, dearest, you are mistaken. You will.

BLOODGOOD: To what purpose?

ALIDA: I want to make a purchase . . . of a husband—a husband who is a gentleman—and through whom I can take my proper place in society. There's the pen!

BLOODGOOD: Is your mind so set on this ambition?

ALIDA: If it cost half your fortune. *(BLOODGOOD signs the paper.)* You won't regret it, daddy. *(She quickly takes letter and heads toward exit.)* I will see that one of the servants delivers this letter immediately. *(She exits.)*

(Shortly after ALIDA exits, BADGER slowly slithers in—startling BLOODGOOD.)

BLOODGOOD: What the devil—Badger! How did you get in?

BADGER: Pardon me, sir, I must have forgotten to knock.

DUF: Knock-knock!

BADGER: But I guess we're beyond that now—ay, sir?

BLOODGOOD: Twenty years beyond—

BADGER: Well, aren't you looking particularly well this fine day? You've hardly aged at all—over these past twenty years.

BLOODGOOD: I could say the same of you.

(ALIDA silently enters and listens.)

BADGER: My dear Gideon, excuse my not calling more promptly, but since my return from California, this is my first appearance in fashionable society.

ALIDA: Who is this fellow?

BADGER: Ah, Alida—how is our sweet little tootles? I don't expect you remember me. The last time we saw one another you were having a profound misunderstanding with your nurse. If you have forgotten me—alack, alas—all is forgiven.

ALIDA: How can I recollect every begging impostor who importunes my father?

BADGER: Charming! As sweet as ever—changed in form—but the heart, my dear Gideon, is hard and dry as a biscuit.

ALIDA: Father, give this wretch a dollar and let him go.

BADGER: Ouch! Miss Bloodgood, when I hand 'round the hat it is time enough to put something in it. Gideon, get this wench to a nunnery!

ALIDA: Is this fellow mad?

BLOODGOOD: Hush, my dear!

ALIDA: Speak out your business. I am familiar with all my father's affairs.

BADGER: All? I doubt that.

DUF: Knock-knock!

ALIDA: Ah, that must be my dressmaker.

LUCY: *(Entering.)* It is the dressmaker, ma'am.

ALIDA: And you are the person I met this morning walking with Mr. Livingstone?

LUCY: Yes—ma'am.

ALIDA: *Hmm.* Follow me and let me see if you can attend on ladies as diligently as you do on gentlemen. *(ALIDA and LUCY exit.)*

BLOODGOOD: So, here you are—again. I thought you were dead.

BADGER: Like a bad shilling, come back again. Your three thousand dollars lasted for some months in California. But, had I known that instead of absconding, you remained in New York, I would have hastened back years ago—to share your revived fortunes.

BLOODGOOD: What do you mean?

BADGER: I am reduced in circumstances and without character.

BLOODGOOD: Mr. Badger, you have always been without character—and I cannot see in what way your circumstances affect me!

BADGER: Can you not? Do you ever read the Sunday papers?

BLOODGOOD: Never.

BADGER: I've got a story ready for one of them. Allow me to give you a sketch of it.

BLOODGOOD: Sir—

BADGER: The story begins in a bank in Nassau Street. Twenty years ago a very respectable old sea captain makes a special deposit of one hundred thousand dollars. Nobody is present but the banker and one clerk. The old captain takes a receipt and is suddenly seized by a fit apoplexy—and he dies on the spot.

BLOODGOOD: Indeed, Mr. Badger, your story is quite original.

BADGER: Ain't it! The banker and his clerk carry the body out onto the sidewalk. The clerk received three thousand dollars hush money and left for parts unknown. The banker remained in New York and established a colossal fortune—to be continued.

BLOODGOOD: And what do you suppose such a story will be worth?

BADGER: I propose to relate that this story is a true account in every particular, and I shall advertise for the heirs of the dead man.

BLOODGOOD: Do you mean to insinuate that this applies, in any way, to me?

BADGER: It rings a distant bell. Ding-dong. Ding-dong.

BLOODGOOD: Your memory is luxurious—perhaps it can furnish some better evidence of this wonderful story than the word of a man of questionable character.

BADGER: My word is worth little. But the receipt, signed by you, is worth a good deal.

BLOODGOOD: You lie!

BADGER: Let us proceed with my story. When the banker and his clerk searched for the receipt, they could not find it—a circumstance that only astonished one of the villains—because the clerk had already retrieved the document.

BLOODGOOD: Villain! Vile, vile villain!

BADGER: You may slander my character however you please, but the moral is: Never destroy a receipt.

BLOODGOOD: What do you demand?

BADGER: Five thousand dollars.

BLOODGOOD: The devil, you say! The dastardly deed of the devil!

DUF: Knock-knock!

PAUL: *(Enters.)* It is I, Paul Fairweather.

BLOODGOOD: What is your business with me?

PAUL: Pardon me, Mr. Bloodgood, but the officers have seized the furniture of our landlord—of your tenant—for a debt owned by my mother. I come to ask your mercy—utter ruin awaits two poor families.

BADGER: *(Aside.)* Oh, Supreme Justice! There is the creditor, and there is the debtor.

PAUL: I plead not for myself, but for my mother and my sister.

BLOODGOOD: I have waited long enough!

BADGER: *(Rising.)* So have I. *(To PAUL.)* Have you no friends or relations to help you?

PAUL: None, sir, my father is dead.

BADGER: Your name is familiar to me—was your father in trade?

PAUL: He was a sea captain.

BADGER: Ah! He died nobly in some storm, I suppose—the last to leave his ship?

PAUL: No, sir, he died miserable! Twenty years ago his body was found on the sidewalk quite close to this bank, where he fell dead by apoplexy.

BLOODGOOD: Ah! My dear Mr. Badger, I do believe we have a little business to settle.

BADGER: Ah, yes, my dear Gideon. *(Aside to BLOODGOOD.)* Stocks have gone up—I want fifty thousand dollars for that receipt.

BLOODGOOD: Fifty thousand?

BADGER: (Aside.) You see the effect of good news on the market—astounding, ain't it?

BLOODGOOD: If you will step into the dining room, you will find lunch prepared. Refresh yourself, Mr. Badger, while I see what can be done for this young man.

BADGER: *(Aside.)* What is he up to? I've got the receipt. He's on the hook! *(Exits.)*

BLOODGOOD: Your situation interests me, but surely, you can find employment.

PAUL: Alas, sir, in these troubled times it is impossible. I would work at any kind of labor if I could save my mother and my sister from want.

BLOODGOOD: Perhaps, I can aid you.

PAUL: Sir, I little expected to find in you a benefactor.

BLOODGOOD: My correspondents at Rio Janeiro require a bookkeeper—are you prepared to accept this situation?

PAUL: Why, yes—

BLOODGOOD: There is one condition—you must be on a vessel that sails tomorrow.

PAUL: Tomorrow?

BLOODGOOD: I will hand you a thousand dollars in advance of salary, to provide for your mother and sister; they had better leave this city until they can follow you. The terms are two thousand dollars a year. Do you accept?

PAUL: *(Seizing his hand.)* Mr. Bloodgood, the prayers of a family whom you have made very happy will prosper your life. God bless you, sir!

BLOODGOOD: Call again in an hour, when your papers of introduction and the money shall be ready.

PAUL: Farewell, sir. I can scarcely believe my good fortune. *(Exits.)*

BLOODGOOD: *(To audience.)* So, now to secure Badger! He must be prevented from communicating with the mother and daughter until they can be sent into some obscure retreat. As for Mr. Paul Fairweather, he will not be taking that job offer after all—seems I've plans to nip that in the bud. I doubt that Badger is in possession of the receipt, but I will take an assurance about that. I will go to the Superintendent of Police while Badger is gorging himself in my dining room. Ha! Badger, when you find the heirs of the estate gone, you will perhaps come down in your terms. *Ha! Ha! Ha! (BLOODGOOD sings.)*

THE MAN WHO BROKE THE BANK AT MONTE CARLO
Words and Music by Charles Coburn

I've just got here, thro' Paris, from the sunny southern shore;
I to Monte Carlo went, just to raise my winter's rent.
Dame Fortune smil'd upon me as she'd never done before,
And I've now such lots of money, I'm a gent.
Yes, I've now such lots of money, I'm a gent.
I stay indoors till after lunch, and then my daily walk
To the great Triumphal Arch is one grand Triumphal march,
Observ'd by each observer with the keenness of a hawk,

I'm mass of money, linen, silk and starch.
I'm mass of money, linen, silk and starch.
I patronized the tables at the Monte Carlo hell
Till they hadn't got a sou for a Christian or a Jew;
So I quickly went to Parie for the charms of mad'moiselle,
Who's the load-stone of my heart. What can I do?
When with twenty tongues she swears that she'll be true?

CHORUS: As I walk along the Bois Boolong, with an independent air,
You can hear them sigh and wish to die,
You can see them wink the other eye,
At the man who broke the bank at Monte Carlo.

LIGHTING dims to BLACKOUT.

END ACT ONE

ACT TWO – *Scene 1*
Olio. A darkened stage.

DUF: Welcome back to the streets of old New York. *(The LIGHTING slowly rises. The ENTIRE CAST strolls out onto the stage to perform the sing-along.)* Please join us in a tribute to the greatest city in the world!

GIVE MY REGARDS TO BROADWAY
Words and Music by George M. Cohan
(These are the original lyrics before the 1918 re-write.)

VERSE 1: Did you ever see two Yankees part upon a foreign shore
When the good ship's just about to start for Old New York once more?
With tear-dimmed eye they say goodbye, they're friends without a doubt;
When the man on the pier, shouts, "Let them clear," as the ship strikes out.

CHORUS: Give my regards to Broadway, remember me to Herald Square,
Tell all the gang at Forty-second street, that I will soon be there;
Whisper of how I'm yearning, to mingle with the old time throng;
Give my regards to old Broadway and say that I'll be there e'er long.

VERSE 2: Say hello to dear old Coney Isle, if there you chance to be,
When you're at the Waldorf have a smile and charge it up to me;
Mention my name ev'ry place you go, as 'round the town you roam;
Wish you'd call on my gal, Now remember, old pal, when you get back home.

CHORUS: Give my regards to Broadway, remember me to Herald Square,
Tell all the gang at Forty-second street, that I will soon be there;
Whisper of how I'm yearning, to mingle with the old time throng;
Give my regards to old Broadway and say that I'll be there e'er long.

LIGHTING FADES to BLACK.

END ACT TWO—*Scene 1*

ACT TWO—*Scene 2*
The drawing room of the Bloodgood home.

DUF: *(Alone.)* Now let us return to the Streets of Old New York. Bloodgood was on his way to see the Superintendent of Police. We return to the drawing room of the Bloodgood home where Bloodgood has returned and is now in his study. Mr. Badger continues to engorge himself on the fine fare in the dining room. Lucy enters. *(Exits.)*

LUCY: *(Enters, speaking to ALIDA who is still offstage.)* I will do my best, Miss Alida, to please you. *(Aside.)* Oh! Let me hasten from this house of evil!

LIVINGSTONE: *(Enters.)* Lucy!

LUCY: Mark!

LIVINGSTONE: What brings you here?

LUCY: What brings the poor into the godless saloons of the rich?

ALIDA: *(Enters, unseen. Aside.)* Mr. Livingstone here—and with this shop girl!

LIVINGSTONE: My dear Lucy, I have news, wonderful news. I am once again rich. But before I relate my good fortune, let me hear from you the consent to share it.

LUCY: Pray tell—whatever do you mean?

LIVINGSTONE: I mean, dearest one, that I love you. I love you with all my reckless, foolish, worthless heart. Oh, my darling, do let me call you sweetheart. (Cue music.)

LET ME CALL YOU SWEETHEART
Words by Beth Slater Whitson, Music by Leo Friedman

LIVINGSTONE: I am dreaming Dear of you, Day by day
Dreaming when the skies are blue, When they're gray;
When the silv'ry moonlight gleams,
Still I wander on in dreams,
In a land of love, it seems, Just with you.

LUCY & LIVINGSTONE: Let me call you "Sweetheart,"
I'm in love with you.
Let me hear you whisper that you love me too.
Keep the love-light glowing in your eyes so true.
Let me call you "Sweetheart," I'm in love with you.

LUCY: Longing for you all the while, More and more;
Longing for the sunny smile, I adore;
Birds are singing far and near, Roses blooming ev'rywhere
You, alone, my heart can cheer; You, just you.

BOTH: Let me call you "Sweetheart," I'm in love with you.
Let me hear you whisper that you love me too.
Keep the love-light glowing in your eyes so true.
Let me call you "Sweetheart," I'm in love with you.

ALIDA: *(Advancing.)* Mr. Livingstone, my father is waiting for
you in his study.

LIVINGSTONE: A thousand pardons, Miss Bloodgood, I was
not aware. Forgive me. *(Aside.)* I wonder if she heard me? *(To
LUCY.)* I will see you again this evening. *(Exits.)*

ALIDA: *(To LUCY, who is leaving.)* Stay, one word with you.
Mr. Livingstone loves you? Do not deny it, I have overheard you
—cooing and wooing and wooing and cooing.

LUCY: Well, Miss Bloodgood, I have no account to render you in this matter.

ALIDA: I beg your pardon—he is to be my husband.

LUCY: Your husband?

ALIDA: Mr. Livingstone is ruined. My father has come to his aid. One word from me and the hand extended to save him from destruction will be withdrawn.

LUCY: But he does not love you.

ALIDA: Pish-posh. What's love got to do with marriage?

LUCY: You have overheard that he loves me. And, you will coldly buy this man for a husband, knowing that you condemn him to eternal misery!

ALIDA: Well, I must. I really must. Let us hope that in time he will learn to endure me.

LUCY: 'Tis his name you require to cover the shame that stains your father's, which all his wealth cannot conceal. His love for me will stop him from such a cowardly scheme.

ALIDA: I will make him rich. What would you make him?

LUCY: I would make him happy.

ALIDA: Will you give him up?

LUCY: Never!

LIVINGSTONE: *(Enters.)* Lucy, dear Lucy, do you see that lady? She is my guardian angel. To her I owe my good fortune. Mr. Bloodgood has told me all. Let me confess, had I not been thus rescued from ruin, I would have no recourse but a Colt's revolver.

LUCY: Mark!

LIVINGSTONE: Yes, Lucy—I could not endure the shame and despair which beset me. But let us not talk of such madness—let us only remember that I owe her my life.

ALIDA: *(Aside.)* And that is one debt I intend to collect.

LIVINGSTONE: I owe to her all the happiness which you will bestow upon me.

LUCY: No, Mark! It is impossible. I cannot be your wife. I—I do not love you.

LIVINGSTONE: You jest, Lucy—yet no—there are tears in your eyes.

LUCY: *(Looking away.)* Did I ever tell you that I loved you?

LIVINGSTONE: No, it is true, but your manner, your looks, I thought—

LUCY: You are not angry with me, are you?

LIVINGSTONE: I love you too sincerely for that, and believe me I will never intrude again on your family, where my presence now can only produce pain and restraint. It will soothe the anguish you have innocently inflicted, if your family will permit me to assist them. I know it will pain you all—but you owe it to me. *(LUCY falls, weeping, in a chair.)* Pardon me, Miss Bloodgood. Farewell, Lucy. I take my leave. *(Exits.)*

ALIDA: He has gone. Dry your eyes you silly girl. I assure you those tears affect me not. I prefer that my husband-to-be have no financial relations with you. *(Offering her purse to LUCY.)* As you are in want, here is some assistance.

LUCY: *(Rising.)* You insult me, Miss Bloodgood. You thought I sold my heart—no—I gave my heart. Keep your gold—it would soil my poverty. Good day! *(Exits.)*

BLOODGOOD: *(Enters from his study.)* What is the matter, my dearest Alida?

BADGER: *(Enters from the dining room.)* Your cook is perfect and your wine the finest.

DUF: Knock-knock!

ALIDA: I'll see to it, daddy dearest. *(Exits.)*

BADGER: Now, where were we, Gideon? Fifty thousand dollars, wasn't it?

BLOODGOOD: I shall give you nothing, sir!

ALIDA: *(Enters, quickly.)* There are policemen outside! They are awaiting the departure of Mr. Badger.

BLOODGOOD: I will give you into custody for an attempt to extort money by threats and intimidation. When they search you they will find a receipt signed by me, which I shall testify was purloined from my desk yonder. *(Aside.)* With the arrest of Badger there's no need to employ that wretched Paul Fairweather. He won't be sailing at my expense!

BADGER: Well played, my dear Gideon, but, knowing the character of the society into which I was venturing, I left the dear document safe at home. *(Moving toward exit.)* Good day, Gideon — *(To ALIDA)* And good day to you, my sweet little tootles. (Exits.)

LIGHTING FADES to black.

END ACT TWO—Scene 2

ACT TWO—*Scene 3*
Outside the Astor mansion on 5th Avenue.

(LIGHTING slowly rises to suggest the cool shades of night. From time to time costumed and masked revelers stroll down the street.)

DUF: It is the night of the Annual Masked Ball at the Astor's 5th Avenue mansion. As our scene opens we discover Mr. Puffy with a pan of roasting chestnuts outside the entrance to the mansion. Paul Fairweather crouches in a corner of the street, asleep.

PUFFY: Lord! I can't sell me chestnuts. I thought if I posted myself just here, so as to catch the grand folks as they go into the Astor Ball, they might fancy to take in a pocketful. *(Spots LIVINGSTONE.)* Hello, stranger. *(Aside.)* Oh my! The poor soul is asleep. I shan't wake him. I'll just leave a nice handful of warm chestnuts in his lap. *(He puts chestnuts in PAUL's lap and exits.)*

(Enter BADGER, very ragged, with artificial flowers and boxes of matches.)

BADGER: *(Hawking to the audience,)* Artificial flowers. You can't go to Mrs. Astor's Ball without a lovely corsage for the ladies—or a nice boutonniere for the gentlemen. Get your artificial flowers here. How about a box of Lucifer's? A hundred per box for three penny. *(Pause.)* Reduced to this by the villainous hands of Gideon Bloodgood. One day I shall avenge his treachery! But now, how 'bout some entertainment? *(Throws his hat onto the ground.)* Bless me with whatever change you can afford.DUF: And now, an act of utter despair as Badger goes into his song and dance. Feel free to sing along and throw those pennies, but please try not to harm our actor!

(*BADGER goes into his song and dance.*)

HELLO, MY BABY
Words and Music by Ida Emerson and Joseph E. Howard

INTRODUCTION: Hello, Hello, Hello, Hello, Hello, Hello,

VERSE 1: I've got a little baby, but she's out of sight,
I talk to her across the telephone.
I've never seen my honey but she's mine all right,
So take my tip and leave this gal alone.
Every single morning you will hear me yell,
"Hey Central! Fix me up along the line."
He connects me with ma honey, then I rings the bell,
And this is what I say to baby mine,

CHORUS: Hello! ma baby, Hello! Ma honey, Hello! ma ragtime
gal.
Send me a kiss by wire, baby my heart's on fire!
If you refuse me, Honey, you'll lose me, then you'll be left alone;
Oh baby, telephone and tell me I'm your own.
Hello! Hello! Hello! Hello there.

VERSE 2: This morning through the phone she said her name
was Bess,
And now I kind of know where I am at.
I'm satisfied because I've got my babe's address
Here pasted in the lining of my hat.
I am mighty scared, 'cause if the wires get crossed,
'Twill separate me from ma baby mine,
Then some other man will win her, and my game is lost,
And so each day I shout along the line,
Hello, hello, hello.
Hello, hello, hello.

CHORUS: Hello! ma baby, Hello! Ma honey, Hello! ma ragtime
gal.

Send me a kiss by wire, baby my heart's on fire!
If you refuse me, Honey, you'll lose me, then you'll be left alone;
Oh baby, telephone and tell me I'm your own.

(Repeat CHORUS after instrumental and soft-shoe dancing interlude.)

MRS. FAIRWEATHER: *(Enters.)* I cannot return to our miserable home without food for my children. Each morning, we separate in search of work, in search of food, only to meet again at night—their poor faces thin with hunger. *(She clasps her hands in anguish.)* Ah! What have we here? Yes, this remains—it is gold!

BADGER: *(Overhearing her last word.)* Gold? Artificial flowers —a box of matches?

MRS. FAIRWEATHER: Tell me, friend, where can I buy a loaf of bread at this hour?

BADGER: There's a saloon open in the 4th Avenue. *(Aside.)* Gold—she said, gold.

MRS. FAIRWEATHER: Will they accept this pledge for some food? *(Shows him ring.)*

BADGER: Let me see it.

MRS. FAIRWEATHER: 'Tis my wedding ring.

BADGER: *(Examining the ring. Aside.)* I could easily make off with it. What will I do?

MRS. FAIRWEATHER: My children are starving. I must part with it to buy them bread.

BADGER: *(Reluctantly, returns ring.)* Go along and buy your children food. Don't show that ring to anybody else. You deserve to lose it for showing it to such a blackguard as I.

MRS. FAIRWEATHER: Thank you, kind sir. *(Exits.)*

BLOODGOOD: *(Enters)* I'm late! So very, very late! What, pray tell, is the time?

BADGER: A boutonniere for the gentleman? Perhaps, some Lucifer's— *(Recognizing him.)* Bloodgood! The devil himself.

BLOODGOOD: Badger! *(BLOODGOOD puts his hand into the breast of his coat).*

BADGER: Take your hand out of your breast! I've a knife up my sleeve that would rip you up like a dried codfish before you could cock that revolver you have there so handy.

BLOODGOOD: You are mistaken.

BADGER: I think not! I did not spend ten years in California for nothing!

BLOODGOOD: What do you want?

BADGER: I want your life—but legally. You have driven me to despair. I am reduced to selling matches and artificial flowers. A week ago, I came out of prison—you had removed the Fairweather family. I could not find a trace of them, but I found the receipt where I had concealed it. Tomorrow I shall place it in the hands of the District Attorney with my confession of your murder of the Sea Captain.

BLOODGOOD: Murder? Demon! Bring that document to my house tomorrow.

BADGER: No, sir—e-e! Once caught twice shy. Come to my house, tonight—and alone.

BLOODGOOD: Where do you live?

BADGER: Nineteen and a half Cross Street, Five Points—fifth floor, back—my name is on the door in chalk.

BLOODGOOD: In an hour I will be there.

BADGER: In an hour. Don't forget to present my compliments to your charming daughter—sweet creature! *(Exit BLOODGOOD. To audience.)* Lucifers—three penny a hundred! Artificial flowers! Get them while they last! (Moving toward exit.) Bloodgood, you will pay for your dastardly deeds! *(Exits.)*

LUCY: *(Enters, stands under lamppost.)* The sisters of charity in Houston Street told me that I might find work at this address. *(Strikes a provocative pose, with innocence.)*

PAUL: *(Rises. To audience.)* My limbs are powerless. How long have I slept there? Another long day has passed. Since Bloodgood withdrew his offer of employment I have crept 'round streets and alleys. I have begged for work—but they laugh at my poor thin form—the remnant of better days hung in tatters about me. My poor mother! My dear sister! Were it not for you, I would lie down here and die—in the streets of New York. *(He staggers and falls to his knees against the lamppost in despair.)*

LUCY: *(Not recognizing him.)* Kind sir, may I be of assistance?

MRS. FAIRWEATHER: *(Enters.)* They refused to take my ring —they said I had stolen it!

PAUL: *(Rising.)* Let me return to our home—perhaps mother or Lucy has found work.

MRS. FAIRWEATHER: Sir! Sir! In the name of your mother—help my poor children.

PAUL: Mother?

LUCY: My brother?

MRS. FAIRWEATHER: My son?

PAUL: Oh, mother! My own Lucy! My heart is broken! *(They embrace.)* Have you concealed from me the extent of your misery?

MRS. FAIRWEATHER: My poor children! I cannot see you die of hunger!

PAUL: Fear not, mother, the wretched have always one resource—they can die! Do not weep, Lucy—in an hour I will be with you. *(Aside.)* I will go and await the crowd as they leave the Astor's—amongst them some Christian heart will aspire to aid me. *(Exits.)*

MRS. FAIRWEATHER: Lucy, start on home. I'll be with you in a minute.

LUCY: Why, mother?

MRS. FAIRWEATHER: I just want one more peek into the Astor's home—to watch the masked partygoers laugh and dance in merriment—at so grand a ball—in their beautiful costumes and masks. I'll only be a minute, Lucy.

LUCY: All right, mother, just a minute. *(She exits.)*

DUF: And now, a song of utter despair and longing, of sadness and tears. The lovely Mrs. Fairweather will give us her rendition of "After the Ball is Over."

(Alone onstage, as the lights dim around her, MRS. FAIRWEATHER sings.)

AFTER THE BALL IS OVER
Words and Music by Charles K. Harris

After the ball is over, after the break of morn,
After the dancers' leaving, after the stars are gone;
Many a heart is aching, if you could read them all;Many the
hopes that have vanished, after the ball.

(Repeat.)

(MRS. FAIRWEATHER exits. Enter ALIDA and LIVINGSTONE. They are in costume and carry their masks.)

ALIDA: How strange that my father has not arrived.

LIVINGSTONE: Allow me to look for the carriage.

ALIDA: I will remain here. *(LIVINGSTONE exits. Aside.)* At last I have won the husband I desire. He is entangled in my father's debt. In one month hence I shall be Livingstone's wife. The best people in New York will be at my feet. The dear Duke still makes love to me—to which Livingstone appears indifferent—so much the better!

PAUL: *(Enters.)* Ah! Miss Alida Bloodgood.

ALIDA: I wonder they permit such vagabonds to hang about the Astor's mansion.

LIVINGSTONE: (Re-enters.) The carriage is ready. *(Recognizing PAUL.)* Paul?

PAUL: Livingstone!

LIVINGSTONE: Great heaven! In what a condition do I find you!

PAUL: We are poor—we are starving.

ALIDA: Pish-posh! Give the fellow a dollar and send him away.

LIVINGSTONE: My dear Alida, you do not know, this is a schoolfellow and old friend—

ALIDA: I know you are keeping me from my carriage. Ah! I see the Duke on the steps yonder. He will see me to my home. Don't let me take you from an old friend. *(Exits.)*

LIVINGSTONE: *(Aside.)* Cold heartless girl! *(Aloud.)* Come, Paul, come quickly. Bring me to where I shall find your mother and your sister. Wait! Let me first go home and get money. I will meet you at your lodgings. Where do you live?

PAUL: Number nineteen and a half Cross Street—Five Points. I will wait at the door.

LIVINGSTONE: In less than an hour I shall be there. *(Exits.)*

(Masked revelers enter.)

DUF: Everybody sing!

(PAUL sings with the masked revelers.)

After the ball is over, after the break of morn,
After the dancers' leaving, after the stars are gone;
Many a heart is aching, if you cold read them all;
Many the hopes that have vanished, after the ball. *(Repeat.)*

LIGHTING FADES to BLACK.

END ACT TWO—Scene 3

ACT TWO—*Scene 4*

*Adjoining attic rooms in a tenement on Cross Street
in the slums of Five Points. The stage is dark.*

DUF: Come now to the rough and tumble, to the dangerous slums of Five Points. Nineteen and a half Cross Street—two adjoining attic rooms. That room belongs to Badger.

(A round pool of LIGHTING opens on one side of the stage. BADGER enters and sits.)

DUF: *(Con't)* And that room to the Fairweather family.

(LIGHTING opens on the other side of the stage. MRS. FAIRWEATHER enters and sits in a chair, followed by LUCY who kneels nearby.)

DUF: *(Con't)* Two adjoining rooms separated by a thin and rotting wall. *(Exit.)*

LUCY: *(Lighting a candle.)* Surely an hour has passed, yet Paul has not returned.

MRS. FAIRWEATHER: Oh, merciful father! Protect my poor children.

BADGER: *(Scraping matches—they do not light.)* One hundred worthless matches. *(Lighting one.)* Oh, lucky chance! Here's one that condescends. *(Lights a candle.)*

MRS. FAIRWEATHER: Day after day with no hope—the future worse than the present. Woe, woe, woe. Bless us and save us. This load of wretchedness is too much to bear.

LUCY: The candle is nearly burned down.

MRS. FAIRWEATHER: So much the better, I shall not be able to see your tears.

BADGER: *(Taking a bottle from his pocket.)* There's the concentrated essence of comfort—the poor man's plaster for the inside.

LUCY: *(Aside.)* Is there no way to end this misery? None but death?

BADGER: *(Finds a slice of bread.)* Here's my supper. *(To imaginary servant.)* James, lay the table, spread the cloth. There's a draught in this room, do take care of it, more champagne, James. Don't let the bubbles expire. Thank you, James. *(Drinks & eats.)*

MRS. FAIRWEATHER: *(Aside.)* If Paul had only Lucy to support, they might live. Why should I prolong my life only to hasten theirs?

BADGER: There are great chinks in the wall. I must see my landlord and solicit repairs. A new family moved into the next room, yesterday. I wonder who they are?

LUCY: *(Aside.)* The wretched always have recourse—they can die.

BADGER: Now let us do a little business, James. Gideon Bloodgood is coming for the receipt bequeathed to me by the old sailor. What price shall we set upon it, James?

LUCY: *(Aside.)* When I am gone, there will be one less mouth to feed.

BADGER: When I am rich, I will dine on the finest steaks at Delmonico's,

LUCY: *(Aside.)* When I am gone, Paul will have but one care to provide for.

BADGER: When I am rich, I will have the respect I deserve.

MRS. FAIRWEATHER: *(Rises. Aside.)* In yonder closet we have some charcoal—there is enough left to bestow on me an easy death. *(Exits into closet.)*

BADGER: All I want is to live the life that every man desires.
LUCY: When I am gone, nobody will even know. *(Rises and moves towards closet.)*

BADGER: I think fifty thousand dollars would be the figure! Oh, what a prospect!

LUCY: *(Looks into the closet.)* What is mother doing? She is lighting the pan of charcoal on which we prepare our food. Ah, the thought! Could I induce her to leave me alone? The deadly fumes of that fuel will bestow on me an easy death.

MRS. FAIRWEATHER: *(Enters. Aside.)* Now, while I have the courage of despair.

BADGER: Fifty thousand dollars! I'll have a pair of fast trotters! James, I think I'll have more bubbly. *(Takes a drink.)* Thank you, my good man—you're a pip of a peach!

LUCY: Mother, I just remembered a friend, a girl at work from whom I may get help.

MRS. FAIRWEATHER: Go, then, my child—yes—go at once.

LUCY: I fear to go alone. Come, you can wait at the corner of the street until I come out.

MRS. FAIRWEATHER: *(Aside.)* When she is out of sight I shall return and accomplish my purpose.

LUCY: *(Aside.)* I will come back by another way.

MRS. FAIRWEATHER: Come, Lucy.

LUCY: I am ready, mother. *(Aside.)* She does not think that we are about to part forever.

MRS. FAIRWEATHER: *(Aside.)* My poor child! She does not think that we are about to part forever.

BADGER: Fifty thousand dollars! I'll be a man among the rich!

(LUCY and MRS. FAIRWEATHER exit. The LIGHTING on their side of the adjoining rooms slowly dims.)

BLOODGOOD: *(Enters.)* Ah, Mr. Badger.

BADGER: Please to wipe your feet before you come in—my carpet is new. I am glad to see you. Do take a seat upon my posh sofa. *(Pointing to floor.)*

BLOODGOOD: Come, sir, to business. You have the receipt with you, I trust?

BADGER: You know I have it or you would not have come.

BLOODGOOD: How much do you want for it?

BADGER: Stay a moment. Let us see. You have had in your possession for twenty years, the sum of one hundred thousand dollars—the profits of one robbery. Well, at eight per cent, this sum would now be doubled.

BLOODGOOD: Let me see the document, and then we can estimate its value.

BADGER: *(Removes the receipt from his pocket.)* Here it is.

BLOODGOOD: *(Springing towards him.)* Let me have it.

BADGER: Hands off!

BLOODGOOD: *(Draws pistol.)* That paper, give it me or I'll blow your brains out!

BADGER: *(Backing away.)* Ah, I expected as much from you! *(Draws pistol.)*

BLOODGOOD: Damnation!

BADGER: Mind you, watch your cussing while you're under my roof!

BLOODGOOD: A thousand curses on you!

BADGER: Derringer's self-cocking. Drop your hand, or I'll blow you into the fires of Satan! *(BLOODGOOD drops the gun.)* So, you took me for a fool—that's where you made your mistake. I took you for a thorough rascal—a vile villain—that's where I did not make a mistake. Now, let us do business.

BLOODGOOD: How much do you want?

BADGER: Fifty thousand dollars!

BLOODGOOD: Be it so.

BADGER: In cash.

BLOODGOOD: Very well. Tomorrow—

BADGER: No, tonight.

BLOODGOOD: Tonight?

BADGER: Yes. I wish to purchase a house on the avenue early in the morning.

BLOODGOOD: Come with me to my house in Madison Square.

BADGER: No, thank you. I'll expect you here in an hour with the money.

BLOODGOOD: *(Aside.)* He has me in his power—I must yield. *(Aloud.)* I will return, then, in an hour. *(Exits.)*

(LIGHTING rises on the FAIRWEATHER room as LUCY Enters.)

LUCY: I took a cross street and ran quickly home. The fumes of the charcoal will soon fill this tiny room. They say it is an easy death—but let me not hesitate—let me sleep the long sleep where there are no more tears, no more suffering. *(Exits into closet.)*

BADGER: So, finally it is settled.

MRS. FAIRWEATHER: *(Enters.)* Poor Lucy! I dared not look back upon her, as we parted forever. Despair hastened my steps. My poor children! I have given you all I had, and now I hope my wretched life will serve you in your terrible need. Come, courage —let me to my deep sleep, and may the Good Lord forgive me.

BADGER: *(Sniffing.)* I smell charcoal—burning charcoal— where can it come from? It's very odd. I've a queer feeling in my head. I must lie down awhile. *(Lies on floor.)*

MRS. FAIRWEATHER: *(Crossing to closet as LUCY enters with charcoal brazier.)* Lucy!

LUCY: *(Sets brazier on floor.)* Mother!

MRS. FAIRWEATHER: My child, what is this? For what purpose are you here?

LUCY: And you, mother, why are you here? Like me, you wished to die.

MRS. FAIRWEATHER: No, no, you shall not die! Oh, my darling child—you are young—life is before you—hope—happiness.

LUCY: The future? The man I love will soon wed another. I have no future.

MRS. FAIRWEATHER: Hush, my child, hush.

LUCY: Is it not better to die thus, than by either grief or hunger?

MRS. FAIRWEATHER: *(Falls into chair.)* Already my senses fail. Lucy, my child, live!

LUCY: *(Falls to her feet.)* No. Let us die together.

MRS. FAIRWEATHER: Oh, merciful Judge in heaven, forgive us—

BADGER: I feel quite sleepy. I must not go to sleep.

PAUL: *(From offstage.)* Mother, open the door! Why is the door locked? Mother, mother! Open the door! *(Bursts into the room—he is followed by LIVINGSTONE. PAUL runs to his mother and sister.)* Too late! Too late! They have committed unspeakable suicide!

LIVINGSTONE: They live still. Quick, cover the burning charcoal, and bear them outside into the air. *(Carries LUCY out while PAUL assists his mother to exit.)*

BADGER: *(Rising.)* I cannot breathe. Have I drunk too much? Let me try my legs a bit. Where's the door. I can't see the door— my head spins 'round! I'm suffocating! I'm going to die, to die just like that old sea captain! Bloodgood will return and find me helpless, then, he will rob me of the receipt. He shall not have it! There is a nook under that floorboard. That is where I shall put it —if I have the strength to reach it. *(Drags himself to the spot and places the receipt under a floorboard.)* Forgive me, Lord. I have led a miserable life of sin. Spare me and I will dedicate my life to helping others—

DUF: *(Enters, wearing angel's wings.)* Will you turn from your life of villainy?

BADGER: I will, sweet angel, I will.

DUF: Will you dedicate yourself to helping the poor on the streets of New York?

BADGER: Yes, sweet angel, yes.

DUF: Sleep. All is forgiven. *(Exits.)*

PAUL: *(Enters adjoining room.)* I heard smothered cries coming from this floor. *(Exits.)*

BLOODGOOD: *(Enters.)* Here I am, Badger. What a suffocating atmosphere! Where is he? Ha! He is intoxicated!

PAUL: *(Rushing into BADGER's room)* Perhaps the cry came from in here.

BLOODGOOD: *(Turning quickly.)* Paul Fairweather?

PAUL: Gideon Bloodgood?

BADGER: *(Raising his head.)* What names were those? Both of them—together here? *(To PAUL.)* Listen—while I yet have breath to speak—listen! Twenty years ago, that man robbed your father of one hundred thousand dollars!

PAUL: Robbed?

BLOODGOOD: Scoundrel!

BADGER: I've got the proof.

PAUL: The proof?

BADGER: You'll find it—it—ah— *(He falls backwards, insensible. PAUL and BLOODGOOD stand aghast.)*

Tableau.

LIGHTING FADES to BLACK.

END ACT TWO—Scene 4

6 FULL-LENGTH PLAYS
VOLUME TWO

Edward Crosby Wells

ACT TWO—*Scene 5*

The Fairweather's old cottage in Brooklyn Heights.

DUF: Now, let us go to Brooklyn Heights, just across the river, overlooking the city of New York and her harbors. You can smell the fragrant flowers in Mrs. Fairweather's garden. Ah! How lovely.

(LIGHTING slowly rises and we see MRS. FAIRWEATHER and PAUL are watching PUFFY as he raises the American flag on the lawn flagpole.)

DUF: *(Con't.)* There is Mrs. Fairweather and Paul, and there is Puffy raising the flag high overhead. It is the Fourth of July. What a beautiful sunny day! And, what a beautiful grand old flag!

MUSIC begins. ALL sing. DUF prompts the audience to join in the chorus.

YOU'RE A GRAND OLD FLAG
Words and Music by George M. Cohan

VERSE 1: There's a feeling comes a stealing and it sets my brain a reeling
When I'm listening to the music of a military band.
Any tune like "Yankee Doodle" simply sets me off my noodle,
It's that patriotic something that no one can understand.
"Way down South in the land of cotton," melody untiring, ain't that inspiring!
Hurrah! Hurrah! We'll join the jubilee, and that's going some for the Yankees, by gum!
Red, white and blue, I am for you.
Honest, you're a grand old flag.

CHORUS: You're a grand old flag, though you're torn to a rag,

And forever in peace may you wave.
You're the emblem of the land I love,
The home of the free and the brave.
Every heart beats true under red, white and blue.
Where there's never a boast or brag;
"But should auld acquaintance be forgot,"
Keep your eye on the grand old flag.

VERSE 2: I'm no cranky hanky panky, I'm a dead square honest Yankee,
And I'm mighty proud of that old flag that flies for Uncle Sam.
Though I don't believe in raving every time I see it waving,
There's a chill runs up my back that makes me glad I'm what I am.
Here's a land with a million soldiers, that's if we should need 'em, we'll
fight for freedom!
Hurrah! Hurrah! For every Yankee Tar, and old G.A.R., every stripe, every star,
Red, white and blue, hats off to you. Honest, you're a grand old flag.

(Repeat CHORUS.)

PUFFY: 'Tis a grand old flag! How is dear Miss Lucy this fine Fourth of July morning?

MRS. FAIRWEATHER: Her recovery is slow—she is still very weak.

PAUL: Her life is saved—for a whole month she hovered over the grave.

PUFFY: But why is it we never see Mr. Livingstone? Our benefactor is like Santa Claus—he showers benefits and blessings on us, yet he never shows his face.

MRS. FAIRWEATHER: He brought us back to this, our old home—he obtained employment for Paul in the Navy Yard.

PUFFY: He set me up again with my very own patented oven, and got me a government contract for Navy biscuits.

PAUL: I will tell you why Livingstone avoids our gratitude: Because my sister Lucy refused his love—because he has sold his hand to Alida Bloodgood—and he has given us the purchase money.

PUFFY: And amongst those who have served us, don't let us forget poor Badger.

BADGER: *(Entering.)* Do I hear my name? They are talking about me.

MRS. FAIRWEATHER: Aye! Who'd forget the man who watched over Lucy during her illness with the tenderness of a brother? A mother never forgets such acts of kindness.

PUFFY: Them's my sentiments to the hair.

BADGER: You shan't have cause to change them.

PAUL: Badger, you're looking well.

BADGER: Indeed! Congratulate me. I have been appointed to the police. The commissioners wanted a special service to oversee the doings in Wall Street. All sorts of shenanigans seem to have concentrated there—and we want to catch a big offender.

MRS. FAIRWEATHER: *(Rises.)* I will tell Lucy that her nurse has come. *(Exits.)*

PAUL: Now, Badger, the news.

BADGER: Bad news, sir. Tonight, just before the great fireworks display, Mr. Mark Livingstone is to be married to Miss Alida Bloodgood.

PAUL: What shall I do? I dare not accuse Bloodgood of this robbery, unless you can produce the proof—and perhaps the wretch has discovered and destroyed it.

BADGER: I think not. When I recovered from the effects of the charcoal, the day after my suffocation, I started for my lodging. I found the house shut up, guarded by a servant of Bloodgood's— the banker had bought the building. But I had concealed the document too cunningly. No, sir, he has not found it.

PAUL: Knowing this man to be a felon, can we allow Livingstone to marry his daughter?

LIVINGSTONE: *(Enters.)* Paul, I have come to bid you farewell, and to see Lucy for the last time—

LUCY: *(Enters.)* For the last time, why so—

PAUL and BADGER rush to her aid.

LIVINGSTONE: Lucy, dear Lucy.

BADGER: Now take care—sit down—

LUCY: Ah, my good and kind nurse—*(She sits.)* You are always by my side.

BADGER: Always ready with a dose of nasty medicine, aint I? Well, now I got another dose ready. Do you see this noble kind heart, Lucy? *(Indicates LIVINGSTONE.)* It looks through two honest blue eyes into your face—tell him, tell him what you see in there . . .

LUCY: Why do you trouble me so?

BADGER: Don't turn your eyes away. The time has come when deception is a crime, Lucy. Look into his face, and confess the infernal scheme by which Alida Bloodgood compelled you to renounce your love.

LIVINGSTONE: Alida!

LUCY: Has she betrayed me?

BADGER: No, you have betrayed yourself. In the ravings of your fever, while I held your trembling hands, I heard the cries that came from your poor wounded heart.

LUCY: *(Hiding her face in her hands.)* No, no.

LIVINGSTONE: Paul, is this true? Have I been deceived?

PAUL: You have—Lucy confessed to me this infamous bargain, extorted from her by Alida Bloodgood—and to save you from ruin she sacrificed her love.

LIVINGSTONE: Lucy. Dear Lucy, look up. It was for your sake alone that I accepted this hated union—to save you and yours from poverty—but whisper one word, tell me that ruin of fortune is better than ruin of the heart.

(LUCY rushes into LIVINGSTONE's arms. BOTH sing.)

BOTH: Let me call you "Sweetheart," I'm in love with you.
Let me hear you whisper that you love me too.
Keep the love-light glowing in your eyes so true.
Let me call you "Sweetheart," I'm in love with you.

(MRS. FAIRWEATHER rushes in with the old sea captain's telescope.)

MRS. FAIRWEATHER: Take a look through this! There seems to be a fire over in New York—Five Points—and if I'm not mistaken— *(BADGER grabs the telescope.)*

PAUL: Now Mark, I can confess to you that a document exists—proof of felony against Bloodgood, which may at any moment consign him to the State Prison and transfer to our family his ill-gotten wealth.

LIVINGSTONE: Proof of felony?

BADGER: *(Looking up from the telescope.)* The fire is in Cross Street!

PAUL: Twenty years ago he robbed my father of one hundred thousand dollars.

BADGER: Damnation! It is our old lodging! And the proof of Bloodgood's felony is yonder, in that burning house—fired by Bloodgood to destroy the evidence! Curses—a thousand curses on him! Quick—for our lives! The fortunes of Lucy and Paul and Mrs. Fairweather are all in that burning house! I go to save it or to perish in the flames!

Tableau.

LIGHTING FADES to BLACK

END ACT ONE—Scene 5

ACT TWO—*Scene 6*
Outside the Cross Street tenement house. The stage is dark.

DUF: What dirty deeds are done in the name of money! Welcome to Number nineteen and a half Cross Street—Five Points.

BLOODGOOD: *(Carries a candle across the darkened stage.)* In a few hours, this accursed house will be in the ruins! The receipt is concealed there—and it will be consumed in the flames! Ha! *(A red burning glow begins to spill onto the street.)* Now Badger—do your worst—I am safe! *(He runs to exit.)*

(The SOUNDS of horns and bells and people shouting 'Fire, fire." BADGER is seen running. He disappears into the burning building. More cries from the crowd—mere shadows on the corner of the street. Loud crashes are heard. Cries of horror are uttered by the mob. BADGER drags himself from the ruins and collapses. LIVINGSTONE, PAUL and PUFFY rush in. PAUL kneels by the still body of BADGER and extinguishes the fire that clings to parts of his clothes.)

PUFFY: Will he live?

PAUL: Only God knows that answer.

Tableau.

LIGHTING FADES to BLACK.

END ACT TWO—*Scene 6*

ACT TWO—*Scene 7:*
An Olio.

DUF: Ladies and gentlemen, Miss Alida Bloodgood—soon to be Mrs. Alida Livingstone—will perform for us her last song of maidenhood.

(A single SPOTLIGHT illuminates ALIDA. She is wearing her wedding dress. ALIDA sings and DUF coaches the audience to sing along with the chorus.)

TA-RA-RA BOOM-DE-AY
Author(s) unknown.

VERSE1: A smart and stylish girl you see,
Queen of swell society,
Not to strict but rather free
When it's on the straight Q.T.

CHORUS: Ta-ra-ra boom-de-ay!
Ta-ra-ra boom-de-ay!Ta-ra-ra boom-de-ay!
Ta-ra-ra boom-de-ay!
Ta-ra-ra boom-de-ay!
Ta-ra-ra boom-de-ay!
Ta-ra-ra boom-de-ay!Ta-ra-ra boom-de-ay!

VERSE 2: But the very thing I'm told,
Not too timid, not too bold.
Just the kind you'd like to hold,
Not too hot and not too cold.

CHORUS: Ta-ra-ra boom-de-ay!
Ta-ra-ra boom-de-ay!
Ta-ra-ra boom-de-ay!
Ta-ra-ra boom-de-ay!
Ta-ra-ra boom-de-ay!

Ta-ra-ra boom-de-ay
Ta-ra-ra boom-de-ay!

LIGHTING FADES to BLACK.

END ACT TWO—*Scene 7*

ACT TWO—*Scene 8:*
The drawing room of the Bloodgood home.

DUF: Here we are in the drawing room of Bloodgood's Mansion, in Madison Square. Soon the Bloodgood home will be a-buzz with the sound of a wedding. And here comes Mr. Gideon Bloodgood, the soon-to-be—but rather reluctant—father of the bride. *(Exits.)*

BLOODGOOD: *(Enters.)* The evidence of my crime is destroyed —no power on earth can reveal the past. *(ALIDA enters, in her wedding gown.)* My dearest child, tonight you will leave this roof; but from this home in your father's heart, none can displace you.

ALIDA: Pish-posh, papa, do take care of my flounces—you men paw one about as if a dress was put on only to be rumpled.

BLOODGOOD: The rooms below are full of company. Has Livingstone arrived?

ALIDA: I did not inquire. Must I do everything? The duke is there. Looking the picture of misery, while all my female friends pretend to congratulate me—but I know they are dying with envy and spite.

BLOODGOOD: And do these feelings constitute the happiest day of your life? Alida, have you no heart?

ALIDA: Yes, father, I have a heart—but it is like yours. It is an iron safe in which are kept the secrets of the past.

(Enter LIVINGSTONE, dressed as he was when last seen.)

BLOODGOOD: Ah! At last! What a strange costume for a bridegroom.

ALIDA: *(Turns and views LIVINGSTONE.)* Had I not good reasons to be assured of your sincerity, Mr. Livingstone, your appearance would lead me to believe that you looked upon this marriage as a jest, or a masquerade.

LIVINGSTONE: As you say, Miss Bloodgood, it is a masquerade—but it is one where more than one mask must fall.

BLOODGOOD: *(Aside.)* What does he mean?

ALIDA: How dare you speak to me in that tone?

BLOODGOOD: Perhaps I had better see Mr. Livingstone alone —he may be under some misapprehension.

LIVINGSTONE: I am under none, sir. Although, I believe you may be. What I have to say demands no concealment. I come here to decline the hand of your daughter.

BLOODGOOD: You must explain this public insult! Guests are gathered below!

LIVINGSTONE: I am here to do so, but I do not owe this explanation to you; I owe it to myself. *(To ALIDA.)* I found myself in your father's debt; he held in pledge all I possessed— all but my good name; the name he wanted to shelter the infamy of his own soiled name. I was vile enough to sell it.

ALIDA: These matters you were fully acquainted with when you sought my hand.

LIVINGSTONE: But I was not acquainted with the contents of these letters—written by you, to the Duke of Calcavella—given me by the Duke himself.

BLOODGOOD: Dare you insinuate their contents derogatory to the honor of my child?

LIVINGSTONE: No, sir, but I think Miss Bloodgood will agree with me, that the sentiments expressed in these letters entitle her to the hand of the duke rather than to mine. *(He hands the letter to ALIDA.)*

ALIDA: Throw him out, father!

LIVINGSTONE: Not yet. You forget that my friends are assembled downstairs to witness a marriage, and all we require is a bride.

BLOODGOOD: Yes; a bride who can pay your debts.

PAUL: *(Enters, followed by MRS FAIRWEATHER.)* No, sir—a bride who can place the hand of a pure and loving maiden in that of a good and honest man.

ALIDA: Pish-posh!

BLOODGOOD: Be still, daughter! *(To PAUL.)* How dare you intrude in this house?

PAUL: Because it is mine—because your whole fortune will scarcely serve to pay the debt you owe the widow and the children of Captain Adam Fairweather!

BLOODGOOD: Is my house to be invaded by beggars? Is there no law in New York for ruffians? I shall summon the police!

BADGER: *(Entering in the uniform of a police officer.)* And here's the police!

BLOODGOOD: Badger!

BADGER: What's left of him.

BLOODGOOD: *(Wildly.)* Is this a conspiracy to ruin me?

BADGER: That's it. We began it twenty years ago. We've been hatching it ever since. We let you build up a fortune—we tempted you to become an incendiary—we led you on from misdemeanor to felony—and that's what I want you for.

BLOODGOOD: What do you mean?

BADGER: My meaning is set forth very clearly in an affidavit, on which the Recorder, at this very late hour and on this day we celebrate American independence, has issued this warrant for your arrest. *(Hands him the warrant.)*

BLOODGOOD: Incendiary? Dare you charge a man of my standing in this city, with such a crime—without any cause?

BADGER: Cause? You wanted to burn up this receipt, which I was just in time to rescue from the flames.

BLOODGOOD: *(Drawing a knife.)* Fiend! You escaped the flames here—now go to those never ending flames in the burning pits of the Hereafter!

BADGER: Not so fast! *(Disarms BLOODGOOD and slips a pair of handcuffs on him.)*

ALIDA: Oh, pish-posh, daddy.

BADGER: Oh, shut up, tootles!

ALIDA: Father—

BLOODGOOD: Alida, my child.

ALIDA: How utterly thoughtless of you! Is this what I have come to? Am I now to be the felon's daughter?

BLOODGOOD: Alida, my child, it was for you alone I sinned—do not leave me.

ALIDA: What should I do in this city? What am I fit for? *(Throws down her bride's coronet.)* —the same fate as you—infamy. Oh, pish-posh! *(She turns and exits.)*

BADGER: Gideon, my dear, shall we depart for the station house.

BLOODGOOD: Take me away; I have lost my child—my sweet Alida!

PAUL: Stay! Mr. Bloodgood, in the midst of your crime there was one virtue: You loved your child; even now your heart deplores her ruin—not your own. Badger, give me that receipt. *(Takes the receipt.)* Do you acknowledge this paper to be genuine?

BLOODGOOD: I do.

PAUL: *(Tears it.)* I have no charge against you. Let him be released. Restore to me my fortune, and take the rest; go, follow your child; save her from ruin, and live a better life. *(BADGER releases BLOODGOOD from the handcuffs.)*

BLOODGOOD: You are a far better man than I. Perhaps there is time yet to teach my daughter of goodness—and the true meaning of riches. *(Exits.)*

LIVINGSTONE: That was nobly done, Paul. Now, my friends, since all is prepared for my marriage let us go down and let the ceremony proceed.

BADGER: But, where is Lucy?

PAUL: Lucy awaits downstairs. Don't you know that it is bad luck for the groom to see the bride before the wedding?

LIVINGSTONE: Come, let us proceed—I mean to claim the delicate hand of my love—Miss Lucy Fairweather—soon to be Mrs. Lucy Livingstone.

(ALL start toward the exit to the ceremony. But they turn and are soon joined by the ENTIRE CAST. LUCY is wearing a wedding dress. DUF enters.)

DUF: Alms. Alms for poor ol' beggar Duf.

BADGER: Come, sir. Take this money *(Hands DUF some folded bills)* and join us in celebration.

MRS. FAIRWEATHER: We'd be honored if you would join our wedding party, Duffy.

DUF: Thank you, ma'am. But, it ain't Duffy—it's just plain Duf.

MRS. FAIRWEATHER: What kind of name is Duf, I wonder?

DUF: Don't know, ma'am. I was raised by pirates—until I escaped. It's the only name I ever knowed. *(Displays his medal on a chain around his neck.)* See this is the patron saint of sailors, Brigid of Ireland, and on the back is my name. See—D-U-F, Duf.

MRS. FAIRWEATHER: Bless us and save us! That doesn't say Duf. Them's your initials, boy—Daniel Ulysses Fairweather— our long lost son—kidnapped by pirates! See. *(Showing him her medal.)* I have a medal just like that, and so does Paul and Lucy, your brother and sister.

DUF: Mother?

PAUL & LUCY: Brother?

MRS. FAIRWEATHER: Bless us and save us, son. My prayers have been answered. *(ALL embrace.)*

BADGER: Oh, joy! Oh, Joy! *(To MRS. FAIRWEATHER.)* You have seen the dark side of life—you can appreciate your fortune, for you have learned the value of wealth.

MRS. FAIRWEATHER: No, we have learned the value of poverty. *(She gives her hand to BADGER.)* It opens the heart.

PAUL: *(To audience.)* Is this true? Have the sufferings we have depicted touched your hearts, and caused a tear of sympathy to fill your eyes? If so, extend to us your hands.

DUF: *(To audience.)* No, not to us—but when you leave this place, as you return to your homes, should you see some poor creatures, extend your hands to them, and the blessings that will follow you on your way will be the most grateful tribute you can pay to the poor—not just the poor of New York—but the poor of America. *(Extends his hand.)* A penny, please. *(A beat.)* Everybody, please join us in song and celebration—

AMERICA THE BEAUTIFUL
Words by Katharine Lee Bates,
Melody by Samuel Ward

O beautiful for spacious skies,
For amber waves of grain,
For purple mountain majesties
Above the fruited plain!
America! America!
God shed his grace on thee
And crown thy good with brotherhood
From sea to shining sea!

(This goes into a MEDLEY of songs sung earlier. When the MEDLEY ends, the SOUNDS and the LIGHTING of fireworks explodes across the stage.)

LIGHTING dims to BLACKOUT

END OF PLAY

3 GUYS IN DRAG
SELLING THEIR STUFF

Dedicated to Frank Calo who helped in giving birth to 3 GUYS, which grew to be something fabulous. Thank you, Frank.

SYNOPSIS: Diva, Lillian, and Tink (three men in drag) are having a yard sale to raise funds for a Faberge egg in which to place the ashes of Diva's dead husband. Diva bosses Lillian, whose principal expertise is making punch with ingredients that could fuel a rocket. Tink is confined to a wheelchair, mostly comatose, but when she does try to make herself heard, the others invariably misunderstand, causing dire consequences. The miscommunications of this misfit trio cause a friend to be run over by a pickup truck while trying to cross the street with her walker. We meet an entire neighborhood of characters through the eyes of the "ladies" during the course of their yard sale, including Diva's mother who has the yard wired with eavesdropping devices and is listening in from her room in a nursing home across the street. Finally, in an explosive climax, the day's *she-nanigans* result in a police shootout when someone plays with a starter pistol filled with blanks. This is a raucous, raunchy, pee-in your-pants, more than a laugh-a-minute play.

3 GUYS IN DRAG SELLING THEIR STUFF, developed and produced by Spotlight On Productions, premiered at the Raw Space Theatre in NYC on January 20, 2000 under the direction of Frank Calo with the following cast and crew:
DIVA: Robert C. Boston, Jr.
LILLIAN: Dana Pointe
TINK: Myles Cohen
Director: Frank Calo
Stage Manager: Sue Marticek
Lighting Designer: Louis Lopardi
Sound Designer: Frank Calo
Set Designers: Tom Barz and Sue Marticek
Costume Designer: Steven Thornburg
Publicity: Calthor Productions

CHARACTERS: DIVA, LILLIAN and TINK. Three elderly women of means. As the title implies, men in drag should play these characters.

SETTING: The action of the play takes place in Diva's front yard somewhere in Suburbia, USA. It is summer. The time is the present. Pleasant weather.

NOTE TO THE DIRECTOR: Keep in mind that the title of this play includes "GUYS" and not "DRAG QUEENS." I have seen numerous productions of this play and can say with certainty that those that worked best, received the biggest laughs, and sold more tickets were played with sincerity. Trust the dialogue. Over-the-top burlesque, buffoonery or drag-queenery, will only turn your audience off and do disservice to the script, the author, and to the humanity of the characters. However, you may include recorded music for the characters to lip-sync anywhere within the play you feel that the dialog/action has something in common with the song. Music, I believe it can only enhance the enjoyment of your production.

A FEW REVIEWS

". . . a trashy delight . . . Diva and Lillian hark straight back to Jackie Gleason and Art Carney . . . And finally, a la South Park, results in a police shootout when someone plays with a cap gun. A satisfying result for a laugh-a-minute, harebrained play. It takes place on a suburban planet of its own." —John Chatterton, OOBR

"With the help of some brilliant dialogue, and the clever antics of the three characters, your mind's eye will create the entire neighborhood including an elderly friend who is hit by a truck, a handsome Greek motorcyclist, and Diva's mother in the nursing home across the street. Lillian's punch, made especially for the occasion, is heavily spiked and the plot gets more outrageous as the "girls" imbibe." —KDHX, St. Louis

"3 Guys in Drag Selling Their Stuff is side-splitting, to say the least . . . wicked wit . . . hilarious. Wells' script is silly, but structured and sprinkled with sensitive moments that further endear his characters to audience members." —Elias Stimac, New York Off-Off Broadway Review

"This play does what Beckett was trying to do, but Beckett was too squeamish to face the facts of the decline of the West. Wells faces them with hilarious completeness, and therefore is able to be both funnier and more tragic than Beckett ever was."—Robert Patrick, Drama Desk and OBIE Award Winning Playwright and Author of Kennedy's Children.

"3 Guys' provides color coordinated joys and sorrows . . . a surreal but touching comedy by Edward Crosby Wells. Whether you call them drag queens or cross- dressers, whether or not you admire their heightened appreciation for the extra dimensions of style in female clothing, these males have all the human emotions of everyone else." —Chuck Graham, Tucson Citizen

"For two hours, we witness the dysfunctional antics of the trashiest members of the Social Register; it's a sort of 'Grey Gardens' garage sale." —James Reel, Tucson Weekly

"A raucous comedy gets unleashed . . . hilarious . . . The unexpected complications create the high humor." —Jesse Greenburg, The Desert Leaf, Tucson

". . . 3 Guys in Drag Selling Their Stuff actually connects to issues that profoundly matter . . . we have a duty to think on these things and do what little we can to make this world a better place."
—Andrew Eaton, The Scotsman, Edinburgh, Scotland

" . . . very, very funny. It is also extremely rude, but if you are broad-minded enough then the one-liners come so thick and fast you barely have time to recover from the last joke before the next one slaps you in the face . . . Like any good play, the audience felt drawn to the characters and by the time they finished with a big show tune the fact that they were men in drag seemed to be the most natural thing in the world." —David Muncaster, The Knutsford Times, England

"Delightful." Deb Flomberg, Denver Theatre Examiner

". . . fun, campy, sometimes poignant. It may not change your life but it may make you change your red muumuu. The show is filled with witty one-liners and the expected crass sex jokes and vibrators. If you are looking for an evening of campy barbs and drag-queen bitchiness, you'll get your money's worth." —Susan Zelenka, Daily Loaf, St. Petersburg, FL

"If you're looking for profound insight into the world of gender bending, well, look elsewhere. This show offers a few profound moments where you really 'get' where it's all coming from, but for the most part, it's a frothy, funny and at moments hammy ode to men in dresses and the bitter travails of yard sales. The play is

by Edward Crosby Wells who has definitely gone for the silly, but the play has sufficient structure and sensitive intimacy to endear these characters to the audience even as they strut and pose and play their roles with farcical physical comedy and sharply witty lines . . . The simple fact of it is that when you hear of a play called 3 Guys in Drag Selling Their Stuff, you can pretty much figure on something witty and a little out of the mainstream. If you think that means good fun, you would be right on the money . . . profound moments . . . but for the most part, it's a frothy, funny and at moments hammy . . . Go, enjoy a guilty pleasure with an offbeat comedy that lets you put your mind in park and laugh." —Lynn Welburn, Daily News, Nanaimo, B.C., Canada

"'Three Guys in Drag Selling Their Stuff' provides comedy, definition of friendship . . . witty . . . a light-hearted, refreshing comedy . . . an airy play to watch . . . constantly keeps the jokes flowing. —Westley Thompson, The Daily Athenaeum, Morgantown, WV

6 FULL-LENGTH PLAYS
VOLUME TWO

Edward Crosby Wells

ACT ONE

Handcuffs, vibrators, chains and whips mixed in with Tupperware, silver trays, crystal figurines, objets d'art and an endless assortment of odds and ends are piled into a child's red wagon. There are mannequins and dress forms covered with wigs, beads, feathers and fabrics. A card table holds yet more items for sale as well as a bowl of punch and a tray of glasses. There are pillars of marble and plaster supporting statues, busts and Chinese vases. There is more "stuff" scattered around DIVA'S front yard. There is a sign that reads "YARD SALE" and another that reads "FREE PUNCH."

(DIVA and LILLIAN are busy sorting through their sale items, marking prices, polishing and admiring. TINK is in a wheelchair with her back to the audience.)

DIVA: *(Looks up quickly as if someone had just yelled something out to her. Directly to audience – to someone in particular.)* What!? What are you? Crazy? Can't you read, you silly shit? Punch! Punch! There's no such thing as a free lunch! Unless, you want Jesus along with your soup. Anyway, that's somewhere else. Another part of town. Certainly not in this neighborhood. No, I am not knocking Jesus. Don't get yourself all puffed up. I was referring to those good Christian missions somewhere down by the railroad tracks. Sir . . . sir, please. Please. Put your finger away. I don't like to be pointed at. . . . Oh . . . well, it looks like a finger. Dear me. . . . Really? With that? I can't imagine it being of much use to anyone. . . . A name? What's that? Pokey? How quaint. . . . It is? You do? With that little. . . ? You want me to what? Sir, the prizes in Cracker Jacks are bigger than that. Sir, please put it away while it's still amusing. . . . Goodbye. Have a nice day. *(She waves and we can see her eyes following this unseen man as he retreats down the street.)*

LILLIAN: Oh, my! I hardly know what to say.

DIVA: Then stop drooling, Lillian! When one doesn't know what to say it is best to say nothing. It has always been a deterrent to hoof in mouth disease. *(She shakes her leg frantically.*

LILLIAN: *(Observing DIVA shaking her leg.)* Looks more like mad cow disease, Diva.

DIVA: Phone.

LILLIAN: Foam in mouth disease?

DIVA: *(Still shaking her leg.)* Telephone! *(Reaches up under her skirt to retrieve her cell phone from under her garter.)* I have it on vibrate. *(Answering her cell phone.)* Diva Hollingsworth here and who might you be? Oh, hello, Carlotta. *(To LILLIAN.)* Carlotta Bean. *(LILLIAN sneers. DIVA speaks into phone.)* Back from Greece so soon? . . . Well, we must get together so you can tell me all about it. The splendor. The wine. The food. The . . . what? You did what? A tourist guide at the Acropolis? He what? Behind a pillar? Oh, no, dear. I wouldn't call that discreet at all. Some might, but most wouldn't – certainly not I. Fairly brazen, if the truth be known. . . . What do you mean he doesn't speak English? When did you learn to speak Greek? . . . Oh. Well, a word or two does not a sentence make, now does it, Carlotta? He is? *(To LILLIAN.)* She brought home some stud she picked up off the streets in Athens. She put him up in the Paisley Room and he's teaching her a little Greek in exchange for rent. (Into phone.) I was sharing the good news with Lillian. Right next to me. We're having a yard sale. *(To LILLIAN.)* Carlotta says hello. *(LILLIAN sneers.)* Hello right back at you. I had a little Greek once –a sailor from Crete. A Cretan Greek . . . and a royal pain in the ass, as I recall. Yes. Well, I'm sure this one is the personification of perfection, dear heart. . . . You don't say. Do tell. He's not? He is? In the kitchen? Doing what in the what? Well, you run right along. Yes, yes hurry. Don't let me detain you. One mustn't keep a naked Greek alone for too long with a pound of feta and a dozen grape leaves. . . . I love you, too. *Ciao.*

(Turns off the phone and puts it back under her garter.) She is such a slut!

LILLIAN: I never could stand the bitch.

DIVA: Me either. *(Calling out to some passing cars.)* Free punch! Free punch over here! *(To LILLIAN.)* Is it time to turn Tink?

LILLIAN: *(Takes a look at TINK.)* She's napping. Maybe we ought to let her be. You know how she likes her beauty rest. Although, at her age, beauty isn't really a major concern, is it?

DIVA: How would I know? And, since I cannot project myself that far into the future, it will – for the time being – remain one of life's many unsolved mysteries.

LILLIAN: I meant, that when you reach her age, just continuing to breathe must pretty much occupy one's mind. All those little synapses pulsating in out, in out, in out. . . .

DIVA: Would you spare us the gory details!

LILLIAN: We'll turn Tink when the sun moves along a bit.

DIVA: Good idea. *(Looking at building across the street.)* That's where I've decided to put her, Lillian.

LILLIAN: Who? Where?

DIVA: Mother. There. *(Points.)* She's become too much of a burden. Last night she urinated on Uncle Sam.

LILLIAN: I beg your pardon?

DIVA: She wrapped her legs around him and took a whiz.

LILLIAN: On purpose?

DIVA: Does it matter?

LILLIAN: One would like to think so. How did he take it?

DIVA: Well, he wasn't happy, if that is what you mean. I dropped him off at the groomers first thing this morning. They'll fluff him up good as new.

LILLIAN: Poor Uncle Sam.

DIVA: Well, she's going in that home over there. I've already begun making arrangements. I will not have my mother urinating on whomever or whatever strikes her fancy. *(Waving downstage to an unseen customer.)* Oh, hello there. See anything you like? . . . Well, of course you can browse. Browse all you want. After all, life's just one big yard sale, isn't it? . . . Well, it can be. . . . I guess it's all in how one looks at it, if you look at it that way. . . . No. I suppose one doesn't have to look at it that way. No one is going to force you to. Unless, you live in China. . . . Of course you don't. . . . Of course this isn't China. I was simply making a figure of speech. *(To LILLIAN.)* Honestly! Dense and literal. Where, pray tell, do people like her come from?

LILLIAN: Just a few blocks over, Diva.

DIVA: She's not quite together, if you ask me. Missing some essential parts, no doubt. *(To customer.)* Just call me if you want anything, dear. . . . Diva. Diva will do just fine. *(To LILLIAN.)* I hope she doesn't die in that condition.

LILLIAN: What condition is that?

DIVA: A total eclipse.

LILLIAN: I don't understand.

DIVA: Of course you don't. And that's because you've been doing too much left brain thinking for your own good.

LILLIAN: How can you tell?

DIVA: How can I tell what?

LILLIAN: Left from right.

DIVA: Simple. All I have to do is remember which hand I use for administering my douche.

LILLIAN: No . . . I meant. . . .

DIVA: Oh, I know perfectly well what you meant. . . but, you're becoming quite tedious. *(To customer.)* What did you say, dear? . . . No. I wasn't talking to you. I was talking to Lillian here. I was telling her that it was she who was becoming quite tedious. Too much red meat. Whether you are or are not remains to be determined. *(To LILLIAN, referring to customer.)* The hearing of a bull elephant. The visage of one, too. *(To customer.)* What's that, dear? . . . No. Certainly not! My bathroom is off limits. . . . Weak kidneys or not, I'm afraid you'll have to devise some other plan for your bladder. *(To LILLIAN.)* The nerve of that woman. Who does she think she is?

LILLIAN: Oh, that's Mrs. Something-or-other. You know the one who headed that concerned citizens' group for a better something or other . . . or maybe they were the ones who boycotted grapes. I just can't seem to remember. *(To customer.)* If you see something you like – anything you can't live without – don't be afraid to haggle. I'm sure we can come to some agreement. . . . Oh, I'm sorry to hear that. We buried our husbands, too. . . . Well, I did. Diva keeps hers in a jar. An old pickle jar, I think. That's why we're having this yard sale. So we can move him out of the pickle jar.

DIVA: And into a proper resting place.

LILLIAN: An egg. We're raising money to put Horace's ashes into an egg.

DIVA: By Faberge. Severely expensive. It would be in very bad taste were I to say exactly how much.

LILLIAN: *Gauche.*

DIVA: *Oui. Tres gauche.* Suffice to say that it is a great deal more than the annual budget of some third world countries. However, due to my wealth and position, only an unremarkable sum in addition to what I've already accumulated is needed. I shouldn't want to dip into my retirement funds, now should I? Of course not. You understand.

LILLIAN: *(To customer.)* What? No! Why would we joke about a thing like that? He died in his sleep. . . . No, mine did. Diva's husband was doing something else altogether.

DIVA: *(To customer.)* In the garden . . . doing sit-ups in the cucumber patch. Just keeled over. . . . No. I haven't done any pickling since. . . . You do? That's nice. Bread and butter or dill?

LILLIAN: *(Ibid.)* They do? Try a half-teaspoon of cloves next time. Oh, yes. That'll brighten them right up. . . . Well, you're very welcome. . . . You, too.

BOTH: *(Watching customer leave.)* Have a nice day.

DIVA: *(Pouring a glass of punch for herself and for LILLIAN.)* Cheapskate! Who did she think she was?

LILLIAN: Is that rhetorical? Or do you actually want me to go ahead and take a guess.

DIVA: Don't guess, Lillian. The odds are not in your favor.

LILLIAN: Neither are the planets.

DIVA: What?

LILLIAN: The planets. According to my horoscope this morning, the planets are not in my favor.

DIVA: What a shame.

LILLIAN: It sure is, Diva. Something terrible will happen if I venture forth into love or business today.

DIVA: Then don't venture forth, dear. Besides, the last time you ventured forth into love Johnny Mathis was on the Victrola and you were on your knees. Anyway, that's a lot of superstitious nonsense and I wouldn't worry about it were I you. You really ought to watch that left brain thinking, Lillian.

LILLIAN: *(After a pause to sip punch.)* So, who do you think she was?

DIVA: Who what was?

LILLIAN: She was.

DIVA: Who she?

LILLIAN: The woman who wanted to use your bathroom. The cheapskate. Who do you think she was?

DIVA: Someone who is directly responsible for the ruination of the American economy.

LILLIAN: Really?

DIVA: Most certainly! One cannot go through life browsing without stopping to buy a thing or two. Do you know what makes our system work?

LILLIAN: I can't say that I do, Diva.

DIVA: Buying! Buying makes our system work. If people don't buy – people can't sell. And if people can't sell, guess what?

LILLIAN: What?

DIVA: Hello China! Some concerned citizen she is! She probably drove her husband to his grave.

LILLIAN: Oh, no. He shot himself in the foot, as I recall.

DIVA: You don't die from shooting yourself in the foot, Lillian.

LILLIAN: You do if you're being attacked by a bear in heat.

DIVA: *(After an incredulous pause.)* Do you make this stuff up as we go along?

LILLIAN *(After a pause to earnestly think.)* No. Not all the time. Only some of the time. I seem to recall there being some truth to this one though. Yes. It was a hot day in the Catskills and. . . .

DIVA: Lillian! Stop it! I no longer have a reliable sense for reality. I don't know if I am coming or if I am going. The woman in the mirror has abducted what was left of an extremely attractive youth. I am losing what little faith I once felt I had in God – and, I am sure He doesn't pay me the attention I feel He ought to be paying one so dearly in need of Him as I. And, furthermore, eighty milligrams of Prozac, daily, has ceased to do its magic! So, please. . . . Don't complicate my life anymore than need be.

LILLIAN: *(After a pause to assimilate.)* That hardly has anything to do with me, Diva.

DIVA: It has everything to do with you, Lillian.

LILLIAN: Yeah? Well, I beg to differ.

DIVA: Don't you get it, Lillian? You're beginning to make sense to me and everybody we know knows you don't make one bit of sense to anybody about anything at anytime! So, where does that leave me? Huh?

LILLIAN: I don't know. I thought you were my best friend.

DIVA: I am your best friend.

LILLIAN: Then, what's the problem?

DIVA: Why am I your best friend?

LILLIAN: Rhetorical?

DIVA: Absolutely. I am your best friend because . . . because. . . .

LILLIAN: I'm the only one who puts up with your shit?

DIVA: Well, yes. But, not only that. Because. . . .

LILLIAN: Because I know that under that reptilian exterior is a fragile little girl?

DIVA: I shall take comfort and interpret that as your unique little way of expressing affection.

LILLIAN: Whatever floats your boat, sister.

DIVA: That was totally uncalled for! You know how I hate popular vernacular! I'm suffering anxiety and you're dishing out nautical cliché.

LILLIAN: I was just getting in practice for our next meeting with Carlotta Bean. Sorry. Take deep breaths. That'll make you feel right as rain. In through your nose . . . out through your mouth.

DIVA: *(Deep breathing.)* Ah. . . .

LILLIAN: Better?

DIVA: Much. *(Hugs LILLIAN.)* Thank you. You're such a treasure.BOTH: *(Calling to passing cars.)* Free punch! Free punch! Get your free punch here!

(Slowly, the wheelchair turns and we see that TINK is in some sort of distress.)

TINK: *(Struggles desperately to speak.) Ja . . . ja . . . ja. . . .*

LILLIAN: Oh, hello, Tink. Did you have a nice nappy-wappy?

TINK: *Ja . . . ja . . . ja. . . .*

LILLIAN: Japanese? Are you trying to say Japanese?

DIVA: Why on earth would she be trying to say Japanese?

LILLIAN: Well, how do I know, Diva? Everywhere you look you see something Japanese. Maybe she wants her hibachi – I don't know.

TINK: *Ja . . . ja . . . ja . . . oow . . . ja . . . oow. . . .*

DIVA: Zsa Zsa! No, Raul! Oh, Raul. Do you remember Raul, Lillian?

LILLIAN: Who?

DIVA: Raul. Tink's gardener. The one with the giant bushwhacker.

LILLIAN: *Ooh . . . ah . . .* oh, yes. He was something, wasn't he? Whatever happened to him . . . and his bushwhacker?

DIVA: They cremated him and it with him.

LILLIAN: He died?

DIVA: Requisite for cremation, Lillian. Of course he died!

LILLIAN: That's too bad. How sad. I think I'm going to cry.

DIVA: Lillian, what is wrong with you? Did you leave home without your head today?

LILLIAN: No. I don't think so.

TINK: *Ja . . . ja . . . ja. . . .*

DIVA: Now, don't get yourself excited, Tink. Raul's no longer with us. In fact, he hasn't been with us since Reagan left office. *(To LILLIAN.)* Now, that was a man after my own heart.

LILLIAN: Reagan?

DIVA: Sure. Why not? He could put his shoes under my bed any day. Besides, what did Nancy have that I don't?

LILLIAN: A red dress?

DIVA: I've got a red dress.

LILLIAN: Size two?

DIVA: I hate you!

LILLIAN: *(Ignoring the last.)* Besides, I never understood a word he said. In fact, I don't really think old Ronnie actually ever said anything . . . just a string of words designed to put you to sleep. Heaven knows he put himself to sleep often enough. Poor thing, couldn't remember himself from one minute to the next. Bless his departed soul.

DIVA: You never liked any of my men, did you?

LILLIAN: Well, let me see. How many of your men did I have?

DIVA: Don't get smart!

LILLIAN: Diva, I hardly think Ronald Reagan qualifies as one of your men. More like an imaginary playmate, I should think. *(DIVA "humphs.")* What about Mister Trump? Is he one of your men?

DIVA: You can die right now, Lillian! A slow and painful death.

LILLIAN: Sorry.

TINK: *Sa . . . sa . . . sa. . . .*

LILLIAN: Salt! She wants salt!

DIVA: I don't think so, Lillian. Has she had her insulin today?

LILLIAN: Of course. While I was waiting to pick her up, Margie was giving her the injection.

DIVA: Who's Margie?

LILLIAN: The new nurse the agency sent over. She's a bit of a bull, but I guess if she's with the agency she knows what she's doing. She says she's really a lady wrestler.

DIVA: What are you talking about? Who's really a lady wrestler?

LILLIAN: Nurse Margie the bull. She said she was between gigs – or, something like that. Her husband's also a lady wrestler. He's between gigs, too. So, he stays home and cooks.

DIVA: How very perverse.

TINK: *Ja . . . ja . . . ja . . . oow . . . sa. Ja . . . oow . . . sa.*

LILLIAN: Joust! She wants to see a joust. Now, if you wanted to see a joust, Diva, where would you go?

DIVA: *(Exasperated.)* For God's sake, Lillian!

TINK: *(Obviously in a panic.) Jaoowsa! Jaoowsa!*

DIVA: JUICE! She needs juice. Quick! Get her some punch! *(LILLIAN goes for the punch.)* Quick, quick, quick! Before she goes into shock! Hurry! Her eyes are beginning to roll back! *(Takes glass of punch from LILLIAN.)* Here you go, Tink. Drink up. *(TINK drinks.)* That a girl. Drink it all down.

TINK: *Mo . . . mo . . . mo. . . .*

DIVA: *(Hands empty glass to LILLIAN.)* Here, Lillian. Get her some more.

LILLIAN: I don't know that this punch is very good for her, Diva.

DIVA: Of course it is. Its got fruit in it, doesn't it?

LILLIAN: Sort of.

DIVA: Sort of?

LILLIAN: Yeah, sort of. Imitation powdered fruit. That's "sort of," isn't it?

TINK: More! More!

DIVA: *(To LILLIAN.)* Quick, quick, quick! *(Takes full glass from LILLIAN.)* Here you go. Here's some more.

TINK: *(Drinks to the dregs. Directly to the audience.)* Would you look at all this junk. What a dump! I think we're having a yard sale—in Appalachia. Shit! I hope they're not selling me. I could demand a pretty penny, you know. I knew somebody who knew somebody who was sold into white slavery once. She was sold as a virgin to a sheik over in one of those Arab countries. I hope he got his money's worth. If she was a virgin I'm ready to be beatified by the Pope. How old am I? How long have I been out here? Are we still on Earth? It's bloody hot out here, I'll tell you that. You can't stick an old lady in a wheelchair made of metal and plastic, cover her up with an old, smelly, blanket, shove her out in the sun, and then expect her to be happy about it. No! I am not one bit happy. Hello. Hello? Is there intelligent life out there? Is my mouth moving? *(She smiles, raises her arms heavenward, closes her eyes and drops her head. Her arms stay raised in the air.)*

DIVA: Tink? Tink? . . . That's a good girl. Sleep tight.

LILLIAN: She's asleep?

DIVA: And as tight as it gets. Just like a baby.

LILLIAN: Her arms. How can she sleep with her arms up like that?

DIVA: At her age people develop all kinds of curious, if not bizarre, eccentricities.

LILLIAN: Well, I find it rather disconcerting. Shouldn't we put them in her lap?

DIVA: Disconcerted or not, you're such a traditionalist, Lillian. I've always suspected that of you. You have these preconceived ideas of how things ought to be and if the world doesn't conform to your silly little notions of acceptable propriety then look out, Henny Penny, here come the sky!

LILLIAN: That's not true.

DIVA: It most certainly is.

LILLIAN: *(Pouring a glass of punch for herself and for DIVA.)* No. It isn't true at all. If I'm such a traditionalist, why did I let you talk me into spending last Christmas in an Arab restaurant with you and your mother?

DIVA: Why? Did she pee on something?

LILLIAN: No. I don't think so. What I meant was, an Arab restaurant is not a traditional dining place for Christmas dinner.

DIVA: That was an experiment. And, you suffered through it rather nicely, I thought . . . getting snarkered and drooling all over those little Arab busboys.

LILLIAN: They weren't little and you started it by telling them how rich you were. It was like throwing raw meat at starving sharks. Who did you think you were – Liz Taylor in Suddenly Last Summer? Besides, they were Italian busboys.

DIVA: Were not.

LILLIAN: Were.

DIVA: Not! What would Italian busboys be doing working in an Arab restaurant? *(Swigs drink.)* And on Christmas?

LILLIAN: I don't see how Christmas has anything to do with it.

DIVA: Lillian, Italians are very religious! Especially on Christmas. They're either praying to the Virgin Mary or they're eating. But they're not going to be bussing tables in an Arab restaurant! You can be sure of that!

LILLIAN: Well, they looked Italian to me. They were cute and they were dark.

DIVA: So are Labrador Retrievers, but I don't throw myself at them like some kind of wanton carnivore in heat every time I pass a pet shop.

LILLIAN: If I knew they were Arabs, I would have kept my hands to myself.

DIVA: Then excuse me. What I meant to say was, "like some kind of discrete, wanton carnivore in heat."

LILLIAN: Have fun at my expense. You always do. *(Pours DIVA and herself another drink. Takes a swig. After a pause.)* Diva, I'm really having a difficult time adjusting to Tink's arms up in the air like that. I really think we should do something about it.

DIVA: All right, if it will make you happy.

LILLIAN: It will.

DIVA: *(DIVA takes hold of TINK'S arms and tries to pull them down without success.)* Oh, my! I don't think she wants to cooperate. Lillian, you better take one wing and I'll take the other.

LILLIAN: *(Taking one of TINK'S arms.)* Okay, Tink. We don't want blood to clog up your armpits, do we? *(THEY huff, puff and struggle until THEY finally manage to get TINK'S arms down into her lap.)*

DIVA: She's a tough old twat, I'll tell you that.

LILLIAN: *(Calling to passing cars.)* Free punch! Big yard sale!

DIVA: *(Ibid.)* Free punch! Big yard sale!

BOTH: Free punch! Free punch!

DIVA: *(Spying a customer.)* Hello, there. . . . No. We're fresh out of Lord Nelson Dolphin tables. Sorry. No Spode, either. Now, let me think. . . . *(To LILLIAN.)* Have we any Baroque walnut three-drawer commodes left?

LILLIAN: Nope. Not a one.

DIVA: *(To customer.)* Sorry, fresh out. Did you try Walmart? . . . Then I don't know what to tell you. Could you use a set of handcuffs? A whip? How about this lovely black leather facial mask? Well, there's certainly no reason for you to take an attitude. You can huff, huff, huff till the cows come home, but it won't change a thing! . . . Don't you stomp your feet at me! Not on my lawn! This is all specially grown blue Bermuda. You can go out in the street and stomp your way to China for all I care! . . . And good day to you, too.

LILLIAN: *(Watching her huff off.)* Have a nice day.

DIVA: Tight ass phonies! You can spot them a mile away. That bitch is such a tight ass only dogs can hear her fart. *(Drinks punch.)* This is good. What's in this, Lillian?

LILLIAN: *(Drinks punch.)* Raspberry Kool Aid, gin, vodka, grain alcohol – one-fifty proof – and a little bit of dry vermouth. *(BOTH refill their drinks.)* She's in the social register.

DIVA: What who?

LILLIAN: Miss Lord Nelson Dolphin tables . . . the tight ass phony. She's in the social register.

DIVA: Oh, her. She knows the printer.

LILLIAN: What?

DIVA: She knows the printer. What other way could the likes of her get into the social register?

LILLIAN: I don't know. How did you get in the social register, Diva?

DIVA: *(After a menacing pause.)* Lillian, I resent the implication of that question. How do any of us get in the social register?

LILLIAN: My great grandfather, the banker, married my great grandmother, the daughter of my great, great grandfather, the railroad tycoon.

DIVA: Well, that's just great, isn't it? I married Horace Hollingsworth the dentist. *(Sips punch.)* This is really good. I want you to write down the exact proportions.

LILLIAN: It's easy enough to remember. Prepare one package of raspberry Kool Aid and mix with a fifth of gin, vodka, grain alcohol and about a mouthful of dry vermouth to taste. *(Pours them each another glass of punch.)* Well . . . being in the social register doesn't really mean anything anyway, does it?

DIVA: Lillian, you're positively jaded. It means everything. . . . What exactly do you mean by "a mouthful of dry vermouth?"

LILLIAN: *(After a pause.)* About a quarter of a cup. . . . Diva, do you mean "know" in the neighborly sense, or in the Biblical sense?

DIVA: What on earth are you talking about?

LILLIAN: You said she got herself in the social register because she knew the printer.

DIVA: That's what I said and that's what I meant.

LILLIAN: Well? In the Biblical or in the neighborly sense?

DIVA: Nothing Biblical about it, dear. On her knees for days! I mean, sexual favors. The open-door, good neighbor policy, if you know what I mean. She married Zilinski the printer.

LILLIAN: Oh . . . then she really does know the printer.

DIVA: That's what I said, didn't I. She knew the printer very, very well, if you catch my drift.

LILLIAN: *(Sees someone across the street.)* Oh, no!

DIVA: *(Thinking LILLIAN'S "oh, no!" was in response to what she had said about the printer's wife.)* She certainly did! I didn't go to her wedding shower, although I did send her a lovely bouquet of calla lilies with a little note: "May all your showers be golden." Not as much as a word of thanks! The bitch! So, I turned down her wedding invitation. Honestly! Holding the reception in the Egyptian Room of the Holiday Inn was an outrage of tastelessness quite beyond my capacity to endure. An experiment in garishness, at best.

LILLIAN: *(In a panic.)* No, no, no! Muffy Hughes – across the street. Quick! Get in front of me. *(LILLIAN tries to hide behind DIVA.)*

DIVA: What is wrong with you?

LILLIAN: I don't want her to see me. Get in front of me! *(Holding DIVA in front of her.)*

DIVA: *(Struggling to get away from LILLIAN.)* I'm not getting in front of anybody, Lillian! Are you out of your mind? Me and King Kong couldn't block you from her seeing you.

LILLIAN: Too late. She's got the eyes of a rodent.

DIVA: And whiskers to match.

LILLIAN: *(Calling over to Muffy.)* "Toodles" to you, too, Muffy. Diva and I are just clearing out some old odds and ends. . . . What? . . . No. Not bed pans. Odds and ends. Out with the old — in with the new. . . . New. . . . New. No. No, I'm over here in Diva's yard. That's why I wasn't home. . . . Yes, of course the doorbell works, but I can't hear it from here. . . . Tink? She's over here with us. . . . Well, I don't know. I imagine her doorbell works, too. . . . Sleeping. . . . Like a log. . . . Log. Log. . . . No, dear. I would never call you a hog . . . not to your face, anyway. Here. In Diva's yard. We've got the little darling for the day. . . . Darling. Darling. . . . For the day. Yes. *(To DIVA.)* She's coming over.

DIVA: *(To LILLIAN.)* Is that a new walker?

LILLIAN: I don't think so. *(To Muffy.)* Watch both ways. *(To DIVA.)* It's just the way the sun's reflecting off of it. *(Calling out to Muffy.)* Watch that car! No, no! The other one. . . .That a girl. You're half way home. . . .Home. *Home.* . . .No, no! I didn't mean for you to go home. . . . *(To DIVA)* What is she doing?

DIVA: She turned around to go back.

LILLIAN: *(Calling out to Muffy.)* Muffy! Muffy! I meant like in home free. . . . Free. Free. *(To DIVA.)* She's coming back. *(To Muffy.)* Watch that car! The other way, Muffy. Wait!

DIVA: *(Rushes downstage with LILLIAN.)* Stop!

LILLIAN: *(The following dialogue should overlap that of DIVA'S below.)* Run! Stay! Your right! Your left! Now! Go! Stay! STOP!

DIVA: Don't run! Go! Your left! Your right! No! Stay! Go! STOP! *(End of overlapping dialogue.)*
(A very long SILENCE as they look toward the street.)

LILLIAN: Oh, dear.

DIVA: Too bad.

LILLIAN: Oh, my.

DIVA: What a shame.

LILLIAN: Oh, Pooh Bear poop.

DIVA: What a mess.

LILLIAN: Is she . . . dead?

DIVA: I don't think so. . . . No. She's moving. . . . Well, she'll need a new walker now.

LILLIAN: I shouldn't be at all surprised. She's had that one a long time. What's happening with that young man on the motorcycle?

DIVA: He's . . . he's . . . ah! He's getting up.

LILLIAN: Good for him. Ooh, isn't he cute! *(Pointing.)* Who's that?

DIVA: Where?

LILLIAN: In the pickup.

DIVA: What pickup?

LILLIAN: The one backing up from out of Doctor Hall's tri-colored hybrid rose bushes.

DIVA: Oh, dear. The old pouf is not going to like that. You know how he covets those roses. What's he doing now?

LILLIAN: Well . . . it looks like he's pulling up next to the hunk from the motorcycle.

DIVA: He ought to look where he's going. He nearly ran over poor old Muffy.

LILLIAN: If he had, it would hardly be his fault, Diva. She ought to stop rolling around like that.

DIVA: How excruciating! She must be in a lot of pain.

LILLIAN: You never can tell with her. She always was big on playacting. . . . Oh, Look at that! He seems to have gotten the motorcycle stud on the back of his truck. . . . And, now he's pushing Muffy up. . . . *(Using her hands to mime pushing Muffy up into the pickup.)*

DIVA: Oh, God! Now, that must smart. I didn't know the human body could bounce like that.

LILLIAN: Wait . . . he's trying again. . . . Oops! She should have stayed with Weight Watchers like I told her to at the time. . . . Now what is he doing?

DIVA: I don't know. It looks like . . . it looks like. . . .

LILLIAN: What? What?

DIVA: It looks like. . . . Oh, my God! It is!

LILLIAN: It is? What? What is it?

DIVA: It's . . . it's a chain.

LILLIAN: A chain?

DIVA: A chain. He tossed a chain over the roll bar and it looks like he's going to. . . .

LILLIAN: WHAT! Going to what!? What, Diva, What!?

DIVA: Yes! He is!

LILLIAN: Oh, bless us and save us! What is he doing?

DIVA: I hope she's wearing her Depends.

LILLIAN: Diva, what is he doing with her legs? Diva? Diva? I knew it! I just knew it! What's he doing with that chainsaw?

DIVA: Nothing. He's just moving it out of the way.

LILLIAN: This is going to be some kind of kinky, perverted, Jeffery Dahlmer thing, isn't it? Quick! Pull up your skirt!

DIVA: What?!

LILLIAN: *(LILLIAN dives for the cell phone. She has her head up under DIVA'S skirt.)* Quick! I need it! Give it to me!

DIVA: *(Fighting her off.)* What are you doing?

LILLIAN: I'm calling 911!

DIVA: There's no need to call 911.

LILLIAN: *(Coming out from under DIVA'S skirt.)* No need? Then why has he got her legs spread apart like that? Oh, no.

DIVA: What?

LILLIAN: She's not wearing her Depends.

DIVA: What a mess. . . . Well, he just tied Muffy's ankles with the other end of the chain . . . and now he's starting to pull . . . pull. . . . Mercy! He must be strong!

LILLIAN: There she goes! . . . She's in!

DIVA: Good. It would've been a shame to leave her rolling around like that. She could have rolled right out into the traffic.

LILLIAN: There they go . . . the leather-clad motorcycle man and poor old Muffy . . . hanging on a chain from the roll bar . . . like an old sow on her way to market. What a sight! And dragging half of the old pouf's rose bushes behind them. Too much excitement.

DIVA: *(Pours them each another punch.)* So . . . why didn't you want Muffy to see you?

LILLIAN: Because every single time she comes around something terrible happens. She is the most accident-prone person I have ever had the misfortune to know.

DIVA: *(Raises her glass in a toast.)* To Muffy.

LILLIAN: To Muffy. *(They clink glasses and drink.)*

DIVA: *(Filling glasses again.)* Better check on Tink.

LILLIAN: Pity she missed all the excitement.

DIVA: Just as well. We'd only have to explain everything in great detail as it was happening and we all know how tiresome that can be.

LILLIAN: I see your point. *(Rolls TINK into a patch of sunlight.)* Here you go. Follow the sun. Oh, we are getting a bit of color, aren't we?

DIVA: Pull her blanket up a bit. *(LILLIAN adjusts TINK'S lap blanket.)* Much better. Move her over there.

LILLIAN: Where?

DIVA: *(Pointing)* There, there. In that patch of sunlight.

LILLIAN: She's already in a patch of sunlight.

DIVA: But it is not a good one.

LILLIAN: Diva, one patch of sunlight is as good as another.

DIVA: Don't let's argue. That one over there looks warmer.

LILLIAN *(Resigned. Mumbling.)* I suppose you're right. You always are . . . even when you're wrong, you're right. Bitch, bitch, bitch. . . .

DIVA: What are you on about?

LILLIAN: Nothing . . . nothing. *(Rolling TINK into another patch of sunlight.)* There you go, Tink. I hope you can tell the difference. I can't. She just has to have her way. Always did . . . always will. Thinks with her twat she does.

DIVA: What? What did you say?

LILLIAN: Nothing.

DIVA: Nobody can say nothing. It is not possible. In fact, nobody cannot say nothing. So, tell me what you said because I heard somebody say something.

LILLIAN: What did you hear? What did it sound like?

DIVA: It didn't sound like you . . . that's for certain. No, not at all like the Lillian we've come to know and love. Maybe it wasn't what I heard it was.

LILLIAN: Maybe, what you heard it wasn't didn't come from me.

DIVA: *(Pours herself some punch.)* Yes. But, maybe, what I heard was and it did. *(Swigs punch.)*

LILLIAN: *(Pours herself some punch.)* That's possible. In an uncertain world, that's really quite possible. *(Swigs punch.)*

DIVA: You're becoming quite tedious, Lillian!

TINK: *(Wakes.) Ha . . . ha . . . ha. . . .*

DIVA: Now, you went and woke Tink. I hope you're happy.

LILLIAN: It wasn't me, Diva. It was you. It's always you! You boss me around. Do this! Do that! Get this! Get that! You're this! You're that!

DIVA: I do not!

LILLIAN: You do too!

TINK: *(Desperate.) Ha . . . ha . . . ha. . . .*

LILLIAN: Ha, ha, ha yourself, Tink! I'm not laughing.

TINK: *Hos . . . hos . . . hos. . . .*

LILLIAN: A horse? *(Looking around.)* I don't see a horse. Do you see a horse, Diva?

DIVA: *(Piqued.)* No, Lillian. I don't see a horse. . . . Leave it to you to change the subject.

LILLIAN: And what subject was that?

DIVA: The subject was me!

LILLIAN: It always is.

TINK: *Hos . . . hos . . . pit . . . pit . . . pit. . . .*

LILLIAN: That's right. Pitty-pat. Horse goes pitty-pat.

DIVA: Horses don't go pitty-pat! They go clip-clop. Pitty-pat was somebody's aunt in *Gone With The Wind.*

TINK: *Hos . . . pit . . . tul. Hos-pit-tul. . . .*

LILLIAN: I know. You're right, Tink. I quite agree. Sometimes, Diva is just not hospitable at all.

TINK: *Hos-pit-tul! Hos-pit-tul!*

LILLIAN: Oh . . . hospital. I understand. No, no. We're not in the hospital. We're in Diva's front yard. *(To DIVA.)* Poor thing. She's having hallucinations. She thinks she's in the hospital. Maybe another glass of punch will straighten her right out.

DIVA: *(Handing LILLIAN a glass of punch.)* I don't know. You think this stuff is good for a diabetic?

LILLIAN: What could it hurt? *(Feeds punch to TINK.)*

TINK: *Na . . . na . . . no!*

LILLIAN: Know? Know what?

TINK: *No, no, no!*

LILLIAN: I know. I know all right. Diva thinks she knows everything there is to know. But you and I know differently, don't we?

TINK: *Hos! Hos! Hos!*

LILLIAN: Hostile? There's no question about it. She can be quite hostile when she wants to be. *(DIVA "humphs!")*

TINK: *Hospital! Hospital!*

LILLIAN: No, no, no. We're in Diva's front yard. Not the hospital. We're having a yard sale. We're raising money for a fabulous egg to put poor dead Dr. Horace in.
TINK: *(Gasping for air. Tries to strangle LILLIAN.)* No, no, no! You goddamned idiot! You haven't got the brains you were born

with! *Hospital! Hospital!* You sorry-ass sack of shit! *(Knocking on LILLIAN'S head.)* Knock, knock!

LILLIAN: Who's there?

TINK: Out to lunch!

LILLIAN: I don't get it.

TINK: *(Directly to audience.)* Are my lips moving? *(Her arms shoot straight up into the air. Her eyes shut and her head slumps over.)*

LILLIAN: That's gratitude for you! Diva, she did it again! I've a good mind to leave her arms up there this time. No. She'll only end up chasing the customers away. *(She tries to get TINK'S arms down, but has no success.)*

DIVA: *(Sees customer 1.)* Oh, hello there. See anything you like? . . . Oh, yes. You missed all the excitement. . . . No, no. That's not for sale. I think that's part of Muffy's walker. If you just sort of prop it up, somebody will be by to pick it up later.

LILLIAN: *(Crosses to customer 1.)* Oh, yes. I'm sure she'll be just fine. Muff's famous for bouncing back like India rubber. . . . Accident? . . . No. That's our friend, Tink. She's taking a nap. . . . I think it's to get rid of the bags under her upper arms. Though I think it's a moot pursuit at this point in her career.

DIVA: *(Greets customer 2)* Hello. If there is anything I can help you with just let me know. . . . Her? She's doing her impersonation of . . . Superwoman. *(To LILLIAN.)* Will you help me get her arms down. She's becoming quite the cause celeb.

LILLIAN: Whatever happened to your nonconformist, anti-traditional intolerance for preconceptions?

DIVA: Lillian! Now!

LILLIAN: *(To customer 1.)* Excuse me. I think I hear someone calling.

(LILLIAN rushes over to TINK and helps DIVA with getting TINK'S arms down. There is a great deal of struggling involved and each end up, at numerous times, in TINK's lap. TINK slips out of the chair and onto the lawn and there is a great deal of schtick involved in getting her back into her chair. Finally, their mission is a success. DIVA and LILLIAN brush themselves off, straighten out their clothes, pat their hair into place and go back to waiting on their customers. The alcohol which DIVA and LILLIAN have consumed has, unmistakably, affected both their speech and their manner.)

DIVA: *(To customer 2.)* Sorry for the inconvenience. . . . Now, wha wha-wha we?

LILLIAN: *(Enter customer 3.)* Hello, there. . . . Yes. That was a piece given me by my late sister-in-law, Blanche Grey-White. . . . Dubious, yes. But she made up for it by being colorful enough for all of us. . . . She was too much the scandal for the hometown crowd. So, she moved to New York City and opened a coffee house in Greenwich Village. It was all the rage. She started the trend, you know . . . oh, yes, she did. Café Cornhole, or something like that. Some say she had an affair with Jack Kerouac. Some say she didn't. Others say it was she who inspired him to write. But, I'm inclined to say that if he was going to write he'd have written anyway and that it was just a ruse on her part to help her sell her coffee. What do you say?

DIVA: *(To customer 2.)* That? That's a wery ware piece of . . . of. . . . *(Calls to LILLIAN.)* Lillian, wha, wha, whass this?

LILLIAN: Let me see. *(DIVA holds up object.)* That's the lid to a Tupperware bowl. I don't know what happened to the bowl. I think Uncle Sam ate it.

DIVA: *(To customer 2)* Tupperware.

LILLIAN: *(To customer 3.)* That is a very strange Pomeranian . . . Uncle Sam. It belongs to the mother of that lady over there. But then, all Pomeranians leave something to be desired, don't you think? *(To DIVA)* It makes a good coaster for something that isn't very hot.

DIVA: *(To customer 2.)* It's a . . . twivet. . . . Twivet! You west stuff on it! . . . A fwisbee? A diaphwagm for a buffalo?

LILLIAN: *(To customer 3.)* No. I'm sorry. I don't know anything about them. Cats have always been a bit too predatory for my taste. A bit too marauding.

DIVA: *(To customer 1.)* It's punch. . . . Wazberry. . . . Fwee. *(Calling out to all in the general vicinity.)* Fwee punch! Fwee punch, evweybody!

LILLIAN: *(Enter customer 4.)* Hi. . . . Oh, yeah. It is good punch. Family recipe. . . . The wagon? No, the wagon's not for sale. . . . Because. . . . Well, because. . . .

DIVA: *(Chiming in.)* Because then we'd have to carry all this stuff back to the house by hand and that is totally unaccepacable! . . . . Well, it won't be the first time his little heart gets broken. *(Swats at child near table.)* Sonny, that's sterling! Sterling does not like to be touched by sticky fwingers!

LILLIAN: *(To customer 1.)* Please don't touch Tink . . . . No, I don't think she'd like it if she awoke to find I've sold her favorite blanket. She brought that back with her from Taos where she was visiting Mabel Dodge Luhan. It has memories . . . moths, too.

I've a nice handmade afghan over here. *(To customer 3.)* Excuse me? . . . No. I don't believe I have. Are they something like Airedales? . . . This is a kind of blanket, madam. An afghan handmade by yours truly.

DIVA: *(To customer 4.)* Madam, would you mind keeping your child away from the merchandise. The fat little bugger doesn't seem to respond to my weqwests. *(She starts shaking her leg. Removes her cell phone from her garter and answers it.)* I know who I am. Do you? Who? Oh, you. How's your Gweek? I'm sworry to hear that.

TINK: *(Directly to audience, unheard by DIVA and LILLIAN.)* There they are, my friends Diva and Lillian.

LILLIAN: Diva, is there something wrong with your mouth?

DIVA: *(To LILLIAN.)* Her Gweek took a hike.

TINK: *(To audience.)* Because of them I no longer have any fear of death.

DIVA: *(Into phone.)* Well, I'll tell you, Carlotta, easy come easy go. *(To child of customer 4.)* I never hit a kwid before, but if you don't kweep your hands off the merchandise I'm gonna wip your fwiggin' heart out and swove it up your ugwy mother's ass!

TINK: *(To audience.)* Because of them death will be a picnic in the park.

LILLIAN: *(To DIVA.)* There definitely is something wrong with your mouth.

DIVA: *(Into phone.)* Not your ugwy mother's ass, Carrotta. I was twalking to somebody else. Besides, I didn't know you had a mother.

TINK: *(To audience.)* And, as far as going to hell, who cares? I've been there. And, it looks a lot like a yard sale.

LILLIAN: *(To DIVA.)* Your mouth, Diva!

DIVA: *(To LILLIAN.)* What's wong wid my mouth? *(Into phone.)* I wasn't twalking to you, Carrotta! Well, I don't like your attitwude, either. Call me back when your swobber! *(Puts phone back under her garter. To customer.)* What are you wooking at?

TINK: *(To audience.)* Like I said, I'm not afraid of death. We all have to go sooner or later. But, in the care of these two morons, I'm liable to go sooner than later! Do you want to know what death is like? Well, I'll tell you anyway. It's a lot like waking up . . . looking around . . . and there it is . . . there you are . . . and there you have it. . . . Hello. Hello. Is my mouth moving? *(Goes back to sleep.)*

LILLIAN: Diva, there's something wrong with your mouth.

DIVA: Wong wid my mouth?

LILLIAN: You've get a tick.

DIVA: A dick?

LILLIAN: A tick.

DIVA: I do?

LILLIAN: *(Pours DIVA some punch.)* This ought to work it right out. *(Hands punch to DIVA.)*

DIVA: *(Swigs punch. After a pause.)* Well? What do you think?

LILLIAN: I think that did it.

DIVA: My tongue went numb.

LILLIAN: That will pass in no time.

DIVA: But, I think it's stuck to the woof of my mouth.

LILLIAN: Say: Rubber baby buggy bumpers.

DIVA: What are you? Crazy? I'm not going to say wubber waby wuggy wumpers! *(Pulling tongue down from roof of mouth.)* Wait. The numbness went. What was that again?

LILLIAN: Rubber baby buggy bumpers.

DIVA: Wubber . . . rrr-uuub-er . . . ba-by . . . buggy bumpers. Rugger buby boggy bompers.

LILLIAN: Rubber baby buggy bumpers.

DIVA: Rubber baby buggy bumpers.

LILLIAN: That's it! You've got it!

DIVA: I've got it!

LILLIAN: *(In a panic.)* Oh, bless us and save us!

DIVA: I don't got it?

LILLIAN: No. Look. Look who's coming back!

DIVA: (Looking.) Oh, no!

LILLIAN: If he exposes himself now with that little kosher pickle of his, we'll lose all our business. *(To customer 2)* Have some more punch. its fwee . . . Free. *(To all.)* Free punch! Free punch, everybody! Free punch!

DIVA: *(To customer 4.)* Madam, I'd put a leash on the little juvenile delinquent were I you. *(Swatting at the child.)* Touch that sterling once more and I'll break every bone in your sickly, sticky little body! *(To customer 4.)* If you can't control the little bugger, may I suggest you put him back in the car. Roll the window down an inch or so and he'll be fine for hours.

LILLIAN: *(To customer 4.)* Please . . . she didn't mean it that way. *(To customer 3.)* She didn't mean it that way.

DIVA: *(To LILLIAN)* I most certainly did. *(To customer 4.)* I'm afraid we've taken everything off the market. Nope. Nothing's for sale. . . . No, not a thing. Horace can just make himself to home in that pickle jar! *(To the flasher.)* Speaking of pickles! Sir? Sir? Please put that away before something dreadful happens to it. . . . Well, that is not an adage that would apply in your case. One could easily chew all of what little there is to bite off.

LILLIAN: Diva! I'm astonished! Don't talk to him. They thrive on that kind of talk. Leave him alone and maybe he'll go home.

DIVA: Wagging his tail behind him? *(To the flasher.)* Sir, please take your hands off that little boy. He may be sticky, but he's all his mother's got. *(To customer 4.)* The Salvation what? My dear misinformed lady, poor people give people like us a reason for being people like us. These are not items one donates to poor people. Why, the silver polish alone would bankrupt them. . . . Well, I am sure that somewhere they must, but I can assure you that nobody in this neighborhood starves.

LILLIAN: *(To Diva)* Honey Aldridge did.

DIVA: Honey Aldridge was different. She had anorexia. Poor people don't get anorexia.

LILLIAN: I didn't know that.

DIVA: Well, now you do. *(To customer 4.)* I am well aware of social issues, madam, and I won't be patronized. I know perfectly well to which side of the wine goblet goes the water glass.

LILLIAN: You didn't two weeks ago when you had that luncheon-orgy for that touring gay mime troupe . . . with Tourette's syndrome.

DIVA: Oh, shut up, Lillian! *(To customer 4.)* Good day to you, too!

LILLIAN: *(Calling after customer 4.)* Oh, madam! Wait! There's a strange man who crawled into the back seat of your car with your little boy! Oh, madam! . . . You-hoo! *(Watching them drive off.)* Have a nice day. *(To customer 1.)* Oh, I see you've discovered poor Aunt Irene's erotic alarm clock. When the alarm rings a little soldier pops out of the top with an erection. . . . That's right. It doesn't stop ringing until you yank on his little peepee. That clock got her up every morning since the day General McArthur came home until the day she died. That was the day Ronald and Nancy Reagan – bless their black little hearts – packed up and went back to the ranch. The thought of their leaving the White House proved to be too much for her. George Bush just wasn't Republican enough for dear old Aunt Irene. It rang and rang and its little erection just stood there waiting to be yanked on that last morning of her pitiful, meaningless life.

DIVA: *(To customer 2.)* Tupperware. . . . T-P-P-R-W-R-E. Tupperware. It's a kind of plastic. . . . From parties. They give parties. . . . I don't know. Look in the phone book. . . . You have a nice day, too. *(She waves "goodbye.")*

LILLIAN: *(To customer 1.)* But, it's a perfectly good clock. . . . Well, how about the one next to it? That was a present to me on my birthday last. It's never been used. No. Not for the sum total of one second. It was given to me by someone I thoroughly detest. They couldn't give me the time of day, so to speak.

DIVA: *(To customer 3.)* Cats? We don't sell cats! What does this look like to you? A pet shop? What are you bothering us for? Are you some kind of lunatic? Go home! Scoot! Scoot! Go home! *(To customer 1.)* Are you going to buy that stupid, ugly clock or what!? Then, put it back where you found it and go home! That's right! Scat! Get! Make tracks! Get my drift!? *(Chases remaining customers.)* Go! Go, go, go, go, go! Get! Good riddance! *(Her leg starts shaking violently. She reaches under skirt and grabs the phone. Into phone.)* I'm Diva and who the hell are you?! . . . Oh, well, I'll pick him up in an hour or so. But, if he still smells like piss your getting the little bastard back. For keeps! *(She turns the phone off and replaces it under her garter.)*

LILLIAN: Good heavens, Diva. What's gotten into you?

DIVA: People! How can they be so inconsiderate?

LILLIAN: Is that another one of your rhetorical questions?

DIVA: We go through all the trouble to drag all this stuff out of the house and nobody buys a thing. Not one thing. They just pick over the merchandise like a flock of vultures! They pick over this and they pick over that . . . sniffing . . . like a pack of hyenas!

LILLIAN: Well . . . yeah. but, the punch sure was popular.

DIVA: Naturally. It was free punch, wasn't it? People will take anything that's free – whether they need it or not. You could put out a sign that said "FREE URINE SPECIMENS" and you can be sure somebody would come along with their hand out! They came for the free punch, Lillian, that's all. And, that's life. They come. They look. They take.

LILLIAN: *(Picks up a figurine.)* But, that's all right, Diva. It was fun. It was a nice afternoon, wasn't it?

DIVA: I suppose.

LILLIAN: There was the sun and the warmth and it was nice.

DIVA: I guess.

LILLIAN: *(Holding figurine.)* Besides, it's hard to let go of things you've been collecting all your life. Isn't it? *(While holding up a figurine to admire, it accidentally falls from her hands and breaks.)* Oh, no! Oh, no! Look what I went and did.

DIVA: That's too bad, Lillian. Is it a total loss?

LILLIAN: *(Picking up the pieces.)* What a shame. I think I'm going to cry.

DIVA: What are you talking about? You were going to sell it.

LILLIAN: No. I only brought it out so people could see it. I never intended to sell it. *(She wraps the pieces of the figurine into a piece of cloth and carefully places it on the table. She seems quite heartbroken.)* I only wanted to show it off.

DIVA: *(Hands LILLIAN a glass of punch.)* Here. Have some punch. It's fwee. *(They chuckle.)*

LILLIAN: *(Taking glass.)* And it's cool. Just what I needed – a glass of something cool. *(Crosses to TINK.)* Tink, how about a nice glass of something cool? Tink? Tink? She seems to be losing her color. Tink? Tink? How about a glass of something cool? . . . Diva, she's awfully pale for someone who's been out in the sun all day. Would you look at her?

DIVA: Oh, for God's sake. *(Crosses to TINK. Holds mirror to her face, Matter-of-factly.)* She's dead.

LILLIAN: What? Tink, are you play-acting for us?

DIVA: She's dead, I tell you. Time to let go.

LILLIAN: *(Pours herself some punch.)* Of all the inconsiderate things one could think to do, she sure came up with a doozy! Didn't she? *(Swigs punch.)* Well, what now?

DIVA: *(Pours herself some punch.)* I don't know. Wait. Just wait. *(After a pause.)* Sometimes I think the whole world is conspiring against us . . . just to make our lives miserable. Why? Why us, Lillian?

LILLIAN: *(After a pause.)* Do you think it's God?

DIVA: God? What's God got to do with anything?

LILLIAN: Testing us. You know, like Job . . . in the Bible. First, He sends that man to expose himself. And then He sends. . . .

DIVA: *(Stopping her)* Lillian, God is not going to send anybody around who exposes himself. Especially someone with such shortcomings.

LILLIAN: Then who?

DIVA: Not God.

LILLIAN: *(Pours herself some punch.)* Well, then how do you explain all this? It can't be anything we've done.

DIVA: I don't know. *(After a pause.)* Do you believe in karma?

BOTH: *(After a pause.)* Naah. *(They clink glasses and chug down their drinks.)*

BLACK OUT

END ACT ONE

6 FULL-LENGTH PLAYS
VOLUME TWO

Edward Crosby Wells

ACT TWO—*Two Weeks Later*

MUFFY (a life-sized dummy) is in a wheelchair in a full body cast. She is quite plump. Her arms are outstretched horizontally and have scarves and beads, etc. hanging from them. There is an outrageous wig plopped on her head. Her face is totally wrapped in gauze with two little holes where her eyes ought to be and there is a slit where her mouth ought to be. She really needs to be believable. Next to her chair are the pieces of her broken walker and a large box of Depends. TINK is in a wheelchair with an IV running into her arm from a bag that hangs from an IV pole. All the "stuff" from the last yard sale is still there along with a different sign that reads: "FREE PUNCH WITH PURCHASE!"

DIVA: *(Behind the table talking into her cell phone.)*   Yes . . . well, I don't see it that way. Besides, I have no idea what a "junk-a-rama" is – 'though I have a pretty good notion you are fully versed in that regard. Oh, please, don't tell me. Let me chew on it awhile. However, if anybody's turning this neighborhood into a junk-a-rama, as you so quaintly put it, then I am sure it is you and not I. Your mere presence in this neighborhood is an abomination of monumental proportions. Were I you, I'd consider moving to Bora Bora or wherever it is they wear rings and bones and things in their noses! Oh? Body art, is it? Then perhaps you should have yourself shellacked and hung in the nearest museum. Well, I suppose if I were Betty White this is where I would tell you to get spayed or neutered! I should get what!? Thank you, darling. I'll be looking forward to that with the anticipation of a schoolgirl. I would tell you to get the same, but I don't really know you that well. *Ciao, Mother! (Turns phone off and puts it under her garter. Waving and shouting across the street.)* I see you too! And stop calling me on my cell phone – you're becoming quite expensive!

LILLIAN: *(Enters carrying more stuff.)* Who are you yelling at?

DIVA: Mother. I knew it was a bad idea putting her in a nursing home just across the street. *(Referring to stuff LILLIAN is carrying.)* Is that the last of it?

LILLIAN: *(Setting down her stuff.)* It is as far as I'm concerned. My heart's about to give out. *(A pause to catch her breath.)* How are the girls?

DIVA: Tink's asleep and Muffy's in a coma.

LILLIAN: I think it's the other way around, Diva.

DIVA: Whatever. They're both quiet. That's all I know.

LILLIAN: Thank heaven for that. A couple weeks ago I was sure poor old Tink had gone to meet her maker.

DIVA: And who would that be . . . Doctor Frankenstein?

LILLIAN: Diva, sometimes your attempt at humor could be mistaken for something offensive. If one didn't know you better, one could find your sarcasm diabolical.

DIVA: *(Humphs.)* Would one?

LILLIAN: *(Backing off from a potential conflict.)* Maybe. Anyway, I'm sure glad you were wrong.

DIVA: *I?* Wrong? About what?

LILIAN: You know, about Tink. You said she was dead. Sometimes it's good to be wrong.

DIVA: Is it?

LILLIAN: Of course it is. We still have our dear old Tink, don't we?

DIVA: *(Without much enthusiasm.) Yeah* . . . we still have our dear old Tink.

LILLIAN: Alive and well. Well . . . alive.

DIVA: So, she's alive. Don't rub it in, Lillian.

LILLIAN: I'm not rubbing anything in, Diva. Why are you in such a terrible mood?

DIVA: Because I nearly became a murderess and that takes a terrible toll on ones sense of self.

LILLIAN: I'm sure it does.

DIVA: I nearly went to prison for the rest of my tender and precious life and all you think about is dear old Tink.

LILLIAN: That isn't true. I think about you constantly. You're on my mind more than I am on my mind – whatever that means. You're my best friend.

DIVA: I guess the fact that you almost lost your best friend to some unspeakable fate doesn't phase you, does it? You don't care that I was a breath away from becoming some hairy-lipped Amazon's girl toy, do you? Some friend you are!

LILLIAN: For Pete's sake, Diva. If Tink had died we both might have gone to prison. It was my punch you force-fed her. You have the strangest way of looking at things sometimes. All I'm saying is thank God you were wrong in your prognosis because everything turned out for the better in spite of it.

DIVA: And, look what we did to poor Muffy.

LILLIAN: We didn't do anything to Muffy. She did it to herself. After all, she was jaywalking, wasn't she? We did warn her. She ought to be grateful that she's still alive.

DIVA: It's hard to tell about some people nowadays.

LILLIAN: It's hard to tell what?

DIVA: Whether they are dead or alive. Exterior signs of life are no longer any kind of guarantee. They can walk and they can talk, but who knows if there's anybody home.

LILLIAN: You're becoming too deep for conscious appreciation, Diva.

DIVA: The late Dr. Hollingsworth was dead three days before anyone took notice.

LILLIAN: Not even you?

DIVA: No, not even I. He was notorious for spending days on end in that cucumber patch out back. I thought he was involved in yet another of his many eccentricities . . . communing with the cucumbers. Some people have an eye for color and some for texture. Dear old Horace had a thing for cylindrical objects of an agricultural nature. Quite demented, if you ask me.

LILLIAN: What nonsense!

DIVA *(Her leg shakes. She reaches under her dress to retrieve the cell phone.)* My God! It's turning into Grand Central Station down here. *(Answers phone.)* Diva Hollingsworth here. Who might you be? *(To LILLIAN.)* Carlotta Bean. *(LILLIAN goes about sorting through stuff.)* You're sounding particularly well today. Yes, it's another beautiful day in the neighborhood. The girls and I are having another yard sale. . . . Didn't I tell you? I need to raise a bit of cash to purchase one of those jewel encrusted, gold Faberge eggs; much like the one you brought back from Russia a couple years ago. Horace needs a permanent resting-place. . . . Well, they have little snaps on them, darling. Doesn't yours open up? Yes, I thought it did. What do you keep in it? M&M's? Oh, dear, how casual can one get? Seen who? Your Greek? I thought it was over between you two. Oh? Making up is always the best part, isn't it? Gone missing, again, has he? If I see him I'll send him right home. What does he look like? Where? Hold on. *(To LILLIAN.)* Go over to that telephone pole and see if there's a missing poster.

LILLIAN: How would I know if it were missing?

DIVA: If what were missing?

LILLIAN: The poster.

DIVA: Lillian! See if there is a poster for a missing Greek!

LILLIAN: *Oh. (Reading from poster on the telephone pole.)* "Missing. One Greek male tourist guide. Large reward for his return. Answers to Laexandros Demosthenes Papadopoulos." *(To DIVA.)* Now, that's a mouthful.

DIVA: Quite a mouthful. *(Into phone.)* No, Carlotta, I was talking to Lillian. No, that is not what I meant by a mouthful. Well, bully for you. Let me just stroll over and take a gander for myself. *(At poster, gasps and nearly faints.)* There is a God! Listen, Carlotta, I'm suddenly feeling faint. Must be the sun. No, I don't think he was abducted by aliens. *Yes.* If I see him I'll send him right home. *(Aside to LILLIAN.)* Over my dead body. *(Into phone.)* Talk at you later. *Ciao,* darling. *(Replaces phone. Climbs telephone pole as her phone vibrates. Vibrating, she does a bit of schtick before ripping down poster and fans herself with it. She climbs down the pole, phone still vibrating. The vibrating stops.)* Quick, Lillian! I need a drink. *(LILLIAN goes to pour DIVA a drink.)* How does she do it?

LILLIAN: I don't know. I've been trying to figure that out for years. Maybe its all that bridgework and all those porcelain crowns Horace did for her. *(Hands Diva glass of punch.)*

DIVA: *(Drinks. Suspiciously.)* You don't suppose that the two of them, Carlotta and Horace. . . . *Naah.* I would have known. A woman knows those things, you know. Besides, I was too much of a woman for him. After all, I am Diva, aren't I? *(Finishes the punch. Pours herself another glass.)* I hope this is the same recipe you made last time.

LILLIAN: Better.

DIVA: Better? What could possibly make it better?

LILLIAN: A fifth of absinthe de wormwood smuggled from Morocco in Pansy Parker's private parts.

DIVA: I beg your pardon—

LILLIAN: She's a big girl.

DIVA: She would need to be. *(Sips punch.)* Oh, it has a slight licorice taste.

LILLIAN: That's the absinthe.

DIVA: Good! I'd hate to think. . . .

LILLIAN: *(Spies a potential patron.)* Free punch!

DIVA: With purchase!

LILLIAN: Free punch!

DIVA: With purchase! *(Taking another sip of punch.)* All I can say is, Lillian, you've outdone yourself again.

LILLIAN: Thank you, Diva.

DIVA: What exactly is it?

LILLIAN: It?

DIVA: Absinthe.

LILLIAN: Well, it's illegal in America – something to do about hallucinations. Sort of like LSD—not that I ever had LSD, at least, I don't think so, but, that would explain alien abductions.

DIVA: Martians?

LILLIAN: Mexicans. Over the wall. Anyway, Dr. Timothy Leary was a great friend of my cousin Gert.

DIVA: I don't remember your ever talking about a cousin Gert.

LILLIAN: That's because she was the black sheep in the family.

DIVA: And all this time I thought you were.

LILLIAN: Oh, no. Gert took the prize for that. She and her husband Charlie founded a retreat near Lake Titicaca in Peru for clairvoyants, spiritualists, astral projectionist and the like.

DIVA: Really?

LILLIAN: It was Dr. Leary's idea. They called it Porta Nostradamus. It was written up in all the important esoteric journals and, for a short time, enjoyed a fashionable reputation as the favored watering hole for some very influential people. Where do you think Shirley MacLaine got all her ideas?

DIVA: At Gert and Charlie's?

LILLIAN: That's right, in Porta Nostradamus. Anyway, it all ended rather badly.

DIVA: How's that?

LILLIAN: Well, one day while Gert was practicing her astral projection, a herd of llama trampled her body to death. So, when she came back from visiting who-knows-who in who-knows-where, she found Charlie crying over a container of ashes. When she realized the ashes were hers . . . well, you can imagine how traumatic that must have been for her.

DIVA: Lillian, I don't believe a word of this.

LILLIAN: It's true. They say her astral form still haunts the grounds where Porta Nostradamus used to stand.

DIVA: Used to stand?

LILLIAN: Yes. Before Charlie threw himself into Lake Titicaca and drowned, he burned the entire establishment to the ground – llama, natives, and all.

DIVA: Oh, dear!

LILLIAN: Anyway, one little fifth isn't about to hurt anybody.

DIVA: *(Looking across the street. Distracted.)* What's that, dear?

LILLIAN: The absinthe. One little fifth isn't about to hurt anybody.

DIVA: No, I suppose not. *(Raises her cup.)* Here's to Gert.

LILLIAN: *(Raising her cup.)* To Gert – wherever you are. *(Cautiously looking around for Gert's specter.)*

DIVA: *(Calling out to unseen passersby.)* Free punch . . . with purchase!

BOTH: Free punch . . . with purchase! Free punch . . . with purchase!

LILLIAN: Diva, do you think we really ought to be hanging things all over Muffy like that?

DIVA: Why not?

LILLIAN: It doesn't seem right somehow.

DIVA: *(Yelling into MUFFY'S ear.)* Muffy! Muffy, darling! Can you hear me?

LILLIAN: They can hear you in Pittsburgh, Diva.
DIVA: *(Ignoring the last. Still yelling into MUFFY'S ear.)* You don't mind if we hang a few things from you, do you, Muffy? *(Putting her ear to MUFFY'S mouth.)* No, no! Not P.U. . . . Do you? Do you mind? *(Listening.)* No, no, no! Not "do you in the hind!" Do you mind? Do you mind if we hang stuff from you? What? What's that? No. Nobody's going to stuff you from behind. Besides, you're all plastered up. Plastered. Plastered, Muffy, plastered. *(Turns to LILLIAN.)* Lillian, we seem to have a bad connection.

LILLIAN: *(Taking charge.)* You're plastered, sweetheart! He'd have to chip away an inch thick of plaster of Paris before he could get his pee-pee even close to you. What? *(To DIVA.)* She said, "start chipping."

DIVA: Oh, for God's sake! Muffy, go back to sleep! Now! *(To LILLIAN.)* Lillian, don't egg her on. Go and see if Tink's still in a coma? Her doctor said she could come out of it at any time. *(To MUFFY.)* Sleep, Muffy, Sleep. Honestly. The things I do for my friends. Florence Nightingale, eat your heart out.

LILLIAN: *(To TINK.)* Wakey, wakey, Tinky-winky.

DIVA: (Spies a potential customer.) Oh, hello there! See anything you like? Well, maybe something you could learn to like? That is, if you took the trouble to look a little closer. *(Crosses to LILLIAN.)* Blind as a bat, she is. *(To customer.)* What's that, darling? No, that's not a mummy. That's a Muffy. You really ought to have your eyes examined. Careful, careful! My, you are blind, aren't you? *(Holding up something.)* Can you see this? No? *(Holding up something else.)* What about this? No? *(Gives her the "middle finger.")* This? Poor thing. Maybe you should get one of those seeing-eye dogs. *(Picks up dildo.)* What about this? Yes! *(To LILLIAN.)* Wouldn't you know it? She's cockeyed! *(To customer – referring to dildo.)* What's that, dear? No, no. Its hardly been used. Practically virginic. Virginic. It's a word of my own divination. What do you mean "fishy?" There's nothing fishy about it. Suit yourself. Well, toodle-loodle to you too.

LILLIAN: *(To unseen retreating customer.)* Have a nice day. *(To Diva.)* Poor dear, not only blind but a bit long in the tooth.

DIVA: A bit? Lillian, she's so long in the tooth she could eat corn on the cob through a glory hole.

BOTH: Free punch . . . with purchase! Free punch . . . with purchase!

TINK: *Pa . . .pa . . . pa . . .*

LILLIAN: Diva! Tink's coming round. It's a miracle.

DIVA: *(Blasé.)* Well, hallelujah. Will miracles never cease? *(Sips punch.)*

TINK: *Pa . . . pa . . . pa . . .*

LILLIAN: *(To DIVA.)* Poor Tink. She wants her Pa. *(To TINK.)* Your Pa's dead, Tink. He died a long time ago . . . in the line of duty . . . with the FBI.

DIVA: Oh, for God's sake, Lillian. He had a heart attack in one of J. Edgar Hoover's dresses.

LILLIAN: Well, I would have too. He had terrible taste in clothes.

TINK: *Pa . . . pa . . . pa . . . cha. Pa . . . cha—*

LILLIAN: Parcheesi? Tink, you're in no condition to play Parcheesi.

TINK: *(Smacking her lips.) Pa . . . pa . . . parched. Parched.*

LILLIAN: Parched! Diva, she's parched. Quick! Get her some punch.

DIVA: You've got to be kidding.

LILLIAN: Huh?

DIVA: Déjà vu? Hairy-lipped Amazon? *Hell-ohhh?*

LILLIAN: What are you talking about?

DIVA: This is how we got into trouble last time.

LILLIAN: Then, go up to the house and get her some water.

DIVA: I don't take orders, Lillian.

LILLIAN: Of course not. I don't know what I could have been thinking.

DIVA: I am sure you don't. Besides, you can't really expect me to walk up that hill just to fetch a glass of water, do you? What do I look like, Jack and Jill?

LILLIAN: What do they look like?

DIVA: Servants, Lillian. They look like servants.

LILLIAN: Oh, well, sorry. I'll go.

DIVA: And leave me alone with the cast from Night of the Living Dead. Suppose we had an emergency while you were gone?

LILLIAN: I never thought of that.

DIVA: Well, that's your trouble, isn't it? You never think. Thinking is a strain on the inseam with you, isn't it?

TINK: Parched. Parched. Parched. *(To audience.)* I'm in hell again, aren't I?

LILLIAN: You're being unfair, Diva. I was thinking of poor old Tink.

DIVA: Pish-posh. You were thinking of yourself. The world is full of people who never think about anybody but themselves. I'm afraid, dearest Lillian, you are just one more in that long chain of thoughtless, selfish-thinking, ne'er-do-wells.

TINK: *(To audience.)* Why does hell look like Walmart . . . with Lillian and Diva as checkout girls?

LILLIAN: As far as people who never think about anybody but themselves, dearest Diva, I think we have a case of the pot calling the kettle beige.

DIVA: Stop trying to be clever, Lillian. It doesn't suit you.

TINK *(To audience.)* I was having this terrible nightmare. I was dreaming that I was. . . . *(Looking around.)* Oh shit! It's not a dream. One of these days I'm not going to wake up. I hope it's on their watch. Think of all that guilt . . . haunting them for the rest of their, trivial, insignificant, dreary little lives. . . . Is my mouth moving? Is any part of me moving? Anything? Any body part at all? Pa . . . pa . . . pa . . . .

DIVA *(Hands LILLIAN cup of punch.)* Here. I don't suppose one little cup could hurt. I'm just a martyr to the cause.

LILLIAN: *(Holding cup for TINK as she drinks.)* There you go. Drinky-drinky, Tinky-winky.

DIVA: Lillian, for God's sake, would you stop talking like some kind of trailer trash breeder.

LILLIAN: Sorry. *(To TINK.)* Drink up, Tink. Diva's on the rag, again. *(To a potential customer.)* Oh, hello. I didn't see you coming. You nearly startled me to death. That? No, that's not a jingle bell. It looks like a jingle bell though, doesn't it? It's made of bronze. Sent to me by a dear friend who went to England to write the great American novel. It predates the time of William Shakespeare. He wrote plays. Elizabethan. No, he was much earlier than Neil Simon. *(Holding up the blackened jingle bell. It is at least an inch in diameter. She jingles it.)* Listen to that. Isn't it beautiful? I think they put these on sheep and goats, or something. Anyway, it's not the thing itself, is it? It's the idea of it. To think that the sound of this little bell has remained the same for hundreds of years; a distinct and audible voice that has spoken with an enduring, everlasting voice since before the Renaissance. Excuse me? The Renaissance? Yes, I've been to the fair. But this was another kind of Renaissance – not a bunch of pathetic geeks in pitiful costumes. I'm talking about a time of reawakening, madame, a time of joy . . . a blossoming of the human spirit. Two dollars? I'm so sorry. You couldn't buy it for a thousand dollars. I'd sooner give it away to someone who understood the significance of it – someone who understood the beauty of a voice ringing unchanged down the centuries. Goodbye to you, too. And, have a nice day!

DIVA: *(Spotting someone across the street.)* Over here! We're having a fabulous yard sale! Free punch . . . *(Under her breath.)* with purchase. *(To LILLIAN.)* Oh my! Isn't he the cause celeb! I think that's the young leather-clad man who rescued our dear old Muffy. *(Looks at poster.)* Oh, my god! One and the same!

LILLIAN: Where's he going?

DIVA: Around the side of Dr. Hall's house, I think. Could it be that he's also one of Dr. Hall's tricks? *(Calling out.)* Oh, hello! Hello! Dr. Hall's away. He's visiting Betty Ford. Can I service you? I mean, be of service? *(Turning to LILLIAN.)* I don't think he heard me.

LILLIAN: *(Looking through binoculars.)* That's because he's on his cell phone. Oh, my! I think you're right. That is Carlotta's Greek.

DIVA: *(Taking the binoculars from LILLIAN.)* And Muffy's leather-clad rescuer – one and the same. Would you look at that basket. Talk about a stimulus package

LILLIAN: What basket? He's not carrying a basket.

DIVA: Lillian, you really have led a sheltered life, haven't you? *(Shakes her leg and reaches under her garter for cell phone. Answers phone.)* Diva Hollingsworth here, and who might you be? What do you want now, mother? Yes, don't you remember? Shortly after the Muffy fiasco when he lost all his rose bushes. He went on such a bender they hauled him off to the Betty Ford Clinic. And would you please stop eavesdropping on every little thing I say! Keep this up, mother, and I'm shipping you off to Idaho with the rest of the skinheads! *(To LILLIAN.)* She's got the whole yard wired for sound! Radio Shack should not be allowed to sell surveillance devices to little old ladies!

TINK: *More. More. More. . . .*

LILLIAN: Not now, Tink. He's on his way over.

DIVA: I've got a man coming, Mother. Over. Coming over! You really need to clean up that act of yours. I've got to go, Mother. *Ciao.* (Turns off phone and replaces it under her garter. She poses sensuously.) Oh, hello there. See anything you like? *(Waving her hands in front of her.)* There are butterflies.

LILLIAN: What?

DIVA: Butterflies, butterflies! There are millions of butterflies. I'm being attacked by a gaggle of butterflies!

LILLIAN: A gaggle of butterflies?

DIVA: A herd? A swarm? A big bunch? Pretty butterflies. *(She waves her hands and fingers in front of her as though they were a swarm of butterflies. She is definitely becoming very stoned on the punch.)* I'm a butterfly.

LILLIAN: You're definitely not a butterfly. Not even close, Diva.

DIVA: I'm not?

LILLIAN: Not in this lifetime.

DIVA: Pity. *(Speaking to young man.)* Are you a butterfly? Then, who the hell are you? Who? The woman you helped onto the truck? That would be Muffy Hughes. No, no. She doesn't live there. *(Finds a sheet and casually throws it over MUFFY.)* That's Dr. Hall's house. Muffy lives two doors over – next to the

Sundowner Nursing Home for geriatric delinquents. But, she's not home. If you don't mind my asking, what do you want her for?

TINK: *More. More. More.*

DIVA: Tink, shut up! Lillian, if she wants more, give her more.

LILLIAN: *(Giving TINK more punch.)* Here you go, Tink. Miss Fidgety-twat's got an itch Quasimodo wouldn't scratch.

DIVA: *(Ignoring the last.)* Well, I will thank her for you the very next time I see her. Where? Umm . . . she went to. . . . Lillian, where did Muffy go after she was released from the hospital?

LILLIAN: Into the care of an evil, old hag from hunger!

DIVA: Hungary. Yes. She went to the goulash-scented hills of Hungary to recover in the care of her sweet peasant family.

LILLIAN: *(To TINK.)* Pig shit.

DIVA: On a pig farm. She needed to get in touch with her roots. It'll help her recovery. Can I offer you some punch? It has absinthe in it. I'm told that it's a lot like LSD. Colored lights, visions, that sort of thing. I never had LSD, but I did see Easy Rider and The Trip with Peter Fonda. Anyway, it's free.

LILLIAN: With purchase.

DIVA: Now, now, dear Lillian. I am sure we could make an exception for this young, young . . . oh, so very young . . . young man.

LILLIAN: *(To TINK.)* That's more "youngs" than in Shanghai!

DIVA: You'll have to excuse my friend. She had a hysterectomy yesterday. You're going to do what? But, you can't do that! It's a long way off. Besides, how do you expect to find her? You've got to be kidding. Hungary's a big place. It would be like finding a . . . a. . . .

LILLIAN: A very large, plump, dull needle in a haystack.

DIVA: Thank you, Lillian.

LILLIAN: Don't mention it.

DIVA: *(To man.)* Well, if you've got to go, go. Don't let me keep you from the love of your life. *(Waving as he leaves.)* Good bye. Good bye, my dear young . . . young . . .

LILLIAN: *(Calling after him.)* Have a nice day.

DIVA: *(Calling after him.)* Wait! Come back!

LILLIAN: Diva, Carlotta will kill you.

DIVA: Well, it won't be the first time. *(To man whom she signals to come closer.)* I'm a filthy rich woman.

LILLIAN: You certainly are.

DIVA: *(To LILLIAN.)* Don't think I don't know what you meant by that, Lillian. *(To man.)* Now, you go up to that house. The door is unlocked. Go up the stairs to the second room on the right and wait for me. Make yourself comfortable. Relax. Take your shoes off. Whatever you like. I won't be long. Remember – I'm very, very rich. *(Blows him a kiss.)* Later.

LILLIAN: Diva, you're no better than Carlotta.

DIVA: Yeah? And your point is? *(LILLIAN shakes her head disapprovingly. DIVA removes sheet from MUFFY.)* How are we doing, Muffy? Sorry. You'll thank me one day. Thank me. I said thank me, not spank me. You have a one-track mind, Muffy, and I'm afraid it runs right into the sewer. Sewer. Sewer. Oh, screw it!

TINK: *(Fully awake. Sings.)* I'M IN THE MOOD FOR LOVE!

DIVA: What?!

LILLIAN: I think she said. . . .

DIVA I know what she said. But, what does she mean?

TINK: *(Sings.)* WHEN THE RED, RED ROBIN COMES BOB, BOB, BOBBIN' ALONG!

DIVA: What's gotten into her?

LILLIAN: I think the punch is kicking in.

TINK: I have always depended on the kindness of strangers. The Tarantula Arms. That's where I took my victims. Rub-a-dub-dub. Three men in a tub, and what a filthy tub!

DIVA: Is it me or is it her?

LILLIAN: I think it's Tennessee Williams.

DIVA: Then, you hear it, too.

LILLIAN: Yes, Diva. I hear it, too.

TINK: *(Definitely a man's voice.)* Diva Hollingsworth! I'm in the garden . . . playing with my cucumber.

DIVA: No, you're not. You're in my yard . . . rotting in your wheelchair.

TINK: Dumplin', it's me. It's your little Mooky.

DIVA: Horace? Is that you?

TINK: I've come to give you a message from the great beyond.

DIVA: Lillian, come here, quick!

LILLIAN: *(Crossing.)* What?

DIVA: (In a loud whisper.) I see dead people.

LILLIAN: What?

DIVA: *(In a louder whisper.)* I see dead people.

LILLIAN: Oh, who doesn't? Have you been to Walmart lately? Dead people. Stupid people. People who probably aren't really people.

DIVA: *(Defensive.)* My mother shops at Walmart, Lillian.

LILLIAN: I rest my case. *(Gulps punch.)* Wow! This stuff has some kick!

TINK: Teeth.

DIVA: Teeth? What about teeth?

TINK: They bite.

DIVA: That's it? They bite?

TINK: That and . . . oh, yes . . . you're going to die.

DIVA: What?

TINK: You're a mean, self-centered, selfish, manipulating, overbearing twit.

DIVA: How can you say such a thing? Who do you think I'm doing all this for? For you, Horace. For you.

TINK: Face the truth, Mooky. You only want that Faberge egg for yourself. What do I care? I'm dead! The pickle jar is just fine. In fact, I like my ashes in a pickle jar. It keeps me close to the memory of what I loved most.

DIVA: Thank you, Horace.

TINK: Not you, you great colossal cow! My cucumbers. I want to live in cucumber fields forever!

DIVA: But, you're dead, Horace. You're dead.

TINK: And, you're not?

DIVA: Of course, I'm not.

TINK: But, you're going to.

DIVA: I am not going to!

LILLIAN: You're not going to what, Diva?

DIVA: I am not going to die.

LILLIAN: Of course not. Well, not right away. But, someday . . . someday you will.

DIVA: *(Real panic.)* I will?

LILLIAN: Most definitely.

TINK: I've got to go now. The great Wisdom Tooth calls.

DIVA: No. You can't go. Come back . . . *(Shakes TINK furiously.)* Come back, Horace! Come back!

LILLIAN: What are you doing, Diva? You're going to kill Tink again! You can't go around shaking people her age.

DIVA: *(Coming to her senses.)* What are you talking about?

LILLIAN: Well, you were talking to Carlotta's Greek and then you—

DIVA: Carlotta's Greek?

LILLIAN: The one in the poster. Don't you remember? You nearly molested the poor man. And, telling him all those things before sending him up to your house to wait for you. I could blush. I really could blush.
DIVA: What are you talking about, Lillian? I was talking to that leather-clad man of Muffy's who's off to Hungary to find her and marry her.

LILLIAN: Diva, I think the punch is having its way with you.

TINK: Why not? Everybody else has had their way with her!

DIVA: There! Did you hear that?

LILLIAN: Hear what?

DIVA: Horace.

LILLIAN: Horace? Where, Diva? Where is Horace?

DIVA: In Tink. Horace is inside Tink.

LILLIAN: It's the punch, Diva.

TINK: It's the punch, you silly cow!

DIVA: *(Screams.)* Oh, my God! I remember!

LILLIAN: What?

DIVA: I'm going to die. Help me, Lillian. I'm going to die.

LILLIAN: You are not going to die.

DIVA: Not today, no. But, one day I'm going to die. You said so
yourself.

LILLIAN: Sweetie, everybody dies sooner or later.

DIVA: It never occurred to me.

LILLIAN: I can't believe that a woman your age never gave any
thought to her own mortality.

DIVA: Believe it! I've been a mean, self-centered twit and I'm
going to die—sobbing.

LILLIAN: *(Hugging and comforting her.)* There, there. You're
not going to die.

DIVA: I've been mean and manipulative and self-centered—

LILLIAN: Like I said, you're not going to die. It's the absinthe in
the punch. Think of something nice and it'll pass.

DIVA: *(Crying.)* I mean, I know people die. People die every
day. But, it's not something I ever thought would happen to me.

LILLIAN: Pull yourself together. Think about something nice. Think about the seashore.

DIVA: The seashore?

LILLIAN: You've always liked the seashore. Think about the waves lapping at your toes . . . your feet . . . your ankles . . . *(DIVA begins to move slowing, feeling the water lapping her feet and rising upwards. She writhes in slow-motion ecstasy. Her arms fly out as though conducting some heavenly orchestra only she can hear. Slowly we see she is on the verge of an orgasm. LILLIAN continues.)* Your legs . . . your knees . . . your thighs . . . your . . . . Diva, what on earth are you doing?

DIVA: Don't stop! Not now! Oh yes! This is it! Oh God! This is good!

LILLIAN: *(Shakes her to her senses.)* Stop! Now! Bad girl! Bad. You've got to get hold of yourself. You could get arrested for feeling what you're feeling in a public place.

DIVA: Arrest me! Put me in handcuffs, in chains . . . do with me what you will! I'm free! I'm free! Over here! I'm free. Free.

LILLIAN: Diva, it's the punch talking. Get control of yourself!

DIVA: I love the night life!

LILLIAN: Of course you do. Are you okay?

DIVA: Okay.

LILLIAN: Okay.

(DIVA starts shaking her leg with uncontrollable fervor. She reaches under her dress and retrieves the cell phone.)

DIVA: *(Answers phone.)* This better be good, Mother! Oh, Carlotta. What do you want? I haven't got your Greek. No, I haven't. What makes you think that? My mother called you, did she? Saw him going into my house? Well, if that's what she told you, then I guess its true – although, I don't remember a thing. No, I have no intention of giving him back. Finder's keepers. Reward? A finder's fee? What kind of a finder's fee? Really? Really? You've got a deal, girlfriend! *(Replaces phone under garter. To LILLIAN.)* Lillian, you'll never believe what just happened? *(Pours herself some punch.)* Carlotta is giving me her Faberge egg in exchange for her Greek. Isn't life wonderful? She wants me to have it for Horace. *(Takes a big gulp.)* Lillian, this is the best stuff I've ever had. *(Spies a potential customer.)*

DIVA & LILLIAN: Free punch . . . with purchase. Free punch . . . with purchase.

LILLIAN: Oh, hello there. Can I show you something? That? That . . . oh dear, it looks like a pistol. Diva, what's this pistol doing here?

DIVA: What do you think it is doing, Lillian?

LILLIAN: What's it doing here, Diva?

DIVA: Waiting to be sold.

LILLIAN: Where did you get it?

DIVA: It's Horace's old starter pistol. He used it over at the community theatre when they did those melodramas. I believe the last time he used it was when he played the sheriff in Dirty Dick from Deadwood. It shoots blanks. But, then, so did Horace.

LILLIAN: *(To potential customer.)* I'm afraid it only shoots blanks. See anything else that interests you? That's a jar of . . . good God! What's in this jar, Diva?

DIVA: Teeth. Molars, bicuspids, canine, wisdom . . . teeth. Horace never could throw anything away. Those represent forty years of extractions. There are probably some contributions from Carlotta Bean in there.

LILLIAN: *(Tries to lift large jar.)* Holy Christmas, this would give the Tooth Fairy a hernia! (To customer.) Now, here's something you might want to invest in. Can I interest you in a genuine pre-Columbian fertility goddess? It was a wedding present. No. We never did have any children. If you like, I'll take off ten percent for impotence. Tools? I don't think so. Diva, do we have any tools?

DIVA: What do I look like, a mechanic? How about a screw? I've got some loose screws from Muffy's walker. Or a vibrator? *(Holds up vibrator – her arms shaking from the vibrations.)* Oh my! That's a perky little number.

LILLIAN: *(As customer leaves.)* Sorry we couldn't help you. Some what? I'm sorry. We don't allow any free punch unless you buy something. Have a nice day.

DIVA: Free loader! My, this vibrator sure has a kick. *(Drops it in TINK'S lap.)*

TINK: *(Wakes. Grabs vibrator and starts to vibrate madly.)* Help! Help!

DIVA: For Pete's sake, enjoy it, Tink.

TINK: Diva, if I wasn't in this chair I'd . . . I'd . . .

DIVA: *(As Bette Davis.)* But you are, Blanche. You are in that chair.

LILLIAN: Diva, you can't leave her vibrating like that. She'll get seasick or something.

DIVA: Let her have her fun. That battery can't have that much juice left in it.

LILLIAN: She's starting to turn blue.

DIVA: She's always had a touch of blue.

LILLIAN: Suppose it's one of those . . . *(She hiccups.)* . . . bunny batteries?

TINK: *(Still vibrating.)* Help! Help!

DIVA: What on earth are you talking about, Lillian?

LILLIAN: You know, the kind that keep going and going and going . . . *(Hiccups.)* . . . and going and going and going—

DIVA: What is wrong with you, Lillian?

LILLIAN: I got the . . . *(Hiccups.)* . . . the . . . *(Hiccups.)* . . . hiccups. You better scare me, Diva.

TINK: *(Still vibrating.)* Help! Help!

DIVA: What?

LILLIAN: I said you better . . . scare me. *(Hiccups.)*

(DIVA picks up the pistol and shoots it into the air. TINK stops vibrating. LILLIAN stops hiccuping. There is a long SILENCE before DIVA'S cell phone RINGS.)

DIVA: *(Lays down the pistol and retrieves the phone.)* Diva, here. Mother, I asked you not to . . . what? What did you call 911 for? No, mother, nobody's being murdered. It was just Horace's old starter pistol. You know, the one from Dirty Dick from Deadwood.

(There is the SOUND of police SIRENS and the red and blue LIGHTS of squad cars flashing across the yard.)

DIVA: Mother, I need to hang up now.

VOICE OVER BULL HORN: *WE HAVE THE PLACE SURROUNDED. PUT DOWN YOUR ARMS AND RAISE YOUR HANDS.*

LILLIAN: How do I do that, Diva? How do I put down my arms and raise my hands?

DIVA: Don't be a ninny, Lillian! *(Holding out the cell phone.)* It's just a cell phone.

VOICE OVER BULL HORN: *PUT YOUR ARMS DOWN AND RAISE YOUR HANDS.*

TINK: *(Holds out vibrator.)* It's just a vibrator.

VOICE OVER BULL HORN: THIS IS YOUR LAST WARNING. PUT YOUR ARMS DOWN AND RAISE YOUR HANDS.

LILLIAN: *(Picks up pistol and points it toward police.)* It's just a starter pistol. It shoots blanks. *(The gun accidentally goes off.)* Oops.

DIVA: *(Into phone.)* Mother, I've got to go now . . . .

(BLACK OUT. The SOUND of a barrage of gunfire.)

End ACT TWO — Scene One

6 FULL-LENGTH PLAYS
VOLUME TWO   Edward Crosby Wells

ACT TWO — *Scene Two, continuous*

Slowly, the LIGHTING returns.

LILLIAN: Thank you, officer, you've been so understanding.

TINK: Holy Tallulah Bankhead! I'm alive.

DIVA: *(Holding something tightly to her bosom. To Muffy.)* Are you in there, Muffy? You didn't get shot, did you? *(Leaning in to listen.)* No, dear. I know how you love men in uniform but this would not be a good time to hit on a policeman. *(To policeman O.S.)* She seems to be fine, officer.

LILLIAN: *(To policeman O.S.)* Oh, I swear, officer, we'll never do anything like that again. Would you like some punch? Sorry, no donuts. Toodles.

ALL: *(Waving "goodbye" to policeman.)* Have a nice day.

LILLIAN: Diva, are you okay?

DIVA: *(Still holding something clutched to her bosom.)* I . . . I . . . I . . .

LILLIAN: You're not having a stroke, are you?

DIVA: NO! LOOK! *(Holds out a large jewel encrusted gold Faberge egg.)*

LILLIAN: Oh, sweet Liberace! It's a Faberge egg. Where did it come from?

DIVA: I don't know. In all the confusion of the gun fire, somebody ran up and put it in my hands.

LILLIAN: Who was it?

TINK: Don't look at me. I don't do running.

DIVA: *(Shaking her leg wildly. To LILLIAN.)* Here hold this. *(Gives egg to*

LILLIAN. Retrieves phone and answers it.) Hello. I'm special and you're not. Oh, it's you, Carlotta . . . *Uh huh . . . Uh huh . . . (Listening. Adding an "uh huh" every so often.)*

LILLIAN: *(Opening egg.)* Oh look. M&Ms. *(Offering some to TINK.)*

TINK: I'm diabetic. Well, maybe one. Oh, a green one. I love the green ones.

LILLIAN: They're all the same.

TINK: Oh, no, there's something about the green ones.

DIVA: *(Into phone.)* It's beautiful! It's wonderful! It's marvelous! Horace will fit very nicely in it.

LILLIAN: Without the M&Ms.

DIVA: *(Into phone. After a pause to listen.)* So it was you! Well, that was fast, Carlotta. *(To LILLIAN.)* She broke into my house and kidnapped the Greek. *(Into phone.)* You're always welcome in my home . . . whether I am there are not. Yes. I love the egg. A Greek for a Faberge egg seems a fair exchange. We will, Carlotta. Yes, of course, we will. And may you and your Greek do the same. Ciao to you too, darling. *(Replaces phone.)*

LILLIAN: What did she say?

DIVA: Carlotta wants to see us be gay. She wants us to sing and dance and be filled with happiness, love and joy. Oh, girls, I have everything . . . the most wonderful friends in the whole wide world . . . and a Faberge egg for Horace. Life is good. *(Spies Mother in window across the street. Yells.)* I see you, Mother. Yes, we're all fine. Thanks for negotiating with Carlotta. *(After a tearful pause.)* I love you, too, Mother.

TINK: The loon has changed her tune.

DIVA: Watch it, Tink! You're not the only bitch on wheels around here!

LILLIAN: So much for gaiety, love and joy.

TINK: Do you remember the routine we did at the Firemen's Ball?

LILLIAN: I just love Firemen's Balls!

DIVA: Of course you do.

(DIVA and LILLIAN pushTINK's wheelchair into a SPOTLIGHT. At this point they lip sync to a song of the DIRECTOR's choosing.)

BLACK OUT.

END OF PLAY

6 FULL-LENGTH PLAYS
VOLUME TWO

THOR'S DAY

Dedicated to Steven E. Thornburg, director of *Thor's Day,* for his
thrilling quintessential production. Thank you, Steven

SYNOPSIS: 2M, One Set, Full Length, 90 Minutes.

Philip, a middle-aged insurance salesman, brings home a gorgeous young man for an afternoon tryst. Their encounter is fraught with pleasure and danger as the clock ticks down to an explosive and unexpected climax. Perhaps possessed with supernatural powers, Buck takes Philip on a breathtaking, life-altering journey into the unexplored territory of his long-suppressed and hidden desires. Intelligent, erotic, powerful, provocative and terrifying, this thriller is sure to keep an audience on the edge of its seat.

THE TIME: It is mid-afternoon on a Thursday in early October. The present.

THE PLACE: Hobbs: A small city in southeastern New Mexico, a mile from the West Texas border.

THERE IS NO INTERMISSION

THOR'S DAY was first presented by Tony Award winning The Glines at the Trilogy Theatre, 341 W. 44th St., New York City, April 30, 1997, under the direction of Steven E. Thornburg with the following cast:

BUCK ROSE: Blake Robbins
PHILIP WINTER: James A. Walsh
Director: Steven E. Thornburg
Stage Manager: George Seylaz
Set: David M. Mead
Lighting: Garth Reese
Costumes: Carla Gant
Music & Sound: Thomas Hasselwander

A FEW REVIEWS

". . . a mysterious and seductive game of rent boy and patron that spirals into an unexpected fight for life and death. Edward Crosby Wells' play is a bit Gods and Monsters and a bit Zoo Story . . . compelling and intriguing drama."
—nytheatre.com

". . . an intriguing mixture of the erotic and dangerous."—HX MAGAZINE

". . . strong, haunting, intense, suspenseful and engaging."—HI DRAMA TV

"A brilliant creation! . . . the heir to Zoo Story . . . Electric . . . The story-telling is assured and highly intriguing. Every behavior leads logically to the next . . . original and universal. This property has a movie in it."—Kenneth Weller, NYC STAGE PAGES

"Each transition, from opening the first beer to pulling the final trigger, had its own psychological logic—a sign of complete commitment by the playwright . . . it's not a show for the faint of heart." —JOHN CHATTERTON, OOBR

". . . a great masterpiece of art." —INSIDER ENTERTAINMENT NEWS

"Edward Crosby Wells is an accomplished and original playwright whose varied works have gained growing esteem over the last few years. He shows remarkable and equal proficiency in comic, dramatic, and fantastic works. One never knows what to expect from each new play of his, except that they always show technical skill, poetic insight, and theatrical acumen."—Robert Patrick, Playwright (author of over 50 published plays including Broadway's Kennedy's Children)

"[Wells'] works are expertly layered and the characters are well thought out, portraying real people. He is equally talented with both comedy and drama. His dramas are beautifully crafted and engrossing and his comedies are arguably the funniest you will ever see."—Frank Calo, SPOTLIGHT ON PRODUCTIONS, New York City

"Brilliant dialogue."—KDHX, St. Louis

6 FULL-LENGTH PLAYS
VOLUME TWO

Edward Crosby Wells

AT RISE – *BUCK is standing behind the sofa. He stretches, looks around the room and examines the gun in his hand before placing it under a cushion of the sofa. He takes a cigarette from out his shirt pocket. He moves about the room searching for some matches. After a while, he finds a gold lighter on a side table and lights his cigarette. He then puts the lighter in his pocket, casually—not the deliberate act of a thief. PHILIP is offstage preparing snacks in the kitchen and will remain there until noted.*

BUCK: Do you hear me?

PHILIP: (*From kitchen.*) What?

BUCK: I said, do you hear me?

PHILIP: Yes. I do now. Go on.

BUCK: Gotta eat. Three kids.

PHILIP: Three.

BUCK: Mind if I take m' boots off?

PHILIP: Not at all. Please, make yourself comfortable.

BUCK: How's that?

PHILIP: I said, please do.

BUCK: (*Sits on sofa, removes his boots.*) One . . . boy . . . eight months. Girl . . . four. Don't be ashamed to tell me if you smell somethin' ripe. Ain't had these here boots off in nearly two years.

PHILIP: Two years?

BUCK: Just kidding. I'm a great kidder. The other . . . six . . . crippled . . . had two operations.

PHILIP: Good God, two.

BUCK: Needs another. Can't walk too good without her braces. Needs new ones. Out-growed 'em. Insurance canceled. If I was to disappear, welfare . . .

PHILIP: I can't hear you.

BUCK: I said, if I was to disappear, or somethin' like that, welfare might start to kick in. Wife. She gets these here headaches, you see. And fits. Terrible fits. Only one kidney . . . and that's gone bad. All over now.

PHILIP: What?

BUCK: I said it's all over now. I shot her in the head this morning. Put her out of her misery.

PHILIP: What?

BUCK: Sent the kids to their Grandma's and shot the old lady.

PHILIP: I can't really be hearing what I'm hearing. Can I?

BUCK: Can't rightly say. I told you I was a great kidder, didn't I?

PHILIP: Yes. Yes, you did.

BUCK: You see . . . my wife . . . she's very sickly.

PHILIP: How sad. I'm sorry to hear that.

BUCK: No need.   Nope.   Gotta eat.   Know what I mean? Yessirree! Gotta eat. Three kids. You?

PHILIP: Me?

BUCK: Kids?

PHILIP: One. He and his wife live in California. He's studying to be an architect. She's a social worker.

BUCK: That's like welfare, ain't it?

PHILIP: She works for the Department of Welfare – or Social Services – if that is what you mean.

BUCK: Givin' handouts to the wrong people.

PHILIP: You'll have to speak louder.

BUCK: I said, that's what I mean all right. He's in college, right?

PHILIP: Berkeley.

BUCK: What's that?

PHILIP: Where he studies.

BUCK: Pretty smart, huh?

PHILIP: He certainly thinks so.

BUCK: You?

PHILIP: Me?

BUCK: What do you do?

(PHILIP enters from the kitchen with some bowls of nuts, chips, pretzels, and some bottles of beer that he places on the coffee table.)

PHILIP: I have an insurance business. *(Crosses to an imaginary downstage window and looks out.)* Looks bad. Looks like we got inside just in time.

BUCK: In time?

PHILIP: For the storm.

BUCK: Yeah. We're due for a good one.

PHILIP: A bad one, you mean.

BUCK: Right. That's what I was fixin' to say. Bad. Somethin' wicked.

PHILIP: Not too wicked, I trust.

BUCK: Wicked enough.

PHILIP: Enough?

BUCK: To be exciting.

PHILIP: Oh. Well. I can handle that. I guess.

BUCK: Maybe. Terrible thing. Tornado.

PHILIP: Tornado? In October?

BUCK: And rain. Hard and heavy rain.

PHILIP: *(Looking out window.)* Look at those clouds. Brown. Brown as brown gets.

BUCK: That's good ol' West Texas dirt sneakin' over the New Mexico border. Probably rain mud all over Hobbs. (*Indicating the watercolors hung about the living room.*) Those yours?

PHILIP: (*Turning from window.   Turns on a lamp or two.*) Excuse me?

BUCK: Them paintin's. You do 'em?

PHILIP: The watercolors. No. My wife. My wife . . . did them.

BUCK: Nice. Flowers. Sunset on the mesa. More flowers. She's an artist. Yes?

PHILIP: Yes.

BUCK: Nice.

PHILIP: Thank you. (*Nervous.*) There's beer and snacks . . .

BUCK: You shouldn't've gone to so much trouble.

PHILIP: It wasn't any trouble. No trouble at all.

BUCK: Good. 'Cause I don't want to put you out or nothin'.

PHILIP: No.   You're not putting me out. I mean, it's my pleasure.

BUCK: Your pleasure. Yes. I can see that.

PHILIP: (*After an uncomfortable pause.*) Where did you park?

BUCK: Around the corner.

PHILIP: (*Nervously.*) Good.

(*A long fidgeting SILENCE.*)

BUCK: How old are you, if you don't mind m' askin'?

PHILIP: (*He does mind.*) No. I don't mind. I don't mind at all. Fifty . . . something. (*A forced smile after trying to make a joke that seems to have gone unrecognized.*)

BUCK: Don't look it.

PHILIP: Thank you.

BUCK: Naah, I'd've taken you for thirty-somethin'. Forty tops.

PHILIP: (*Flattered.*) Thank you.

BUCK: Twenty-five.

PHILIP: Twenty-five?

BUCK: Me. I'm twenty-five. Would be twenty-six in two weeks.

PHILIP: Twenty-six. (*A beat.*) Would be?

BUCK: In two weeks – if I was to live that long.

PHILIP: Of course you'll live that long.

BUCK: Will I?

PHILIP: I'm sure of it.

BUCK: You're sure of it?

PHILIP: Well, pretty sure.

BUCK: Pretty sure?

PHILIP: I think it's safe to assume . . .

BUCK: It ain't safe to assume nothin'. Ain't safe no way.

PHILIP: I only meant . . .

BUCK: I know what you meant.

PHILIP: Do you?   That requires an assumption on your part, doesn't it?

BUCK: Nope. Just me knowin' somethin' that you don't.

PHILIP: And what's that?

BUCK: That's the thousand-dollar question, man. That's the thing for me to know and you to find out.

PHILIP: Really?

BUCK: Really. (*Wanting to change the subject.*) I'm what you call your Libra. You?

PHILIP: Aquarius.

BUCK: When's that?

PHILIP: February.

(*A pause while BUCK stares as though waiting for more.*)

PHILIP: (*Continues.*) The eleventh. Day before Lincoln's.

(*BUCK continues to stare.*)

PHILIP: (*Continues.*) Abraham . . . Lincoln . . . President.

BUCK: Yeah, I know. Shot, right?

PHILIP: Shot, yes.

BUCK: Do you put much stock into that kind o' thing?
PHILIP: What kind of thing?

BUCK: Signs. Like Libra and Aquarius.

PHILIP: Oh. I suppose there may be something to it. I don't know, really.

BUCK: Yeah, I feel the same way. I don't know – really. (*Sings.*) THIS IS THE DAWNING OF THE AGE OF AQUARIUS AGE OF AQUARIUS AHH-QUAR-REE-US . . . (*Speaks.*) That's an old hippy song.
PHILIP: Not so old. (*A nervous attempt at making conversation.*) You sing.

BUCK: All my life. You?

PHILIP: Sing? No. Like to though.

BUCK: Then, why don'tcha?

PHILIP: Can't. In the shower maybe. Otherwise, can't.

BUCK: Course you can. Everybody can.

PHILIP: But not well.

BUCK: Well . . . that's a whole other matter, ain't it? Sing somethin'.

PHILIP: No. Really. I can't.

BUCK: Come on. There's nobody here.

PHILIP: (*Embarrassed.*) No. Please . . .

BUCK: Come on. Ain't nobody to hear you now.

PHILIP: There's you.

BUCK: Ain't nobody, I say. Sing.

PHILIP: I can't.

BUCK: Sing.

PHILIP: (*Firmly.*) I don't want to.

BUCK: That's different.   If you don't want to, I understand (*After a pause – with a big, boyish grin.*) You sure?

PHILIP: As sure as sure gets.

BUCK: (*Shrugs.*)   Suit yourself.   (*Sings.*)   THIS IS THE DAWNING OF THE AGE OF AQUARIUS AH-QUAR-REE-US AH-QUAR-REE-US (*Speaks.*) Like movies?

PHILIP: Used to.

BUCK: Don't make 'em like they used to, huh?

PHILIP: No. I mean, I don't get out much.

BUCK: Should. There's more out there than the eye can see.

PHILIP: Is there?

BUCK: Worlds and worlds.

PHILIP: Really?

BUCK: You'd be surprised.

PHILIP: Would I?

BUCK: You'll think you died and gone to heaven.

PHILIP: Will I?

BUCK: Guarantee it.

PHILIP: (*Uncomfortable – guarded.*) It's . . . it's difficult.

BUCK: What's that?

PHILIP: Getting out. Doing things.

BUCK: Sick?

PHILIP: No.

BUCK: Work hard, huh?

PHILIP: Yes.

BUCK: Tired, huh?

PHILIP: Sometimes.

BUCK: Sometimes?

PHILIP: Often. I feel locked into it. My life . . . the order . . . the order of my life. The routine.

BUCK: I don't get out much myself. 'Cept to make my deliveries. Very routine. Junk food, she calls it.

PHILIP: Who?

BUCK: The ol' lady.

PHILIP: Your mother . . .

BUCK: My wife.

PHILIP: Of course.

BUCK: Of course?

PHILIP: You'll have to excuse me. I'm . . . I'm . . . sorry.

BUCK: What are you sorry for?

PHILIP: Umm . . . not paying attention, I guess.

BUCK: Maybe you're paying too much attention.

PHILIP: I don't see how that's possible.

BUCK: 'Cause you're lookin' to close.

PHILIP: You think?

BUCK: Yeah . . . I do.

PHILIP: Sorry. (*After a pause.*) Your wife.

BUCK: Never know when one o' those fits is gonna come upon her. (*He lights a cigarette with the gold lighter. PHILIP does not notice that it is his. BUCK pockets the lighter.*) I almost forgot.

PHILIP: What?

BUCK: Nothin'.

PHILIP: Nothing? It had to be something.

BUCK: Maybe. Maybe not. Anyway, I took care of it. All over now. She's gone.

PHILIP: Your wife?

BUCK: My wife.

PHILIP: She's gone?

BUCK: All gone.

PHILIP: She left you?

BUCK: We had this arrangement. First she'd go then I'd follow . . . just after I did some business.

PHILIP: Business?

BUCK: Tying up some loose ends – if you know what I mean.

PHILIP: No. I don't know what you mean.

BUCK: How could you?

PHILIP: You could explain.

BUCK: I could.

PHILIP: (*Waiting for BUCK to say more, but he doesn't.*) I see . . . I guess. Whatever. I hope it works out for you.

BUCK: It will. I promise. Visiting some Roman Catholics who speak Latin backwards.

PHILIP: I don't understand.

BUCK: Me neither. Guess speakin' it forwards is hard enough, huh? (*He finds this very funny. He is amused with himself.*)

PHILIP: (*Puzzled.*) I guess.

BUCK: Ain't no guess about it.

PHILIP: (*After a nervous pause.*)   Look.   I think I made a mistake. Perhaps we ought to . . .

BUCK: (*Cutting him off.*) No mistake. Everything's copacetic. Relax. She went to visit some of her kinfolk who used to live next door to a whole coven of witches. They're gone now. Got burned out in the night. But when they was alive you could hear them chantin' Latin, backwards. That's what devil worshipers do, you know? They chant Latin backwards. You could hear them through the paper-thin walls whiles you were lyin' in bed beatin' your meat – or slippin' it to the old lady, the wife – in the middle of the night. (*After a pause.*) *Yessirree!* Three kids make you older. Know what I mean?

PHILIP: I know one does.

BUCK: How's that?

PHILIP: Well . . . *ah* . . . on birthdays. On his birthday, I mean. My son's. They always seem more traumatic than my own.

BUCK: Traumatic?

PHILIP: I feel my age more . . . my youth . . . or rather, lack of it.

BUCK: I wouldn't worry 'bout that.

PHILIP: I'm not exactly worried. (*Indicating beer and snacks.*) Please. Help yourself.

BUCK: Don't mind if I do. (*Chugs beer. Takes another.*) Drink beer and pee, huh?

PHILIP: What?

BUCK: Piss, man. Some guys like to get pissed on.

PHILIP: Not me.

BUCK: Wanna see my dick?

PHILIP: (*Nervous. Uncertain as to what he's gotten himself into.*) I'm not that way. I just had the afternoon free. My wife was out. I saw you. I thought . . .

BUCK: I know what you thought.

PHILIP: No, you don't. You don't know at all what I thought.

BUCK: Bet me.

PHILIP: Huh?

BUCK: Bet me.

PHILIP: Bet you what?

BUCK: Bet me one hundred dollars that I don't know what you were thinking when you picked me up.

PHILIP: I didn't exactly pick you up. You asked if you should follow me home.

BUCK: Whatever, man. Bet me.

PHILIP: One hundred dollars?

BUCK: That's my price.

PHILIP: Your price?

BUCK: Don't believe it when they tell you the best things are free, man. They ain't. They ain't free at all. One hundred dollars . . . cash.

PHILIP: (*Nervously.*) Well, I uh . . . well, I think I've got that much in the house. Sure. Why not?

BUCK: Why not?

PHILIP: Okay.

BUCK: (*Takes a long swig of beer.*) Here goes . . .

PHILIP: But if you lose?

BUCK: If I lose you get me, man. However you want me – you get me. I mean, even if you want me to piss on you. Okay?

PHILIP: I don't want you to piss on me.

BUCK: But if you do. I don't mind. I mean, I like it, man. I really can get into it. Some guys like to drink it. *Ooh* . . . I like that, man. I fuckin' love it, you know?

PHILIP: I don't.

BUCK: Whatever, man. Okay?

PHILIP: Okay, but how will you know if I'm telling the truth or not?

BUCK: I'll know.

PHILIP: How?

BUCK: I'll know, man. I'll know.

PHILIP: All right. You're on.

BUCK: (*Takes a moment to think.*)   When you see me – when our eyes meet – you say to yourself, do I dare?   Should I try? What would he want with me?   I'm just an old geezer.   Or somethin' like that. I don't think you love yourself, man.

PHILIP: I like myself all right.

BUCK: I said love.   It's already a fact how you don't like yourself.   But hey, don't get upset.   Nothin' personal.   Let me finish.

PHILIP: It feels personal.

BUCK: Sure it does.   The whole world can seem like that sometimes, but it ain't. No offense. All right? C'mon. C'mon. No pouting, all right?

PHILIP: I'm not pouting.

BUCK: Yes, you are. You're just a big ol' pouter.

PHILIP: Go on with your story.
BUCK: It's your story. And, we're gonna see just how much you love yourself—and pretty soon.

PHILIP: We are?

BUCK: Yeah. Anyway. He's young and hot and full of life, you say to yourself. And then, maybe – maybe he's dangerous. I could get him home and he could kill me. Right? Grab a baseball bat, a lamp, or a poker and bash my head to bloody pulp. Right?

PHILIP: Well, I . . . *uh* . . .

BUCK: Yes or no?

PHILIP: More yes than no, I suppose.

BUCK: This guy's gonna cost me, you say to yourself. He ain't gonna come cheap, I can see that. Nope. Not cheap at all. And maybe . . . maybe he's got a knife, or a gun, hidden somewhere. Wanna frisk me? Maybe I'm sittin' on it . . . sittin' on the thing that's gonna kill you, man. Wanna check me out? Check me out real good?

PHILIP: No. It's all right.

BUCK: You don't know that. Not really. (*Rubbing his thighs and crotch.*) Go ahead. A free frisk. On the house.

PHILIP: It's all right, really.

BUCK: Your choice, man. Suit yourself. (*After a pause.*) And then you think about your wife . . . the poor unsuspecting woman . . . gone for the day. Got this golden opportunity. A plum dropped right in your lap. Can't pass this one up. Nope. Not once the blood starts to flow . . . makin' you hard as a rock. Achin' for some relief from all your one-hand fantasies. Can't pass this one up, you say to yourself. Can you, man? Where?

PHILIP: Where? I don't understand.

BUCK: The wife! You ain't listenin', man. Where is she?

PHILIP: I don't know why you need to know.

BUCK: (*Sharply.*) Where the fuck is mommy?

PHILIP: What?

BUCK: (*Less threatening.*) Where're you keepin' her, man?

PHILIP: (*With renewed anxiety.*) She's . . . she's in the hospital. My wife is in the hospital. Look, I don't see what this has to do with . . .

BUCK: (*Cutting him off. With seeming concern.*) Sorry, man. Ain't nothin' serious, I hope.

PHILIP: No. No, she'll be just fine. Veins. Some veins in her legs. They're removing them today. Did. A couple hours ago. And then they're going to run some tests. Nothing really. Just in overnight. Maybe, a couple days. We'll know better tomorrow.

BUCK: But long enough.

PHILIP: Long enough?

BUCK: For us. Long enough for us.

PHILIP: Yes.

BUCK: Now. Where were we? Oh, yeah, don't tell me. I got the house all to myself, you say to yourself. Business is slow. Maybe I'll call in and take the afternoon off. If I don't do it now I may never get another chance. Least, not anytime soon. Right?

PHILIP: Something like that. Close enough.

BUCK: Close enough?

PHILIP: To the truth.

BUCK: The truth. I've just begun.

PHILIP: Then continue. Please

BUCK: Here comes a big one. I'm not queer, you tell yourself. Not really. It's just that once in a while I like to get off with other men. I'm bi, right?

PHILIP: Right. Bi. That's right, bi.

BUCK: Ain't nothin' wrong with that. And all the while our eyes haven't broken contact. See? Like now. Should I look away, you ask yourself? Should I just roll up my window, turn the key and drive off – and miss my chance for the fuck of a lifetime? No. Maybe I'll just keep starin' till one of us breaks contact. One of us has gotta. Sooner or later. 'Sides, he must be interested or else why hasn't he broken contact? Should I smile, you ask yourself? Just a little one because there's somethin' very threatening about this whole thing – two guys, eyes locked, starin' at each other in the parking lot of the porno store . . . and neither of 'em really knowin' what's goin' on in the other ones mind. And Christ! I've got this load just achin' to explode . . . right here . . . now . . . in my pants. (*Grabs his cock and squeezes.*)

PHILIP: (*Apprehensive.*) I don't remember thinking that.

BUCK: You don't?

PHILIP: No. I don't.

BUCK: I guess you win, man. Keep the hundred. Whatever you want. I'm all yours. Even if it's . . . you know . . . odd . . . strange . . . something you've thought about, but never could say because the shame was too much. Maybe somethin' a little more unspeakable than piss. Know what I mean? Whatever you like, man, you got it.

PHILIP: That's it? Just like that?

BUCK: That's it. Just like that.

PHILIP: That's too easy. There's a catch, right?

BUCK: You don't like it easy? Maybe you like to make it hard on yourself, huh?

PHILIP: I like it fair. I believe in fair play.

BUCK: Really? We'll just have to see about that, won't we?

PHILIP: I don't see how . . .

BUCK: (*Cutting him off.*) So, what do you do, man?

PHILIP: Well, that all depends on what you . . .

BUCK: (*Stopping him.*) No. Work. What do you do for work?

PHILIP: Work? *Oh . . . well . . . ahh* . . . insurance. I thought I told you. House, car, life. You know. Insurance.

BUCK: Yeah, you did. It don't always pay up.

PHILIP: Well, I'm sure if you had a policy with me . . .

BUCK: You're uptown, right?

PHILIP: My office is on North Dal Paso, if that's what you mean.

BUCK: I'd've thought you was in the oil business.

PHILIP: Oil? No. Not even snake oil. Insurance. I'm in the insurance business.

BUCK: Could've fooled me. Drivin' a nice car and all like you do. I'd've taken you for some big shot oil dude. Maybe havin' some wells of your own pumpin' away . . . linin' your pockets.

PHILIP: Don't I wish.

BUCK: (*Purposefully flattering.*) Then, hearing how old you are, not that fifty-something's old . . . and seeing how defined you are – good definition for a man of fifty-something – I figured you worked-out or did some kind of manual labor to keep yourself in such great shape.

PHILIP: (*Flattered.*) Thank you. I do go the gym every so often. I mean, I used to. I do things around the house, you know? I repair things, take on projects . . . physical projects . . . and get a lot of exercise at the same time.

BUCK: You see, I figured somethin' like that. There you are. Doing whatever it is you do to keep yourself fit. Solid. You look solid. I saw that right away. I said to myself, that man looks solid, real solid. Here. Let me feel. (*Feels PHILIP's shoulders and arms.*) Yes. See? Just what I thought. Solid as a man half your age. (*Moves right up close to PHILIP.*) Here. Feel. Go ahead. Don't be shy. (*PHILIP feels BUCK's muscles.*) See? Solid. But no more solid than you, man. Well, maybe just a little. There you are. I figured somethin' like that.

PHILIP: How? How did you figure something like that?

BUCK: I've a nose for people. A natural gift. (*Takes another beer. After a pause.*) What's her name?

PHILIP: Whose? Whose name?

BUCK: The ol' lady's. The missus.

PHILIP: Day. Daisy.

BUCK: Yours?

PHILIP: Philip. Philip Winter.

BUCK: Winter. *Ooh*, cool subject. Stay cool, I like to say. (*Laughs.*) That's a joke, Philip. Told you I was a kidder. You're awful serious, Phillip. You know that?

PHILIP: I've been told that before.

BUCK: Bet you have.

PHILIP: Not as often as you'd think, perhaps.

BUCK: Let's hope not, Philip. (*After a pause.*)   Philip Winter . . . sad and serious among the scrub pine and the cactus in a field of dying pumpjacks.

PHILIP: Excuse me?

BUCK: Philip Winter. He holds his head high in the desert where he waits for the sun . . . this season of death and nothingness . . . sad and serious among the scrub pine and the cactus in a field of dying pumpjacks. Philip Winter. Your name . . . and you.

PHILIP: And me?

BUCK: You give me that impression.

PHILIP: I never thought . . . Sad. But nice. Poetic. Beautiful, really.

BUCK: Yes. (*After a pause.*) Buck.

PHILIP: I beg your pardon?

BUCK: Buck. That's m' name. Buck Rose.

PHILIP: Nice to meet you. (*A conservative laugh.*) Now, that's really silly. I mean, after all this time. It's like "have a nice day" isn't it? (*Stiffening.*) I'm sorry. (*Relaxes.*) Buck Rose. I like the sound of that. Buck. The masculine. The stag. Rose. Not feminine – but beautiful. Beauty is neither feminine nor masculine, it just is. Don't you think?

BUCK: Of course. And you know what? You're not so bad yourself. I mean, to look at you, nobody'd guess you were . . . well, you know . . . fifty-something . . . and bi . . . like you say (PHILIP forces a smile. After a pause.) So . . . she won't be home till tomorrow. (*A beat.*) Nice house.

PHILIP: (*With renewed caution.*) Yes . . . thank you.

BUCK: (*Offering a cigarette.*) Smoke?

PHILIP: Thank you, no. Trying to quit.

BUCK: Good for you, Philip. Good for you. (*Lights cigarette with gold lighter, then puts the lighter back into his pocket. PHILIP still does not notice that the lighter is his own.*) I've been thinking about quitting myself.

PHILIP: What the hell. Give me one. (*BUCK gives PHILIP a cigarette that he lights from off the end of BUCK's. An ember falls into PHILIP's lap.*) Damn!

BUCK: Burn yourself?

PHILIP: No. Someone's telling me not to smoke, that's all. (*He puts his cigarette out, then brushes the ember off, checking to see that everything is all right.*) It'll be all right.

BUCK: (*Places his hand just above PHILIP's knee.*) Can't never be sure. (*Rubs the spot sensuously.*)

PHILIP: (*Nervously.*) No. One can never . . . be. (*A pause while BUCK's fingers caress PHILIP's thigh, moving upward.*) I'm always so afraid . . .

BUCK: Of getting burned?

PHILIP: Yes.

BUCK: It could smart real bad.

PHILIP: Yes. You'd think I would have learned by now. Clumsy me.
(*BUCK's hand works its way up PHILIP's thigh, then onto his crotch. THEY kiss. Nervously, PHILIP pushes him away.*)

BUCK: I can make it feel better.

PHILIP: All the years?

BUCK: Now. Just now.

PHILIP: I'm sorry. Look, I'm really not certain that we . . .

BUCK: (*Putting a finger to PHILIP's lips.*) Shhh. Don't say nothin' that you won't have a way out of later on. (*After a pause.*) You ain't from these parts, are you, Philip?

PHILIP: No. We came down from Madison, Wisconsin just after Phil Junior was born.

BUCK: Been a long time.

PHILIP: Over twenty-two years.

BUCK: Almost a native. You ought to be talkin' like one o' us by now.

PHILIP: Yes. (*A beat.*) You mean, I don't?

BUCK: Hell no! I mean, we use the same words and all, but we got a different sense for them.

PHILIP: A different sense?

BUCK: A different understanding 'bout a lot 'o the things we say.

PHILIP: Surely, not that different.

BUCK: Like night and day. You can be sure o' that. (*After a thoughtful pause.*) You have a northern accent. I bet you think it's me got the accent, right?

PHILIP: (*Amused.*) Oh . . . I suppose.

BUCK: Yeah. See? I know how you think.

PHILIP: Stop saying that!

BUCK: What?

PHILIP: That you know things about me. That you know what I think. You don't. You don't know the first thing about me, or how I think!

BUCK: Philip, I think you are very sensitive. (*PHILIP does not reply. After a pause.*) Like the Great Southwest?

PHILIP: Excuse me?

BUCK: The Great Southwest. Do you like it?

PHILIP: It's all right, I guess.

BUCK: You guess?

PHILIP: I'd prefer it better upstate, I think.   Maybe, Albuquerque. Santa Fe, perhaps. I don't know, really. But, my business is established . . . doing well . . . and . . .

BUCK: Insurance, right?

PHILIP: Winter Insurance Agency . . . yes.

BUCK: Winter Insurance Agency.   Sounds like it means somethin' different from what it says. But then, a lot does, don't it?

PHILIP: I'm sorry. I don't follow you.

BUCK: Some hear one thing . . . some another.

PHILIP: You're in my head! I'm afraid. What are you doing? I'm really confused.

BUCK: I was makin' a joke, Philip. I told you I was a kidder. I mean, there's fire insurance, life, health, theft, but whoever heard of insurance against winter?

PHILIP: Ah, yes. (*Chuckles.*) A lot of claims to pay there!

BUCK: That's the spirit!   (*A beat.*)   I'm a vendor.   Candy. Crackers. Chips. Jerky.

PHILIP: That sounds . . . interesting.

BUCK: It is. You get to meet a lot of interesting people. Not as interesting as the ones you meet at the porno store, hey?

PHILIP: Like me?

BUCK: Exactly like you. You can bet on it. Very interesting. (*Indicates kitchen.*) You don't got another beer or three out there, do you? Maybe some trail mix? Or somethin' like that?

PHILIP: Now, isn't that a coincidence?

BUCK: What's that, Philip?

PHILIP: I was just thinking about trail mix. (*Rises, crosses toward, then exits into the kitchen.*) I picked some up at the health food store earlier. You know, the one on Turner. In fact, that's where I was coming from before going to . . . you know, where we met.

BUCK: The porno store.

PHILIP: There, yes.

BUCK: The porno store.

PHILIP: That's right. (*Enters from the kitchen with more beer and a bowl of trail mix.*) In the parking lot of the porno store.

BUCK: (*After a pause.*) You into health foods?

PHILIP: No. Not really. Although, I was a vegetarian once. (*BUCK stares at him blankly.*) I mean, I didn't eat meat.

BUCK: Not even chicken?

PHILIP: No.

BUCK: Why?

PHILIP: Why didn't I eat chicken?

BUCK: Why didn't you eat meat?

PHILIP: I don't know, really. (*After a pause.*) Well, I suppose I do. I mean, there's the obvious – the price of meat.

BUCK: The price of meat . . . (*He stretches his legs out in front of him.*) I hear that.

PHILIP: What I mean to say is that it may well have been economics that led me to give some thought to a more humane, if you will, ideal. You know, when you don't have much money you have to keep questioning your motives for giving up whatever it was you've given up in the name of morality, humanity, Christianity, what-have-you. (*BUCK stares at him blankly.*) Well, I mean, it's very easy to tell yourself you're doing something for some great and noble principle when, in fact, you're doing it out of necessity.

BUCK: (*Glancing around the room.*) Necessity?

PHILIP: We had hard times, struggles, Day and me. Don't think we didn't.

BUCK: Day. Daisy. Your wife.

PHILIP: Yes.

BUCK: Times change.

PHILIP: Yes. Times change. Besides, this was a long time ago I'm talking about. I was single then – a student in Madison.

BUCK: Wisconsin, right?

PHILIP: Yes, Wisconsin.

BUCK: Hear tell it's cold up there. Lots of snow.

PHILIP: Oh, yes.

BUCK: Even for a man named Winter? Hey! (*Amused with himself.*) That was a good one, wasn't it? Even for a man named Winter.

PHILIP: Yes. That was a good one.

BUCK: (*Arches his back, stretches, lets his hands rest in the vicinity of his thighs – smiles.*) No meat, huh?

PHILIP: (*Watches BUCK, nervously.*) No.

BUCK: (*Stiffens his legs, arches his back, runs his hands, palm down, along the outer seam of his jeans, then back along the inner seam until his thumbs come to rest hooked over his belt buckle. PHILIP watches nervously.*) Ain't never knowed nobody what didn't like a taste of meat every now and again.

PHILIP: (*The nervousness of insecurity. The excitement of the unknown object of desire.*) Well, I do . . . now. But, then . . . I asked myself what I would do were I stranded on an island and actually had to kill for a meal. Would I do it? No. You go to the supermarket and you pay somebody else to do it for you. Your killing. Your murder.
BUCK: (*Momentarily taken aback. After a pause.*) It ain't murder to kill if you got a good cause.

PHILIP: So I am told. But at the meat case you don't really make the same connection.

BUCK: What connection is that?

PHILIP: The one you would make if you were stranded on an island.

BUCK: Or in the desert?

PHILIP: Yes. Or in the desert . . . and face to face with the thing whose ground flesh you just threw into the shopping cart without question.

BUCK: Sounds serious.

PHILIP: You never really know if your sacrifice is out of some great and noble principle, or what?

BUCK: Is that somethin' anybody needs to know?

PHILIP: It helps. Yes.

BUCK: Who? Certainly not the animal.

PHILIP: No. But me . . . and you. Anyone who questions their motives, their reasons . . . themselves. It gives us an insight into what kind of human beings we've become.

BUCK: What kind is that?

PHILIP: For me, one who cares, I hope. One who tries to do the best he knows, who tells the truth at all times, except when it may hurt another unnecessarily.

BUCK: Or yourself?

PHILIP: Myself?

BUCK: You wouldn't tell the truth if it was gonna hurt you, would you? I mean, you'd lie if you needed to protect yourself, right? Maybe if it would save your life?

PHILIP: To save my life? Yes, probably . . . no doubt, I'd lie.

BUCK: Like all the rest of us.

PHILIP: Yes, like all the rest of us.

BUCK: (*Hooks his thumbs over his belt buckle, letting his fingers dangle over his crotch.*) Powerful serious.

PHILIP: I suppose if there was no alternative – eat meat or die – I owe it to myself to survive.

BUCK: That's the bottom line, ain't it?

PHILIP: It does seem that way.

BUCK: There's a killer in all of us.

PHILIP: Yes. To a certain extent. Something carried over from the old days. But, I couldn't do it for pleasure. Not like some hunters seem to do.

BUCK: Not for sport, huh?

PHILIP: I see nothing sporting about it. It's no longer necessary. Civilization is beyond that, don't you think?

BUCK: Too deep for me, Philip.

PHILIP: When deer season opened my dad would go off with his buddies and shoot us a buck. He'd tie it on top of that old gray Oldsmobile of his and come driving, lickity-split, up the dirt road of our farm . . . honking his horn for all the neighbors to see his dead trophy . . . pull up next to the house and yell for me to come out and help him string it up on the front porch, where he would rub my face with its blood as he gutted it . . . laughing, because he thought it was funny. Saying, "I'm going to make a man out of you, yet. Before I die . . . if it's the last thing I do . . . I'm going to make a man out of you." Mother would come out and scold him, but she was afraid to really challenge him. He'd beat the crap out of her just as sure as he would out of me. She cooked it and we ate it. All fucking winter we ate that trophy of his. It became impossible to swallow. I've never been able to eat venison since. (*After a pause.*) Anyway, I gave it up.

BUCK: (*Running his hands down his thighs, then back to his belt buckle.*) Meat.

PHILIP: No. I gave up giving up, so to speak. I mean, my giving up meat wasn't going to stop the slaughter of livestock, was it?

BUCK: S'pose not.

PHILIP: Besides, I know now that I can do it. I know that I can give it up if I want to, or have to . . . again. I know that I can muster the strength of some of my convictions for at least some of the time. There's some small salvation there. Funny, isn't it?

BUCK: Don't rightly know. I ain't laughin'. I don't think we share the same sense of humor, Philip.

PHILIP: I was being rhetorical. Sorry.

BUCK: Nothin' to be sorry for. The thing is, when you got five mouths to feed you don't got time to think of those things.

PHILIP: No. I suppose not.

BUCK: Nope. Not when you got five mouths to feed. You'll kill. A rabbit here, a buck there . . . and any man who tries to keep you from it. You'll kill. I promise.

PHILIP: Surely, you don't really mean that?

BUCK: When a man gets hungry he's gotta eat.

PHILIP: I'd never get so hungry that I'd kill a man.

BUCK: No? A body can get mighty hungry for life.

PHILIP: Nothing is so important that I'd kill another human being for it. I'd rather die first.

BUCK: You think so?

PHILIP: I believe so, yes. I couldn't hate that much.

BUCK: Hate? Off the ranch altogether! Hate ain't got nothin' to do with it.   People who hate don't kill nothin', 'cept maybe themselves. You gotta love to kill, Philip.

PHILIP: I don't see the sense of that.

BUCK: No?   You gotta love yourself enough when you're hungry. You gotta protect the things and the people you love. When somebody you love is in pain and dyin' right before your eyes – you gotta kill and take the misery away.

PHILIP: Ah . . . you mean euthanasia.

BUCK: I mean knowin' what love is all about, really about.

PHILIP: (*Shivers. Crosses to window.*) I'm cold. You frighten me with this talk.

BUCK: Don't mean to.

PHILIP: (*At window – looking out.*) All heaven is about to break open. Strange. All that sand and water up in those clouds. You wonder how it all stays up there. My God, the sheer weight of it!

BUCK: It don't.

PHILIP: (*Turning from window.*) What?

BUCK: It don't.   When all that sky gets heavy enough it just busts open and lets loose.   Like widow's tears at a funeral. Pourin' down to beat the band. 'Fore you know it, the rain and a little bit o' Texas will come down a-pourin'.

PHILIP: (*Sotto voce.*) A little bit o' Texas.

BUCK: It's 'cause o' all those cotton farmers and peanut farmers turnin' up all that land 'cross the border . . . and the wind whippin' it up into the skies. 'Fore you know it, there's a little bit o' Texas here . . . there. Why, Philip, I bet there's a little bit o' Texas comin' down on Wisconsin right this minute.

PHILIP: (*A long, wistful sigh.*)   Wisconsin.   (*After a pause.*) Sometimes I think how nice it would be to survive without compromise . . . to live in a world of our own making . . . to be our own creation, but I suppose this is all our own doing anyway, isn't it?

BUCK: 'Stead o' God's?

PHILIP: With God. Hand in hand with God.

BUCK: Don't seem natural.

PHILIP: To really have free will.   Free choice.   To build upon what God has already created.

BUCK: Don't seem natural.

PHILIP: Of course it is.   We're caretakers of sorts, aren't we? Our body – our planet. (*He looks to BUCK who does not reply. After a pause.*) Maybe choice is a luxury of perfectly free time. Nothing to get in the way. Who knows? If you haven't the time to think about the quality of your life, you're probably too busy doing the best you can just to survive.

BUCK: I hear that.

PHILIP: I think it's natural.   As natural as growth, growing, becoming, being.

BUCK: S'pose so.

PHILIP: We just take what comes along and we make the best of it. At least, we should. Shouldn't we?

BUCK: What else is there?

PHILIP: Something better.   There must be something better.

BUCK: There's magic.

PHILIP: Not in my life.

BUCK: It ain't over, yet.

PHILIP: No, that it's not.

BUCK: Maybe it's all around you, hidin' in plain sight.

PHILIP: I don't see it.

BUCK: (*Moving in on him.*)   That don't mean it ain't there. Maybe you don't know where to look . . . how to pay attention. You gotta have faith. You gotta have faith that it's there. And then you gotta reach out and grab it.   Take it in your hands, Philip. Go ahead. Grab it, Philip. Make it yours. It's right there waitin' for you, Philip. Come on. Touch it. It aches, Philip. It wants you to touch it so bad.

PHILIP: (*Confused. After a pause.*) What exactly are we talking about?

BUCK: Magic. Magic, Philip, magic.

PHILIP: I thought. Never mind. (*After a long reflective pause.*)
You know, there's something hypocritical about it all.

BUCK: Hypocritical?

PHILIP: My not eating meat. After a year of vegetarianism I
ended it with a hot dog from a street vendor. That's a laugh. No,
I'm not much into health food. But, they've got the best trail
mix in that health food store on Turner. And from there it's just a
short drive to where we met.

BUCK: In the parking lot of the porno store.

PHILIP: Yes. In the parking lot of the porno store.

BUCK: I made my last delivery at Allsup's and thought I'd
swing by. And there we were . . . pullin' into the porno store at
the same time . . . parkin' right up next to each other.

PHILIP: Coincidence.

BUCK: Two things happenin' at once. (*He snuffs out the last of
a cigarette between his index finger and thumb, then drops it into
an ashtray.*)

PHILIP: You'll burn yourself!

BUCK: Ye of little faith. (*Showing him his thick, dark-stained
fingertips.*) Calloused.

PHILIP: (*Sitting – sips beer.*) I'm not much of a drinker. Too
strong. I mean, in the afternoon.

BUCK: Yes.

(*In the SILENCE that follows, BUCK starts to light a cigarette. PHILIP recognizes the lighter, checks the side table to make certain. The cigarette doesn't get lit.*)

PHILIP: How did you . . ?   That was on the . . . Look, I think you'd better . . .

BUCK: (*Cutting him off. Putting on his charm.*)   Wait a minute! Now, hold on. It ain't how it seems.

PHILIP: Oh, it's how it seems, all right!

BUCK: No, sir. You're jumping the gun.

PHILIP: Am I?

BUCK: Yes, sir. Things ain't as they seem. I promise. Things ain't at all what they seem.

PHILIP: I know that lighter was right there on that table. That's where I keep it— a reminder that I don't smoke anymore.

BUCK: You sure got funny ways, Philip.

PHILIP: Well, they're my ways.

BUCK: I wasn't gonna keep it.

PHILIP: Oh?

BUCK: You thought I was a . . . well, shame on you, daddy.

PHILIP: I'm not your daddy.

BUCK Then stop actin' like you wanna be. I was just lookin' for a light, that's all. And you was in the kitchen getting' us all these nice snacks and such and I couldn't find a match to save my life.

So, I started to look around. (*Moves around the room, playfully, making a game of his search. Lifting objects here and there.*) High and low. Here. Nope. There. Nope. Nothin'. Nothin', nothin', nothin'. And then, low and behold! What do you think I saw?

PHILIP: (*Amused by his boyish manner.*) The lighter?

BUCK: Plain as day! Hidin' in plain sight! Like a whole lot o' things . . . hidin' in plain sight.

PHILIP: I'm sorry.

BUCK: No! I'm the one who's sorry, daddy.

PHILIP: Really, it's all right.

BUCK: Oh, no! It's not all right. Not by a long shot. (*Handing him the lighter.*) Take it. I'm sorry. My daddy brought me up better than that. I'm really, truly sorry.

PHILIP: I'm sure you didn't mean to . . .

BUCK: No, sir. (*After a pause.*) You don't want to spank me, do you?

PHILIP: (*Chuckles.*) No, not this time.

BUCK: (*Holding cigarette. After a pause.*) I don't suppose you have a book o' matches, do you?

PHILIP: (*Handing him back the lighter.*) Here. Use this. It was really very silly of me.

BUCK: Oh, no. Weren't silly at all. Thank you, Philip. (*Lights cigarette and, with an obvious gesture, he places the lighter on the coffee table.*) If ever I took somethin' what didn't belong to

me, may God cut my hands off as quick as . . . (*Raises his arm.*)
That! (*Snaps his fingers.*)

(*A great bolt of LIGHTING flashes just outside the window. In a
moment, THUNDER.*)

PHILIP: (*Startled.*) Good God!

BUCK: (*Moving closer to PHILIP.*) It's all right, Philip.

PHILIP: (*Recovering.*) Scared the bejesus out of me.

BUCK: Just a coincidence. Two things happenin' at once.

PHILIP: One would think you were Thor himself.

BUCK: Thor?

PHILIP: A god in Norse mythology, dealing out lightning and
thunder with a snap of his fingers.

BUCK: Powerful.

PHILIP: Indeed. In fact, today is Thor's day. Thursday.

BUCK: Thursday. Thorsday. I get it. That's a new one on me!
That goes back a ways, don't it?

PHILIP: A long way. Named after Thor. Are you interested in
things mythological?

BUCK: What do you mean?

PHILIP: Myths. Creation stories . . . like Genesis in the Bible.

BUCK: I believe in Jesus.

PHILIP: Yes, of course.   But, there are other cultures. Civilizations. Some with as many gods as . . .

BUCK: (*Cutting him off.*) I believe in Jesus.

PHILIP: But, before Jesus there was . . .

BUCK: (*Stopping him – firmly.*) I said, I believe in Jesus.

PHILIP: (*Nervously.*) Well, I suppose I do, too. (*After a pause.*) I don't know why that sounded like an admission of guilt.

BUCK: We're all guilty, Philip.

PHILIP: (*Reflective.*) You're probably right about that.

BUCK: Tell me about your guilt, Philip.

PHILIP: My guilt?

BUCK: Yeah. What's the worst thing you ever did?

PHILIP: I don't know. Lying, I suppose.

BUCK: Lying?   That's the worst thing you ever did?   Wow, man! I could tell you some doozies!

PHILIP: I mean, to myself. Have you any idea how evil . . . what a treacherous undertaking it is to lie to oneself?

BUCK: I don't know. Evil? Treacherous? Those sound like pretty serious words, Philip.

PHILIP: They are.

BUCK: Then why do you do it?

PHILIP: I don't. Well, I do . . . but I'm not aware that I'm doing it till after I discover that I am. Lying, that is. I don't set out to lie. I just realize at certain times in my life that I do . . . that I am.

BUCK: Accept him, Philip. Let him into your heart.

PHILIP: Who?

BUCK: Jesus. Jesus is for sinners.

PHILIP: (*Uncomfortable.*)   Sinners, yes.   (*Pause to collect himself.*) I was only making reference to the lightning when you snapped your fingers.

BUCK: Like this? (*Snaps his fingers.*)

(*LIGHTNING.*)

PHILIP: (*Startled.*) Jesus H. Christ!

BUCK: It weren't nothin' but one o' them coincidences.

(*The SOUND of THUNDER.*)

PHILIP: You. Who in hell are you?

BUCK: *Shhhh.* Buck's here.

PHILIP: Who in hell are you?

BUCK: I'm your friend, man. I'm the fuck you've been waitin' all your life for. Whoever you want me to be . . . that's who I'll be, man. C'mon. You're freakin' out over nothin', man. Absofuckinglutely nothing.   Just a little ol' lightnin' and thunder. Mother Nature havin' herself a little hissy fit.
PHILIP: It frightens me . . . you . . .

BUCK: (*Comforting.*) Ain't nothin'. It's natural, that's all. You gotta connect with it. Don't let it get the upper hand. (After a pause.) You and me . . . we use the same words, man . . . but I don't think we always speak the same language. Know what I mean?

PHILIP: I do. Actually, I believe I do.

BUCK: Good. That's a start. Feel better?

PHILIP: Yes. Thank you.

BUCK: Don't mention it. M' uncle Kirby's the same way. He's a man among men. Nothin' girlish about him. Nosirree! A fuckin' man. All balls. Know what I mean? If it has a pussy he'll have his way with it, I can tell you that.

PHILIP: Really?

BUCK: You can bet your ass on it. But for some reason God only knows, he was scared of thunder and lightnin'. That was until m' aunt Opal and me cured him for good.

PHILIP: And how did you do that?

BUCK: Well, we went out on the Carlsbad Highway one night and gathered ourselves up a whole tin of tarantulas.

PHILIP: What?

BUCK: You know, the kind that fruit cakes come in 'round Christmas time?

PHILIP: Is this a joke?

BUCK: No, sir. I'm the one drove ol' Opal out there. Sometimes those tarantulas are so thick on the highway the crunchin' under the truck wheels like to turn your stomach. And vinegaroon scorpions! We gathered up about a dozen big ol' scorpions and mixed 'em in with the tarantulas. Then we let 'em loose one night in the bedroom whiles he was sleepin'.

PHILIP: Good God! That's terrible!

BUCK: Naah. They're harmless as horny-toads. Anyways, after we locked him in and made a lot of noise so he'd wake up, we waited outside . . . till the screamin' stopped.

PHILIP: (*Disturbed.*) And? What happened?

BUCK: Nothin' happened. Broke him of it, that's all. Things what don't mean him no harm don't frighten him no more.

PHILIP: That's horrible.

BUCK: It worked.

PHILIP: You could have frightened him to death . . . given him a heart attack.

BUCK: That ol' geezer's been right as rain ever since.

PHILIP: Still, it could have killed him . . . driven him mad.

BUCK: So could lightnin', daddy. But, it ain't likely.

PHILIP: (*After a pause.*) Well, I see your point . . . I guess. (*Inhales deeply. Exhales.*) I'm sorry.

BUCK: Ain't nothin' to be sorry for.

PHILIP: I've always been like this. Ever since I was a kid I've been like this. I feel I'm connected to it.

BUCK: To what? Thunder and lightnin?

PHILIP: To the weather in general. It's like the weather outside and I, in here, are one. Does that sound strange?

BUCK: Is it the truth?

PHILIP: I . . . I don't know. It's my truth, I guess.

BUCK: Do you know how you feel?

PHILIP: How I feel? Yes. I know how I feel.

BUCK: (*Reassuring.*) That's it then. That's all you need to know, Philip. That's all there is to know.

PHILIP: (After a pause.) Do you really think a tornado is coming?

BUCK: Yup. There's a tornado comin' all right.

PHILIP: Then, you see, I feel I'm responsible.

BUCK: How's that?

PHILIP: That it's my fault somehow . . . my doing.

BUCK: Don't seem possible.

PHILIP: I know it doesn't. But it's how I feel goddamnit! That's how I feel.

BUCK: *Shhhh.* You just got worked into a state.

PHILIP: Sometimes, I'm in a crowd somewhere . . . or in Furr's cafeteria with Day, or just walking in the mall, where my office is, when it happens. I'm connected to them. All these people, and events. They're pieces of me and I'm a piece of them. Connected. And, I'm thinking that they can hear what I'm thinking.   And, I'm hearing what they're saying as what I'm thinking.

BUCK: (*Comforting.*) It's all right.

PHILIP: It's real. There's something very real about it.

BUCK: It's all right.

PHILIP: No, it's not all right.   I'm connected to the whole of everything. We all are. And I can't free myself of it.

BUCK: Then why try?

PHILIP: I want my own will!   Don't you understand what I'm trying to tell you?

BUCK: Sure. You're scared o' bein' alone when the end comes.

PHILIP: No. I want to be alone. It's something else. I want to be in control. But I'm afraid of the responsibility of control.

BUCK: You want to be God?

PHILIP: No. I'm afraid that I may discover that I am God!

BUCK: That's a lonely place to be, Mr. Winter.

PHILIP: Yes. Yes it is.

BUCK: Best you relax. (*Comforting.*) *Shhhh.* Buck's here.

PHILIP: And when I try to talk to somebody I hear . . . no, feel . . . I feel an exchange of information taking place that has nothing to do with the actual words themselves.   Sometimes it is like there are layers and layers of meaning in the same sentence. Like an intuitive language is being spoken. Good God! I don't know what I'm saying anymore. What are you doing to me?

BUCK: Ain't doin' nothin', daddy.

PHILIP: Please. Don't call me daddy. I feel old enough as it is.

BUCK: But you could be my daddy.

PHILIP: If you mean age-wise . . . yes . . . yes, I could.

BUCK: But you don't wanna be, right?

PHILIP: Right.

BUCK: How 'bout I be your daddy?

PHILIP: I don't see how that could be possible.

BUCK: Philip. Phil. May I call you Phil?

PHILIP: If you like.

BUCK: Phil. This is a world in which anything is possible.

PHILIP: Theoretically, perhaps. In the abstract. Certainly not literally. One cannot imagine a world in which anything is literally possible. That would be chaos.

BUCK: It would be heaven.

PHILIP: I don't think so.

BUCK: You'll see. Time will tell. (After a pause.) Feelin' better?

PHILIP: Yes.

BUCK: Good, Phil, 'cause you're a nice man and you oughta feel good. It don't feel good when you're scared and alone.

PHILIP: No. Not at all.

BUCK: I mean, you could be surrounded by everybody in the world and you'd still be scared and alone.

PHILIP: It seems that way.

BUCK: People can go out of their way to love you . . . yet; you're so deep . . . so far into yourself . . . you can't really be touched by it . . . by love. You can't love and you can't be loved. That's scary. That's alone. Unreachable. Untouchable.
PHILIP: Is that what you see? Is that how you see me?

BUCK: Well, son . . . quite frankly, yes. You break my heart, boy.

PHILIP: I see. I guess I'm to be an object of pity, huh?

BUCK: You see? There you go. Nobody's pitying you, man. 'Cept maybe yourself. You need one of m' aunt Opal's remedies. That's what you need all right. You're like in a prison, man. You're hidden away behind bars of fear, man.

PHILIP: How? How did it happen?
BUCK: Shame. Guilt. Lying to yourself. Who can say, really?

PHILIP: (*Takes a long, deep breath.*) And you. You are right out there. On the wing. What you see is what you get, right? You've got youth, looks, strength, charm. Ah, yes . . . a most disarming charm. Afraid of nothing and nobody, right?

BUCK: That's not true. Not true at all.

PHILIP: What's a strapping young man like you afraid of?

BUCK: Lots o' things.

PHILIP: What kind of things?

BUCK: Dark things. Evil things. The devil's things.

PHILIP: (*Unsure.*) You're kidding. The great kidder, right?

BUCK: No, sir. There ain't no kiddin' when it comes to the powers of darkness.

PHILIP: You believe that?

BUCK: Yes, sir. That's why I accepted Jesus as my Savior.

PHILIP: You don't strike me as a man who has accepted Jesus as his Savior.

BUCK: I don't?

PHILIP: No . . . not Jesus.

BUCK: Why is that, Philip?

PHILIP: You know . . . the things you say . . . the things you like.

BUCK: What things, Philip?

PHILIP: You know. You don't need me to tell you what you already know.

BUCK: Maybe I do.

PHILIP: Well . . . like . . . like pissing on people. There. I said it. You said you liked to piss on people.

BUCK: You're a brave man, Philip. I bet that was real hard for you to say.

PHILIP: I was only repeating.

BUCK: And Jesus?

PHILIP: What about Jesus?

BUCK: He don't like to piss on people?

PHILIP: I don't know. How would I know a thing like that?

BUCK: Yeah. How would you know a thing like that?

PHILIP: I don't. I don't know. I don't want to know a thing like that.

BUCK: You don't want to know Jesus?

PHILIP: I don't want to know those kinds of things about Jesus.

BUCK: You mean, you want to know what you are prepared to accept and nothin' else. Right?

PHILIP: I don't want to argue.

BUCK: Then believe me when I tell you I am born again . . . baptized with the holy water of Jesus Himself.

PHILIP: Born again? What exactly do you mean by that?

BUCK: What I mean is what I say.

PHILIP: You needn't be defensive.

BUCK: I'm not.

PHILIP: It's just that I've heard that phrase "born again" used so often and so loosely . . . I don't have a sense for it. I don't know what it means.

BUCK: I guess you gotta be to know. Before I was born again I was a dead man. I was walkin' the earth without the breath of Jesus in me. I was a dead man walkin' in the darkness. And darkness, Philip, is pure evil . . . and sexy.

PHILIP: Sexy?

BUCK: Ain't nothin' so sexy as pure evil. (*Matter-of-factly.*) Once, I killed a man in Lubbock, Texas.

PHILIP: I don't think I want to hear this.

BUCK: Of course you do.

PHILIP: No, really.

BUCK: You do, Phil. I guarantee it. Pure evil, Phil. There ain't nothin' like it! And sexy.

PHILIP: I really don't want to hear it.   Let's talk about something else.

BUCK: No, no, no. You gotta hear it. You gotta face it. You gotta come right down to it, Phil, before you can be born again. You're not exactly the happiest camper on the block no, are you? (*PHILIP does not answer.*) Well, you're not. Take my word for it. You see, Phil, evil is darkness. Pure darkness. And it's sexy because in pure darkness you can do anything your heart desires. Who's gonna see you? Who's gonna tell? God? (*A pause for PHILIP to answer but he doesn't.*) So . . . I drove on over to Lubbock—this was years ago before I found Jesus—and I found myself in an alley behind this porno movie theater getting' myself a blow job. Oooh boy! It was a good one! You

see, it was my first. Ain't never had a blow job like that since.
Ain't nothin' like the first time. Is there, Phil?

(*PHILIP tries to speak, but nothing comes out.*)

Anyway . . . this guy – this older gentleman – he's down on his
knees. I'm pushed up against a dumpster . . . smell of somethin'
foul, somethin' maggoty-rotten in the air . . . jeans down around
my boots . . . and then we both hear somebody comin' our way . .
. outta the shadows. The old man starts to get up, but I'm startin'
to cum, you see, so I push his head down hard on my prick . . .
and I shoot a long, heavy load down his throat. Oh, God, it was
good! Next thing I know there's this other guy – this younger
guy – and he's *standin'* right in front of me . . . behind the old
man who's still slurpin' up the last o' my wad. And this younger
guy . . . he's got a baseball bat.

(*PHILIP cringes and shivers.*)

Suddenly, the bat cracks the skull of the old man . . . everything
goes into slow motion. He looks up at me . . . cum runnin' down
the sides of his mouth . . . and he smiles. He smiles like he's
seein' an angel or somethin' . . . and I'm that angel. And then he
falls over, sideways, into the dirt. Dead. Me . . . I'm still standin'
there with my jeans down around my ankles . . . my prick still
drippin' when I grab the fucker's bat and, before he has a chance
to run, I give him what he gave the old gentleman. Next thing I
know I got a hard on like nobody's ever had a hard on. I raise
the bat and I smack him again! Again! Again! Again! Again!
Shit, man! Shit! I'm gonna cum! Every fuckin' time I hit the
sonofabitch I'm that much closer t' cummin'. Here I just had my
first blow job – shot my biggest wad ever – and I'm startin' to
cum again. One last crack of the bat and I explode, man . . .
shootin' my load all over the stupid bastard. It felt like a fuckin'
cup-load man! Like the fuckin' universe was explodin'. I
thought it would never stop. And then . . . then I took a piss,
man.

PHILIP: (*Dazed, shaken – on the verge of tears.*) What?

BUCK: I pissed all over that sonofabitch! I drunk a shit load o' beer so I was pissin' like a race horse. I washed the smirk off his sorry face, I'll tell you that. Shit, man! I never felt anything like it . . . before or since. I'd've taken a dump on him if I could have. Yup. If I could have, I sure as hell would have. Then . . . then I pulled up my jeans, got in my truck and got the hell out o' Dodge. I took the bat with me. Prints, you know. Burned it when I got back to Hobbs. I still get a hard on every time I think about it. (*After a pause to rub his crotch.*) Scary stuff, *huh*, Philip? (*PHILIP begins to cry.*) But that was before I was born again. (*Touching PHILIP.*) C'mon. C'mon. You're takin' this all too seriously. You gotta lighten up. Chill out. Stay cool, man. C'mon, you're gonna be okay.

PHILIP: (*Wiping his tears.*) I don't know who you are.

BUCK: I told you. Whoever you want me to be. 'Sides, do you really know who anybody is? Take your time. Think it over.

PHILIP: What are you going to do with me?

BUCK: What do you want me to do with you, Philip?

PHILIP: Magic. Earlier you told me to reach out and touch it. Well, I'm ready to touch it.

BUCK: I bet you are! (*He raises his arm.*) Coincidence? (*He snaps his fingers and there is a sudden flash of LIGHTNING.*) Two things happening at once!

(*The LIGHTING from the lamps goes out. This should not effect the LIGHTING too much, as it is still mid-afternoon. It is, however, darker outside than would otherwise be normal for this time of day—This time of year. Every so often throughout the remainder of the play the SOUND of gusts of wind can be heard howling, accompanied by the SOUND of a tree's branch scratching against the windowpane.*)

PHILIP: (*Rises. Crosses to window.*) The electricity's out!

BUCK: (*Rises. Follows him.*) It'll be back on in no time.

PHILIP: (*Looking out window.*) I don't think . . .
(*Suddenly, the LIGHTS flash back on, followed by the SOUND of THUNDER.*)

BUCK: See? Magic.

PHILIP: (*Soto voce.*) Yes. Magic.

BUCK: (*Looking out the window from over PHILIP's shoulder.*) They come in hard and fast. Go out the same way. (*While standing behind PHILIP, he has unbuttoned his shirt. As he turns from the window, he pulls his shirt out of his jeans. He is bare-chested.*) You don't mind if I get comfortable?

PHILIP: (*Turning from window. Getting a good, hard look at him.*) No. Not at all.

BUCK: (*After a pause.*) Storm's makin' it dark out there.

PHILIP: Yes.

BUCK: Be pitch black before you know it.

PHILIP: Yes.

BUCK: There's a lot o' scared and lonely out there . . . in the darkness. (*Removes his shirt and throws it aside.*)

PHILIP: Yes.

BUCK: Yes. (*Begins to unbutton PHILIP's shirt.*) Your wife. She doesn't come home till tomorrow, right?

PHILIP: Yes.

BUCK: Yes. All the time in the world.

PHILIP: Time?

BUCK: For us. For magic.

PHILIP: Magic. Yes.

BUCK: Yes.

PHILIP: I . . . I never did anything like this before.

BUCK: Before?

PHILIP: Now.

BUCK: Like what?

PHILIP: This.

BUCK: This?

PHILIP: You know.

BUCK: Yes. I know, Philip. (*Removes PHILIP's shirt and throws it aside.*)

PHILIP: I never asked a stranger into my home before.

BUCK: I ain't no stranger. Why, we been getting' on 'bout all kinds o' things all afternoon.

PHILIP: You know what I mean.

BUCK: Yes. I know exactly what you mean.

PHILIP: I don't know what possessed me.   (*Runs his hands along BUCK's body.*)

BUCK: Do you hate her?

PHILIP: (*Shudders.*) Her?

BUCK: Your wife . . . the old lady.

PHILIP: No. I love her. Do you . . . love your wife?

BUCK: Love's funny. It comes. It goes.

PHILIP: Yes.

BUCK: Yes. (*He undoes his jeans, steps out of them and throws them aside.*)

PHILIP: Yes.

BUCK: Yes. (*He removes his underwear.*)

PHILIP: Yes.

BUCK: (*Running his hands over the length of his own body.*) Do it much?

PHILIP: No.

BUCK: Been a long time, right?

PHILIP: Yes. A very long time.

BUCK: Yes.

PHILIP: (*Having second thoughts.*)   Music.   Would you like some music?

BUCK: I don't mind.

(*PHILIP crosses to the radio and turns it on. The MUSIC is a slow, sensuous tango.*)

PHILIP: How this? It's the Roswell station.

BUCK: (*Moving close to PHILIP – pulling his body up against his own.*) Not bad.

PHILIP: Want to hear something else? I can change it.

BUCK: Relax. (*A pause to listen.*) It's one o' them tangos.

PHILIP: Yes. I believe it is.

BUCK: Can you do it?

PHILIP: The tango?

(*BUCK nods "yes."*)

PHILIP (*Continues*) Well, I haven't danced in years.

BUCK: Me neither. Wanna try?

PHILIP: With a man?

BUCK: Take a good look at us, Philip . . . and then tell me you still have a problem with that.

PHILIP: No. I guess not.

BUCK: Good.

PHILIP: You lead?

BUCK: Naturally.

(*BUCK and PHILIP begin to dance a slow, sensuous tango. Their dialogue should be stretched out over periods of dancing.*)

BUCK: Dangerous.

PHILIP: Yes.
BUCK: Seductive.

PHILIP: Yes.

BUCK: Precise.

PHILIP: Yes.

BUCK: Powerful!

PHILIP: Yes!

(*LIGHTNING.*)

BUCK: Yes!

(*LIGHTNING.*)

PHILIP: Yes! Yes!

(*The SOUND of THUNDER. The MUSIC and the LIGHTS go out. PHILIP slides to his knees and, with BUCK's back to the audience, PHILIP buries his head in BUCK's crotch.*)

BUCK: (*Holding PHILIP's head and pushing his crotch into PHILIP's face.*) YES. YES. SWEET JESUS! YES! YES! YES. . ! (THUNDER! LIGHTNING! THUNDER!) YES! GOD! SWEET JESUS! YEEEESSSS . . !

(*A long SILENCE.*)

PHILIP: (*Slowly rises.*) The electricity . . .

BUCK: *Shhhh . . .*

PHILIP: (*Crosses to window.*) The storm . . .

BUCK: (*While putting on his underwear and jeans.*) That was nice. Fucking nice! Sweet Jesus, that was beautiful! (*Gets a cigarette.*)

PHILIP: (*Disturbed.*) How can you say such a thing?

BUCK: (*Lighting a cigarette, slipping the lighter into his pocket.*) Such a thing as what, Philip?

PHILIP: (*Reluctantly.*) "Sweet . . . Jesus."

BUCK: Ain't he sweet?

PHILIP: I don't know. I . . . I just don't think that it's appropriate, that's all. (*Realizes that BUCK has, once again, pocketed the lighter.*) Please give me the lighter, Mr. Rose.

BUCK: *Huh?*

PHILIP: The lighter. You just put it in your pocket.

BUCK: (*Feeling his pocket.*) So I did. Why don'tcha come on over here and get it? C'mon. Just reach your hand right down in there and lift it out, daddy.

PHILIP: No.

BUCK: Your warm hand . . .

PHILIP: No.

BUCK: Slidin' hot. Slippin' it out.

PHILIP: Stop it!

BUCK: C'mon. (He extends his arms outward from his sides, pushing his pelvis forward.) Slip your bisexual hand in there and feel around for it. C'mon.

PHILIP: Stop it!

BUCK: What in hell's wrong with you, man? Shame? Guilt? Maybe you're not bi at all. Maybe you're just plain queer.

PHILIP: I'm not queer.

BUCK: Ain'tcha?

PHILIP: (Standing firm.) The lighter. Please.

BUCK: That's it. You're all-hog queer, ain'tcha?

PHILIP: I'm married. I have a son. I never did anything like today before in my entire life! The lighter, Mr. Rose.

BUCK: Buck. Nobody calls me Mister Rose. That's what they call m' daddy.

PHILIP: (After a pause.) Buck . . . please. It's getting late. Please give me the lighter . . . and leave.

BUCK: Leave? Just like that? (He snaps his fingers.)

(*LIGHTNING.*)

PHILIP: (*Panicked.*) Oh, my God!

BUCK: Yes, Philip Winter. Yes.

(*The SOUND of THUNDER.*)

PHILIP: Oh, God!   (*Backing away.*)   Don't hurt me.   Please
don't hurt me.

BUCK: (*Moving toward him.*)   Ain't nobody gonna hurt you,
Philip.

PHILIP: (*Backing away. On the verge of tears.*) You can have
the lighter. Keep it. Just leave me alone, please.

BUCK: (*Grabbing his hand, forcing it to his pants' pocket.*) You
want it? Huh, queer? Dig for it, queer!

PHILIP: No!

BUCK: (*Holding PHILIP's hand firmly against his thigh.*)   I
said, dig for it!

PHILIP: Please . . . please don't do this.

BUCK: *Ahhh* . . . C'mon faggot. You love it.

PHILIP: No. I don't. Honest to God, I don't.

BUCK: I'm the fuck you've been waitin' for all your life, man.

PHILIP: Stop it!   (*Pulls away. Raises his fists into BUCK's
face.*) All right! That's it! You want to fight, fucker? I'm not
afraid of you!

BUCK: (*Laughs.*) You're not, huh? (*Raises his hand and snaps his fingers.*)

(*LIGHTNING. PHILIP lowers his fists. THUNDER.*)

BUCK: Now that's a good boy, Phil.

PHILIP: (*Frightened – backing away.*)   Please.   I'm sorry. Please.   Look, if it's money you want . . . if it's that hundred dollars . . .

BUCK: (*Sparring.   Punches PHILIP several times.*)   I don't want none o' your money, faggot! I just saw an old dead queer. Walkin' dead.

PHILIP: Fuck you!

BUCK: No, faggot. I fuck you. (*Punches PHILIP again.*)

PHILIP: STOP IT!

BUCK: You ain't never been alive. Have you, faggot?

PHILIP: I don't know what you mean. Of course I've been alive . . . I mean, I am alive.

BUCK: Are you? (*Punches him.*)

PHILIP: Yes. Stop hitting me. I'm alive, goddamnit! I'm alive!

BUCK: Hear and now . . . maybe.   But it's my breath you're breathin'.   Maybe you feel alive now 'cause you're thinkin' I'm here to take it.   Maybe I'm the angel of death. *Huh,* faggot? Fight back, faggot!

PHILIP: No. You want my life, take it! I'm not going to fight you for it!

BUCK: Your life. It's like cummin' for the very first time. You don't really feel it till it's almost over . . . all over. Snap! (*Snaps his fingers. LIGHTNING.*) And then, by God, you want it to last forever. Snap! (*THUNDER.*) But it don't, man. It just don't last forever. Snap! (*LIGHTNING.*) You're already dead, man. Dead meat hangin' in the closet, man. Snap! (*THUNDER. He removes the lighter from his pocket.*) Here! Here's your lighter. (*Extends it to PHILIP who is backing away.*) Here. Take it. Go on now. Take it! Take it! (*Following PHILIP as he backs away.*) You wanted it, faggot. Now. Take it!

PHILIP: (*Grabs the lighter from out of BUCK's hand.*) Thank you. Now. Please. Leave, Mr. Rose.

BUCK: Buck.

PHILIP: What?

BUCK: Buck. Say it!

PHILIP: What? What do you want me to say?

BUCK: BUCK. BUCK. My name is Buck. Say it, queer. Say it!

PHILIP: (*With renewed fear. Sotto voce.*) Buck.

BUCK: Again!

PHILIP: (*A little louder.*) Buck.

BUCK: AGAIN.

PHILIP: Buck!

BUCK: That's better. Again.

PHILIP: Buck! Buck, Buck, Buck! All right?

BUCK: (*A big, boyish grin.*) That's m' name, faggot. That's m' name.

PHILIP: (*Regaining composure. Truly alarmed.*) Yes.

BUCK: Yes? Yes what?

PHILIP: Yes, Buck.

BUCK: Yes. That's nice, Philip. Philip Winter. Sad and all alone in the darkness of the desert.

PHILIP: (*Placating.*) Yes, Buck. Sad. Alone. Buck.

BUCK: Good. (*After a fearsome pause.*) Y'all better leave now.

PHILIP: (*Stunned.*) What?

BUCK: I said, it's time for you to go.

PHILIP: Go? Go where?

BUCK: Git!

PHILIP: Where? What are you talking about? You're the one who needs to go.

BUCK: (*Sternly.*) Git outta this house.

PHILIP: (*Dumbfounded.*) What?

BUCK: (*A deep, threatening, resonate voice.*) GET . . . OUT . . . OF . . . THIS . . . HOUSE.

PHILIP: This is my house, Mr. Rose!

BUCK: BUCK!

PHILIP: Buck. This is my house. You don't order me about in my house!

BUCK: *Snap!* (*LIGHTNING.*) This ain't your house. This is my house. You live in a closet, man. *Snap!* (*THUNDER.*)

PHILIP: You're crazy.

BUCK: Am I . . . faggot? (After a pause.) Git out!

PHILIP: No!

BUCK: (*Snaps his fingers.*) Go!
(*LIGHTNING and HOWLING WIND.*)

PHILIP: No.

BUCK: You ain't nothin' but a dead old man.   Walkin' around . . . livin' in the closet . . . hangin' from your daddy's porch . . . gutted . . . stinkin' up the place.

(*The SOUND of THUNDER.*)

PHILIP: No.
BUCK: Can't love 'cause you don't know how. Can't be loved 'cause you don't know who. Who are you man? You're so busy tryin' to figure out who I am . . . when you don't even know who it is you are.

PHILIP: Maybe. Maybe not.

BUCK: Fuck you! You're a faggot, man. A queer! That's who you are! And you know what?

PHILIP: No! God damn it! What?

BUCK: It's okay. It's fucking okay, man. Just be it. Stop the bullshit. All right? Philip? Stop the fucking bullshit. Are you listening to me?

PHILIP: Yes, Buck. I'm listening.

BUCK: Then stop it, man. Stop lyin' to yourself.

PHILIP: (*Breaking down, realizing that there may be some truth to this; a truth he does not want to hear – much less, face.*) I'm not lying to myself.

BUCK: Dead and stuffed and still walkin'.

PHILIP: No . . .

BUCK: You gotta be born again!

PHILIP: No! I don't want to be! (*After a pause.*) It's a lie!

BUCK: What is? What's a lie, Philip?

PHILIP: You. Being born again. Everything. Everybody! It's all a lie.

BUCK: Who, Philip? Who?

PHILIP: Me! (*After a pause.*) Me. My life, goddamnit! My life.

BUCK: So . . . are you tellin' me you're not bi, Philip? That maybe you're queer?

PHILIP: I suppose that I am. Yes.

BUCK: When did you discover this about yourself?

PHILIP: Now. Just now.

BUCK: No bullshit. Remember?

PHILIP: Twelve. Maybe thirteen. I knew I was different. I just didn't know how I was different. I was a loner. Isolated. I was filled with . . . with . . . rage. Rage and desire.

BUCK: Rage and desire? For what?

PHILIP: I don't know.

BUCK: Love?

PHILIP: Yes. I had love. Love for anyone who could end my isolation . . . who would take even the slightest interest in me. It was Bobby who took that interest. It was Bobby who took my love. (*After a pause.*) Bobby was the most beautiful human being I had ever seen . . . until you, Buck. Bobby had . . . he's dead now . . . he had gray eyes. Gray eyes that saw through lies and deceptions. They kept me on my toes by forcing me to think – actually think for the first time in my short-lived life – by making certain I spoke the truth. You see I couldn't help but speak the truth when looking into those magnificent gray eyes of his. There was some sort of silent understanding. A kind of natural hypnosis. There could be nothing but truth when looking into Bobby's eyes. They were magic. And I knew that I loved him with all my heart. He was lean, solid, muscular. He was caring, thoughtful, full of life, full of promise. He was everything I was not. And everything I longed to be – to possess. (*After a pause.*) Until you.

BUCK: I wouldn't be getting' no ideas if I was you. (*After a pause.*) You said he was dead?

PHILIP: Yes. We were walking home from school. He had detention. I sat with him. It was dark already. Winter. Snow.

Blowing. Bitter Wisconsin cold. Ice. The road was covered with ice. Packed now. We slipped several times. We helped each other up. It was downhill to the farm where we both lived. His was the next house over. Someone suggested we race. We did. He fell . . . and slid under an oncoming car that never stopped. No one ever found out who it was killed him. My love.

BUCK: Who suggested you race?

PHILIP: Does it matter?

BUCK: It might.

PHILIP: I don't remember.

BUCK: I bet you do. In fact, it was you. Wasn't it, Philip? (*No answer. After a pause.*) Wasn't it, Philip?

PHILIP: (*Sotto voce.*) Yes.

BUCK: I can't hear you.

PHILIP: Yes. It was me. All right? It was me. So what? We were kids. Twelve. Maybe thirteen.

BUCK: And you died with him. At twelve. Maybe thirteen.

PHILIP: Yes. (*After a pause.*) Oh, God! I just want to touch someone else's soul. I want to really touch someone outside my body. I want to know.

BUCK: What's that, Philip? What do you want to know?

PHILIP: (*Through tears.*) God! I want to know God! God . . .

BUCK: Poor, poor, old man Winter. (*Softly.*) It's time for you to leave, Mr. Winter.

PHILIP: No. You have no right. I'm calling the police.

(*PHILIP crosses to the telephone. BUCK crosses to the sofa and removes the handgun from where it was hidden.*)

BUCK: (*Crossing to PHILIP.*)   Run, Philip.   (*Rips cord off telephone.*)

PHILIP: (*Sees the gun.*) Oh, my God!

BUCK: Run. You don't love, man. You don't know how.

PHILIP: (*Backing away.*) I do! I do!

BUCK: You're trapped, Philip. Trapped.

PHILIP: No . . .

BUCK: Who do you love, Philip? Who do you love?

PHILIP: I love you! I love you!

BUCK: Bullshit!

PHILIP: No. I do. I love you, Buck Rose. I love you.

BUCK: Too late, man. Too fucking late!

PHILIP: Don't hurt me. Please . . .

BUCK: He's dark. He's evil. The son o' Satan!

PHILIP: Who? Who are you talking about?

BUCK: Me, man! Who the fuck else?

PHILIP: I don't think you're evil.

BUCK: No? How about sexy? You think I'm sexy, Philip?

PHILIP: Yes.

BUCK: Yes?

PHILIP: Yes. Very.

BUCK: You never know whose eyes he's gonna show up behind.

PHILIP: Who?

BUCK: God. Satan. Bobby. My wife.

PHILIP: Your wife?

BUCK: I told you. I had to shoot her, man. She was in pain, man. Terrible fucking pain! What else was there to do?

PHILIP: You said you were kidding. The great kidder, right?

BUCK: I don't kid.

PHILIP: But you said . . .

BUCK: Fuck what I said!

PHILIP: You're crazy. You're a goddamned psychopath.

BUCK: With a gun, cocksucker. (*He grabs PHILIP.*)

PHILIP: Let me go! Leave me alone!

BUCK: Time to go.

PHILIP: (*Struggling, breaks free and falls to the floor.*) HELP!

BUCK: (*Straddling him.*) Shhhh. You've been in the closet too long.

PHILIP: (*On his back.*) Shoot me! Shoot me! Go ahead. Shoot me you sonofabitch! Shoot me if you're going to. Shoot me.

BUCK: (*On his knees, tracing PHILIP's face with the barrel of the gun.*) I'm sorry, Philip. But it's time for you to meet Jesus. (*Gives PHILIP a long, hungry kiss.*) Now. Suck on it man!

PHILIP: *What?*

BUCK: (*Shoves the barrel of the gun into PHILIP's mouth.*) Suck on it! (*PHILIP does and gags.*) That's good, man. Real good. Run your tongue along the barrel, boy. Yeah. Oh, shit, man! I'm cummin'! Oh, God! I'm fuckin' gonna cream, man. YES! (*He withdraws the gun from PHILIP's mouth.*) Now you better get the fuck outta here, man.

PHILIP: Where? Where should I go?

BUCK: Away from here. Outta the closet.

PHILIP: I can't.

BUCK: Yes. You can.

PHILIP: (*Resigned.*) Okay. You'll let me go, right?

BUCK: You should o' left whiles you had the chance, Philip.

PHILIP: What do you mean?

BUCK: Too late now, Philip. I can't let you go now. *Listen.*

PHILIP: What?

BUCK: *Shhhh. Listen* (*He rises and kneels beside PHILIP. The SOUND of the TORNADO, like a freight train, moves slowly toward the house.*) *Listen.*

PHILIP: (*Rises to his knees.*) What? What is it?

BUCK: The voice of God . . . tornado.

PHILIP: Oh, my God!

BUCK: He's coming, Philip. He's coming to wash away the sins of the world.

PHILIP: Stop it! Stop it!

BUCK: I can't.

PHILIP: Yes! Yes, you can. I know you can.

BUCK: No, Philip. Only you can stop Him now.

(*The SOUND of the TORNADO grows LOUDER.*)

PHILIP: How?

BUCK: Here. (*He offers PHILIP the gun.*) Take it.

PHILIP: No.

BUCK: Take it!

PHILIP: (*Grabs the gun and points it at BUCK.*) Please. Please leave. I'm afraid—

BUCK: Me, too, Philip. Me too. (*Pause.*) *Shhhh. Listen* (*The SOUND of the TORNADO grows louder.*) Sweet Jesus! Save these poor servants . . . trapped . . . with nowhere to go! Save us, Lord! Save us!

PHILIP: Stop it!

BUCK: Show us the way, Sweet Jesus. Show us the way!

PHILIP: Stop it!

(*The SOUND of the Tornado grows louder.*)

BUCK: Show us the way! Show us the way!

PHILIP: We're going to die!

BUCK: We're all going to die!

PHILIP: I don't want to.

BUCK: Are you born again?

PHILIP: I don't believe!

BUCK: Are you ready for the rapture?

PHILIP: No!

BUCK: We're here, Lord! Come and get us!

PHILIP: No! You can stop it. You can stop the tornado. Now.

BUCK: With a snap of my fingers?

PHILIP: Yes.

BUCK: Too late. (*Backing away from where PHILIP kneels on the floor, stretching out his arms as if crucified.*)   Dear Lord, there ain't nothin' on this ol' planet of yours but shit!   Piles and piles of shit!

PHILIP: Please . . .

BUCK: Can you love?

PHILIP: Yes.

BUCK: (*Heavenward.*) You hear that, Lord? He can love! (*To PHILIP.*) Can you love yourself?

PHILIP: Yes, yes!

BUCK: Kill me!

PHILIP: WHAT?

BUCK: KILL ME!

PHILIP: No!

BUCK: Show me your love, Philip. Show me your love!

PHILIP: I don't know how!

BUCK: Shoot me! Set me free, Philip! Let me fly!

PHILIP: I can't!

BUCK: Show him the way, Sweet Jesus. Show him the way!

PHILIP: Oh, God. Help me.

BUCK: (*Wails.*) Do you hear me, Lord?   (*He turns toward PHILIP with his arms outstretched as if crucified.*) I said, do you hear me? (*The TORNADO has reached the house. The*

SOUND is a deafening rumble.) DO YOU HEAR ME? Hear me, Lord! Hear me! (*PHILIP pulls the trigger. SILENCE. The TORNADO is gone. BUCK stands stunned with a contented smile. Softly, at peace.*) Sweet. Philip, I love you man. (*He falls to his knees.*) Sweet Jesus . . . you give me a hard-on. (*He keels over - dead.*)

(*LIGHTNING and the far off rumble of THUNDER. The electricity returns and the LIGHT of the lamps and the MUSIC of a tango resumes. PHILIP kneels paralyzed in place, horrified, with the realization of what's just taken place. The SOUND of a gentle rain beginning to fall. The LIGHTING slowly dims to the MUSIC of the tango. BLACK OUT and CURTAIN.*)

END OF PLAY

WAIT A MINUTE!
A fun-packed play in 30 skits

SYNOPSIS: (Ensemble, Minimum 3/M and 3/W, One Set, Full Length.)

WAIT A MINUTE!! is a fun-packed play of 30 witty, smart, laugh-out-loud skits—and all with twists and surprising endings. Skits range from 1 to 5 minutes each. It is intended to be presented as a complete play.   Individual skits are not to be performed separately without written permission from the author.

ACT ONE

A REALLY BIG BOAT
AH, SHUCKS!
OIL SPILL
A WOMAN ON THE MOON
SMALL POTATOES
HOW DID THAT GUN GET IN MY POCKET
BURNING ISSUES
THE EUPHEMISM
SIX MINUTE MEN
TEDDY'S BEAR
GARDEN TALK
THE VIRGIN AND THE VAMPIRE
THE MADAME AND THE MOUSER
CIAO, MARCELLO
FISHIN' NO-SEE-'EMS
A FLY IN HER EAR
THE RECRUIT
EIGHTY-EIGHT

ACT TWO

WAITING FOR LUGGAGE
GRANNY GETS THE BIRD
BLACK CANDLE
TOONGA NUFEELA
JANUS WATCH
PETER & JUDY
POLYPHEMUS
MONSTER UNDER THE BED
TWISTER
HANGING JUDGES
A THUMB'S STORY
WAIT A MINUTE!

ACT ONE

A REALLY BIG BOAT

(BASIL and NIGEL, two men of flamboyant character, are leaning over the railing of the Titanic and sipping champagne. It is night.)

BASIL: *(Raises glass to make a toast.)* Happy anniversary, love.

NIGEL: Chin-chin, darling. *(They drink.)* I say, who ever would have imagined we'd be celebrating our first anniversary on this really big boat, the Titanic? I feel like the queen of the world!

BASIL: Careful, love. Somebody will hear you.

NIGEL: Oh, bother! As a member of the Oscar Wilde Society, I am coming out of the armoire! Hear me, world! Hear me roar! *Grrrr . . .*

BASIL: Oh, dear!   That champagne is going directly to your head, Nigel.

NIGEL: Out of the armoire, boys, and into the streets!

BASIL: *(Spots something off in the distance.)* Oh, I say, what is that, dear chap?

NIGEL: What is what, Basil?

BASIL: *(Pointing.)* That. Out there, darling. It looks like . . . Oh, Zeus on Olympus! It looks like a giant penis.

NIGEL: Oh, I say! It is a giant penis, what? Pray tell, however do you suppose a giant penis floated out into the middle of the north Atlantic?

BASIL: And whose penis do you suppose it is? I mean, that ought to be the really huge question.

NIGEL: No one I know, darling. It must be fifty feet tall. Quick, Basil! Get those really big oars out of that really big lifeboat over there.

BASIL: *(Retrieving oars.)* Whatever do you plan to do with these?

NIGEL: We're going to row, darling. We're going to row this really big boat over to where we can get a really good look at that really big penis.

(They put the oars in water and row.)

BASIL: Oh, Mary Queen of Scots, this is exhausting!

NIGEL: We're almost there. Row, darling, row! Row your little, round, firm tushy off! Look at that! *(They stop rowing.)* It . . . it's . . . it's an iceberg.

BASIL: Still . . . it looks like a penis.

NIGEL: Kind of . . . I mean, if you squint.

BASIL: Big.

NIGEL: Really big.

BASIL: Nigel.

NIGEL: Basil?

BASIL: I think it is going to hit this boat, what?

NIGEL: I think you're right.

(*The SOUND of the iceberg hitting the Ship. BOTH hold onto the railing for dear life.*)

BOTH: OOPS . . .

NIGEL: Quick!   Get rid of the evidence.   Throw the oars overboard.

BASIL: NO. We'll need them for the lifeboat. *(Spots someone he recognizes on the deck.)* I say, there's that busybody American woman over there.

NIGEL: Who?

BASIL: Molly somebody. Ah yes! Brown . . . Molly Brown from Denver, Colorado. Very rich. Loves the royals.

NIGEL: Then she'll love us!

BASIL: *(Calling out to her.)* Hello, Molly! Over here! Care to share a lifeboat?

NIGEL: Wait a minute!   Don't run!   We'll save you, Miss Brown! You'll be safe with us!

END

6 FULL-LENGTH PLAYS
VOLUME TWO

AH, SHUCKS!

(EDDIE and SUSIE are at a bus stop.)

EDDIE: Howdy, Susie.

SUSIE: Howdy right back atcha, Eddie.

EDDIE: So where ya'll headed?

SUSIE: Yonder.

EDDIE: I 'spects I ain't never been to Yonder.

SUSIE: Gots me a cousin up in Yonder.

EDDIE: Really? I gots me one down Nowhere.

SUSIE: I've been to Nowhere. Couldn't wait to get out and get to Somewhere.

EDDIE: That's where most o' my folks live. Nice place.

SUSIE: Some say.

EDDIE: Some disagree.

SUSIE: *Yup.*

EDDIE: Yup. I was born and raised in Somewhere. Were you always from Here?

SUSIE: Nope. I moved to Here from Yonder.

EDDIE: Yonder's nice.

SUSIE: *Yup*. Some say it is.
EDDIE: Yup. That's what some say.

SUSIE: I like Hither better. Got an uncle in Hither.

EDDIE: I gots me an aunt in Hither. Here it is. There's m' bus.

SUSIE: Yup. There it is.

EDDIE: Yup.

SUSIE: Mine too.

EDDIE: Really?

SUSIE: Yup. Only I'm goin' in the opposite direction.

EDDIE: Wait a minute! Then you best be gettin' on first.

END

OIL SPILL

(MUFFY and DARLING are standing and looking through the fourth wall.)

DARLING: Stand back, Muffy. It's all covered in oil. Look at that poor bird. Don't stand so close. It'll give you nightmares. Some things should not be seen by polite society.

MUFFY: It's really dreadful, Darling—that wretched bird in all that oil. The man on the boat seems to be cleaning one of them —a pelican, I think. One can assume that eventually he'll get round to the big one. Oh wait! It's a child. Why isn't he helping that darling child first?

DARLING: You need glasses, sweetie. It's a seal. It looks to be dying, however. Probably can't breathe in all that oil.

DARLING: It's downright irresponsible.

MUFFY: Felonious. We should get a closer look.

DARLING: No, stand back. Everything appears less frightening from a distance. Living a good life is all a matter of perspective. One must always keep her distance from society's dregs. That's why we're here and they're there. It's a matter of finding ones place and sticking to it.

MUFFY: I remember a time when no one saw anything like this. It didn't exist. None would have it. When the establishment tended to the environment and we in the Junior League were patrons of the Arts. We are no longer the cultural beacons we once were. Now we are reduced to cookbooks and silent auctions.

DARLING: We need to put our collective foot down and make a difference. Restore culture to its former heights. Civilizations have come and gone for far less.

MUFFY: Those poor birds—and, of course, the seal. Drowned in all that oil. A catastrophe.

DARLING: Stop looking. It'll haunt you forever.

MUFFY: Those poor innocent animals. But, the frame's nice.

DARLING: Yes, the frame's nice. Wait a minute! I'll have a word with the curator. What a colossal waste of perfectly good oils.

END

A WOMAN ON THE MOON

(Two women, GLORIA and BETTY, are seated at a table tallying the check from their luncheon.)

GLORIA: Did you watch the moon landing the other day, Betty?

BETTY: No, Gloria. I didn't care to see a man lay claim to yet one more piece of real estate. You had the fruit salad. Men already think they own the world . . . and now they've got to have the moon, too. I had the three-bean soup. "One small step for man; one giant leap for Mankind." Give me a break! I wonder who wrote that bit of misogyny? Sixty cents for the soup. That's mine. Do you know why they didn't send a woman to the moon? Seventy-five cents for the fruit salad. That's yours.

GLORIA: No, why is that?

BETTY: Imagine how those men in Washington would react to hearing, "One small step for woman . . .?"

GLORIA: They'd freak.

BETTY: You bet they'd freak. Egg salad sandwich, ninety-cents. That's mine. One day it will be our turn. Fried bologna on rye, seventy-five cents. That's yours. One day there will be a woman on the moon. That will be a day to celebrate!

GLORIA: I'd be happy to get to Las Vegas one day. Too many seeds in the rye and he never did bring the horseradish. My bra is killing me. I think I'm going to buy one of those living bras.

BETTY: What?

GLORIA: Yeah, it's called a living bra and it's supposed to hold your breasts gently, but firmly. Like it had a mind of its own.

BETTY: Now, isn't that just what I need—something with a mind of its own holding up my . . . *euphemisms.* The side order of slaw was forty cents. That's yours.

GLORIA: But you ate it.

BETTY: Okay, we'll split it. Twenty cents you owe and twenty cents I owe. One hot tea with lemon, a quarter. That's mine. One day I'd like to burn mine.

GLORIA: Burn your what, your tea?

BETTY: My bra, Betty. One day I'd like to burn my bra.

GLORIA: Why?

BETTY: Gloria, do men wear bras?

GLORIA: No, not even when they obviously need them.

BETTY: Well, that's my point! One coffee, black. That's yours. Twenty-five cents. So, what's in Las Vegas?

GLORIA: *Huh?*

BETTY: You said you wanted to go to Las Vegas. You do know that women are enslaved in Las Vegas, don't you? The fruit cup was mine—forty cents. Haven't you ever heard of showgirls?

GLORIA: Sure. I wanted to be a showgirl when I was a little girl.

BETTY: That's like wanting to be a performing dog!

GLORIA: It's not the same thing!

BETTY: It certainly is! Miss Gloria Steinem, the show dog!

GLORIA: Don't call me that! I hate it! Miss implies that there is a man lacking in my life. How much was the rice pudding, Miss Friedan?

BETTY: Sixty cents! Don't change the subject!

GLORIA: How about Mizz? Not Miss or Missus. That way you're not being defined as being manned or manless. You ate some of my rice pudding.

BETTY: Ten cents! I didn't eat more than ten cents worth! Mizz: M-I-Z-Z. I like the sound of that. All right. Rice pudding—you —sixty cents. Rice pudding—me—ten cents. Let's see. That comes to one dollar and fifty-five cents each.

GLORIA: Wait a minute! That's not right. You charged me more somewhere. Give me that check. *(Grabbing check.)* Now, let's see. You had the three-bean soup—sixty cents. We split the slaw fifty-fifty, which means you owe twenty cents and I owe twenty cents, right?

BETTY: *Right.*

END

6 FULL-LENGTH PLAYS
VOLUME TWO

Edward Crosby Wells

SMALL POTATOES

(TRAVIS and JW are sitting on a bench, a rock, something. Late afternoon. West Texas.)

TRAVIS: *(Gulping beer.)* Seven months and I ain't touched 'er in three. Know what I mean?

JW: *Yep.* They're kind of scary when they start to show like that. *(Finishes his beer, smashes the empty can on his head, collapsing it, then reaches for another.)*

TRAVIS: It don't feel right doin' it with her in that condition and all. Liable to damage the baby or somethin'.

JW: You think that's possible?

TRAVIS: Of course it's possible.   Shows you how little you know me. *(Smashes beer can, belches and opens another.)* Last night I was fixin' to slap her good. All I wanted was a steak and a baked potato. Is that too much to ask for?

JW: Ain't nothin' like a juicy steak and a baked potato—unless it's mashed, or whipped. *Whipped.* I like the sound of that.

TRAVIS: Since she got herself all swelled up with the kid and all, she's gone on some kind of health kick. I guess that's all well and good for her, but I ain't gonna be turned into some kind of New York food sissy. So she says somethin' about bad starch and, "Potatoes are delicious, but are they really necessary?" Damn straight they're necessary! There's always a meat, a vegetable and a potato. Though sometimes you can do away with the vegetable. That's what God intended. Know what I mean?

JW: Yep. Unless you're havin' spaghetti.

TRAVIS: Spaghetti's different, JW. You're still gettin' your meat with your spaghetti—unless it's canned. Mamma *(Pronounced: Ma'am ah.)* used to make canned spaghetti and fried hot dogs. That's good eats.

JW: The wife wants to eat out every other night—Taco Bell, Billy's B-B-Q, McDonald's—she's got no idea what us roustabouts do for our money. Put her out in the oil field for a day, then she'd change her tune.

TRAVIS: You got that right!

JW: Are you gonna marry her, Travis?

TRAVIS: Wait a minute! I don't rightly know, JW. What with the baby on the way, and her cookin' and all—I'm not so sure it'll work out. She might do better elsewhere. Women are funny things. You give them all you got, you try to be nice to them, and what do they do? Next thing you know you'll be eating steak with rice. Can you imagine that? Nope. Marriage wouldn't be fair to her. 'Sides, what do I look like to you, *huh?* Know what I mean?

END

HOW'D THAT GUN END UP IN MY POCKET

BUDDY: *(Reading newspaper.)* *"How'd that gun end up in my pocket?"* Can you imagine that?

MARGE: What?

BUDDY: The fool said that to the arresting officer after he shot his wife.

MARGE: *(Reading letter.)* Some people, Buddy. Some people. Cousin Harriet and that woman she said was her *"roommate"* exchanged vows in Amarillo, Texas the week before last. I can't imagine.

BUDDY: Another scandal rocks Washington after lobbyist agrees to murder wife of Senator in exchange of vote on oil drilling in Alaska. I can imagine that.

MARGE: The house next door to Dolly—she's the one made my wedding dress—burned to the ground killing a family of five. All Dolly's orders for prom dresses got smoke-damaged and now she doesn't know who to sue.

BUDDY: SWAT team assassinates Postal worker eating gun made of licorice. That's hard to swallow.

MARGE: Was that a joke, Buddy?

BUDDY: *(After a pause.)* I think it was, Marge. It just came out without thinking about it. It took a awhile to get it, but I got it. I believe I finally found some humor in the world. It feels . . . it feels miraculous.

MARGE: Aunt Opal's best friend's grandson was so badly eaten by bedbugs they had to send him home from school. Always thought that kid was buggy. *(She bursts out in laughter.)*

BUDDY: Harvard professor develops cure for flatulence. Now he is working on cure for an alarming rise in halitosis. *(BOTH explode in laughter.)*

MARGE: Sister wants to know if we're coming home for Butch's graduation from beauty school. *(She cannot control her laughter.)*

BUDDY: Terrorists steal thirty pounds of plutonium and hold grammar school children hostage. Governor demands proof that they are really weapons of mass destruction. President appoints commission to look into the matter. *(BOTH laughing uncontrollably.)*

MARGE: Uncle George may have chicken flu. That would be the first time a chicken flew!

BUDDY: America invades third world country where everybody is starving and there is no oil. *(Stops laughing. Seriously.)* Huh? That doesn't make any sense.

MARGE: *(Equally serious.)* Wait a minute! Who'd believe that?

END

BURNING ISSUES

GEORGE: *(In chair, reading newspaper.)* Gracie, it says that marijuana may soon be legal.

GRACIE: *(Feather dusting.)* Thank goodness! I never thought I'd live to see the day.

GEORGE: But you don't smoke marijuana.

GRACIE: That's right, George, but poor old Aunt Pansy does.

GEORGE: I didn't know you had an Aunt Pansy.

GRACIE: We don't like to talk about her. She's been smoking the stuff since her hippy days. Maybe now she'll be able to get back on the apple cart.

GEORGE: You mean, back on the wagon?

GRACIE: Nope, back on the apple cart. The evil weed ruined Uncle Arnold's cider business. She went astray with quite a few of Arnold's apple pickers. Get stoned and get loose.

GEORGE: She was a bad apple, huh?

GRACIE: You shouldn't make jokes about the weakness of others. Besides, if she hadn't been such a good church-going Christian, she may never have fallen by the wayside.

GEORGE: Off the apple cart.

GRACIE: And right into the gutter.

GEORGE: But what has the church got to do with her falling by the wayside?

GRACIE: She fell right in with the preacher's wife.

GEORGE: One would think that falling in with a preacher's wife would be a good thing.

GRACIE: Oh no, George. There's nothing more tempting to the Christian soul than prohibiting something. She fell off the apple cart when she fell in with the preacher's wife who ran off to Chicago. Then she got a tattoo and ended up behind bars and all because marijuana was illegal. Once it becomes legal people will lose interest. If they don't make it legal, I don't believe the poor thing will ever be born again—especially since she took up stripping right after getting out of jail.

GEORGE: Wait a minute! Stripping in a sleazy strip bar?

GRACIE: Nope—in a parking lot of a strip mall.

GEORGE: Poor thing. We shouldn't want her stumbling in the dark, waiting to be born again. Won't do Uncle Arnold or the apple pickers any good.

GRACIE: I wouldn't worry about that, George. Uncle Arnold is dead. *Dead as a doornail.*

GEORGE: How?

GRACIE: He went to Chicago looking for Aunt Pansy and fell in with the wrong crowd—*her friends.* Seems they were connected with the Colombian drug cartel and he must have said something they didn't like.

GEORGE: So they . . . I see your point. Say goodnight, Gracie.

GRACIE: Good night, Gracie. It all goes to show.

GEORGE: It all goes to show what?

GRACIE: That sometimes the righteous are more dangerous than the sinner. Say goodnight, George.

END

Edward Crosby Wells

THE EUPHEMISM

(Olivia, Tish and Zoe are three middle-aged women having afternoon tea.)

OLIVIA: Wait a minute! Not really?

ZOE: True. Really.

TISH: Hard to believe, but true.

OLIVIA: It is difficult to imagine, don't you think?

ZOE: However difficult to imagine, I'm not making this up.

TISH: I'm sure you're not, dear. Wouldn't you all agree?

OLIVIA: Let's move on, shall we?

ZOE: Let's. We've lots of business to discuss.

TISH: Indeed we do. Where should we begin?

OLIVIA: How about the euphemism?

ZOE: The euphemism? You mean that son of—

OLIVIA: Our waiter might be listening, mightn't he?

ZOE: He might. But, *the euphemism* had it coming!

OLIVIA: I'm sure it did, but the question at the moment is how to get rid of—*it*, isn't it?

TISH: It certainly is the question—getting rid of the euphemism.

ZOE: Where should we start?

OLIVIA: How about what are we going to do with it?

TISH: We could put *it* in the trunk and drive *it* to the garbage dump, or maybe the lake.

ZOE: Three hundred pounds—dead weight. A perfectly good shower curtain, wasn't it?

TISH: Perfectly good—Bed, Bath and Beyond. I needn't remind you ladies that we're doing my euphemism next month.

OLIVIA: *(Calling out.) Waiter! Check please! (To Tish.)* Then do put your *euphemism* on a diet.

END

SIX MINUTE MEN

(GUY 8 and GUY 9 are sitting at a table, each wearing a name badge.)

GUY 8: You can learn a lot about woman on a six minute date. Take it from big twelve.

GUY 9: Big twelve? Your badge says "nine."

GUY 8: But my friends call me big twelve. Know what I mean? *(A wink.)* You like magic?

GUY 9: Sure. Everybody likes magic.

GUY 8: I got this levitating act that drives the ladies wild—that's why they call me big twelve.

GUY 9: I don't see the connection.

GUY 8: You could. We'll see how it goes with the ladies first. Know what I mean?

GUY 9: What's your real name?

GUY 8: Weren't you here for the orientation? No names—don't ask, don't tell.

GUY 9: Why is that, do you suppose?

GUY 8: Ever seen *Fatal Attraction?* You don't want to end up getting your rabbit boiled, do you?

GUY 9: I don't have a rabbit. Do you have a rabbit? I had a rabbit when I was little. Mother boiled it for a stew. That made me feel really bad, but it kind of made me feel really good too.

GUY 8: Feeling bad makes you feel good?

GUY 9: I like a good spanking every now and again. Number fourteen looked like a real good spanker. I asked her if she'd like to spank me and she slapped my face.

GUY 8: That's a start.   You can't have everything. I asked number seven if she'd like to see some magic. She said yes, so I rubbed the old magic levitator and before you could say *shazaam* the table rose six inches off the floor. She'll be back. *Yup.* Tonight was a bust, if you know what I mean. All those women and every one a loser—not an honest one in the bunch. Ready? *(Rises to exit.)* The wife's got dinner on, I expect.

GUY 9: Mine too. *(Rises to exit.)*

GUY 8: Maybe I'll run into you again next week *(Gesturing.)* You first. I'll follow.

GUY 9: Wait a minute! Not too close.

END

TEDDY'S BEAR

(TEDDY and CHARLIE, two young men, are sitting outside their tent, warming in front of a fire.)

TEDDY: That mountain looks so daunting, but I'm determined to climb it.

CHARLIE: There ain't no climbing, Ted. There's a path goes right to the top.

TEDDY: Still, it's uphill all the way.

CHARLIE: Everything's uphill in this neck of the woods. Ain't nothin' worth anything if you don't head for the heights. Think of the thrill when you reach the top and look out over the whole valley.

TEDDY: I suppose, but what if a bear kills us on the way up? Shouldn't we have protection?

CHARLIE: How about a ham sandwich?

TEDDY: No, thanks. Still full from the beans and franks.

CHARLIE: For the bear. If we stumble upon one, we give it a sandwich and he'll go on his way.

TEDDY: Suppose he doesn't like ham? Suppose he'd rather have berries, or honey.

CHARLIE: We don't have berries or honey. We got Spam, but I don't think he'll wait till we get the can open. *(As to a dog.) We got Spam, little guy. Just wait and don't eat us. Give me time to open it.*

TEDDY: Bears don't eat people, they claw you to death. They sneak up on you and it's all over.

CHARLIE: That's life and that's why you should always carry a ham sandwich.

TEDDY: *(Spotting something.) Shhh.* There's something out there.

CHARLIE: There's always something out there. Is it a bear?

TEDDY: I don't think so. It's fat and ugly, and it's carrying a banjo.

CHARLIE: I don't see anybody. It's probably just another camper. Maybe he's lost.

TEDDY: I don't think so. He's staring at me and licking his lips like he's gonna eat me, but I don't think he's got any teeth.

CHARLIE: Wait a minute! You're making this up.

TEDDY: Nope.

CHARLIE: Then you're imagining things.

TEDDY: Nope. *(The strumming SOUND of a banjo) Quick! Give me a ham sandwich.*

END

GARDEN TALK

(MARGE and ARTHUR are in their garden, gathering flowers.)

MARGE: This one has a nice thick stem. Don't cut it. It won't topple like the limp ones. Sunflowers make such nice arrangements. A pity their heads get so big. They collapse under their own weight.

ARTHUR: A pity, indeed. Wait a minute! Before I forget, don't mention Larry's malpractice suit tonight. For all his bragging about being Chief of Surgery, that won't last long, will it?

MARGE: Leaving all that hardware in a patient isn't going to bode well when he goes before the Board. Don't tell any of your jokes in front of Roger. You know how he can get. Oh my, look at all those pansies—still in bloom and with all those lovely painted faces. I hope Roger doesn't critique the entire menu as he did last time.

ARTHUR: Pansies seem to thrive on nothing, don't they? Pansies are the first to come and the last to go. They lay so close to the dirt, the only thing that seems to kill them are stepping on them and grinding them into the ground. I will have a talk with Roger about that.

MARGE: I'm glad you did. It was embarrassing. Delphinium and Snapdragons are always a bit festive. Cut a few, Arthur. It was a good idea to make the dinner party formal. Maybe Minnie won't show up in her Hawaiian moo-moo this time. Look at our hollyhocks, so tall and erect—and what endurance! They last so long. Honestly, I cannot imagine what Howard sees in her.

ARTHUR: We'll forego the asters. They spread and fall helter-skelter however the wind blows. Quite annoying, aren't they? Did you really have to invite the Cutlers? They're both a bit extreme, don't you think? I don't believe calling yourselves "artists" gives one free reign to do and say whatever comes to mind. There seems a faulty connection between the brain and the mouth.

MARGE: Quite right. I wish the lilacs hadn't died. They come and go so quickly. We could have done a nice bouquet of only them. Lilacs add a splash of passion and some sweetness to the air. By the way, your secretary called again. She said you needed to come in to work on some papers.

ARTHUR: What did you tell her?

MARGE: I told her the papers could wait till after the weekend. She calls too often, if you ask me.

ARTHUR: The Rosenthal case is rather prickly. There are all those depositions to go over. What do you think of those marigolds?

MARGE: Nobody brings marigolds into the house. Have you no sense of decency? They stink.

ARTHUR: The moonflowers are abundant this year. Poisonous, of course, but you'd have to eat a great many before they killed you. However, they could be ground into a paste and mixed in with mashed potatoes or something, couldn't they?

END

THE VIRGIN AND THE VAMPIRE

SHE: *(Sitting on loveseat.)* Would you care for some coffee?

HE: *(Sitting next to her.)* I love coffee, but I can only drink it when the world is asleep.

SHE: The world? Surely there is always somebody awake in the world.

HE: Most assuredly, but I am an artist and artists need a safe haven from the sound of Human thought. Their minds are never still and it destroys the creative process.

SHE: That pretty much rules out coffee, doesn't it? There must be something I can offer you.

HE: Perhaps there is.

SHE: And what would that be?

HE: We'll see. Ask me again later. Maybe I'll be hungry then.

SHE: Are you making advances towards me?

HE: I was thinking about it, yes.

SHE: You stop it right now. I'm not the kind of lady you think I am.

HE: The seduction is the most pleasant part of the game, isn't it?

SHE: You have much experience with the seduction?

HE: I seduce the muses.

SHE: What do you use for bait?

HE: My talent. I have a very large talent.

SHE: *(Moves closer to him.)* Do you really?

HE: Oh, yes. I am considered by many to be a genius.

SHE: Seductive bait, indeed. Alas, I shall never get the opportunity to see your work.

HE: Of course you will. There's always tomorrow evening.

SHE: For some. Other than wooing me with your huge talent, how many unsuspecting women have you seduced?

HE: I can't really say.

SHE: *That many?*

HE: I'm afraid you're the first.

SHE: That's so nice to hear. *(SHE leans in, bites his neck, HE screams as the LIGHTING dims.)*

END

THE MADAM AND THE MOUSER

(MADAM is hovering over the MOUSER who is on his hands and knees.)

MOUSER: *(Holding out a piece of cheese.)* They say the bell tolls for thee, but I can't find thee anywhere. Come out, wee mousey. I've got Huntingdon Stilton on a stick. *Yummy, yummy.*

MADAM: Not too much cheese, Mouser, we shouldn't want to spoil him. Had he not swallowed an entire diamond bracelet I'd be inclined to let him go about his business.

MOUSER: And what business would that be, Madam?

MADAM: You should know far better than I, Mouser.

MOUSER: Indeed I should, Madam. That would be making more wee mouseys. 'Tis what they do, Madam. The Missus has a mouse coat. I bring home the mouses and she tans their little hides. Which reminds me, Madam, would you mind terribly if I were to take him home with me?   That is, after the little scoundrel has been apprehended.

MADAM: And my bracelet has been extracted. Will you be needing pliers?

MOUSER: *(Crawling along floor.)* Not at all, Madam. I once extracted a baby's rattle and a toe.

MADAM: A toe! *Wait a minute! A baby's toe?*

MOUSER: No. Just the rattle belonged to the baby. The toe belonged to the Missus. A great many body parts can be found inside a mousey, Madam. I once captured a mousey with a mousey inside and another mousey inside him. Like those Chinese boxes, Madam.

MADAM: Do find our culprit. I'm becoming ill.

MOUSER: Sorry, Madam. There's a great deal of brainwork goes into mousing. One needs to think like a mousey and of course one needs the right bait. Ordinary cheese won't cut it, Madam. They have discriminating palates. Though I did catch one who dined entirely on earwax.

MADAM: Please hurry and catch the little beggar.

MOUSER: I'm doing my best, Madam.

MADAM: I don't care about the bracelet, Mouser. Here, take your payment and depart. All this intestinal talk is more than I can bear.

MOUSER: If Madam is sure. *(Rises and takes the money. Moves towards exit. Removes mouse from pocket. To mouse.)* Nice wee mousey. Gets them every time. Now open up. That's it, nice and wide. *(Removes bracelet, holds it up to have a look and exits.)*

END

CIAO, MARCELLO!

(Two young women, TIFFANY and BRITTANY, are standing on a sidewalk in Rome.)

TIFFANY: So I said to Danny, Danny, you really don't get it, you just don't get it, know what I mean? So he says to me, Tiffany, if you go to Rome you go without me. Well, here we are and— Brittany, quick! Take a picture of him.

BRITTANY: Who? Where?

TIFFANY: *(Pointing.) Right there.* In front of that stupid fountain with all those naked babies and things. He looks gorgeous. Use your zoom. I love Italians . . . pasta, sausage, Italian men.

BRITTANY: I see him. I'm zoomed in as close as I can get. We can enlarge it later. *(Click.)*

TIFFANY: Did you get it? Let me see.

BRITTANY: Me first. Just hold on. *(Examining camera screen.)*

TIFFANY: Well, well? Is he gorgeous or what? Wait till Danny sees this. This'll make him jealous. I told him, Danny, they've got the World Series on Italian television and he says, but not in English. How much English do you need to watch a ball game? He'll never get to see the Eiffel Tower.

BRITTANY: That's in Paris.

TIFFANY: Wherever. Give me that camera. I want to see him. They say a picture's worth a thousand words.

BRITTANY: Yeah, but I can't find my picture. There's nothing. Maybe the batteries are dead.

TIFFANY: For God's sake, Brittany! Put some fresh ones in. *Quickly, quickly* before he leaves.

BRITTANY: I don't have any. I'll have to buy some.

TIFFANY: He's not going to stand there while you run off to get batteries. Besides, remember what they said about the hair dryer? Electricity is different over here, so the batteries won't work either.

BRITTANY: I never thought of that.

TIFFANY: There's a gorgeous man across the street and you—

BRITTANY: *(Correcting her.)* Piazza.

TIFFANY: *Whatever.* Over there is an Italian hunk and you've got dead batteries. I bet he doesn't have dead batteries! How sad is that?

BRITTANY: *Sorry.*

TIFFANY: *(Raising her arm and waving. Shouts.)* Ciao, Marcello!

BRITTANY: What are you doing? You're embarrassing me. I could die. I really could. Besides, how do you know he's gorgeous?

TIFFANY: He's Italian.

BRITTANY: So was Mussolini.

TIFFANY: *Whatever. (Waving and shouting.) Ciao, Marcello!*

BRITTANY: And how do you know his name is Marcello? It could be anything—Dino, Guido, Roberto, Mario....

TIFFANY: I get it already. I heard it in one of those movies you have to read. He was on a train and it was pulling out of the station. She was on the platform waving and shouting, *Ciao, Marcello!* I've wanted to shout *Ciao, Marcello* ever since. I think he heard me. He's on his way over. How do I look?

BRITTANY: Like a Valley Girl in heat. Wait a minute! I think it's—

TIFFANY: *Wait a minute! It's Danny.*

END

6 FULL-LENGTH PLAYS
VOLUME TWO

Edward Crosby Wells

FISHIN' NO SEE 'EMS

(JOE BOB and SKEETER are sitting on a river's bank fishing. There are tiny flying insects constantly pestering them. BOTH swat at them, slapping themselves throughout the play—even when not noted.)

JOE BOB: *(Swatting.)* If it ain't the heat, it's the tomato bisque that'll kill ya.

SKEETER: *Huh? (Swats.)*

JOE BOB: That was one of Grandma's favorite sayings, before she drowned. Then grandpa got to sayin' it and the preacher even said it at the service. *Yup.* There's a headstone where her body outta be. *If it ain't the heat, it's the tomato bisque that'll kill ya.*

SKEETER: What's it mean?

JOE BOB: It means—well it means if it ain't one thing it's another. In grandma's case it was the undertow.

SKEETER: Oh. *(After a pause.)* What's tomato bisque?

JOE BOB: Somethin' you make with tomatoes.

SKEETER: That sounds about right. *(Slapping himself.)* Nasty gnats!

JOE BOB: I think I got one. Oh boy, he's a big one. *(Reeling in fish.)*

SKEETER: Take it slow. Ya don't wanna lose 'im.

JOE BOB: I got 'im. I got 'im. *(A beat.)* He got away.

SKEETER: Next time

JOE BOB: If it ain't the heat, it's the tomato bisque that'll kill ya.

SKEETER: *Yup.* If it ain't one thing it's another. *(Slaps his face.)*

JOE BOB: Nope. If the fish ain't bitin' or they get away it's all the same.

SKEETER: It kind of changes, don't it?

JOE BOB: All the time. Saying sometimes mean one thing and other times somethin' else altogether. That's the beauty of it. Grandma was very smart that way.

SKEETER: *(Pulling on his pole as if it were being tugged.)* I got one!

JOE BOB: Bring 'im in nice and slow.

SKEETER: It's a big one, Joe Bob.

JOE BOB: *(Stands behind SKEETER and gives him a hand pulling it in.)* I hope it ain't a gator.

SKEETER: You think it's a gator? *(Slaps himself.)*

JOE BOB: Could be. I'd get ready to run just in case. What did you use for bait?

SKEETER: Chicken guts.

JOE BOB: Fresh or old?

SKEETER: Fresh of course.

JOE BOB: It just could be a gator, Skeeter. Get ready to run.

SKEETER: Don't worry 'bout me. Pull.

(They BOTH pull on the fishing pole, reeling it in.)

JOE BOB: *Wait a minute!*

SKEETER: What? What is it?

JOE BOB: If it ain't the heat, it's the tomato bisque that'll kill ya.

SKEETER: *Yup.* If it ain't a fish it's a gator.

JOE BOB: *Nope.* It's grandma.

END

6 FULL-LENGTH PLAYS
VOLUME TWO

A FLY IN HER EAR

(MARGARET and LOCKLEAR are standing on a bare stage.)

MARGARET: All these flies in my ear, and fly swatters only give me migraines!

LOCKLEAR: Have you lost your mind? What are you talking about?

MARGARET: Your words. They're like buzzing pests asserting themselves into my thoughts. They aggravate and irritate. When I try to swat them from my consciousness they only buzz louder and give me headaches—exquisitely painful headaches.

LOCKLEAR: Perhaps it is the roasted lamb speaking, or perhaps the wine is causing you to speak in tongues.

MARGARET: The lamb had nothing to do with it.   It was cooked to perfection. The wine delighted. No, it is your words buzzing like flies I cannot swat from my thoughts. I do not speak in tongues. I t was metaphor, plain and true.

LOCKLEAR: Neither plain nor true, Madam.

CHARLES: *(VOICE O.S.) Wait a minute!* Stop! *Ma'am! Ma'am! Ma'am!* How many times do I have to tell you the word is *Ma'am* and not Madam

LOCKLEAR: What's the difference, Charles?

CHARLES: *(VOICE O.S.)* The difference, darling, is that one runs a whorehouse and the other does not.

MARGARET: Are you going to let him call you "darling."

LOCKLEAR: He's called me worse.

MARGARET: I think the playwright is responsible for all the confusion. Who cares if it's *Ma'am* or *Madam?*

CHARLES: *(VOICE O.S.)* I care, dear heart. Every time we work together one of you deigns to rewrite the script. Why do I continue to cast either one of you?

LOCKLEAR: Good question, Charles. Why do you?

MARGARET: I'd like to know the answer to that.

CHARLES: *(VOICE O.S.)* Now you're both giving me a migraine! This is a period piece—a farce—so just stick to the script.

LOCKLEAR: This is becoming tiresome.

MARGARET: If it is, you have not been listening beyond what mere words imply.

LOCKLEAR: And you would know something about that, would you? I think you're in the throes of dementia . . . *Ma'am.*

MARGARET: You should know well about that. How long was your last bout in the—they still call it a *"sanitarium,"* do they not?

LOCKLEAR: It was a retreat.

MARGARET: Call it what you will. It was where they put you after running through town three o'clock in the morning, naked and screaming.

LOCKLEAR: I was drunk.

MARGARET: You were mad!

LOCKLEAR: I was locked out . . . *Ma'am.*

MARGARET: With the cat, no doubt.

CHARLES: *(VOICE O.S.)* Enough! May we get back to rehearsal?

LOCKLEAR & MARGARET: Yes, Charles.

MARGARET: All these flies in my ear, and fly swatters only give me migraines!

HOWARD: *(VOICE O.S.)* Okay, gang. Let's wrap it there. The two of you were splendid. Charles, that goes for you too.

LOCKLEAR & MARGARET: Thank you, Howard.

CHARLES: *(VOICE O.S.)* Same here, Howard.

LOCKLEAR and MARGARET EXIT.

END

6 FULL-LENGTH PLAYS   Edward Crosby Wells
VOLUME TWO

THE RECRUIT

(SIR, holding a yellow legal pad, standing over MAGGOT who is doing pushups.)

SIR: Three more, Maggot!

MAGGOT: *(Exhausted.)* Ninety eight . . . ninety nine . . . *(Collapses.)*

SIR: What happened to one hundred, Maggot?

MAGGOT: I can't do it, Sir.

SIR: Do it, Maggot!

MAGGOT: I can do it, Sir. *(Does one last pushup.)* Thank you, Sir.

SIR: Good Maggot. Stand for jumping jacks!

MAGGOT: *(Standing in jumping jack position.)* How many, Sir?

SIR: Until I tell you to stop. *(MAGGOT begins jumping jacks. SIR makes notes on his legal pad.).* Any history of debilitating, life-threatening disease, communicable or non-communicable? You're slowing down. Jump, jump, jump, Maggot!

MAGGOT: As healthy as a horse, Sir.

SIR: Ever steal, rob or burgle?

MAGGOT: No, Sir,

SIR: Ever commit a felony?

MAGGOT: No, Sir.

SIR: Touch another man's genitals?

MAGGOT: No, Sir.

SIR: What about your own?

MAGGOT: That would be unavoidable, Sir.

SIR: Perfect, Maggot. Now is the golden time for recruitment.

MAGGOT: Why is that, Sir?

SIR: Because now is the only time and it's always time to recruit fresh meat. Jump!

MAGGOT: Fresh meat, Sir?

SIR: Into the grinder of our Commander and Chief.

MAGGOT: Grinder, Sir?

SIR: At ease, Maggot! *(MAGGOT takes the "at ease" position.)* What did you think you was here for, Maggot?

MAGGOT: To serve our country, Sir.

SIR: You got that right, Maggot. You serve our country and our country will service you.

MAGGOT: I don't like the sound of that, Sir.

SIR: *(Circling MAGGOT.)* I don't like the sound of squishy feet in the shower with eleven other men. Do you hear me complaining?

MAGGOT: No, Sir.

SIR: You bet your ass you don't. Sometimes those men make squishy sounds from other body parts. Do you make squishy sounds, Maggot?

MAGGOT: I don't think so, Sir.

SIR: We'll see about that when we get you in the shower, Maggot. We're the elite. No smelly parts here.

MAGGOT: Sir, I think I forgot to check the box.

SIR: What box is that, Maggot?

MAGGOT: Where it asks about my sexual—

SIR: Wait a minute! Stop right there, Maggot! *Did I ask?*

MAGGOT: No, Sir.

SIR: *Then don't tell!*

MAGGOT: But I don't want to be fresh meat for the grinder. Besides, I've got lots of smelly parts, Sir.

SIR: Head for the showers, Maggot! We're the elite and you're fresh meat for our Commander and Chief's grinder. I don't ask—and you don't tell! Now, head for the showers . . . double time! *(MAGGOT does.)* I'll be right on your tail.

END

6 FULL-LENGTH PLAYS
VOLUME TWO

EIGHTY-EIGHT

(The CHARACTERS are SWEETIE and HONEY, two young women. The SETTING is the shoulder of a highway. HONEY has arms raised high overhead. She parts her arms then closes them to clap her hands together. Each time she claps her hands she repeats "eighty-eight." She does this continuously. She spots cars from time to time and her head moves to follow them. After a while we see through HONEY that a car has stopped. Shortly thereafter SWEETIE enters.)

SWEETIE: Ha-loo, ha-loo.

HONEY: Ha-loo right back atcha, Sweetie.

SWEETIE: Likewise, I'm sure. Watchyadoin', Honey?

HONEY: Counting.

SWEETIE: On the highway?

HONEY: There's no better place.

SWEETIE: Really?

HONEY: Want to try it?

SWEETIE: Far too physical for me. I like to do my counting sitting down, but you go right ahead, Honey. *(HONEY continues her "counting." After a pause to watch her.)* I thought you were signaling distress.

HONEY: Distress?

SWEETIE: That's why I pulled over.

HONEY: *(Continues her "counting.")* Eighty-eighty, eighty-eight, eighty-eight. I wish you'd join me. You would not believe how exhilarating it is till you try it.

SWEETIE: My hair—I just had it done. Besides, I'll look silly.

HONEY: To who?

SWEETIE: People—people coming down the highway.

HONEY: So you think I look silly, do you?

SWEETIE: *No, no, no.* I thought you were in distress. It never crossed my mind that you looked silly. I mean, you didn't. Just distress, that's all. Certainly not silly.

HONEY: I see. *Eighty-eight, eighty-eight, eighty-eight . . . .*

SWEETIE: I thought you were counting.

HONEY: I am. *Eighty-eight, eighty-eight, eighty-eight . . . .*

SWEETIE: No you're not. You're just repeating "eighty-eight" over and over again.

HONEY: That's the name of the game.

SWEETIE: What game?

HONEY: It's called "Stuck." It's a numbers game. Right now I'm *stuck.*

SWEETIE: That's very odd, Honey. So how do you get unstuck?

HONEY: One has to have a partner. You can do it really slow. You won't sweat and you won't mess your hair.

SWEETIE: Oh, all right—but just for a minute. What do I do?

HONEY: You put your arms over your head and every time you slap your hands together you say "eighty-eight."

SWEETIE: And that will get you unstuck?

HONEY: Yes, always say eighty-eight. Then I'll move my feet again.

SWEETIE: Your feet?

HONEY: They're stuck too.

SWEETIE: Okay, here I go—just till I get you unstuck. *(She raises her arms and begins.) Eighty-eight, eighty-eight, eighty-eight . . .*

HONEY: I'm beginning to feel better already.

SWEETIE: This is kind of fun.

HONEY: It sure is, Sweetie. I don't want you to stop. You're doing great. *Eighty-eight, eighty-eight, eighty-eight.* That's wonderful. Go to the middle of the road.

SWEETIE: *What?*

HONEY: The acoustics are better there.

SWEETIE: You think? *Eighty-eight.*

HONEY: *Eighty-eight.* I do.

SWEETIE: Alright. *(Begins backing out onto the highway.) Eighty-eight, eighty-eight—*

HONEY: That's it, Sweetie. *Eighty-eight.* A little bit further.

SWEETIE: Are you unstuck yet? *Eighty-eighty, eighty-eight—*

HONEY: Almost. Further. Just a little bit more. Eighty-eighty.
SWEETIE: *(Offstage.) Eighty-eighty, eighty-eight—*

BOTH: *Eighty-eighty, eighty-eight, eighty eight—*

HONEY: *Wait a minute!*

*(The SOUND of a THUD followed by a truck SCREECHING to
a stop.)*

HONEY: *(Con't.) Eighty-nine, eighty-nine, eighty-nine.*

END ACT ONE

ACT TWO

WAITING FOR LUGGAGE

(MAN and CLERK (M or F) are at an airline service counter, conversation in progress.)

CLERK: I told you, sir. You'll have to wait until the plane from Dallas arrives.

MAN: *(Shouting.)* Why is my luggage in Dallas?

CLERK: Please, sir. Shouting will get you nowhere. Besides, it is not in Dallas. *(Looking at watch.)* It's in the air.

MAN: I'm going to sue you!

CLERK: That will be nice, sir.

MAN: Did you hear what I said?

CLERK: With both ears, sir. You're going to sue me, wasn't it?

MAN: Are you retarded or something . . . *backwards?*

CLERK: My life is so backwards that I find myself standing on my head when I least expect it. In the service industry it is often required.

MAN: Standing on your head?

CLERK: I'm very good at it, sir. I find myself in that position one or two times a day. Shall I show you? *(Begins bending to show him.)*

MAN: *(Looking around.)* You'll embarrass me.

CLERK: I cannot imagine that, sir. I could bend over backwards if you like. *(Starts to bend backwards.)*

MAN: Stop it! Are you crazy?

CLERK: It's this job, sir. It's required of me.

MAN: What am I supposed to do without my luggage, *huh?*

CLERK: It will be here in two hours, sir.

MAN: I have a meeting in one.

CLERK: Is it a short meeting?

MAN: Relatively.

CLERK: Relative to what?

MAN: To how long I've been waiting for my luggage.

CLERK: The plane arrives in two hours. Your luggage should be on it.

MAN: *Should? Aren't you certain?*

CLERK: Unless there was a mix-up, sir.

MAN: *(Shouts.) Mix-up!*

CLERK: Please keep your voice down, sir. It could be an act of God.

MAN: What has God got to do with my luggage?

CLERK: Maybe you weren't meant to have that luggage, sir.

MAN: Stop it! Go ahead and stand on your head. I'd rather talk to your feet anyway.

CLERK: Too late. Would you like to watch me bite a tongue, sir?

MAN: Do you actually work here?

CLERK: Where's that, sir?

MAN: Are you really a customer service clerk.

CLERK: Indeed I am. I have a badge to prove it.

MAN: Then where is my luggage?

CLERK: It went to Dallas, sir.

MAN: Why?

CLERK: Why indeed. I've never thought Dallas an agreeable destination. I'm going to bite my tongue. Stand back.

MAN: Stand back?

CLERK: I don't want to get blood on you, sir.

MAN: I certainly don't want your blood on me either.

CLERK: *Wait a minute! Did I say mine?*

END

6 FULL-LENGTH PLAYS
VOLUME TWO   Edward Crosby Wells

GRANNY GETS THE BIRD

(GRANNY and JENNY are tossing bird seed to the chickens that are scurrying about; getting between there legs and under their feet causing them to jump and move awkwardly from time to time.)

JENNY: The end of the world is here, and I'm still waiting for my bicycle.

GRANNY: It'll be over before you know it. Be patient. Won't be a long to wait. *Chick, chick, chick.* Eat your supper. The end is near. Praise the lord!

JENNY: Praise the Lord. How will it end, Granny?

GRANNY: A baptism of fire. Flesh melting off the bone. *Hallelujah!*

JENNY: Oh, no. If I don't get my bicycle soon I'll scream bloody murder.

GRANNY: Won't do you a lick of good. Feed the chickens. It'll keep your mind off the bicycle, but be careful not to take it off the chickens. My babies don't care about the world coming to an end. It's feeding time and all they know is they gotta eat. *Here chick, chick, chick . . . .* Come to Granny. Praise the lord.

JENNY: What about me? When do I get my bicycle? If it don't come soon, it'll be too late.

GRANNY: Soon enough. Patience is a virtue, child. *Chick, chick, chick . . . .*

JENNY: How do I get it?

GRANNY: The hard way seems to be the only way. It's a learned virtue.

JENNY: Oh, Granny. I'm just waiting for a bicycle.

GRANNY: We're all waiting for something. *Chick, chick, chick.* Feed the chickens, Jenny. Patience comes easier when you're doing something else. *Chick, chick, chick.*

JENNY: Well, let's see. *Chick, chick, chick. Chick, chick, chick.*

GRANNY: That's it. You mustn't dwell on the end when it's near. *Hallelujah!*

JENNY: *Chick, chick, chick.* I think it's working!

BOTH: *Chick, chick, chick.*

JENNY: *(Pointing off into the distance.)* Look! There's Bubba with the bicycle! He's in time for the end of the world.

GRANNY: Praise the lord and hallelujah! *Chick, chick, chick. (She wrestles an invisible chicken to the ground, seizing it by the neck and then twists it, killing it.)* Praise the lord. *The end is here.*

JENNY: Poor chicken.

GRANNY: We all have to go sometime. You and Bubba can pluck the feathers.

(THEY move towards the exit.)

JENNY: *(Calls to Bubba.) Wait a minute!* You give me my bike, Bubba, and start pluckin'!

END

BLACK CANDLE

(MIMSIE is sitting holding a black candle watching HEATHER make a big circle with a stick on the ground. They are BOTH within the circle. Night SOUNDS of the woods.)

MIMSIE: *(Examining the candle.)* Do you think this will kill 'em.

HEATHER: *(Sitting.)* Guaranteed.

MIMSIE: They suck your blood. I'm too young to die, Heather. I'm afraid. I don't want my blood sucked. I'm anemic, you know.

HEATHER: Calm yourself. That's a very special black candle and it'll keep us safe.

MIMSIE: I hope so. *(Hands candle to HEATHER.)* I'm feeling drained already. I'm getting chills. I think I have a fever. Goose bumps! I've got goose bumps! Feel my head.

HEATHER: *(Feeling her head.)* Mimsie, you're just fine.

MIMSIE: The thought of getting my blood sucked is making me ill.

HEATHER: If this works the way it's supposed to neither of us will be getting our blood sucked.

MIMSIE: I hope it's big enough to last all night.

HEATHER: It'll last, Mimsie.

MIMSIE: You can't be too sure. *(A thoughtful pause.)* Heather, the salesman gave me a funny look. *Askance,* if you know what I mean.

HEATHER: He couldn't help it, Mimsie, he was walleyed.

MIMSIE: *Oh.* Then I guess it's all right. He should hang more pictures, if you ask me. Give him something to look at. Well, I hope the black candle lives up to its hype. *(Shivering.)* My flesh is crawling.

HEATHER: This candle is guaranteed. It's time to light it. Stay in the circle. It won't work unless you're in the circle. And, whatever happens, do not step outside the circle.

MIMSIE: *(Blessing herself with the sign of the cross.)* Whatever you say.

HEATHER: Gotta light?

MIMSIE: It's in your other hand.

HEATHER: Ah. So it is. *(She lights the black candle.)*

MIMSIE: I hope it doesn't take too long.

HEATHER. Be patient, Mimsie! Some things cannot be rushed.

MIMSIE: What do you think they'll be like? Tail and horns? I heard they can be huge and ugly and they bite something wicked. Suck your blood in no time flat, they do.

HEATHER: Doubtful. I think that's just a myth among the country folk in these parts. Now keep quite.

MIMSIE: *(After a long shivering pause.)* Wait a minute! I'm feeling something. *(Shivering shoulder shrugging chills.)* It's getting cold.   Something's happening, Heather. I'm getting scared! *(She starts to rise to leave the circle.)*

HEATHER: *(Grabbing MIMSIE'S wrist, preventing her from getting up.)* Stop it! There is nothing to be scared about! It's a slight breeze, that's all. *(Pointing.)*

MIMSIE: Well don't let the candle blow out. We'll get invaded from outside the circle and we'll be dead by dawn *(A whining cry.)* Oh my God, they're gonna suck me dry . . .

HEATHER: We've got the black candle, don't we? It's guaranteed, isn't it? He said if it didn't work he'd give us our money back.

MIMSIE: A lot of good that will do! If it doesn't work we'll be dead! Besides, how are we going to get any sleep?

HEATHER: There's plenty of room to lie down within the circle. We'll be protected. The candle will draw them to it and when they get within the circumference of the circle they'll drop like flies.

MIMSIE: Like flies?

HEATHER: Mosquitoes, Mimsie. They're just mosquitoes. Honestly, I am never going camping with you again!

END

Edward Crosby Wells

TOONGA NUFEELA

WOMAN: *(Behind desk.) Wait a minute!* Don't you take that tone with me, sir!

MAN: *Toonga nufeela.*

WOMAN: Don't you toongy nufeely me, mister.

MAN: *Nufeela. Nufeela. Goondeed. Tilly tit!*

WOMAN: Did you just call me by a body part? Because if you did I'm calling 911. *(Reaches for telephone.)*

MAN: *No-o-o-o-o. No oddy art.*

WOMAN: Then behave yourself! This is America. In America we speak English. You people come over here and think we owe you something. Well, we don't! We don't owe you a thing, mister. Speak English or stay home. You're in America now. Not some third-world welfare state.

MAN: *Ahm ho! Ahm ho!*

WOMAN: Did you just call me a ho?

MAN: *No-o-o-o-o. Ahm ho! Ahm ho!*

WOMAN: Men can't be hos. Well, maybe where you come from. You people disgust me.

MAN: *No ho. Ho-o-o ma.*

WOMAN: Homo? *Sexual deviant. (Picks up telephone and begins dialing.)*

MAN: *Nufeela. (Sticking his tongue out.)*

WOMAN: You disgusting little man! *(Into phone.)* Security, I have a homosexual sex maniac here in my office sticking his tongue out at me. Please hurry. He's making rude gestures as we speak. Yes, that's what I said. A homosexual. He's acting lewd. Well, who knows!? Maybe where he comes from they like women! That's make him a homosexual homosexual, doesn't it? *(Hangs up phone. To MAN.)* You people come over here and assault our women. Bankrupt our welfare system. Put our workers on unemployment. Too lazy to learn English. You . . . you . . . *alien.*

MAN: *E-e-e-e. Yo-o-o-o . . . ba, ba, ba . . . oss.*

WOMAN: Right. E...I...E...I...O. The farmer in the dell. Security will be here any moment, sir—and I use "sir" very loosely. If you know what is good for you, you'll go.

MAN: *Yo-o-o-o-o ired! (Grabs pad and pencil from desk. Scribbles something and then hands it to her).*

WOMAN: *(Reads what is written on the pad. Picks up the telephone. Pushes button. Speaks into phone.)* Mr. Jones, the . . . the . . . the . . . ne . . . ne . . . new . . . ow . . . owner is . . . he . . . here to . . . to see you. Yes, I . . . I . . . I know sir. He's late because he . . . he . . . he had to have a too . . . tooth pulled. Tha . . . tha thank you, sir. *(To MAN.) You ma . . . ma . . . may ga . . . ga . . . ga in now, si . . . si . . . sir . . . .*

END

JANUS WATCH

(Two uniformed and armed soldiers at a border crossing standing back to back, either sex. BOTH stare directly ahead.)

SOLDIER ONE: *(A long SILENCE.)* I apologize if my honesty disturbs you.

SODIER TWO: *(Wounded.)* It need not have been so blunt.

SOLDIER ONE: I needed a way to reach you.

SOLDIER TWO: You did.

SOLDIER ONE: I know.

SOLDIER TWO: What now?

SOLDIER ONE: We wait.

SOLDIER TWO: How long?

SOLDIER ONE: Until—

SOLDIER TWO: Honestly, I hope it is soon.

SOLDIER ONE: Do you have it?

SOLDIER TWO: In my pocket. *(Reaches into pocket.)*

SOLDIER ONE: *(Looking about nervously.) No! Not now.*

SOLDIER TWO: I wasn't going—*(Disappointed.)* What do you take me for?

SOLDIER ONE: I wanted to be certain. I didn't think you would, but I wanted to be certain.

SOLDIER TWO: Are you?

SOLDIER ONE: *Umm—*

SOLDIER TWO: We need to find a way to reach the others without others hearing.

SOLDIER ONE: Yes. Some hear only a snatch here and there and then they begin to suspect.

SOLDIER TWO: It's more like paranoia than suspicion.

SOLDIER ONE: Their imaginations get the better of them.

SOLDIER TWO: Then they become a danger to us.

SOLDIER ONE: They do indeed.

SOLDIER TWO: Yes. That's been the problem all along, hasn't it?

SOLDIER ONE: Yes. It has.

SOLDIER TWO: My watch is nearly over. I'm tired.

SOLDIER ONE: Yes. *(Seeing in the distance.)* Your replacement is coming. You'll be relieved of duty soon enough. *Quickly!*

SOLDIER TWO: Wait a minute! Don't let them see us.

SOLDIER ONE: *(After a pause.) Now!*

SOLDIER TWO: *(Reaches into his pocket, removes an envelope and passes it back to SOLDIER ONE.)* All the names. You will help them cross, yes?

SOLDIER ONE: For the love of freedom.

SOLDIER TWO: Yes. For the love of freedom.
(Back to back, BOTH rotate slowly and each ending up in the other's former position. They stare directly ahead while walking to exit.

END

6 FULL-LENGTH PLAYS
VOLUME TWO

PETER & JUDY

(PETER sounds suspiciously like Cary Grant and JUDY like Bette Davis. Their dialogue should run the gamut of emotions.)

PETER: Ju-dee?

JUDY: Pee-tah?

PETER: Ju-dee, Ju-dee.

JUDY: Pee-tah, Pee-tah.

PETER: Ju-dee, Ju-dee, Ju-dee.

JUDY: Pee-tah, Pee-tah, Pee-tah.

PETER: Judy!

JUDY: Peter!

PETER: *Ju-dee.*

JUDY: *Pee-tah.*

PETER: JUDY.

JUDY: PETER.

PETER: Judy?

JUDY: Peter?

PETER: Judy. Judy.

JUDY: Peter. Peter.

PETER: Judy, Judy, Judy!

JUDY: Peter, Peter, Peter!

PETER: Oh, Judy.

JUDY: Oh, Peter.

PETER: Oh, oh, oh, Judy.

JUDY: Oh, oh, oh, Peter.

PETER: Oh, Judy!

JUDY: Oh, Peter!

PETER: *Judy!*

JUDY: *Peter!*

PETER: Ah, Judy.

JUDY: Ah, Peter.

PETER: JUDY.

JUDY: PETER.

PETER: Judy?

JUDY: Peter?

PETER: Judy, Judy.

JUDY: Peter, Peter.

PETER: *Judy, Judy, Judy.*

JUDY: *Pee-terr . . . Wait a minute!*

PETER: *Yes, yes, yes . . . .*

JUDY: *Yes, yes, yes . . . .*

PETER: Cigarette, my dear?

JUDY: Thank you, dah-ling.

END

POLYPHEMUS

(The characters are POLYPHEMUS, CHORUS, ULYSSES and PENELOPE.)

POLYPHEMUS: I am Polyphemus.

CHORUS: The one-eye.

POLYPHEMUS: Looking out from all.

CHORUS: I am the collective.

POLYPHEMUS: Without end.

CHORUS: Without beginning.

POLYPHEMUS: Seeing all.

CHORUS: Knowing all.

POLYPHEMUS: Being all.

CHORUS: We are one.

ULYSSES: *(Enters.)* I am Ulysses.

CHORUS: The two-eyed.

ULYSSES: The two-eye lives in one body.

CHORUS: Lives then dies.

ULYSSES: As every mortal must.

CHORUS: The two-eye kills.

ULYSSES: As every mortal does.

POLYPHEMUS: Go back to your ship.

CHORUS: Go back to your wife.

POLYPHEMUS: Leave this island.

CHORUS & POLYPHEMUS: We are Polyphemus.

ULYSSES: I am Ulysses.

CHORUS & POLYPHEMUS: *(Ibid.)* We are Polyphemus.

(CHORUS and POLYPHEMUS exit. PENELOPE enters.)

PENELOPE: Wait a minute! Who are you?

ULYSSES: I am your husband.

PENELOPE: I am Penelope and I do not remember you.

ULYSSES: I am Ulysses.

PENELOPE: Prove it.

ULYSSES: Have you gone blind?

END

MONSTER UNDER THE BED

LITTLE KID: Why is the sky blue?

BIG KID: 'Cause.

LITTLE KID: 'Cause why?

BIG KID: 'Cause it is.

LITTLE KID: That's not an answer.

BIG KID: Course it is. Some things just is.

LITTLE KID: Ain't!

BIG KID: Is!

LITTLE KID: *(After a thoughtful pause.)* Mommy said we was gonna have a new brother.

BIG KID: Or sister.

LITTLE KID: I don't want a sister. If a sister comes we should send her back.

BIG KID: Once she comes she's here and once she's here ya can't send her back.

LITTLE KID: Why not?

BIG KID: 'Cause.

LITTLE KID: 'Cause why?

BIG KID: 'Cause ya can't.

LITTLE KID: Can!

BIG KID: Can't!

LITTLE KID: *(After a thoughtful pause.)* Where do I come from?

BIG KID: Mommy and Daddy.

LITTLE KID: But before Mommy and Daddy?

BIG KID: Dust. You come from dust.

LITTLE KID: From dust?

 BIG KID: 'For you was here you was nothin' but dust.

LITTLE KID: Nothin' but dust?

BIG KID: Nothin' but dust. Everybody comes from dust.

LITTLE KID: Everybody?

BIG KID: *Yup.* Everybody.

LITTLE KID: So where do everybody go after here?

BIG KID: Back to dust. You come from dust and you go back to dust.

LITTLE KID: Wait a minute! *(Screams and starts to run.) C'mon!*

BIG KID: Where?

LITTLE KID: To my bedroom! I want you to see somethin' under my bed.

BIG KID: What's under your bed?

LITTLE KID: I don't know, but I think somebody's comin' or goin'.

END

TWISTER

(JUNIOR and MISSY are riding a roller coaster. They are holding on to the invisible safety bar for dear life. They lean and sway one way and then another, in unison. The ride is wild and intense.)

MISSY: *Wait a minute!* I've changed my mind.

JUNIOR: Too late. Here we go!

MISSY: I'm going to be sick.

JUNIOR: Marry me.

MISSY: HELP.

JUNIOR: Is that a "yes?"

MISSY: *Oh, God! There go my tits!*

JUNIOR: Where?

MISSY: I don't know where! *They're just gone.*

JUNIOR: We'll get you new ones. *Hold tight!*

MISSY: *Oh my god!* I want my old ones.

JUNIOR: Here comes a big one! HOLD ON.

MISSY: I am holding on!

JUNIOR: Will you marry me?

MISSY: I've got no tits!

JUNIOR: You've got tits. Centrifugal force has had its way with you.

MISSY: What are you saying? *Help!* They're broke!

JUNIOR: You broke your tits?

MISSY: They exploded. They exploded and now I'm going to die.

JUNIOR: Maybe they imploded.

MISSY: *What's the difference, you dumb shit?*

JUNIOR: You needn't call me names. *Oh my god! I didn't see that coming!*

MISSY: Me either. I'll never do this again! HELP!

JUNIOR: Hang on! We're almost over the last hump!

MISSY: Over the last hump my ass! HELP!

BOTH: HELP!

JUNIOR: *Ow, ow, ow!* I think I twisted my—

MISSY: *What?*

JUNIOR: My manhood. Hold on!

MISSY: To your manhood?

JUNIOR: I think I crushed—

MISSY: Oh, look. We're coming in. I am glad that's over.

JUNIOR: My nuts.

MISSY: Now, what did you ask me?

(BOTH stand and head toward exit.)

JUNIOR: *(In pain.)* I asked if you would ma . . . ma . . . merry-go-round. Would you like to go on the merry-go-round next?

END ACT ONE

ACT TWO

THE HANGING JUDGES

(AT RISE: The setting is an art gallery. The fourth wall is hung with unseen paintings being judged by CARLOTTA BEAN, HONEY ALDRIDGE and DOCTOR HALL. They are bunched at far left or far right stage—the idea is to have them move their way across the stage to the opposite end by the end of the play.)

CARLOTTA: *(Facing the audience.)* We ought to start somewhere and it might as well be here.

HALL: What is your verdict, Honey? Is it a nay, or is it a yea?

HONEY: I don't much care for storms or seascapes. Never have. This one has both storm *and* seascape. A bit of a mish mash, if you ask me. *Nay.* A definite nay.

CARLOTTA: Let me have a look.

(HONEY moves on to the next painting, pressing her nose against it followed by CARLOTTA and HALL. CARLOTTA bobs up and down.)

HALL: Why are you bobbing up and down like that?

CARLOTTA: It requires my eyes to be level with the painting. I'm teetering on the brink of a decision.

HALL: I always stand at a respectable distance. *(Moves upstage.)* See? This . . . oh, how shall I say? This is the proper way to view a work of art.

CARLOTTA: It appears to be a rendering of Gainsborough's Blue Boy.

HONEY: Are you sure it's not brown and yellow clouds over a raging blue sea?

HALL: It looks like a Smurf. *Nay.*

HONEY: *(At the next painting.)* Oh, my! That's frightening. I'm afraid it's a nay.

CARLOTTA: I certainly agree. We are all well into the twenty-first century—most of us, anyway—and there is no longer any point to pointillism. Say *nay, nay, nay.*

HONEY: I quite agree. *Nay*

CARLOTTA: *(Watching HONEY who is already at the next painting.)* Honey, stop rubbing your nose all over the paintings. *(Handing HONEY a tissue.)* Look at yourself. The paint wasn't dry on that one.

HONEY: *(Rubbing the paint from off her nose.)* So, that's why there are so many trails going through that woodland pastoral.

HALL: I think it is ruined, ladies.

CARLOTTA: Nonsense. Get me a brush, Honey. There's dozens in the backroom.

HONEY: I'm on it. *(Exits and quickly returns with two brushes.)*

CARLOTTA: Look at how she obeys. One can't help but love her.

HALL: Perhaps you should get yourself a poodle, Carlotta.

CARLOTTA: *Humph!*

HONEY: *(Rushing in.)* I brought you two, Carlotta.

CARLOTTA: *(Grabs one from HONEY'S hand.)* Now, let's see. *(Applying the brush to the painting.)* Maybe if we extend this branch. This tree seems to have a road going right through it.

(They ALL move in on the painting.)

HALL: I think that tree is *supposed* to have a road going through it.

CARLOTTA: Nonsense. *(Begins filling in the gap.)*   There— look how much better that is—no more hole. There's still those trails going through the sky.

HONEY: They could be airplane trails.

HALL: Of course. Mucus-filled airplane trails. Just extend that cloud, Carlotta.

CARLOTTA: Like this? *(She paints.)*

HALL: Now see what you've done. It looks like a giant rabbit hopping over a redwood forest. You've got the bunny's feet caught in the branches. What's this?

CARLOTTA: A power line.

HALL: It used to be the horizon.

CARLOTTA: Now it's a power line.

HONEY: *(Stepping up to the painting. While the others brush away, she moves the paint around with her finger.)* Maybe we could get rid of the power lines by *(Finger painting.)* blending this into that.

HALL: You just blended that family of bears into the giant rabbit.

CARLOTTA: Oh, well, if you ask me it's a much better painting.

HALL: It looks like . . . oh, how shall I say? It looks like a rabbit on an aquarium filled with brown and green fish swimming under a power line.

CARLOTTA: Let's give it a yea and get out of here!

HALL: *Driving Through a Redwood* by Dottie Beach receives unanimous yeas.

CARLOTTA: It's the least we can do—considering.

(CARLOTTA and HALL hurry offstage.)

HONEY: *Wait a minute!* Wait for Honey. *(She runs offstage after them.)*

END

A THUMB'S STORY

MILLIE: *(Standing at butcher's block.   Back to audience. Raising high a meat cleaver over a quartered chicken.) I hate him. (The thwack of the cleaver separates a leg from a thigh.)* I wanted eighths not quarters. *I hate him!*

HANK: *(Sitting. Reading.)* The last I heard the butcher was putting his thumb on the scale.

MILLIE: Don't you listen to a thing I say? He wasn't putting his thumb on the scale.

HANK: Oh, I thought—

MILLIE: Don't think!

HANK: I'll try not to, dear.

MILLIE: He didn't put his thumb on the scale. He chopped it off!

HANK: He chopped it off?

MILLIE: Why do I have to repeat everything with you? He chopped it off and it fell onto the chicken while he was quartering it and then he threw it on the scale without quartering it again. Why can't people follow directions?

HANK: Damned if I know.

MILLIE: Why is it always about you? Anyway, there lay the bloody thumb.

HANK: Didn't he feel it—scream and carry on?

MILLIE: Everyone isn't you, Hank. Stop trying to make this all about you! He felt nothing. He looked at it laying between the breast and the hindquarter and he said nothing—like it happens everyday. Though if it did he would have run out of thumbs by now.

HANK: I should think so. The poor man just chopped his thumb off. Well? What happened to his thumb?

MILLIE: It's still there. Nearly wrapped it in with the chicken until I had to ask him to remove it. I don't know how to cook thumb.

HANK: I don't imagine.

MILLIE: That's your problem. You have no imagination! Now there's thumb blood all over our chicken. I washed it real good, but I keep detecting a slight whiff of the butcher.

HANK: *(Looking towards the butcher block. Horrified.)* That's the same chicken? You brought the same chicken home?

MILLIE: I certainly did.

HANK: I'd be happy with meatloaf.

MILLIE: For Pete's sake, Hank! Tuesday is meatloaf. Tonight is chicken.

HANK: Still, I don't think I'll be able to eat it knowing what I know.

MILLIE: What do you know, Hank?

HANK: What you told me.

MILLIE: What a dummy you are! You only know what I tell you. I may not have told you the truth.

HANK: In that case, I may well be a dummy.

MILLIE: Don't get smart with me. You're just a big dumb nothing.

HANK: Then there wasn't a thumb?
MILLIE: Of course there was a thumb. I always tell the truth. It's my nature. Do you think I could stand here and tell you I hate the butcher if there wasn't a thumb? I don't hate that easily. I always lean toward love.   It's a slight, but discernible inclination.

HANK: *(Sotto voce.)* Could have fooled me.

MILLIE: What did you say?

HANK: Yes, dear—like the Tower of Pisa. Couldn't we send out for pizza?

MILLIE: We could, but we won't. I'll wash the chicken in mouthwash.   Will that make you happy? I could use rubbing alcohol. You know what your problem is?   You have no sense of adventure.

HANK: You almost brought a man's thumb home! That's adventure enough for the both of us.

MILLIE: Always with your nose in a book.   That's as close as you ever get to an adventure. What are you reading?

HANK: *(Picks up book.) Martha Stuart's Untraceable Poisons for a Perfect Garden.*

MILLIE: I'm not much into horticulture.

HANK: You should be. There are so many ways to eliminate bothersome creatures. For instance, when a leech grabs hold and sucks the life right out—you need to know the best poison to take care of the problem.

MILLIE: You wouldn't know the best of anything.

HANK: You've kept me under your thumb since the day we met.

MILLIE: Don't be ridiculous.

HANK: You're the one who's ridiculous. Give me your thumb.
MILLIE: What?

HANK: *(Goes to butcher's block and retrieves the cleaver.)* Give me your thumb.

MILLIE: Why?

HANK: I'm going to chop it off—be free of you.

MILLIE: Don't be stupid.

HANK: Stupid? It's the smartest move I'll ever make.

MILLIE: *(Begins backing away.)* You're beginning to scare me. Back off, Mister!

HANK: I don't think so.

MILLIE: All right. You've made your point. We don't need to have chicken. A meatloaf sounds pretty good right now.

HANK: *(Raises cleaver.)* I want to be out from under your thumb. Give me your hand.

MILLIE: How about deli? We could send out for deli.

HANK: I've lost my appetite.

MILLIE: I'll cook whatever you like. *Anything.* Tell me what you want. Pork? Lamb? How about lasagna?

HANK: *(Raises high the cleaver.)* I want out from under your thumb!

MILLIE: Wait a minute!

(Quick BLACK OUT. The SOUND of the thwack of the cleaver.)

MILLIE: *(Con't.) Ouch.*

END

6 FULL-LENGTH PLAYS
VOLUME TWO   Edward Crosby Wells

WAIT A MINUTE!

(AT RISE: NEXT, 12, 13 and 14 are in a waiting room. After a long SILENCE.)

12: Seems like we've been here forever.

14: How long has it been since anyone's been called?

NEXT: I fell asleep and lost track of the time.

13: Did everybody take a number?

12: I did. *(Examines ticket.)* I'm number twelve.

14: Fourteen. My ticket says fourteen.

NEXT: Who am I?

12: You're eleven. You were the only one here when I came in.

NEXT: That doesn't mean anything. I could be seven and let eight, nine, ten and eleven go ahead of me.

12: Why would you do a thing like that?

NEXT: I fell asleep. I could have been taken advantage of in my sleep.   Strange things happen to people while they're sleeping. It's an opportune time for negative forces.

14: Like what?

NEXT: Like dreams and nightmares and spirits from the other side.

13: What other side?

NEXT: Of the door. Slipping in while you are least aware. Making yourself their home. Living in your body.   Dictating your every move.   Your life is no longer your own. Stranger things have happened. Oh, the horror! *The horror!*

13: *(Shivering.)* I've got to get out of here.

14: *(Ibid.)* Me too.

12: Hogwash! *(To NEXT)* Look at your ticket.

NEXT: I don't want to look at my ticket. I'm next and that's all anybody needs to know.

14: Did anyone knock on the door?

12, 13, NEXT: Nope.

14: Why not?

12: Scared.

13: Scared.

NEXT: I was asleep.

14: They could have forgotten that we're here.

13: You only just got here. What's your hurry?

14: I hate waiting.

NEXT: Get used to it! I'm next. So relax. Everybody here knows I'm next.

14: You were all here when I got here. Any one of you could be next. Sooner or later, we all get to be.

NEXT: Don't try any funny stuff! I'm next and that's all there is to it!

12: *(To NEXT.)* If you'd only show us your ticket.

NEXT: I know what my ticket says. I could sell one of you my ticket.

14: How much?

NEXT: I need to think about it.

12: Careful, 14's a malcontent.

NEXT: Then he'd better start a riot 'cause the deal's off!

14: I might. I just might be forced to riot.

12: One alone cannot riot. It would look like St. Vitus Dance.

13: I knew a man who blew himself up once.

NEXT: Only once? Why did he blow himself up . . . *once?*

13: He was trying to make a point.

14: A moot point, indeed. Who's next?

NEXT: I'm next!

12: Show us your ticket.

NEXT: I ate it.

13: What kind of person eats their ticket?

12: People can't do whatever they please.

14: That's for sure.

NEXT: Why not?

12: I don't know why not. But, there must be a reason.

14: There's always a reason.

13: *Always.*

NEXT: Nope. There ain't always a reason. You can go to the bank on that. *(NEXT crosses to door and knocks.)*

VOICE: *(From the other side of the door.) Wait a minute!*

(SILENCE as ALL stare at the door. BLACK OUT.)

END OF PLAY

TALES FROM
DARKEST SUBURBIA

Tales from Darkest Suburbia premiered at the Riverfront Playhouse in Aurora, IL where it opened on March 20, 2009 with the following cast and crew:

Marla Holman	Minnie Swisher
Carol Townsend	Sissie Brockman
Gary Krolik Jr.	Judge Rudolph Bleeker
Brandon Vanlear	Harley Bean, Dr.
Swisher	
Robert Richardson	Sid Dumpling, Dr. Hall
Sarah Odenbach	Sylvia Dumpling
Nikki Edwards	Millie Slaughter
Gary Riggle	Hank Slaughter, Smith
Tristan Porter	Moe Beach
Jill Kustush	Carlotta Bean
Vicki White	Honey Aldridge
Jana Sanders	Rosy Bleeker
Tim Curtis	Narrator
Director	Shawn Dooley
Assistant Director	Tim Curtis

TALES FROM DARKEST SUBURBIA
Review by David Muncaster
Amateur Stage Magazine, U.K.

Tales from Darkest Suburbia consists of seven interconnected
stories that give us a glimpse of what the author describes as
"typical" American life. You know the sort of thing: Murder,
adultery, blackmail, kidnapping. Oh yes, and cannibalism,
dismemberment and a flesh eating poison. All very much the
sort of thing that passes for normal in American suburbs. Well, it
does in the mind of Edward Crosby Wells anyway.

The first of our stories explores friendship: The kind of deep
personal friendship that is built on a mutual contempt for each
other, where the only things that bonds is the "love of the game
and a taste for blood. Across the tablecloth that features a
rubbing of Tallulah Bankhead's gravestone, Sissie exploits her
knowledge of something that Minnie is desperate to keep secret.
The seemingly pleasant chatter is full of veiled threats and a deal
is done. In the next tale a judge discusses with an attorney the
outcome of a murder trial, involving Minnie's husband, before it
has been heard in court. Having enjoyed the first tale I found the
second even better, and so this continued as each of the tales
surpassed the previous for ingenuity and humour. What I really
like about this play though, is that the characters, however
surreal, are still believable. Their conversation flows naturally
and we gradually become embroiled in their extraordinary lives.

Tales from Darkest Suburbia is a remarkable achievement.
Although each story works very well on its own and could be
presented independently as a short play; as a complete piece it
comes together very well, is most satisfying and very funny.

CHARACTERS
(in order of appearance)

NARRATOR
MINNIE SWISHER
SISSIE BROCKMAN
JUDGE RUDOLPH BLEEKER
HARLEY BEAN
SYLVIA DUMPLING
SID DUMPLING
HANK SLAUGHTER
MILLIE SLAUGHTER
DOCTOR PETER SWISHER
MOE BEACH
CARLOTTA BEAN
HONEY ALDRIDGE
DOCTOR HALL
ROSY BLEEKER
SMITH

ACT ONE—SYNOPSES

Scene One – *The Rubbing*

2W, 1 table set with tea things, 2 chairs. Sissie Brockman has invited her friend Minnie Swisher for afternoon tea and to show off her rubbing of Tallulah Bankhead's gravestone that also serves as the tablecloth upon which they have their tea. Minnie would do or give anything to keep Sissie from revealing that she had been having an affair with Moe Beach who was recently shot under suspicious circumstances. Sissie explores options for using the situation to her own advantage.

Scene Two – *The Sullied Robe*

2M, 1 desk, 2 chairs. A judge and a defense attorney meet in the judge's chambers just before going to trial.   The judge desperately tries to remove a stain of unknown origin from his robe using a variety of cleaning solutions.   They discuss the merits of the defense attorney's client charged with murder compared to the merits of the victim until they finally predetermine the outcome of the trial.   This is obviously an amusement performed on numerous occasions.

Scene Three – *The Dumplings*

1M/1W, 1 small table, 2 lounge chairs. Sid and Sylvia dumpling kidnap Lydia a well-known TV chef and have her on a chain in the kitchen where she is forced into cooking for them. Bound in the basement is Chef Pierre, another TV chef who refused to cook and went on a hunger strike. Though the characters of Chef Pierre and Lydia are never seen they are often heard as mumbles from behind duct tape. The Dumplings are now faced with the immediate dilemma of what to do with the chef in the cellar— less immediate is what to do with Lydia.

Scene Four – *The Butcher's Thumb*

1M/1W. A kitchen table, 2 chairs, a butcher's block. Hank and Millie Slaughter are having a conversation concerning the butcher's severed thumb and the evening's menu. The question is, who's really the butcher and whose thumb is it anyway?

ACT TWO—SYNOPSES

Scene One– *The Session*

1W/1M, two chairs or a chair and a couch. Moe Beach is hearing a strange voice. Doctor Swisher thinks Moe may be having an affair with his wife. The good doctor has an unconventionally diabolical approach to therapy. The line between patient and doctor becomes blurred when, together, they delve into the nature of reality. The cure may be far worse than the disease.

Scene Two – *The Hanging Judges*

2W/1M, Bare stage. Three conniving judges of a local art competition, each with their own devious agenda, select the winning entrees for a forthcoming exhibition.

Scene Three – *The Gazillion*

1W/1M, 3 chairs. Rosy is waiting for her plane to board that will begin her journey around the world. Smith wishes he had never sat next to her as Rosy terrorizes him in her own inimitable style. Both have something to hide.

6 FULL-LENGTH PLAYS
VOLUME TWO

.

ACT ONE—Scene One

The Rubbing

AT RISE: The setting is the dining room of SISSIE BROCKMAN. Two chairs and a cloth-covered table set with tea things. SISSIE is alone and putting the finishing touches on her carefully arranged table. After awhile, MINNIE SWISHER bursts into the room. She is wearing formal gloves.

NARRATOR: Volumes upon volumes could be written on the dynamics of friendship. Friends come and friends go. Some stay and it seems they'll be here forever. Then forever ends and everything changes—friendships vanish. Some we outgrow and some outgrow us. It could be something so simple as one no longer liking how the other sees them. It gets in the way of change—of growth. Some have friends they've had for so long they've become tolerated fixtures, like dripping faucets. They're annoying but not enough to do something about it. Then there is a very special kind of friendship—a kind based on mutual contempt. What binds them is their love of the game and a taste for blood. Sissie Brockman and Minnie Swisher are an example of this special kind of bond. Beneath the surface of their agreeable civility lurk lethal obstacles to uneasy compromise.

MINNIE: *(Announces.)* So sorry I'm late, but Doctor Hall had his sprinklers going and I had to walk all the way down the block just to cross the street. And, when I did, I ran into cunning Carlotta feigning shock over the Art Society's choices for this year's hanging. I guess I know what that means.

SISSIE: *Indeed.* Carlotta Bean is just being—Carlotta Bean, I suppose. Rather ill mannered, but we love her just the same. By the way, what a pity I left the front door unlocked.
MINNIE: A pity?

SISSIE: Because it just saddens me not to have had the opportunity to open the door and properly escort you in.

MINNIE: You're such a treasure, Sissie—always thinking of others.

SISSIE: It's my nature. I can't seem to do otherwise. *Tea?*

MINNIE: Of course. *(Sitting.)* What a beautiful table—and your "special occasion" china. *(Quickly remembering.)* How was your trip to Alabama?

SISSIE: Poor Uncle Willard has completely recovered and Aunt Martha—well, Aunt Martha being Aunt Martha was Aunt Martha. One lump or two?

MINNIE: Fake sugar, I'm afraid.

SISSIE: Of what?

MINNIE: Just one of those casual sayings.

SISSIE: *Ahh. (Holding a small sandwich.)* Chicken Liver?

SISSIE: Yes. With watercress.

MINNIE: Nice.

SISSIE: This one is egg salad.

MINNIE: Yes, I see it is. *(An uncomfortable pause.)* I really need to talk to you about something.

SISSIE: Of course, Minnie. What is it?

MINNIE: You remember what I told you before you took the bus to Huntsville—before your uncle had his heart attack?

SISSIE: Last time you'll catch me on a bus.

MINNIE: Well . . . you do remember what I told you?

SISSIE: I'm not sure, Minnie.

MINNIE: You know—about Moe? You couldn't have forgotten already.

SISSIE: Moe? Moe Beach—the plumber?

MINNIE: Yes.

SISSIE: I seem to recall something. What was it again?

MINNIE: About our, you know—Moe and me? For God's sake, Sissie, we *did it.*

SISSIE: Did what?

MINNIE: *It.* You know what *it* is.

SISSIE: Indeed I do.

MINNIE: Several times.

SISSIE: He hardly seems worth several times—once, maybe twice in a wanton moment. Do you think that was wise?

MINNIE: It's a little late for that, isn't it? Anyway, you may have heard that Moe is deceased.

SISSIE: Danny may have called me in Alabama to share the news. In your husband's office, wasn't it? How sad it must be for you—and Doctor Swisher, of course.

MINNIE: He didn't do it.

SISSIE: Never thought he did.

MINNIE: Moe barged into the office, knocked my husband unconscious and then proceeded to go through his drawers until he found the gun he keeps in case of an emergency.

SISSIE: Like a riot or something?

MINNIE: It's possible.

SISSIE: Moe Beach being Moe Beach leaves nothing unexpected—not even suicide, does he? It all makes perfectly good sense to me. Besides, if there weren't something unusual about him in the first place, he wouldn't have been seeing a psychiatrist, would he?

MINNIE: A good observation. I never thought of that.

SISSIE: That's why I'm here—to help my friends. It's my nature.

MINNIE: He must have been insane to begin with.

SISSIE: Not a totally unfounded assumption.

MINNIE: However, the thing is—because of Moe and me—

SISSIE: Don't explain. My lips are sealed.

MINNIE: It wouldn't help my husband's case—it might look like he was defending my honor.

SISSIE: Like your honor needed defending.

MINNIE: Thank you. You know what I think?

SISSIE: I wouldn't presume.

MINNIE: I think Moe was distraught over my telling him I didn't want to see him anymore.

SISSIE: So he shot himself with Doctor Swisher's gun.

MINNIE: Yes. Poetic, isn't it?

SISSIE: More Dorothy Parker than Walt Whitman, I would say. Did he ever finish working on your plumbing?

MINNIE: Yes, thank God—that's why I didn't want to see him anymore.

SISSIE: Great reasoning. It'll all work out for the best. Isn't that how the cliché goes? Let's get our minds away from such dreary thinking. Did you notice anything unusual?

MINNIE: *(Looking around.)* No. Everything appears to be the same, Sissie.

SISSIE: Look down—on the table.

MINNIE: *(Looking down.)* I see your "special occasion" china.

SISSIE: For the love of God, Minnie, look at the tablecloth.

MINNIE: *(Moving plates around to examine the tablecloth.)* That's interesting. What is it?

SISSIE: A rubbing of Tallulah Bankhead's grave stone.

MINNIE: You're kidding?

SISSIE: While in Huntsville, I went over to Tallulah Bankhead's grave and did a rubbing.

MINNIE: Tallulah Bankhead? I've heard the name. She was an actress, wasn't she?   In fact, I seem to remember hearing something about her being a tramp—more a slut, actually.

SISSIE: She was far from being a tramp or a slut!   Were you there?

MINNIE: No, of course not.

SISSIE: Then you shouldn't spread undocumented rumors.

MINNIE: I'm sure there are no documents that say Tallulah Bankhead was a slut.

SISSIE: There you have it. She was a great movie star. More famous than—oh, I don't know . . . Lady Gaga.

MINNIE: Lady Gaga's a singer.

SISSIE: *Whatever.*

MINNIE: *(Looking closely at tablecloth. Reading.)* Tallulah Brockman Bankhead. You have the same name.

SISSIE: The Brockmans are *Cause Celebes* in Alabama.

MINNIE: *Cause Celebes, huh?* I didn't know that.

SISSIE: I only mention it because it is a fact. Personally, I've never let it go to my head—that goes against my nature, as it were.

MINNIE: *(Sweetly, coyly.)* You are truly self-focused.

SISSIE: I suppose I am. We are very closely related, you know.

MINNIE: Really?

SISSIE: Oh, yes—once removed . . . on my father's side, of course.

MINNIE: Of course.

SISSIE: I share her love for Noel Coward—what a man he was. I share her love for drama, for theatre, for literature, for life, for—

MINNIE: For literature? How would you know that?

SISSIE: She was Noel Coward's best friend, wasn't she? And, Noel Coward being who he was, is world renowned for his literature. I share so many things that are Tallulah. Tallulah being Tallulah is much the same as me being me being Tallulah. I'm— what do the Italians call it? *Simpatico!* Cousin Tallulah and I are *simpatico.* After all, we do share the same blood, do we not?
MINNIE: Yes, once removed.   There's a lot of shared blood when you're only once removed.
SISSIE: There you have it. After our little tea I'm taking it to Honey Aldridge to be framed.

MINNIE: She's blind as a bat, you know.

SISSIE: Yes, but she owes me a favor and free of charge being free of charge, seems a fair price.

MINNIE: I can see that. Be careful going past Doctor Hall's.

SISSIE: Thank you for the warning. If anything were to happen to it—well, I shan't allow myself to think about it.

MINNIE: Then, you shouldn't. But why on Earth are you using it as a tablecloth?

SISSIE: It seemed a casual statement at the time.

MINNIE: A little too casual, if you ask me. *(She places her cup in the saucer in the manner of one who has decided, out of fear, not to touch another thing on the table.)* Where will you be hanging it?

SISSIE: I thought it might be a nice gesture if I allowed the Art Society to hang it in their little gallery.

MINNIE: That's—nice.

SISSIE: Me being me, I cannot fight the desire to share a good thing with others. It displays a kind of grandness befitting a close relative of Tallulah, wouldn't you agree?

MINNIE: I must agree with that.

SISSIE: A good example, don't you think?

MINNIE: Exemplary.

SISSIE: Darling, you're not drinking your tea. And, there are all those wonderful little sandwiches.

MINNIE: They do invite, don't they?

SISSIE: They scream to be eaten.

MINNIE: We can't have that. *(She reaches for a sandwich, knocks over her cup, spilling tea over the charcoal rubbing. In her rush to clean it she destroys the rubbing and knocks a teacup to the floor—breaking it.)* Oh my God! How clumsy can I get? These fingers sometimes—they fumble so. Can you ever forgive me? *(Picks up pieces of broken cup.)*

SISSIE: How stupid, stupid, stupid, stupid . . . *of me.*

MINNIE: I can't tell you how much—

SISSIE: No, it was my fault. *Mea culpa.* It was very stupid of me to use the rubbing for a tablecloth. I just wanted to make some sort of a casual statement.

MINNIE: You did, Sissie. It was a very grand statement . . . and casual.

SISSIE: I shouldn't want you to feel badly. Besides, I will rub another when poor Uncle Willard has his next heart attack. My only regret is that I will have nothing to lend the Art Society. Do be careful with that cup—I shouldn't want you to cut yourself and bleed all over those lovely gloves.

MINNIE: *(Getting up from picking up the pieces.)* I am so sorry, Sissie. Are these cups open stock?

SISSIE: I'm afraid not—*discontinued.*

MINNIE: I'd better go before I destroy something else.

SISSIE: Think nothing of it. I'll just sit here and assess the damage. I'm sure the front door is still unlocked. By the way, when is the good doctor's trial?

MINNIE: No date is set yet.

SISSIE: You let me know because I want to be there for moral support.

MINNIE: Thank you. I'm sure it will be appreciated.

SISSIE: It just worries me.

MINNIE: Of course, it must.

SISSIE: I pray to Heaven that my better nature will allow me to stay mum.

MINNIE: *(Sitting.)* *Mum?* What kind of mum?

SISSIE: Nothing really. It's just that if someone in authority should ask me if I had any information to add—well, me being me, I must confess that I have never lied before.

MINNIE: Nobody is going to ask you anything. I only mentioned it because it would be best for all concerned if you did not offer such personal information.

SISSIE: Not information that would help your husband's current predicament, I'm sure.

MINNIE: What exactly are you telling me?

SISSIE: Nothing. Don't worry. Everything will work out for the best, as it should. Forget I ever mentioned anything. *(Holding up pot of tea.)* *Tea?*

MINNIE: Yes. And a sandwich if you don't mind—chopped liver.

SISSIE: Of course. *(Pouring tea.)* You know me, *(Handing SISSIE a sandwich.)* forgive and forget.

MINNIE: *(Casually.)* I came across something very curious while you were bussing off to Alabama.

SISSIE: Do tell.

MINNIE: While doing my everyday routine duties, I ran across something very disturbing while doing my research over at the Historical Society.

SISSIE: *Oh?*

MINNIE: We've been best friends for how long, Sissie?

SISSIE: Ever since Danny and I moved here from up north.

MINNIE: Then it could not have been you and Danny.

SISSIE: Danny and I?

MINNIE: Because this was concerning two women who live, or lived in the south.

SISSIE: North. We're from the north.

MINNIE: What a coincidence. Would you believe that there is another Agnes "Sissie" Brockman and another Danielle "Danny" Coon, two women and "longtime companions" living down south?

SISSIE: We never lived a mile south of here—except, of course, when I was a little girl growing up in Alabama. Coincidences happen everyday.

MINNIE: To make the coincidence yet more intriguing, Danny was also a high school athletic coach. That stretches the imagination, doesn't it? May I please try the egg salad—and I wouldn't mind a bit more tea.

SISSIE: Certainly. Have you ever heard of *doppelgängers?*

MINNIE: *(Munching sandwich.)* I'm not sure.

SISSIE: They say we all have a double somewhere on Earth— each and every single one of us.

MINNIE: That's probably it. The odd thing is—

SISSIE: Isn't it odd enough?

MINNIE: The down south Brockman was released from prison for manslaughter in a bar brawl, shortly before you came to town.

SISSIE: Makes one think, doesn't it?

MINNIE: There was, as I recall, some accusations—unsubstantiated I must add—concerning Coach Coon's relationship with a member of the girls' basketball team.

SISSIE: Shocking!

MINNIE: We'll just chalk it up to the mysterious—like Ripley's Believe It Or Not.

SISSIE: When did you say your husband's trial was?

MINNIE: I didn't. It hasn't been determined yet.

SISSIE: I'm really worried about my Aunt Martha. She was looking rather pale last I saw her. I really should go and stay with her until I'm sure she's in the pink.

MINNIE: When would you do that, Sissie?

SISSIE: I really cannot say. I only hope it is not during your husband's trial.

MINNIE: Let us hope not, but if it should work out that way, you can be sure we'll be secure in the knowledge of your best wishes.

SISSIE: True. Very true.

MINNIE: Oh, dear. Look at the time. *(Rises.)* I really must be off, Sissie.

SISSIE: *(Rises.)* You take care and do give my best to your husband. And about the rubbing—don't give it another thought.

MINNIE: Still there's that teacup.

SISSIE: It's just a teacup. I've never really put much stock into material possessions.   Me being me has always worked to elevate my higher nature.

MINNIE: I can see that.

SISSIE: I shall miss you while I'm gone.

MINNIE: And I you.

SISSIE: There's no telling how long I'll be in Huntsville. I can make all the rubbings I want.

MINNIE: You're such a treasure. *(She hugs SISSIE.)*

SISSIE: *(Hugging back.)*   And so are you, sweetie.   It's not everyday two friends understand each other so completely. Thank God for friends like you.

(They continue to embrace as the LIGHTING FADES to BLACK OUT.)

ACT ONE —Scene Two

The Sullied Robe

AT RISE: The setting is JUDGE RUDOLPH BLEEKER'S chambers. It is early morning and BLEEKER is seated at his desk frantically trying to rub a spot from his robe. There is an array of cleaning supplies cluttering his desk. Throughout the course of the play he angrily struggles to remove that stain. There is a chair nearby. After awhile HARLEY BEAN, Esq. enters carrying a briefcase.

NARRATOR: The understanding that Sissie and Minnie have come to agree upon is the glue sealing their friendship. Proof positive of the closeness of enemies. The fate of Minnie and her husband, Doctor Peter Swisher, is in the hands of Harley Bean, their attorney, and Judge Rudolph Bleeker. This could or could not be a good thing. Blind justice may hold her scales with fairness and compassion to all as she balances truths and facts, but sometimes those dispensing justice have their fingers on her scales. Guilt or innocence can also be decided by malicious caprice.

BLEEKER: So?

BEAN: So?

BLEEKER: Sit.

BEAN: *(Sitting.)* I'm sitting.

BLEEKER: I see. And, on today's docket?

BEAN: The People versus Peter Swisher.

BLEEKER: Doctor Swisher?

BEAN: Psychiatrist.

BLEEKER: Charge?

BEAN: Murder.

BLEEKER: Did he do it?

BEAN: Some say he did, Your Honor. Some say he didn't. He, of course, agrees with the latter. The prosecution will speak to the former.

BLEEKER: Of course. And, the victim?

BEAN: Moe Beach. Naturally, he has nothing to say for himself.

BLEEKER: Naturally. That wouldn't be the plumber Moe Beach, would it?

BEAN: That's the one. You've used him?

BLEEKER: When Rosy clogged the toilet.

BEAN: Oh?

BLEEKER: Too much exotic cuisine.

BEAN: I see.

BLEEKER: She spells it with Y, you know.

BEAN: What?

BLEEKER: Her name—Rosy.

BEAN: Yes, some do and some don't.

BLEEKER: She does—but most aren't so militant about it.

BEAN: Militant?

BLEEKER: Nearly killed an auto mechanic when he called her Rosy with an I-E.

BEAN: Called her? You mean he only spoke her name?

BLEEKER: That's what he did, all right.

BEAN: He didn't write it for her to see?

BLEEKER: Didn't need to. She can hear the difference.

BEAN: Between I-E and Y?

BLEEKER: Every time.

BEAN: Astounding.

BLEEKER: *Eerie.*

BEAN: *Wives.* Who can figure?

BLEEKER: Yours?

BEAN: Carlotta?

BLEEKER: Do you have another?

BEAN: No, just the one—Carlotta. She recently assumed the position of head of our local Art Society.

BLEEKER: Nice assumption.

BEAN: Bossy bitch! I'm thinking of killing her.

BLEEKER: How?

BEAN: I haven't decided yet. Something painful, I imagine.

BLEEKER: That's always a nice touch. It helps them understand the unfortunate choices they have made. Just make sure you do it in my jurisdiction.

BEAN: Of course. I wouldn't want anyone other than you as the presiding judge.

BLEEKER: *Slam-dunk.* Kill the bitch.

BEAN: Maybe for her birthday.

BLEEKER: Won't that be a surprise. *(Pause.)* What do you know about removing stains?

BEAN: What kind of stains?

BLEEKER: Don't know.

BEAN: What did you have for breakfast?

BLEEKER: Don't remember.

BEAN: Maybe the stain will remind you. Take it off.

BLEEKER: I'm trying to take it off.

BEAN: I mean the robe.

BLEEKER: You know as well as I that I'm naked as a jay bird under this robe.

BEAN: Ever wonder what that means?

BLEEKER: What what means?

BEAN: "Naked as a jay bird."

BLEEKER: They're naked, aren't they?   Well—except for the feathers.

BEAN: Why not naked as a goose—or, naked as a vulture, or a cockatoo?

BLEEKER: Cockatoo doesn't seem . . . *seemly,* does it?

BEAN: I suppose not. I know it gives you pleasure.

BLEEKER: What?

BEAN: Being naked as a jay bird.

BLEEKER: More than you know.

BEAN: You can take it off. I won't look.

BLEEKER: I'd rather leave it on. Bloated. Not a good day.

BEAN: In that case—

BLEEKER: Another time, maybe.

BEAN: I can wait. It may need dry cleaning.

BLEEKER: *What?*

BEAN: Your robe. *(Picking up a bottle from desktop.)* Try this. *(Reading from bottle label.) Dry cleaning without the expense of dry cleaning.*

BLEEKER: Already did. It doesn't work and I can't take the bench like this.

BEAN: Nobody will see it.

BLEEKER: I will.

BEAN: Don't look down.

BLEEKER: I'll know. It's been sullied. I can't pass judgment in a sullied robe.

BEAN: Of course you can. *(Picks up another bottle.)* This is interesting. *Endless Wind—the dirtier you are the cleaner you smell.*

BLEEKER: Ah, yes, a recent investment. It's a man's cologne and woman's perfume in one.

BEAN: It looks like a powder.

BLEEKER: Exactly. *(Raises his arm to show BEAN his armpit.)* Come here?

BEAN: Sir?

BLEEKER: Smell my armpit.

BEAN: But . . .

BLEEKER: *Now.*

BEAN: Yes, Your Honor. *(Rises to sniff BLEEKER'S armpit.)* *Wow.* You smell divine. *(Buries his nose in BLEEKER'S armpit.)*

BLEEKER: *(Pushing BEAN away.)*   Thank you, Bean.   I'm going to make a fortune on this—*a gazillion.*

BEAN: What exacting is it?

BLEEKER: Living microbes. You lightly dust them under your arms and in all your private places. As they eat the germs and bacteria on your body they put out a sweet floral gas.

BEAN: Are you telling me that what I'm smelling are microbe farts?

BLEEKER: Well, if you have to put it that way—yes, I suppose I am.

BEAN: Nice. Very nice, Your Honor. May I take another sniff?

BLEEKER: *Certainly not.* Now, if only I could get this spot out.

BEAN: *(Picking up another bottle.)* How about this? *(Reading label.)* Oh, wait. This is for cleaning guns.

BLEEKER: *(Reaching for it.)* I was looking for that.

BEAN: *(Hands BLEEKER the gun cleaner.)* I didn't know you had a gun.

BLEEKER: It's the only way I can keep my wife out of my bedroom.

BEAN: With a gun?

BLEEKER: It works. Don't question it.

BEAN: Carlotta and I have talked about separate rooms.

BLEEKER: Stop talking and do it. Sex is better with separate rooms.

BEAN: Really? How?

BLEEKER: We don't have any.

BEAN: How is that better?

BLEEKER: Is that rhetorical?

BEAN: Not by intention.

BLEEKER: *(Opens another bottle and begins to use it on the stain. After a pause.)* So, what do you say?

BEAN: About what?

BLEEKER: The value of a plumber's life.

BEAN: Oh, I don't know. I suppose that depends on how good a plumber one is.

BLEEKER: He wasn't much of a plumber—this Moe Beach. He had to use a ten-foot electric vibrating snake to penetrate my wife's stools.

BEAN: Good god! But, how was that his fault?

BLEEKER: It wasn't. The fault was in telling Rosy she took the biggest dump he had ever seen in twenty years of plumbing. That accolade didn't set well—even with her uncompromising competitive spirit. *(Throwing down his cleaning rag.)* This crap doesn't work either!

BEAN: Excuse me?

BLEEKER: Nothing works on this stain.   My robe is sullied, Bean.

BEAN: Wear another.

BLEEKER: They're all sullied.

BEAN: Odd.

BLEEKER: Indeed.

BEAN: You'll need to take them to the cleaners.

BLEEKER: One day I will, perhaps.   So, what is the value of a doctor's life?

BEAN: He's a psychiatrist.

BLEEKER: He loses points for that.

BEAN: I'd say they're pretty much even, what with Moe insulting your wife's bowel movement. Where should we start?

BLEEKER: Let's give them ten points each.   Where does that put us?
BEAN: I'd say we deduct two each.

BLEEKER: Okay.   That takes them down to eight points each. What do you know about Doctor Swisher's wife?

BEAN: I've heard she has a history.

BLEEKER: That will lose the good doctor a point. He's down to seven. And, Missus Beach?

BEAN: Missus Beach keeps to herself mostly.   If she has a history, nobody knows it—or, perhaps she's adept at revisionism.

BLEEKER: Oh, I like that. That's one point for the victim. What do we have?

BEAN: Swisher, seven points. The victim, nine points.

BLEEKER: It's not looking good for the defendant. Especially since I can see the value of Rosy seeing him.

BEAN: Missus Bleeker needs a psychiatrist?

BLEEKER: I think so.

BEAN: In that case I think we ought to give a point to Swisher.

BLEEKER: Good. Doctor Swisher eight and Moe Beach nine. *Damn this spot! Out, out, out!*

BEAN: *(Handing BLEEKER another bottle.)* Try this.

BLEEKER: *(Reading.) Do not use in an enclosed space.*

BEAN: I wouldn't worry about that. They're probably just being over-cautious. You know, like *cigarettes may be damaging to your health.*

BLEEKER: So, what exactly happened to the victim?
BEAN: Swisher says Moe burst into his office, rushed over to his desk and pulled a gun from out the top drawer and shot himself.

BLEEKER: What was the doctor doing with a gun in his desk?

BEAN: I asked him that too. He told me there were too many crazies going in and out of his office.

BLEEKER: Good answer—though it is the nature of the business, isn't it? Let's give him another point. What have we got?

BEAN: Nine to nine.

BLEEKER: *Wait.*

BEAN: What?

BLEEKER: If the patient shot himself, the doctor couldn't have been doing too good a job curing him. Deduct two points.

BEAN: Fair enough.

BLEEKER: What does the prosecution say?

BEAN: Swisher cold-bloodedly shot Moe as part of his therapy.

BLEEKER: He sounds *perfect* for my little Rosy.   That's two points for the good doctor. What's the tally?

BEAN: Nine each.

BLEEKER: This is going to be a tough one, Bean.

BEAN: *(Rises.)*   Your Honor—good people of the jury, Doctor Peter Swisher has been an active member of our community, a model citizen and a generous contributor to the political machine of our community.

BLEEKER: Try *generous contributor to our political landscape.* "Machine" sounds cold and calculating, don't you think?

BEAN: Okay—a model citizen and a generous contributor to our political landscape. Much better, very humanizing.

BLEEKER: What if the plumber should accumulate more points?

BEAN: Your Honor—ladies and gentlemen of the jury, Peter Swisher may not have been all things to everyone in our community. But, he is a good man. He may have contributed to a political party many of you may not agree with—but he deserves as fair a hearing as we would give the lowliest vagrant squatting in the restrooms of our local bus station. But, he is still a human being, isn't he? *(A beat.)* Your Honor, you're rubbing—

BLEEKER: I beg your pardon?

BEAN: You're rubbing a hole in your robe.

BLEEKER: *Oh*—so I am. Mustn't do that. Wouldn't want anybody to see what's not underneath.

BEAN: Why don't you try a little *Endless Wind* on that stain?

BLEEKER: You think?

BEAN: It might.

BLEEKER: *(Putting some on the stain.)* We'll see.

BEAN: It's gone, Your Honor!

BLEEKER: I see that it is, but I'm feeling all tingly. I feel wonderful.

BEAN: I've never smelled anyone so heavenly.

BLEEKER: Now you have.

BEAN: May I? Just one more sniff?

BLEEKER: *No.*   And now I'm ready to take the bench.   Nine each, *huh?*

BEAN: Yes. It's a tie.

BLEEKER: Got a coin?

BEAN: *(Reaching into pocket.)*   A dime.   *(Hands it to BLEEKER.)*

BLEEKER: Call it.

BEAN. Tails.

(As LIGHTING dims, BLEEKER tosses the dime into the air.)

NARRATOR: Imagine, your fate could be decided by the toss of a coin. And you'd never really know, would you?

BLACK OUT.

6 FULL-LENGTH PLAYS   Edward Crosby Wells
VOLUME TWO

ACT ONE—Scene Three

The Dumplings

AT RISE: The setting is a living room with no set other than a couple comfy chairs and a table with a telephone and a stack of empty bowls that once held spaghetti. Seated are SID and SYLVIA DUMPLING. A conversation is in progress.

NARRATOR: In another part of town thoughts are on fine dining. Sid and Sylvia Dumpling, an unassuming suburban couple whom neighbors would say are likable and friendly, take their food very seriously. Some might say too seriously. *Haute Cuisine* plays a disproportionate role in their lives as they go on a quest for that ultimate gastronomical ecstasy. Very few appreciate the subtleties of the palate as much as Sid and Sylvia Dumpling.

SYLVIA: *(Eating a bowl of pasta, which she does throughout the play, even during her dialogue.)* About the chef—

(SID puts down the newspaper that had been hiding his face. There is spaghetti hanging from a corner of his mouth. He too eats a bowl of pasta throughout the play. BOTH often sip wine. At the moment, SYLVIA gives SID a scrutinizing glance then taps the side of her mouth. It takes him a while to "get it" before he wipes the dangling spaghetti away.)

SID: *(Cleaning his mouth with a napkin.)* In the kitchen?

SILVIA: In the cellar.

SID: *Oh, him.*

SILVIA: Pierre.

SID: *(Mimicking a highbrow gesture and tone.) Chef Pierre.*

SILVIA: Told you.

SID: You told me nothing. After the fact you told me . . . and you told me, and you told me again.

SILVIA: I knew before we chained him to the—

SID: Why didn't you tell me then?

SYLVIA: You never listen.

SID: *(Shrugs.)* So you knew, so what?

SILVIA: Told you.

SID: *(Resigned.)* I know.

SYLVIA: Got to think of something.

SID: We will.

SYLVIA: When?

SID: When we do.

SYLVIA: He'll starve to death.

SID: His choice.

SYLVIA: He's very proud. You know the French.

SID: See where it got him.

SYLVIA: We can't just let him go. He'll head right to the police.

SID: We could put him in a box—

SYLVIA: What kind of box?

SID: Wooden, I suspect. Ship him somewhere.

SYLVIA: China. He'll never find his way home.

SID: Maybe. Maybe not. Where in China?

SYLVIA: Where the crispy duck comes from.

SID: Beijing.

SYLVIA: Peking.

SID: Beijing, Sylvia—Beijing.

SYLVIA: I never heard of Beijing duck—Peking.

SID: Peking has been renamed and is now Beijing, but I'm sure the duck is just as crispy.

SYLVIA: Whatever. I wonder if Lydia makes Peking . . . I mean, Beijing? *(Calling to kitchen.)* Lydia? *(A mumbling comes from the kitchen.)* You haven't taken that tape off have you? *(More mumbling from behind duct tape.)* Good, good. You know what will happen to you if you take the tape off. *(Mumbling.)* Good, good. You don't happen to make Beijing duck, do you? *(More mumbling.)* Thought not. *(Turns to SID.)* Italians. All they know how to cook is Italian. Who eats Italian seven days a week?

SID: Italians?

SYLVIA: Lucky guess. *(Banging the floor with her shoe.)* Hey you! *(Mumbling comes from the basement.)* You don't cook

Chinese, do you? *(Mumbling.)* Beijing duck? *(More mumbling.)* No, Beijing. There is no more Peking. Don't you know anything? I'm beginning to think you're a phony. *(More mumbling. To SID.)* The French—who can understand a word they say?

SID: The French.

SYLVIA: They're *too* French, if you ask me.

SID: What do you expect?

SYLVIA: Nice sauces 'though. They do make nice sauces.

SID: Very nice.

SYLVIA: Have you finished thinking about it?

SID: *It?*

SYLVIA: Chef Pierre.

SID: Oh, him. We could eat him.

SYLVIA: *Sidney Dumpling!* He's a human being. He comes from France, not the stockyard.

SID: They eat snails—who eats snails?

SYLVIA: Somebody who was starving, I imagine. And then convinced somebody else they were the posh thing to eat.

SID: You are what you eat, I always say.

SYLVIA: *Ewww.* Then I certainly wouldn't eat him.

SID: For Pete's sake, Sylvia. I wasn't serious.

SYLVIA: Thank heavens.

SID: What do you take me for?

SYLVIA: *(After a pause to stare at him.)* Well, what are we going to do with him? *(Banging on floor.)* Hey you! What are we going to do with you? *(Mumbling from below.)* How does China sound? *(Mumbling.)* How about we eat you? *(She giggles. She waits but there is only SILENCE.)* Hello? Hello down there. *(Pause.)* The French—who can figure.

SID: I told you a long time ago it was a bad idea.

SYLVIA: *Pish-posh.* I don't remember your saying a thing.

SID: You never listen.

SYLVIA: I most certainly do. *(A pause.)* What exactly are you saying, Sid?

SID: You're always making me do things. Do this, do that—

SYLVIA: You're going to give me a sick headache.

SID: I thought it was a bad idea to kidnap the chef.

SYLVIA: I distinctly remember you saying that you'd kill to have Chef Pierre cook for you. Didn't you? Did I take offense? Wasn't my cooking good enough for you?

SID: Of course your cooking was good enough for—I didn't mean to be taken literally.

SYLVIA: Well, you were. *(Banging floor.)* Hey, you! *(Mumbling from basement.)* How would you like to go to China? You could learn to cook Chinese. *(Mumbling.)* Don't get huffy with me. I'm only trying to expand your horizons. *(To SID.) Ingrate.*

SID: That's the French for you. Just as well, if you ask me. Postage would cost a fortune. Besides, eventually he'd make his way back here and then where would we be?

SYLVIA: Let's not think about it. I hate thinking about things. It gives me a sick headache.

SID: Par for the course.

SYLVIA: What is that supposed to mean?

SID: Nothing.

SYLVIA: Don't give me a sick headache.

SID: Mustn't do that.

SYLVIA: Don't you love me, my little apple dumpling?

SID: *(Having trouble saying it.)* Of course I love you, my little squash blossom. But, we're in a fine mess and it's your fault.

SYLVIA: Lydia's in the kitchen cooking up a storm. I see you don't mind eating all her goodies.

SID: Waste not, want not.

SYLVIA: Besides, I think she likes it.

SID: How could anybody like being chained to the water pipe?

SYLVIA: There are people into that sort of thing. I'm told there are people who love being chained—handcuffs, whips. They do it all the time.

SID: I never knew that.

SYLVIA: Now you do. *(Yells to kitchen.)* Lydia, don't you love cooking for us? *(Mumbling.)* No, we are not going to kill you. Honestly, who do you think we are? *(To SID.)* We're not going to kill her—are we?

SID: We've got to do something.

SYLVIA: Why does everybody make the worse of what I say?

SID: I don't know.

SYLVIA: I'm a good person, aren't I?

SID: A regular Mother Theresa.

SYLVIA: I'm not torturing anybody, am I?

SID: Not Lydia—'though most people don't much care for being in chains.

SYLVIA: A minor inconvenience. *(A beat.)* We might make her an offer she can't refuse. The Italians understand that sort of thing.

SID: What kind of offer?

SYLVIA: I'll have to think about it.

SID: Careful. I wouldn't want you to get a sick headache.

SYLVIA: I'll think about it in small doses. All I know is when you say, "I'll make you an offer you can't refuse," Italians seem to have a sixth sense for what that means.

SID: What *does* it mean?

SYLVIA: Something scary, I believe. I seem to remember that it involves the head of a horse.

SID: You think she'll go for it?

SYLVIA: Watch this. *(Crosses to kitchen.)* Lydia. *(Mumbling.)* Would you run away if you had half a chance? *(Mumbling.)* All right—if you had a whole chance? *(Mumbling.)* Don't make fun of me, Lydia. I'm dead serious. *(Mumbling.)* That's not the answer I wanted to hear. Suppose I made you an offer you couldn't refuse? *(Mumbling.)* Now, that's more like it. *(Crossing back to chair. To SID.)* You see? Didn't I tell you? *Didn't I?*

SID: Yes, Sylvia, you told me.

SYLVIA: I don't like that tone. You're really giving me a sick headache.

SID: Sorry.

SYLVIA: Don't be sorry. Just do better.

SID: Yes, dear. Why don't you give Doctor Hall a call before your headache sets in?

SYLVIA: I don't need a doctor. I need quiet understanding.

SID: Yes, dear.

SYLVIA: You're right on the edge, Sid—right on the edge. You know how I am when I get a sick headache.

SID: You turn into someone who's not you.

SYLVIA: You better believe it.

SID: I do. I certainly do. The last time you had a sick headache you nearly gutted me with a boning knife. Doctor Hall had to give me thirty-nine stitches.

SYLVIA: You exaggerate. Besides, that wasn't me.

SID: It sure looked like you.

SYLVIA: Well, it wasn't!

SID: Okay, it wasn't.

SYLVIA: It was an inner urge. It only looked like me on the surface. So don't make me have a sick headache.

SID: I'll do my best, dear. But, we do need to deal with the chef in the basement.

SYLVIA: Maybe we won't have to do anything. He seems determined to starve himself to death. We should stay the course and let Nature take her course. *(A beat.)* I wish we had gotten a German. We could get the house cleaned in the bargain. Spic and span! You know how *they* are.

SID: We'd need a longer chain.

SYLVIA: Just a thought. Besides, I don't think that television food show has any German cooks.

SID: Too many sausages.

SYLVIA: Just a thought.

SID: Besides we are not kidnapping another chef.

SYLVIA: I said it was just a thought.

SID: Would you like me to tell you what *I* think?

SYLVIA: Sidney, I'm in no mood to be bored.

SID: I won't bore you this time. I promise.

SYLVIA: Well, if you must, you must.

SID: We've got to let them go.

SYLVIA: Are you crazy? What kind of a stupid thought is that?

SID: It's for the best.

SYLVIA: Not for our best! You're giving me a sick headache. *(She jumps up and runs around the room like a wild woman.)* *Ow, ow, ow!* Now you did it. *Ow, ow, ow!*

SID: Sylvia, get hold of yourself. I think we ought to call the police and turn ourselves in.

SYLVIA: *Ow, ow, ow! (She goes behind his chair and picks up the telephone. After a pause.)* Okay—I'm beginning to see the wisdom of your ways.

SID: That's a new one.

SYLVIA: *(In pain.) Ow, ow, ow!* I'll call them right now.

SID: Good idea.

SYLVIA: *Ow, ow, ow! (Banging on the floor.) Hey, Frenchy!* You want to go home? (Mumbling.) Just what I thought. I have such a headache.

SID: Try taking something—an aspirin, maybe. *(Sotto voce.)* *Rat poison.*

SYLVIA: What did you say?

SID: Nothing, dear.

SYLVIA: They don't come any dumber than you, do they?

SID: Is that rhetorical?

SYLVIA: You know what I think?

SID: There you go thinking again.

SYLVIA: I have been struck by inspiration. I have the perfect
idea.

SID: What's that, dear?

*(SYLVIA suddenly wraps the phone cord around his neck. A very
animated struggle ensues. In the end she manages to strangle
him to death.)*

SYLVIA: Lydia! *(Mumbling.)* Stop whatever you are doing.
We're changing the menu. *(Mumbling from kitchen. She dials
the phone. Into phone.)* Rosy, is that you? Are you sure this is
Rosy with a Y? Good, good. You didn't sound like yourself. I
don't know, dear. Somebody other than you—a Greek or a
Puerto Rican, maybe. You know how fast they talk. What's that,
dear? *(Glances toward SID.)* He's good. How is His Honor? I'm
sorry. Tell him I hope he recovers soon. So, what are you doing
tonight? *Wonderful.* Why don't you tuck Judge Bleeker in and
pop on over for dinner? Good, good. How's six for cocktails?
What's that, dear? *French.* We're having French. *(Looking at
SID.) Provincial.*

*(As she hangs up the phone the LIGHTING fades to BLACK
OUT.)*

6 FULL-LENGTH PLAYS
VOLUME TWO

ACT ONE— Scene Three

The Dumplings

AT RISE: MILLIE is standing at a butcher's block. HANK is sitting and watching television.

NARRATOR: So much for *haute cuisine*. If our last tale was to your taste, we have another little gastronomical delight for your dining pleasure. This time it is served up by Hank and Millie Slaughter.

MILLIE: *(Raising high a meat cleaver over a quartered chicken.) I hate him. (The thwack of the cleaver separates a leg from a thigh.)* I wanted eighths not quarters. I hate him!

HANK: *(Looking up.)* Who?

MILLIE: You know who.

HANK: How should I know who? Put that down.

MILLIE: From what I've been telling you. Makes you nervous, does it? *(Lays cleaver on butcher's block.)*

HANK: The last I heard was, "the butcher put his thumb on the scale."

MILLIE: He didn't put his thumb on the scale. It fell onto the chicken while he was quartering it and then he put it on the scale without quartering it again. Why can't people follow directions?

HANK: Some can.

MILLIE: Why is it always about you? Anyway, there lay the bloody thumb.

HANK: You're making this up.

MILLIE: Why would I make up a thing like that?

HANK: Didn't he feel it—scream and carry on?

MILLIE: Everyone isn't you, Hank. Stop trying to make this all about you! He felt nothing. He looked at it laying between the breast and the hindquarter and he said nothing—like it happens everyday. Though if it did he would have run out of thumbs by now.

HANK: I should think so.

MILLIE: You should indeed. I'm not paying for that chicken, says I. Once I cut it, Missus Slaughter, you own it, says he. So I says, you got to be kidding? And he says, I just cut off my thumb with a meat cleaver—do I look like I'm kidding? Have you done it before, says I? Nope, first time, says he. It was then —that moment—I decided to hate him.

HANK: Decided?

MILLIE: I chose.

HANK: You could have chosen otherwise.

MILLIE: I could have, but I didn't.

HANK: Why?

MILLIE: His attitude.

HANK: But the poor man just chopped his thumb off.

MILLIE: I don't care if he beheaded himself.

HANK: Not very likely.

MILLIE: It's a figure of speech.

HANK: *Yeah.* Go figure.

MILLIE: I was talking about the weight of his thumb, fat galoot that he is. That thumb must have weighed a quarter pound. Big as a Whooper, it was.

HANK: Surely you exaggerate.

MILLIE: *Whatever.* But given the price of meat nowadays—

HANK: Well? What happened?

MILLIE: What happened with what?

HANK: His thumb.

MILLIE: It's still there. Nearly wrapped it in with the chicken until I had to ask him to remove it. I don't know how to cook thumb.

HANK: I don't imagine.

MILLIE: You should. That's your problem. You damn well should imagine. I've never seen thumb on the menu. I really hate that man.

HANK: Because you chose.

MILLIE: Because I can.

HANK: Why?

MILLIE: You're repeating yourself. There's blood all over our chicken. I washed it real good, but I keep detecting a slight tinge of red and whiff of blood.

HANK: *(Looking towards the butcher block. Horrified.)* That's the same chicken? You brought the chicken home?

MILLIE: I certainly did.

HANK: And that's the same chicken?

MILLIE: You really should stop repeating yourself. Of course. Tonight is chicken night.

HANK: I'd be happy with meatloaf.

MILLIE: For Heaven's sake, Hank! Tuesday is meatloaf. Tonight is chicken.

HANK: We could change every so often. Maybe give up chicken altogether.

MILLIE: Nobody's gonna give up chicken! You're gonna eat it and like it.
HANK: Still, I don't think I'll be able to eat it knowing what I know.

MILLIE: What do you know, Hank?

HANK: What you told me.

MILLIE: What a dummy!

HANK: That's not very nice.

MILLIE: You are. You really, really are.

HANK: Why? Why am I a dummy?

MILLIE: You're predisposed to it.

HANK: *Bull.*

MILLIE: You only know what I tell you.

HANK: In that case, I may well be a dummy.

MILLIE: Don't get smart with me, Mister.

HANK: I think I'll pass on chicken tonight.

MILLIE: No substitutions!

HANK: Fine with me.

MILLIE: You'll go to bed hungry.

HANK: Won't be the first time.

MILLIE: What is that supposed to mean?

HANK: Nothing.

MILLIE: Nothing is right. You're just a big dumb nothing. You don't know anything except what I tell you.

HANK: Then there wasn't a thumb?

MILLIE: Of course there was a thumb—big as a tuba. Do you think I could stand here and tell you I hate the butcher if there wasn't a thumb? I don't hate that easily. I always lean toward love. It's a slight, but discernible inclination.

HANK: *(Sotto voce.)* Could have fooled me.

MILLIE: What did you say?

HANK: Yes, dear—like the Tower of Pisa.

MILLIE: You got that right. That's what I thought you said.

HANK: Couldn't we go out to dinner?

MILLIE: We could.

HANK: *Great.*

MILLIE: Hold on. I didn't say we would. I said, we could.
There's a chicken on the cutting board and it's not going to
waste.

HANK: We could give it to some needy family.

MILLIE: We are some needy family.

HANK: Maybe a family more needy.

MILLIE: I'll wash it in mouthwash. Will that make you happy?

HANK: Mouthwash?

MILLIE: Yeah, mouthwash—*gargle, gargle.*

HANK: Wouldn't that taste terrible?

MILLIE: How would I know?   I never ate chicken in
mouthwash.

HANK: I think I'll have a peanut butter sandwich.

MILLIE: No substitutions!

HANK: Does it have to be mouthwash?

MILLIE: I could use rubbing alcohol.   You know what your problem is?

HANK: No. What's my problem, Millie?

MILLIE: You have no sense of adventure.

HANK: You almost brought a man's thumb home!   That's adventure enough for the both of us.

MILLIE: Always glued to that television. That's as close as you ever get to an adventure.

HANK: I agree with you. No argument from me.

MILLIE: Well, pass the ammunition.

HANK: What does that mean?

MILLIE: Does it matter?

HANK: I suppose not.

MILLIE: What are you watching?

HANK: Martha Stuart.

MILLIE: I knew it was something felonious.

HANK: Today's show is about untraceable poisons for a perfect garden.

MILLIE: I'm not much into horticulture.

HANK: You should be. There are so many ways to eliminate bothersome creatures. For instance, when a leech grabs hold and sucks the life right out—you need to know the best poison to take care of the problem.

MILLIE: There are no leeches in our garden—*how disgusting.*

HANK: And there's nothing disgusting about dismembered thumbs?

MILLIE: It's more understandable than garden sucking leeches.

HANK: I see. You wanna hear something about thumbs?

MILLIE: From you? I'm sure it'll be a kicker.

HANK: It will be. I'm tired of your thumb. *No.* I'm sick of it! *(Jumping up!)*

MILLIE: *What?*

HANK: You've kept me under your thumb since the day we met.

MILLIE: Don't be ridiculous.

HANK: You're the one who's ridiculous. Give me your thumb.

MILLIE: What?

HANK: *(Goes to butcher's block and retrieves the cleaver.)* Give me your thumb.

MILLIE: Why?

HANK: I'm going to chop it off—be free of you.

MILLIE: Don't be stupid.

HANK: Stupid? It's the smartest move I'll ever make.

MILLIE: Well, you can't have my thumb. Get somebody else's.

HANK: I want yours.

MILLIE: *(Begins backing away.)* You're beginning to scare me.

HANK: *(Moving in.)* There's a switch.

MILLIE: Back off, Mister!

HANK: I don't think so.

MILLIE: All right. You've made your point. We don't need to have chicken. A meatloaf sounds pretty good right now.

HANK: Forget about it.

MILLIE: Anything you want, dear.

HANK: *(Raises cleaver.)* I want to be out from under your thumb. Give me your hand.
MILLIE: You can't have it.

HANK: *Now.*

MILLIE: How about deli? We could send out for deli.

HANK: I've lost my appetite.

MILLIE: I'll cook whatever you like. *Anything.* Tell me what you want.

HANK: You've had your pound of flesh! *(Grabs her hand and pins it to the butcher's block.)*

MILLIE: Pork? Lamb? How about lasagna? We could send out for pizza—

HANK: *(Raises high the cleaver.)* I want out from under your thumb!

(Quick BLACK OUT. The SOUND of the thwack of the cleaver.)

MILLIE: *Ouch.*

END ACT ONE

ACT TWO—Scene One

The Session

AT RISE: The setting is the psychiatric office of DOCTOR PETER SWISHER where a conversation with MOE BEACH is in progress.

NARRATOR: The friendship between Sissie Brockman and Minnie Swisher is well intact. All those lethal obstacles threatening to undermine their solid relationship have been carefully maneuvered into safe waters. Judge Bleeker and Harvey Bean have already decided the fate of Doctor Swisher. Justice, as it were, has been dispensed prior to the fact. Sylvia Dumpling has strangled her husband, Sid, in a moment of uncompromising values prior to sitting down to dine on an exotic French meal with her best friend Rosy, Judge Bleeker's wife. Since the doctors grafted Millie Slaughter's thumb back on she's been the perfect wife. From a casual glance, all is well in darkest suburbia. As for the facts surrounding the death of Moe Beach— judge for yourselves.

MOE: A voice from within—but I don't remember.

DOCTOR: *(Writing on yellow pad.)* You don't remember the voice—

MOE: What the voice said.

DOCTOR: Of course.

MOE: But it said something.

DOCTOR: They usually do.

MOE: I think it was trying to give me advice.

DOCTOR: They usually are. What kind of advice?

MOE: I don't remember. Seemed relevant then—*real.*

DOCTOR: And now?

MOE: I'm not sure.

DOCTOR: Sure?

MOE: It was real.

DOCTOR: *Ah. (Smiles.)*

MOE: But it seemed relevant.

DOCTOR: Of course. *(Throws pencil on the floor.)* Pick that up.

MOE: Excuse me.

DOCTOR: For what?

MOE: I don't think I heard you correctly.

DOCTOR: Of course you did. *(A pause.)* These sessions are expensive, Mister Beach. Stop wasting our time.

MOE: *(Crosses to pick up pencil.)* It looked like you threw it.

DOCTOR: I didn't throw it.

MOE: *(Retrieves the pencil and returns with it.) Here.*

DOCTOR: Now, where were we?

MOE: I don't remember.

DOCTOR: Correct. You don't remember, but I do. You hear voices.

MOE: Just one voice.

DOCTOR: Are you certain that it was only one?

MOE: Isn't that enough?

DOCTOR: Why do you ask?

MOE: It seems like it ought to be.

DOCTOR: Ought to be?

MOE: Enough to make one wonder.

DOCTOR: One shouldn't—

MOE: *Wonder?*

DOCTOR: I should think not.

MOE: So you agree—

DOCTOR: Of course not.

MOE: It seemed so important.

DOCTOR: So did my wife's webbed fingers.

MOE: Mrs. Swisher has webbed fingers?

DOCTOR: You didn't know?

MOE: How would I know a thing like that?

DOCTOR: Of course, you wouldn't. That's why she wears gloves year 'round.

MOE: I thought she was just being fashionable.

DOCTOR: Let's not change the subject. Tell me more about the voice, what it said.

MOE: What it said?

DOCTOR: That's the question. You said you don't remember what—

MOE: *It said.* I know. I just can't remember.

DOCTOR: So you said.

MOE: What do you suppose it means, Doctor Swisher?

DOCTOR: I'd have to hear it first.

MOE: Yes. *(A pause. Makes an eerie high-pitched sound.)* *Eeeeee-ahhhhh-ipper, ipper, yahhhhh-ooooh*—it sounded something like that.

DOCTOR: *Hmm,* then I don't believe it actually said anything.

MOE: It made perfect sense to me, at the time.

DOCTOR: So did intelligent design until I took a good look at most of my patients.

MOE: I sometimes feel—

DOCTOR: You *say* you feel—

MOE: Sometimes—

DOCTOR: You feel. *(A pause. Sighs.)* Is this one of those times?

MOE: Yes.

DOCTOR: And, what is it you feel?

MOE: I don't know to say.

DOCTOR: But, you know you're feeling something. Is that correct?

MOE: Yes. Once you're no longer there it's gone—you forget.

DOCTOR: What?

MOE: *There.* I forget there.

DOCTOR: *There*— Where is "there?"

MOE: Where I am no longer—where I do not remember.

DOCTOR: What do you think that means?

MOE: I don't know.

DOCTOR: You seem to know little to nothing.

MOE: Yes.

DOCTOR: There you have it! You don't know. *That's* your problem. *(Throws yellow pad on floor.)* There's a strong wind blowing. Pick that up.

MOE: There's no wind. We're inside. *(Moves to pick up pad.)*

DOCTOR: There is always a wind—moves right through you.

MOE: I don't feel it.

DOCTOR: *I know. (Snatches pad from PATIENT. A beat.)* Where were we?

MOE: You were telling me what my problem was.

DOCTOR: And what is that?

MOE: I don't know.

DOCTOR: Exactly.

MOE: What about the voice?

DOCTOR: What about it?

MOE: I can't put my finger on it.

DOCTOR: Nobody can.

MOE: Really?

DOCTOR: Who can put a finger on—

MOE: A voice?

DOCTOR: In your head.

MOE: It's quite familiar.

DOCTOR: That can be annoying—*eeeee-eeeee-ya-ya-yo-yo*—

MOE: It was more like—

DOCTOR: I don't care! Why have you been sneaking about with my wife?

MOE: I haven't been sneaking about with your wife.

DOCTOR: Somebody has.

MOE: Not me. I was only at your house to fix your plumbing.

DOCTOR: Don't change the subject. We're talking about your voices.

MOE: Voice—just one voice.

DOCTOR: Whatever.

MOE: After it's been in your head awhile you can't tell if you recognize it as something from reality—

DOCTOR: Reality?

MOE: What we agreed upon.

DOCTOR: We agreed upon reality?

MOE: Didn't we?

DOCTOR: You tell me.

MOE: A long time ago.

DOCTOR: You and I?

MOE: All of us. We decided to call it a rock and the rock became real.

DOCTOR: Rocks are real.

MOE: Yes, because we all recognize them.

DOCTOR: Rocks?

MOE: *As* rocks.

DOCTOR: How's that?

MOE: From the beginning we are taught.

DOCTOR: Rocks?

MOE: Reality.

DOCTOR: So, are saying that rocks are real because we recognize them? Aren't they real without us?

MOE: Are they?

DOCTOR: You tell me.

MOE: I think they are. I seem to remember they are. But, the voice—

DOCTOR: Is real?

MOE: Maybe. Or, something I only imagined.

DOCTOR: I see. We are all in agreement when it comes to rocks being real. However, a question remains when it comes to a voice you may or may not have heard in your head—especially one that sounds like a pig call.

MOE: Yes. Although we haven't agreed upon the voice yet.

DOCTOR: Do you think we ever will?

MOE: It's possible.

DOCTOR: And when we do—

MOE: It becomes real. DOCTOR: Voices or rocks?

MOE: The voice. Just one voice.

DOCTOR: In your head?

MOE: That's where my ears are.

DOCTOR: Most people have ears attached to their heads.

MOE: Naturally.

DOCTOR: But yours are *in* your head.

MOE: That's where I hear.

DOCTOR: *Eeeeyayayoyoscubbydubbydoo—*

MOE: And other things.

DOCTOR: Ghosts? Satan? God?

MOE: Doorbells. Phones. Horns.

DOCTOR: You hear doorbells?

MOE: The chimes—the ringing. I've heard the ringing—never the doorbell itself.

DOCTOR: Often?

MOE: Sometimes.

DOCTOR: In your head.

MOE: Through my ears.

DOCTOR: Relax. Imagine a quiet meadow—rolling hills of green—

MOE: Can't.

DOCTOR: *Won't.*

MOE: It's not my kind of place.

DOCTOR: And, what is your kind of place?

MOE: I generally know when I'm there but when I leave I don't know anymore. I forget. However, I always know when it isn't.

DOCTOR: Imagine that.

MOE: That's hard to imagine, but when it isn't, I know it isn't, you know?

DOCTOR: Do I?

MOE: You must.

DOCTOR: Or you'll do something felonious like you did to my wife?

MOE: I don't know what you're talking about. I barely know your wife.

DOCTOR: Barely.

MOE: Hardly at all.

DOCTOR: Hardly—

MOE: At all.

DOCTOR: You know she has webbed fingers.

MOE: Only because you told me.

DOCTOR: You know she's never seen in public without gloves.

MOE: Everybody knows that.

DOCTOR: Who's *everybody?*

MOE: Everybody who knows her. We thought it was just your wife's style.

DOCTOR: Minnie certainly has style. Suppose you tell me how you know my wife.

MOE: I wouldn't know how—

DOCTOR: To say?

MOE: Wouldn't know where—

DOCTOR: To begin?

MOE: She's a friend of my wife's.

DOCTOR: Don't change the subject.

MOE: Sometimes, I really don't feel—

DOCTOR: You only feel sometimes. You don't know what you think and you don't know whose gibberish is jabbering in your head. Reality requires majority approval. You hear the ringing but not the bell. You only know where you are when you are no longer there. You only know what is when it isn't and you claim not to have had carnal knowledge of my wife. Next you will be telling us you don't know why you are here.

MOE: Isn't that what you are supposed to tell *me?* I thought you already knew—

DOCTOR: *Surprise.* I am not here to know. I am here to assist you with exploring your problems.

MOE: My problems—

DOCTOR: You weren't expecting a euphemism, were you?

MOE: No.

DOCTOR: I find it best to treat the patient with a hard dose of reality.

MOE: I appreciate your directness.

DOCTOR: Then we agree.

MOE: Agree?

DOCTOR: On reality. It goes right to the heart of the matter.

MOE: I see your point.

DOCTOR: Do you?

MOE: I think so—I guess.

DOCTOR: Spoken with certitude.

MOE: Perhaps something less than that.

DOCTOR: Not so sure?

MOE: I don't think so—it moves so quickly it becomes a blur. I can't see it anymore.

DOCTOR: It?

MOE: *The train. The thought. The thread.*

DOCTOR: And with it your vision—

MOE: Yes.

DOCTOR: Yes—

MOE: Is my time up?

DOCTOR: When I say it is. *(A beat.)* Get on the floor.

MOE: What?

DOCTOR: Lick my boots.

MOE: Is this part of the therapy?

DOCTOR: *Down.*

MOE: *(On the floor.)* I can't see what—

DOCTOR: Lick!

MOE: I don't know—

DOCTOR: Let's see some tongue-action, boy!

MOE: *(Licks boots.) Why?*

DOCTOR: Get up.

MOE: I was only getting started. *(Getting up.)* I didn't mind—
really.

DOCTOR: Really?

MOE: Not at all. I've often thought of—

DOCTOR: Licking my boots?

MOE: Not *your* boots necessarily. Boots in general.

DOCTOR: You would lick just anybody's boots?

MOE: Absolutely not—not just anybody's boots, sir.

DOCTOR: Then whose, boy?

MOE: Certainly not just anybody's, sir.

DOCTOR: Did you lick my wife's boots?

MOE: I certainly did not! *(A pause.)* Does your wife wear boots?

DOCTOR: Don't change the subject. Take this.

MOE: What is it?

DOCTOR: A pill. And, don't ask for what.

MOE: Why?

DOCTOR: Take it.

MOE: I need something to wash it down.

DOCTOR: Spittle.

MOE: I don't think—

DOCTOR: Swallow. *(MOE does.)* Good. Now tell me why you are here.

MOE: The voice—

DOCTOR: Go on.

MOE: At night, when I'm walking down Main Street—

DOCTOR: At night?

MOE: Coming home from work.

DOCTOR: I see.

MOE: Outside the super market.

DOCTOR: I've gotten your point.

MOE: I hear the voice most everywhere.

DOCTOR: *Eeeeee-ahhhhh-ipper, ipper, yahhhhh-ooooh.*

MOE: That's it! That's exactly how it sounds. How did you ever? That's amazing.

DOCTOR: Can you see who it is?

MOE: Who what is?

DOCTOR: Speaking.

MOE: Now? No.

DOCTOR: *Then! Then, you idiot!*

MOE: It was just a disembodied voice. More like sound and light —kind of weird. *(A beat.)* I don't think a doctor should call his patient an idiot.

DOCTOR: I don't think a patient should secretly meet with his doctor's wife.

MOE: That's not true!

DOCTOR: Stop trying to change the subject. Was the voice male or female?

MOE: Does it matter?

DOCTOR: What do you think?

MOE: I don't think it matters.

DOCTOR: Are you bisexual?

MOE: Absolutely not.

DOCTOR: Are you sure?

MOE: I would know a thing like that, wouldn't I?

DOCTOR: One would think. Do you suppose my wife knows your sexual preference?

MOE: Doctor Swisher, I told you that I am not having an affair with your wife.

DOCTOR: Mr. Beach, did I ever mention "*affair?*"

MOE: You insinuated—

DOCTOR: I'm merely trying to establish the gender of the voice and which gender it is that holds more of an attraction to you.

MOE: It wasn't sexual—the voice.

DOCTOR: Would it matter if it were?

MOE: If it *were*—it might matter. I might respond differently.

DOCTOR: To the voice—

MOE: Yes. *(A beat.)* Isn't my time up yet?

DOCTOR: Did I say it was?

MOE: No. I was only thinking—

DOCTOR: Stop thinking. When your time is up you will know.

MOE: You will tell—

DOCTOR: It will be obvious.

MOE: You're not going to charge me—

DOCTOR: Extra?

MOE: Yes.

DOCTOR: You're thinking. I told you to stop thinking.

MOE: I can't help it.

DOCTOR: Draw!

MOE: What?

DOCTOR: Your gun—

MOE: I don't have a gun.

DOCTOR: *(Shoots PATIENT with imaginary gun.) Bang! You're dead!*

MOE: I get it. *(Does likewise.)* Bang—you're dead too.

DOCTOR: No I'm not.

MOE: Of course not.

DOCTOR: You're imagining things—*again.*

MOE: But you—

DOCTOR: *I?*

MOE: Pulled a gun—

DOCTOR: A finger.

MOE: Yes. Of course.

DOCTOR: Are you sure?

MOE: Of?

DOCTOR: The difference.

MOE: Of course.

DOCTOR: Good for you. I could have pulled a rock—or a stiffy.

MOE: That would be nonsense.

DOCTOR: Really?

MOE: I think so, yes.

DOCTOR: I told you to stop thinking.

MOE: Sorry.

DOCTOR: *Now—*

MOE: Now?

DOCTOR: The session is over.

MOE: So soon?

DOCTOR: We're finished.

MOE: Am I better?

DOCTOR: Than what?

MOE: Than before?

DOCTOR: You tell me. *(Pointing finger as a pretend gun.) Bang, bang!*

MOE: You're doing it again.

DOCTOR: Doing it?

MOE: Pretending your finger is a gun.

DOCTOR: Then you know the difference?

MOE: Naturally. Is this part of the therapy?

DOCTOR: Do you want it to be?

MOE: *(Shrugs.)* Sure. Why not? *(Points finger as a pretend gun.)* Bang, bang! You're dead!

DOCTOR: No, I'm not.

MOE: Of course not. It's just a game. It's not real.

DOCTOR: *(Pulls out a real gun.)* What about this? Is this real?

MOE: Good grief! That's a gun!

DOCTOR: Are you sure?

MOE: Of course I'm sure.

DOCTOR: It could be a rock—or the wife's vagina.

MOE: It could be but it happens to be a gun.

DOCTOR: Then we agree that it's real.

MOE: Yes, it's real. But, I wish you'd put it—

DOCTOR: Away?

MOE: Yes.

DOCTOR: Did you put it away with my wife?

MOE: I don't know what you're talking about.

(DOCTOR pulls the trigger and MOE falls to the floor.)

DOCTOR: Now it's away.

MOE: You shot me.

DOCTOR: Yes I did.

MOE: You shot me for real.

DOCTOR: Wise *and* correct—two admirable attributes.

MOE: *Why?*

DOCTOR: They just are. You don't think so?

MOE: It doesn't matter at this point.

DOCTOR: I suppose you're right.

MOE: Why did you shoot me?

DOCTOR: It's part of the therapy.

MOE: Shooting your patients is part of the therapy?

DOCTOR: It works, doesn't it?

MOE: No. It doesn't work. I'm dying.

DOCTOR: That's what you are supposed to do.

MOE: But I'm dying. I'm dying for real.

DOCTOR: That's good.

MOE: *Good?* What's good about getting shot and dying?

DOCTOR: It goes to show.

MOE: *(Gasping.)* Show me what?

DOCTOR: You've always known the truth.

MOE: *Truth?*

DOCTOR: What's real.   What's not.   The consequences of adultery.

MOE: I'm going to die.

DOCTOR: Of course you are.

MOE: I don't want—

DOCTOR: Who does?

MOE: This is it, isn't it?

DOCTOR: Yes. The session is over. You may leave now.

MOE: I won't pay for this session. *(Gasps and dies.)*

DOCTOR: Nobody ever does. *Eeeeee-ahhhhh-ipper, ipper, yahhhhh-ooooh—*

(LIGHTING slowly dims to BLACK OUT.)

ACT TWO—Scene Two

The Hanging Judges

AT RISE: The setting is an art gallery. The fourth wall is hung with unseen paintings being judged by CARLOTTA BEAN, HONEY ALDRIDGE and DOCTOR HALL. They are bunched at far left or far right stage—the idea is to have them move their way across the stage to the opposite side by the end of the play.

NARRATOR: Despite all the facts in the case, the jury will decide for themselves the predetermined guilt or innocence of Doctor Swisher. Somebody once said that art is the food of the soul.   In suburbia the Art Society provides the soul with more than enough nourishment. There are painting classes year-round, holiday crafts classes, painting classes, Christmas gift wrapping classes and much more—all provided by the local Art Society. Their premier event is the annual art contest.   Entries pour in every year from the far corners of suburbia, but only the best of the best are hung for all to see and to satisfy their hunger as souls are fed with much needed sustenance.

CARLOTTA: *(Facing the audience.)* We ought to start somewhere and it might as well be here.

HONEY: Where is here, Carlotta?

HALL: *(Rather fey. Holding a clipboard.)* Here is right where you are, Honey. Right in front of you. Step forward, my dear. *Careful* —don't walk into the wall.

HONEY: *(She walks into the wall, bounces off, then sticks her nose against the painting. After a pause.)* Oh yes. One can nearly smell the texture.

CARLOTTA: I bet one can.

HALL: What is your verdict, Honey? Is it a nay, or is it a yea?

HONEY: I don't much care for storms or seascapes. Never have. This one has both storm *and* seascape. A bit of a mish mash, if you ask me.

HALL: Do we have a nay?

HONEY: Well—all the colors seem to look like real colors. The blues are blue, the yellow is yellow—but, I don't think that's enough to give it a yea. It's a bit small for a seascape *and* a storm. One or the other would have sufficed. Besides, it should be wider than it is tall.

CARLOTTA: For pity's sake, would you please give Doctor Swisher's lively rendition a yea or a nay?

HONEY: Doctor Swisher? I wouldn't give that quack the time of day. *Nay.* A definite nay.

HALL: That's one nay for the quack. *(Putting a check mark on the clipboard.)*

CARLOTTA: Let me have a look. *(A pause. Impatient.)* Honey.

HONEY: What?

CARLOTTA: Move on to the next painting please. The good doctor and I need to judge this one.

(HONEY moves on to the next painting, pressing her nose against it as she does with all that follow.)

HALL: I must contemplate this one.

CARLOTTA: Contemplate away. *(Bobbing up and down, she adjusts herself so that her eyes are level with the painting.)*

HALL: *(Watching her. After a pause.)* How shall I say?

CARLOTTA: How shall you say what, Doctor Hall?

HALL: I was just wondering—why are you bobbing up and down like that?

CARLOTTA: It requires my eyes to be level with the painting. I know of no other way to fairly judge the worth of art—especially when done by my psychiatrist.

HONEY: You go to a psychiatrist?

CARLOTTA: Just for the Prozac, Honey.

HALL: He did murder one of his patients, didn't he?

CARLOTTA: Some say he did and some say he didn't. I just don't know what to say. Besides, as you all perfectly know, my husband is his attorney.

HONEY: I don't much care for the quack, but in all fairness, one should give him the benefit of the doubt, shouldn't we?

CARLOTTA: That would be the proper thing to do, wouldn't it?

HONEY: I heard it was suicide. Moe Beach walked into Doctor Swisher's office and then Moe shot himself dead. Poor Mrs. Beach—she'll surely miss him.

CARLOTTA: I imagine.

HALL: Carlotta, is it a yea or a nay?

CARLOTTA: Don't rush me—like you do all your patients. I've decided to do the right thing and wait until the trial and then we shall see what we shall see.

HONEY: I think that's best, Carlotta.

CARLOTTA: However, with his attorney being my husband, I'm expecting a positive result.
HALL: What about the painting? Surely we won't have to wait until the trial to get a yea or a nay on the painting.

CARLOTTA: Give me time. I'm teetering on the brink of a decision. I need to get close to it. *(She moves forward.)*

HALL: I always stand at a respectable distance. *(Moves upstage.)* See? This . . . oh, how shall I say? This is the proper way to view a work of art.

HONEY: Art and I need to be quite close.

CARLOTTA: You really ought to have those cataracts attended to.

HONEY: I like to see the stroking.

HALL: The stroking?

HONEY: The way the brush makes its way across the canvas.

HALL: I thought . . . oh, how shall I say? I thought you meant—

CARLOTTA: I'm sure you did. Your mind is *"oh, how shall I say,"* subterranean.

HALL: That's hardly polite, especially for a woman in your condition.

CARLOTTA: In my condition?

HALL: The results are in on your yeast infection—

CARLOTTA: *(Quickly changing the subject.)* Honey, this appears to be a rendering of Gainsborough's Blue Boy.

HONEY: Are you sure it's not brown and yellow clouds over a raging blue sea?

CARLOTTA: Certain.

HALL: He looks like a big blue *poof* to me.

CARLOTTA: Everybody looks like a *poof* to you.

HALL: I meant the original. This one looks like a Smurf.

HONEY: *(Giggles.)* You're so funny, Doctor Hall. You always make me laugh.

HALL: Thank you, Honey. They say that laughter is the best medicine.

CARLOTTA: For what?

HALL: For dreary occasions and unsatisfied conclusions, Carlotta. I say nay.

CARLOTTA: That's one nay for Doctor Hall and one nay for Honey Aldridge. Therefore, since we won't be hanging poor Doctor Swisher's little masterpiece, I'll have to say yea. He would die of a broken heart if he ever found out that his favorite patient didn't fight the tides of his misfortune and vote yea. Besides, I'm almost out of Prozac. I don't know what I'll do if he gets the electric chair.

HALL: *(To CARLOTTA.)* Are you sure there's not . . . how shall I say—a bit of Hieronymus Bosch lurking behind that Rubenesque exterior?

CARLOTTA: *(Ignoring the last. Moving to next painting.)* Have you made a decision on this one, Honey?

HONEY: Oh, my god! That's frightening. I'm afraid it's a nay.

CARLOTTA: I certainly agree. We are all well into the twenty-first century—most of us, anyway—and there is no longer any point to bloody pointillism. And, I do mean bloody.

HALL: I quite agree. That's three nays for Sylvia Dumpling's *Pork Chops in Handcuffs with a Hatchet in a Side Dish.* Let's move on, ladies. I'm becoming nauseous *(ALL quickly move on.)*

CARLOTTA: What have we here? *Pigs in a Blanket* by Heinz Fleishmann. Oh, our butcher. Not bad for someone without an opposable thumb.

HALL: Yes, it's a shame about his thumb. I could have reattached it if he hadn't dropped it in the meat grinder.

HONEY: It ended up in my meatloaf. His thumbnail—I thought it was a piece of onion, at first.

CARLOTTA: How tragic for you, dear.

HALL: I reattached Millie Slaughter's, you know.

CARLOTTA: Even with an opposable thumb she can't paint. I sent it back. We couldn't have it hanging in our little gallery. So what do you think of Fleishmann's *Pigs in a Blanket?*

HONEY: Yea.

HALL: Yea.

CARLOTTA: That's three yeas. Move along, Honey. You're in the middle of the road.

HONEY: Sorry.

(ALL move to the next painting.)

HALL: Let's see. This one is titled *Portrait of Picasso's Portrait of Gertrude Stein as Done by Jackson Pollack* by Danny Coon. Dear me, how shall I say?

CARLOTTA: Say *nay, nay, nay.* Gertrude Stein never had a mustache.

HONEY: How do you know, Carlotta?

CARLOTTA: Because if she did, Picasso would certainly have put one there.

HALL: She might have been a secret shaver.

CARLOTTA: Moving on. *(Moves to next painting.)* I will need to disqualify myself from this one.

HALL: What have we here? *A Night at the Acropolis* by Carlotta Bean. *Mon Dieu,* naked Greeks. Did you paint this from memory?

CARLOTTA: It's a metaphor—the unashamed freedom of the Greek psyche.

HONEY: Is that you, Carlotta?

CARLOTTA: Many *artistes* place themselves in their work.

HALL: But, pray tell, how did you manage to place yourself in that position?

CARLOTTA: It's called artistic license, Doctor Hall.

HALL: As a doctor, I must inform you that the human body cannot assume that position.

HONEY: Looks like an orgy to me.

CARLOTTA: Well, it's not! Is it yea or what?

HALL & HONEY: Yea.

CARLOTTA: It appears to be a tie. In that case, according to our bylaws I am required to break it—*yea.* Now it's unanimous. *Next. (At next painting.)* Oh my God! This looks like it was painted with a sponge mop.

HALL: We have here *Wall Surrounding The Virgin Mother Nunnery for Wayward Girls* by Honey Aldridge. That explains the penguin in the lower corner.

HONEY: She wandered into the picture.

CARLOTTA: It's not like a photograph, Honey. You didn't need to paint her in.

HONEY: I know, but she was there and then she wasn't there and I couldn't get her out of my mind.

CARLOTTA: I'm sure that makes perfect sense to you. It's a very large canvas, isn't it? It does crowd out the other paintings, doesn't it? How would you say, Doctor Hall?

HALL: Well, how shall I say? Large—quite large. Honey, what exactly *did* you paint this with?

HONEY: A sponge mop.

HALL & CARLOTTA: *Brava, brava.*

CARLOTTA: I'd say that's two yeas, wouldn't you, Doctor Hall.

HALL: Absolutely.

CARLOTTA: Then, two yeas it is.

HONEY: And I say yea.

CARLOTTA: You don't get to say yea, Carlotta.

HONEY: It was a tie, wasn't it?

CARLOTTA: Only the president of the Art Society gets to break a tie. Hal, I give the Virgin two yeas. Let us move on please. *(At next painting.)* What have we got here? *Taking Heart to Give a Heart* by Doctor Feh. *Feh, Feh?*— who's Feh? I don't know a Feh.

HALL: *Frederick Edward Hall.*

CARLOTTA: And a lovely painting it is. A bit heavy on the dripping blood. But, I like it—very medical.

HONEY: Is it going into the patient or coming out of the patient?

HALL: That's . . . how shall I say? A mystery. Something to tantalize the observer and leave them to arrive at their own conclusions. As an artist, I merely ask the questions.

CARLOTTA: And, such a profound question it is. I'm sure we all agree that it's a yea.

HALL: You humble me.

CARLOTTA: *(Watching HONEY who is already at the next painting.)* Honey, stop rubbing your nose all over the paintings.

(Handing HONEY a tissue.) Look at yourself. The paint wasn't dry on that one.

HONEY: *(Rubbing the paint from off her nose.)* So, that's why there are so many trails going through that woodland pastoral.

HALL: I think it is ruined, ladies.

CARLOTTA: Nonsense. Get me a brush, Honey. There's dozens in the framing room.

HONEY: *(Running to exit.)* I'm on it. *(Exits.)*

HALL: Yes, but what is she on? You know, Carlotta, you really shouldn't tamper with another person's art. It's . . . oh, how shall I say—

CARLOTTA: Can it, Hall!

HONEY: *(Enters with two brushes)* Soft or stiff?

HALL: *Stiff.*

CARLOTTA: Just hand me a brush. *(Grabs one from HONEY'S hand.)* Now, let's see. *(Applying the brush to the painting.)* Maybe if we extend this branch so that it covers—

HALL: I can't watch.

CARLOTTA: This tree seems to have a road going right through it. That'll never do.

(They ALL move in on the painting.)

HALL: I think that tree is *supposed* to have a road going through it.

CARLOTTA: Nonsense. *(Begins filling in the gap.)* There—look how much better that is—no more hole.

HONEY: Oh, thank you, Carlotta.

CARLOTTA: I'm not finished yet. There's still those trails going through the sky.

HONEY: They could be airplane trails.

HALL: Of course. Mucus-filled airplane trails. Just extend that cloud, Carlotta.

CARLOTTA: Like this? *(She paints.)*

HALL: Now see what you've done. It looks like a giant rabbit hopping over a redwood forest.

CARLOTTA: Quite surreal—reminiscent of Dali.

HALL: *(Grabbing the other brush from HONEY'S hand and begins painting along with CARLOTTA.)* You've got the bunny's feet caught in the branches. What's this?

CARLOTTA: A power line.

HALL: It used to be the horizon.

CARLOTTA: Now it's a power line.

HONEY: *(Stepping up to the painting. While the others brush away, she moves the paint around with her finger.)* Maybe we could get rid of the power lines by *(Finger painting.)* blending this into that.

HALL: You just blended that family of bears into the giant rabbit.

CARLOTTA: Oh, what the hell. If you ask me it's a much better painting.

HALL: It looks like . . . oh, how shall I say? It looks like a rabbit on an aquarium filled with brown and green fish swimming under a power line.

CARLOTTA: Give it a yea and let's move on.

HALL: *(Takes CARLOTTA'S brush and along with his own, attaches them to his clipboard.) Driving Through a Redwood* by Dottie Beach receives unanimous yeas. *(Making three check marks.)*

CARLOTTA: It's the least we can do for the poor grieving widow—considering what Honey did to it. Thank goodness we were able to salvage it.

HALL: I quite agree.

CARLOTTA: Honey, try and keep your nose off the paintings from now on. *(Handing HONEY a huge handful of tissues from out her jacket pocket, or elsewhere.)* Here, clean your hands.

HONEY: Sorry. *(Cleaning her hands.)*

CARLOTTA: *(At the next painting.)* What a beautiful frame.

HONEY: I framed that.

CARLOTTA: You did good, Honey. Hal, look at this frame. I say yea just because I like the way it's hung.

HALL: I can't argue with that.

HONEY: Does being hung well make it art?

HALL: One could argue that case.

CARLOTTA: You certainly could.

HALL: A definite yea.

HONEY: Another yea here

CARLOTTA: Moving on. *(ALL move on to the next painting which happens to be offstage.)* Shameful!

(The LIGHTING begins to FADE.)

CARLOTTA *(Con't.)*: That's not art—that's an insult to art lovers everywhere. If Minnie Swisher thinks we'll show sympathy just because she has webbed fingers and her husband may or may not be headed for the electric chair, she's got another think coming.

BLACK OUT.

ACT TWO—Scene Three

The Gazillion

AT RISE: The setting is a bare stage except for a row of seats in an airport. ROSY BLEEKER and SMITH are seated with a chair between them. They each have carry-on luggage.

NARRATOR: There seems to be a penchant for predetermined results in suburbia. The dilemma of what is worthy and best appears to be resolved by special interests and by the voice of persistence. Residents of suburbia love to travel. Leaving suburbia for short periods of time only serves to make home that much more attractive upon their return. Many spend the entire year planning those excursions that will net them souvenirs and photographs to share with family and friends throughout the following year. The most serious traveler of all must surely be Rosy Bleeker who, with style and flare, is about to fly to destinations unknown as she bids a fond farewell to suburbia before setting out to journey around the world.

ROSY: *(To SMITH.)* I'm Rosy with a Y. Everybody thinks it's I E, but it's not. It's Y. It is astonishingly difficult to tell one way from the other when one is speaking, of course. One can, however, when it is written—if it is legible. I get angry when somebody puts I E when it ought to be Y. *Why?* Because it is my name. I'm over-sensitive. It's a gift. I hear I E in the voice, in the way the second syllable is pronounced. *Rosy, Rosy, Rosy*—that's the sound of Y. *Rosie, Rosie, Rosie* has the definite ring of I E— and who are you?

SMITH: *(Reading newspaper. Uncomfortable.) Ah . . . Smith.*

ROSY: Good, good. Brevity and a real American name—solid, rock solid. Good for you. I'm all-American too as was my late husband the judge—that's rather *as is* my late husband, isn't it?

One only gets to be late once. He moved on. *Where?* I don't know where. How should I know where? *(Pointing upward.)* Somewhere up there, I suppose. Who knows? At least he had the good sense to know that someday he would actually transition. Some don't know that, you know. He did, however, and he enjoyed a sense for the depth of my grieving after his departure. He left me with a gazillion. Invested in a very expensive fragrance. Perhaps you've heard of it—*Endless Wind?*

SMITH: I do believe I have.

ROSY: It made a gazillion.

SMITH: *(Sudden interest. Stops reading newspaper.) A gazillion?*

ROSY: I Exaggerate. Enough to do what I've always wanted to do. He rarely spoke, you know. *Why?* More than likely he had little to say—at least to me. However, that's then and this is now and I'm ready to begin my great adventure.

SMITH: What might that be?

ROSY: No *might* about it. I'm going 'round the world, Smith—outward bound, alone and on my way. Have you ever been 'round the world?

SMITH: Can't say I have.

ROSY: I can't say I have either, but I will a year or so from now, from where it all began right here, right now.

SMITH: Have you ever considered investing some of your money?

ROSY: Maybe I have, but it is doubtful.

SMITH: I know of several sure-thing opportunities—

ROSY: Sure thing? How silly you are. I'd much rather prefer less "sure things." Those are the things that make life exciting. You would agree, of course. Where are you headed, Smith?

SMITH: Home.

ROSY: Is that euphemistic or metaphoric?

SMITH: I don't understand.

ROSY: Sorry. Is home where your heart is or is it where we're all headed—far, far away—when the mortal coil is shed, as it were?

SMITH: Jersey City.

ROSY: That really shouldn't be either one of those choices, should it? Of course it shouldn't but sometimes it is.

SMITH: You mentioned a gazillion.

ROSY: Give or take a few.

SMITH: Where do you . . . *ah* . . . keep it? Where is it invested, if you don't mind my asking?

ROSY: Of course I mind. It's in a safe place, Smith. *(A beat.)* Jersey City, *huh?*

SMITH: Have you ever been to Jersey City?

ROSY: If I had, I have the good fortune of having no memory of it—the more exotic local for Rosy. I'm a voluptuary, you know.

SMITH: That must take a lot of money. I'm sure I could be of great service to—

ROSY: Must it? Of great service? I might be interested. I'll let you know when I am—if I am.

SMITH: Perhaps, today?

ROSY: One should never say one way or the other, but I will keep you posted as time goes by.

SMITH: I am at your disposal.

ROSY: Yes, I can see that.

SMITH: I could double your money.

ROSY: Double it?

SMITH: Maybe triple it.

ROSY: You certainly are an extravagant talker. We'll see, Smith. Perhaps, if you could triple—

SMITH: Quadruple even—depending on how much you are willing to invest, of course.

ROSY: I'm thinking about gold.

SMITH: Not a good investment.

ROSY: See this pin? *(She moves into the middle chair, leans toward SMITH and shows him the pin on her breast.)* Can you read it?

SMITH: I can barely make it out.

ROSY: *(Grabs his head and pulls it towards the pin.)* How about now?

SMITH: "Rosy around the world." *(Pulling back.)*

ROSY: My best friend Sylvia Dumpling gave it to me. It's a going 'round the world gift. Solid gold, you know. Don't you love the color gold? That's rhetorical—everybody does.

SMITH: I could really help you with setting up a trust—

ROSY: I trust no one, Smith. *(She moves back into her seat.)* That's why it is carefully concealed.

SMITH: Concealed?

ROSY: *(Adjusting her breasts.)* Concealed.

SMITH: You mean?

ROSY: I do.

SMITH: How much?

ROSY: That's a bit personal, don't you think?

SMITH: But the x-ray—

ROSY: They match the pattern of my . . . *(She gives her breasts a boost upwards.)*.

SMITH: *Ah . . . I see.* Maybe you could make an exception in my case. I could invest as little as you like. Show you my worth, so to speak.

ROSY: I believe I already know your worth, Smith.

SMITH: I'm very trustworthy.

ROSY: Trust is the quickest way to misfortune, Smith. I've always found trust a disappointing virtue.

SMITH: Perhaps you could learn to trust me.

ROSY: The impossible happens everyday, Smith.

SMITH: I think I could relieve you of some worry.

ROSY: I am already certain of that.

SMITH: Get it off your chest, so to speak—your worry.

ROSY: I don't worry. I haven't the time to worry. I'm off on safari into Darkest Africa. Why do you suppose they call it Darkest, Smith?

SMITH: From how it looks under all those jungle trees.

ROSY: Is that your guess? If it is, I'm sure that's not it. It must be something else. There always is, you know—something else.

SMITH: The amount of sun it gets?

ROSY: I'm sure it gets the same sun as any other part of Africa. There must be something else—another meaning, I think. I'll come to it—you can be certain of that. *(Looking to the side.)* Is that a policeman?

SMITH: I believe it is.

(BOTH hide behind their newspapers.)

ROSY: *(After a pause.)* Is he gone?

SMITH: *(Looking out from over the paper)* I don't see him.

ROSY: But, is he gone?

SMITH: I suppose he is. There's something blue going down the moving sidewalk.

(BOTH lower their newspapers.)

ROSY: It's a little game I like to play.

SMITH: A game?

ROSY: Policeman peek-a-boo. Sylvia and I play it all the time. It helps pass the time. I see you play it too.

SMITH: Yes. Yes, I do.

ROSY: I didn't know it had reached Jersey City.

SMITH: A long time ago.

ROSY: I should have patented it, eh Smith?

SMITH: Things travel around the world. They take on a life of their own. Take you and your gazillion for instance. Know what I mean?

ROSY: I do indeed, Smith. The question remains—do you? Everything has many meanings, don't you think?

SMITH: I do.

ROSY: See how clever you are.

SMITH: Thank you. About your money—the gazillion—

ROSY: *(A sudden realization.) Oh, no!*

SMITH: I only meant that perhaps I could be of some service—

ROSY: *No, no, no.* Darkest Africa. I know it means.

SMITH: What does it mean?

ROSY: I can't say it. It has the potential of being politically incorrect. There are others listening.

SMITH: I don't see anybody listening.

ROSY: Is that a fact—what you do not see *isn't*?

SMITH: There's nobody within earshot.

ROSY: There could be listening devices. Security is extremely important nowadays. One never knows what foreign company could be managing this airport. They could be listening through hidden microphones in our chairs.

SMITH: I don't think so.

ROSY: There you go not thinking again. I think there could. We had best change the subject before they come and get us.
SMITH: Nobody's going to come and get us.

ROSY: You're just full of assertions, aren't you? Besides, after Darkest Africa I'm moving on to Casablanca. That means *white house,* you know. You *should* know. If you do not I certainly don't want to hear about it. There's nothing politically incorrect about a white house, is there?

SMITH: *Ah*—

ROSY: That's rhetorical. Besides, I'm getting tired of what you don't think. Nobody cares what anybody doesn't think.

SMITH: All that money—before or after taxes.

ROSY: That's a bit too familiar, don't you think?

SMITH: Forgive me. *(After an uncomfortable pause.)* So, now you're going 'round the world?

ROSY: Indeed I am. Have you got chewing gum in your ears? Everybody ought to go 'round the world at least once, but then everybody wasn't married to Rudolph. I wasn't married to Rudolph. Of course I was but we had separate rooms you know. *(A beat.)* I wonder what his room looked like? I never took as much as a peek—afraid I'd catch him doing something felonious.

SMITH: *Felonious?*

ROSY: Like peeking back. Oh, well—when I return home, it'll still be there—his late room. Neither euphemism nor metaphor there—this is home. Always has been. My heart is in suburbia. Never wanted to go anywhere unless it was 'round the world. Why do anything half posterior? Anybody can go from here to there. If you're going to go somewhere you ought to go all the way—'round the world. Do you believe in going all the way, Smith?

SMITH: I suppose.

ROSY: *Suppose?* You really ought to learn to think—at least learn to say yes or no a bit more often. Until you do you'll never go 'round the world, Smith.

SMITH: Maybe I don't want to go around the world. I'm a financial investment broker.

ROSY: Is that what you call it?

SMITH: Well—

ROSY: *Tut, tut, tut. Rhetorical again.* I'd be very uncomfortable wearing your shoes. I've walked in many a shoe—never yours. I would have remembered I can assure you of that—I never forget a thing. Is that euphemistic or metaphoric—to walk in ones shoes? Can you answer me that?

SMITH: I'm not sure.

ROSY: Give it the old college try.

SMITH: Euphemistic?

ROSY: *Wrong.* I should have said give it the old high school try. Do you have any money, Smith?

SMITH: Some.

ROSY: On you?

SMITH: Maybe.

ROSY: Either you do or you don't.

SMITH: A bit.

ROSY: How much?

SMITH: I'm not sure.

ROSY: Can't be much.

SMITH: It isn't.

ROSY: That doesn't speak well for your investment abilities. How do you expect me to put my trust into a pauper?

SMITH: I do better with other people's money.

ROSY: I'm sure you do.

SMITH: Does that mean you've decided to let me handle your fortune?

ROSY: We shall see what we shall see. *(A beat.)* I don't use a *(Covers her mouth)* gun *(Uncovers her mouth.)* you know.

SMITH: *(Defensively.) A gun?*

ROSY: It's not that kind of safari. *Cameras.*

SMITH: I didn't think—

ROSY: *Shhh*—nobody cares what you didn't think. We use cameras—like those up there. *(She points upwards.)* Whatever you say make your lips move like you're saying something else.

SMITH: Why?

ROSY: Because they could be reading lips. *(Covering her mouth.)* Guns *(Uncovering her mouth.)* could be an easy one to spot especially because they're looking for things like that. One must cover one's mouth when saying something provocative. Like this, *(She covers her mouth.)* guns, bombs, knives, machetes, con artists, jagged-toothed saws, blow-torches, ice picks and gold digging gigolos. *(Uncovers her mouth.)*

SMITH: I'll try and remember.
ROSY: Do that. I remember everything, as you already know. Besides, as I have already told you, it's not the kind of safari that uses *(Covers her mouth)* guns. *(Uncovers her mouth.)* I think *(Covers her mouth.)* guns *(Uncovers her mouth.)* should not to be in the hands of the general public. Rudolph believed otherwise, but look where it got him.

SMITH: Where did it get him?

ROSY: *(Covers her mouth.)* Dead. *(Uncovers her mouth.)* You really don't listen well, do you? Some kind of obstruction. Did you have a terrible childhood? Molested by the town idiot, I suspect. I sold all his stock in *Eternal Wind* the day after he died. And not a moment too soon.

SMITH: *Eternal Wind?* I've heard something else about it. A cologne or perfume isn't it? In fact, I think I heard there was some kind of scandal concerning it.

ROSY: You sure did. A week after I dumped the stock, a mysterious flesh-eating bacteria started eating all those who had worn it.

SMITH: You're joking, right?

ROSY: Wrong. Do I look like a woman who would joke about hundreds, maybe thousands of people being eaten alive—flesh oozing from off their bones?

SMITH: No, I guess not.

ROSY: Good guess. Anyway, to make a long story short, you couldn't squeeze a nickel out of Rudolph. I would have been lucky to get a new pair of panty hose while he was alive. His motto was, one must buy only what one needs—everything else is extraneous. That's why I told him it was a waste of money to buy that gun—who would burgle us? The living room only has two chairs and an orange crate.

SMITH: You don't really mean—

ROSY: Don't you tell me what I really mean, Smith. I told Rudolph over and over again that nobody's going to burgle us. This isn't New York City, is it? That's rhetorical. This is suburbia and nothing like that happens in suburbia. He was cleaning his gun and I forgot to tell him I filled it with bullets— *just in case.*

SMITH: *In case?*

ROSY: One never knows—even here in darkest suburbia. First time I ever forgot anything. *Odd, isn't it?* I'm not one to forget anything, am I? *(Glances down.)* Is it hard? It appears a bit stiff —you'll never be able to squeeze it in however hard you push. It's a bit large—too oversized. They'll never let you on the plane with that.

SMITH: You're making me blush.

ROSY: Surely you know that won't fit into the box.

SMITH: *Box?*

ROSY: The one that tells you what size is allowed. Luggage that large ought to have been checked in. I could be wrong— completely erroneous—although unlikely. Sometimes they let one break the rules and sometimes not. They're not consistent— just indiscriminate. Much like those who sometimes choose to end Rosy with an I E and only sometimes Y. Say Rosy.

SMITH: Excuse me—

ROSY: Not once have you said my name. Say Rosy.

SMITH: *(Hesitantly.)* Rosy.

ROSY: Thank you, Smith, you remembered. That was a definite Y. *(Panicked. Covers her mouth.)* That's not a policeman coming this way, is it?

(BOTH cover their faces with newspapers.)

SMITH: *(Carefully looks over the top. Squints. Relieved.)* That's just somebody in a cheap blue suit. *(Puts the newspaper away.)*

ROSY: *(Lowers her newspaper.)* Of course I wasn't worried. It could have been a policeman and I certainly would not have cared one way or the other—not in the least. It is not like I've got a *(Covering her mouth.)* bomb *(Uncovering her mouth.)* strapped around my waist, is it? Of course it isn't, Smith. Don't you just love policeman peek-a-boo?

SMITH: My favorite game.

ROSY: Play it often?

SMITH: Often enough.

ROSY: Now, all there is to do is wait. Soon it begins.

SMITH: *Begins?*

ROSY: My adventure into the unknown. Haven't you been listening? *(She moves into the seat next to SMITH, grabs his head with both hands and shoves his face into her breasts.)* Here, read the pin.

SMITH: *(Struggling. Gasping for air.)* I can't breathe.

ROSY: Of course you can't. I said it before, Smith, and I'll say it again and I'll say it one last time—Rosy's going 'round the world. *(She releases him.)*

SMITH: *(Jumps up and grabs his luggage.)* You're crazy, lady! Keep your gazillion! *(He runs to exit.)*

(ROSY looks about until she spots the audience.)

ROSY: *(To audience.)*   Hello there. I'm Rosy with a Y. Everybody thinks it's I E, but it's a Y. It is astonishingly difficult to tell one way from the other when one is speaking. One can, however, when it is written—

(ROSY continues moving her mouth silently as the NARRATOR speaks. The LIGHTING begins to FADE.)

NARRATOR: The misfortunes of some become the fortunes of others.   Some fly off to distant ports while others grind away from day to day and nothing changes until that moment when the unexpected happens and *everything* changes. Some take comfort from the illusion of security in the complacency of their ineffectual suburban lives. Hidden in plain sight are ordinary thugs executing ordinary evils daily as ritual. Few see them of course. They are hidden in the light of the sun—in the fanciful tales from darkest suburbia.

BLACK OUT

END OF PLAY

6 FULL-LENGTH PLAYS
VOLUME TWO

Edward Crosby Wells

POET'S WAKE
monologs for the dead

SYNOPSIS: Full length, 33 characters, 14M/11F/8E, with doubling. It is possible to perform *Poet's Wake* with as few as 8 actors. That would be my preference.

We are at the wake of a Poet Laureate. Mourners come and go, delivering monologues. We learn, through the mourners, about the life of the poet and about the mourners themselves. Some define us by the people in our lives. The life of the celebrity after death is too often defined by those who are left behind. Some have axes to grind. Some speak out of ignorance. Although each may believe they are telling the truth, but it is the teller's truth—truth is subjective. The artist's work is too often overshadowed by the tales and the writings of the survivors. In the end we must discover, uncover or simply choose and decide the truth ourselves. The truth of others and the truth of oneself is, perhaps, merely a matter of perception. *Poet's Wake* might even show us a bit of truth about ourselves.

THE CHARACTERS IN ORDER OF APPEARANCE

THE UNDERTAKER
THE WIDOW
THE OTHER POET
THE BEST FRIEND
THE BORROWER
THE YOUNG FAN
THE REMORSEFUL CRITIC
THE WOMAN IN THE BLACK-RIMMED HAT
THE WOMAN WITH A PAST
THE OTHER WOMAN
THE CABBIE
THE WIDOW'S LOVER
THE PUBLISHER
THE LAWYER
THE NAVAJO GIFT-BEARER
THE SISTER
THE VOLUNTARY MOURNER
THE AGENT
THE MAN FROM THE BAR
THE FIRST WIFE
THE DAUGHTER
THE STUDENT
THE PETRIFIED FLORIST
THE EMPATHETIC MOURNER
THE CONSTANT INITIATE
THE INFREQUENT LOVER
THE INTENTIONAL WRITER
THE NOT SO VERY REVEREND
THE DISENCHANTED PRIOR NUN
THE SON
THE POET'S ANGEL
THE PLAYWRIGHT
THE CORPSE

6 FULL-LENGTH PLAYS
VOLUME TWO

Edward Crosby Wells

POET'S WAKE
monologs for the dead

Somewhere a lone casket, open. The CHARACTERS come and go. Perhaps this is a darkly somber place, a smoky cabaret, a carnival midway, the raw stage of an empty theatre, or perhaps —

THE UNDERTAKER: The terrible pain of Being diminishes the dreadful anxiety of death. They come one after the other and they each are the thing they dreaded most. They are dead. All knew they would cease to be. But nobody believed it. Take yourself, my friend. Did you envision yourself here? Did you envision yourself a corpse under the care of your kindly undertaker? Did you envision yourself laid out for all to see how there are worse things than the miseries of life? All know they could be you. And will. One day. The corpse. They take heart. Your friends. Your relatives. Your admirers. Your enemies. All who are gathered here in your name. They take heart and they depart feeling a little bit more of life. A bit of appreciation for it. And the pain of their Being is diminished. A corpse gives one pause to think. Doesn't it?

THE WIDOW: You're dead. Very. Very dead. D-E-A-D. Dead. And I'm not. I never liked you very much. No. Not as much as you led yourself to believe. If you ever believed. Who am I kidding? You never believed. *Never.* All that arrogance and yet you never did. In yourself or in anyone else for that matter.   Certainly not in me. Your wife for more years than I remember. Or care to remember. I knew you far better than you knew yourself and since I never liked myself very much. Thanks to you.   I never could trust the things I knew.   The things I believed. You always reminded me. Constantly reminded me to hate myself. I had to change you said. Repeatedly. I had to change. *Change*. From what? Into what? And why? To suit you? What about myself? You never let me show you who I was. Really was. *Am*. You never let me show you. Show me. *I am*. Look at you now. 'Though that's not you now. Is it? You're gone and I guess most of me is in there with you. Wherever *there* is. All the years. Our years. My years. In this coffin. The two of us. Move over. But don't expect a single tear from me. All dry. Brittle. Used. *Jesus*. Look at yourself. Why in hell did you have to die that way? Have you ever considered anyone other than yourself? *Damn you.*Sometimes when you draw in one of those. *Drew*. Drew in one of those deep breaths in your sleep. I'm suddenly awakened from the sound of your not breathing. I strain to hear for signs of the living coming from your side of the bed. The other side of the bed. What was I expecting? Did I ever mention love? No. Never did. It doesn't matter. It's over. No more words.

THE OTHER POET: What were we saying? You know. When we were. In the beginning. I was a poet too. Something more than just your cheerleader. You in the sun. Me in your shadow. Whatever did we find to talk about?   When we had those

preternatural dreams of immortality. Forgetting we were mortal
just long enough to launch our little ship upon the sea of
disbelief. Before some sorry bastard felt it necessary to remind
us of our folly. *Memento mori.* Before. Before then. Before
our dreams became mediocrity. Well. Mine did. You fared
pretty well. I slipped into a quiet resignation. An anesthetic for
the body. The mind. The spirit. My soul. Lost. The long slow
acceptance. The fear and the trembling that besets an age when
one can no longer move forward with the grace of a questioning
child. Nor backwards into the arms of an all-forgiving parent.
That's a bitter realization you wouldn't know anything about.
That's not fair. Of course you would. It was in your poetry. You
knew how to make us want to listen. I never figured that out.
We're all at sea. Closer to some sort of perfection? Or farther
away? Adrift? Too soon we begin to slow and grind to a halt on
unseen shoals. At some point. Still in life. We stop. Grounded.
Beached. The world stops and we take a chair and a blanket and
a soft pillow and we sit. Patiently. Two old souls. Asses gone
lazy. Mules refusing to budge. Watching. Waiting for the world
to rouse itself from sleep. To commence spinning once again.
For all the ships in all the waters to set forth upon the waves.
Driven by lusty winds. Lusting for recognition. For immortality.
Something beyond here and now. Dreams. Warmed in the sun.
There is a point. A point in life. There is a point. God damn it!
There is a point. When the sun above warms the body and the
sun below warms the heart. The spirit. And when we come to
that point we stop. *Memento mori. No.* That was never you.

That was me. *Me.* My poetry. *Mine.* All that time it was me. All in one inspired breath. Never you. I was a poet too. I have no idea who you were.

THE BEST FRIEND: It hurts something awful to see you this way. I have so few friends. Acquaintances for the most part. You were my only true friend. You were the best. My very best friend. Until we meet again I shall miss you terribly. I heard something in your voice. When I got off the phone from talking with you last week I thought about how sad you sounded. In pain. Distant. How I wish I had some magic solution. Some magic incantation that would simplify and take away all life's pains. Or maybe some kind of insight. Some wisdom. Some truth that once heard would ring bells. Open doors. Provide options. Give us choices. Free us. A truth that would brush away cobwebs from years of unknowing. A truth that would cause us to see clear to the heart of the matter. No matter what that matter might be. To see clearly the reality of the moment. At any given moment. And in that transcendental overview all the options and choices would avail themselves to the seer. To you. To me. When we are in the dark and trying to make our way through a maze of life's obstacles the only option we have is to feel our way towards freedom. Our ultimate destination. Finding freedom only in death. Listening to you on the phone last week I heard something in your voice. I heard you bumping into things and coming up against walls. I sensed feelings you did not understand. I felt your frustration. Your resignation.

One wall too many. I heard it in your voice. Listening to you I heard the voice of someone trapped. No clear vision to help you avoid the obstructions along your path. Your way. We come to relationships with baggage. You had yours. I had mine. That baggage is the past. The most difficult obstacle to overcome. But we overcame it. There were moments. There were so many moments in our friendship when we were free to have a loving relationship. Spontaneous communion. Interaction with another soul. A real friendship. I will miss that for the rest of my life. You used a gun. You used a gun to clear the path you were following. And one of those obstacles along the path was yourself. You used a gun and it killed something in me. The *you* in me. Why? My dear friend. I would rather you shot me instead. So much sadness. So much pain. I heard it in your voice.

THE BORROWER: *Sucks!* Don't it? Not bad. Really. You look good. A damn sight better than the last time I saw you. A damn sight. Is that make-up on your? You look good but. *Shit!* Did they have to use so? Don't look like yourself. Not at all like. The way they filled in the bullet hole. Don't get me wrong. You look good. Better than good. Too good maybe. For a dead man. All that make-up. Look at you. *Unnatural.* So I borrowed a couple bucks from you. I told you I'd give you a little something when I. Didn't I? I kept running into problems. You know. Maybe you don't. The old curve ball. Unexpected. Maybe you don't know what it's like to walk in other people's.

Did you ever try? At least I tried for God's sake. I could barely scrape enough together for. *I tried.* But no. It's your way or the highway. All or nothing. That's not my way. Never could figure you. *I tried.* Don't forget that. *Christ.* You got one bad mean streak. *Shit!* For a while I thought. *The man. Mister Big.* Was it worth it? Was it? Those who didn't want to be with you wanted to be you. I wanted. I know. You can't have both. But you were bigger than life. A force of nature big. *What happened?* All that make-up. *Jesus Christ!* Did you ever wonder? I mean. If you had just. I meant to. I mean I really meant to. What the hell. I guess I'll keep it. You've got no use for it *now.*

THE YOUNG FAN: You don't know me but I know all your poems by heart. Every one. Maybe not every one but most. *Some.* Certainly *some* of your poems. Were you conscious of them? They seemed channeled. Certainly inspired. Stream of consciousness. Were you in control when you were writing them? So many variables. Sometimes they take control. The muses. They must. Isn't that genius? All the unknowns. The sense of eternity balanced on a single moment in time. *Now. Then. Forever.* I know all your poems. To know one of your poems is to know all. To know you. Can you hear me? Right now? This moment? I love the one about. You know the one. I thought it was about me. Are you in there? In your poems? Or were they in you?

THE REMORSEFUL CRITIC: I'm sorry. It was my first assignment. Critic at large. I wanted to make a name for myself. That required defaming yours. Or so I thought. I had no idea what you were saying. And I didn't really care. It all sounded so strange and unimportant. *Gibberish.* How was I supposed to know? I didn't know anything about poetry. It was just a job. An assignment. I was going to be clever. And I was. I loved that review. I looked so important. I cannot read it now. I wince. I am embarrassed. I am sorry. Sometimes we need others to show us the way. Others to tell us what to like and what not to like. That's how it works. Isn't it? Who in hell would like Cummings, Ferlinghetti, Blake, Eliot or Whitman if others hadn't told us to. What is greatness? Who decides? The critic with the loudest voice? The one with the most influence? The one working for the most prestigious publication? Who decides? Who decides the literature? The plays? The poems that are taught in our schools? Who discourages young minds from deciding who's who for themselves? Could it be that educators don't teach *how* to think? But *what* to think? I'm sorry. Don't blame me. I'm not responsible. You must understand that it wasn't my fault. I'm the victim here. It's the fault of the system. Hell. I don't know what to think anymore. All I am now is sorry.

THE WOMAN IN THE BLACK-RIMMED HAT: They all came out for this one I see. What an array. The old enemies sniffing about like a pack of hyenas. How fortunate they only growl just loud enough to let you know where they are. They always show themselves at these affairs. One last deception for the melancholy living. Petty tyrants walking about with human excrement shoved deep into their collective nose. Or is it *noses?* Seeking information to decipher. To unravel the mysteries of your poetry. Especially those you wrote in Venice. *"Demons gather round/ in basic mourning-black/ lean o'er my remains/ and by their silence betray themselves."* I'd call that prophetic. Wouldn't you? What an array. All the elements gathered in celebration of a life few knew. Fewer understood. How carefully they wear their masks. Chins buried. Seldom daring to make direct eye contact for fear of having to conjure insincere tears best shed for themselves. From the shame of betraying their foul and bilious souls. *Hyenas.* They eat the dead by beginning at the rectum. Oh my god! Look at the time! *Ciao my darling. Bravo you!*

THE WOMAN WITH A PAST: *"Much of what I wrote early in my career has proven to be the seeds and reminders of futures to come. I have been repeating myself since I can remember, and learning to say what I had to say in so very many ways until I too could hear it—and move on."* Those are your words. Not mine. There comes a time. Deep inside the darkest heart. Beyond the word. Into the essence of meaning itself. Where words implode from the weight of. What? Gravity? How quickly the senses embrace the next revelation. We're like flies. You and I. Buzzing and flitting about. Waiting for the next sensation. The next time we touch. *Yes.* You touched. Deeply. *Yes.* Many times. *Yes.* You touched. *Yes and no.* You thrust yourself upon me. Deep into my trembling and anxious flesh. Wanting you. Fearing you. Not knowing what to expect. Afraid of losing myself. Losing you. *You. Yes.* You forced yourself into me and I couldn't resist. I wanted you deeper and deeper and then I didn't want you at all. I allowed you to happen and you happened. When the mere idea of you had me beside myself. I allowed you to happen. *What awareness is this?* We're like flies. You and I. Drawn to the sweet-scent of decay.

THE OTHER WOMAN: I can't look. I really don't want to. Just a body. Tell yourself it's just a body. You there. Me here. I really don't want to be here but. A body. Just a body. Oh God. Look at you. I think music thinking of you. I wasn't going to come today. Not here. Not to this place. Not now. I didn't want to see you. Not with your wife here. Not with you. You know. Dead. I wanted to remember you in feelings. In light. In the quiet of my mind. Somehow differently. Somewhere differently. Not like this. *A body. Just a body.* Not you. Not the essence of you. How could I hope to? How could I be heard by? How could I? *No.* Those days in New Mexico when we read D.H. Lawrence. Did you remember them from time to time? Those days? It was a secret ritual. Paying the desk clerk. Letting us into the backroom with the Lawrence paintings. Those the English hadn't shredded. Burned for their painted villainy. Pagans and demon-worshipers. Naturalists they were. Naked bodies dancing in a forest under a brilliant moon. Happy. Wide-eyed and happy. Weren't we? Happy? I heard new sounds that day. They came from you. We drove to that little shack of a guest house where Lawrence wrote. Where his ashes were captured in cement. One day those ashes will rise. Like the Phoenix. *Just a body.* Later. Another day. That same summer perhaps. We drove to Sitting Bull Falls. Parked at a roadside picnic area and watched *life.* You were reading *The Plumed Serpent.* Remember? You turned to me and said *I need a sign.* You wanted to know if Lawrence was inside. Had he gone into the heart of darkness? Then there were the screams of young boys coming from the water fountain over there. *Rattlesnake!* They screamed. *Rattlesnake!* They ran away and returned with sticks and rocks. A rifle in the arms of some brat's father. You ran and stood between the frightened child of a snake and the venomous mob. You begged the snake to slither away while you warned the gathering mob to retreat. You were beautiful that day. *Later.* On our way back down from the falls. *The rabbits.* It took forever going down that mountain road. I suggested we stop and pitch our tent. You were afraid of wolves and so we continued. Applying the brakes as we sputtered and stopped our way downward. There were thousands of rabbits. Some stopped. Blinded and frozen in the beams of our light. In disbelief. In the middle of the road. In the middle of the night. In the middle of the world. *Trembling.*

THE CABBIE: So I'm sittin' wid da wife readin' da paper. And there's your picture. Like a movie star. Like Stallone. De Niro. I says to da missus I know dis guy. So I'm rackin' the old noodle. Where ya know da dead guy from? Then it hits me. *Pow!* Like a steel-toed boot in da noggin. You was da fare that left da package o' papers in my cab. *Poems.* A whole pile of *poems.* So I goes to the Algonquin where I picked ya up that morning.   Da guy behind da desk sends me up and you're standin' there in your robe crying. I'd cry too. I've seen closets bigger than dat room. Hope ya didn't pay through da nose. Ya looked like a crazy man. I thought you was gonna kiss me. But I ain't into that. Nope. I ain't inta dat and I ain't inta *poems.* You'd think I was bringin' back your kidnapped baby. Or your long lost mother. *But poems?* Go figure. Three hundred and sixty-seven dollars. And fifty cents. *For poems.*   Now I don't know from poems but dat was one big tip. Every penny you could scrounge up. *For poems.* I'd of taken a thank you. Or just a couple of bucks. You know. For the missus. My niece. She writes *poems.* Maybe one day she'll end up like you. Not dead. Famous I mean. And rich. Stayin' at the Algonquin. A bigger room next time I hope. *From poems.* What a world. Only in America. I best be headin' downtown. I wonder if anybody here needs a cab? *From poems.*

THE WIDOW'S LOVER: Your wife. She never liked you very much. Men are so easily deceived. You were. You didn't know she was in love with me. Me. Another woman. She told

me she thought you knew. Did you? Is that why you shot
yourself? I'd like to think it was. What an insignificant little
man you were. And a coward. Only cowards take their own
lives. Did you think it would make you more precious? Did you
think it would ensure your place in history? Did you know your
poetry was sexist? That's right. Sexist and demeaning. There's
no place in history for a sexist poet. You'll go up in flames and
as quick as that you'll be forgotten. Who in Hell was he? She
never liked you very much. Your wife. You couldn't pleasure
her. Not as I could. Men are so insensitive to a woman's needs.
It's all in the foreplay and it begins long before the bedroom. It
begins with a gentle touch after dinner. A touch of her cheek. A
gentle hand sliding down her throat. A caressing of her breasts.
Pulling her into you. Lips pressed tightly upon lips. Tongues
exploring. Tasting. And then the sitting on the sofa. Thigh
against thigh. Touching. Caressing. Taking in the scent of her.
Foreplay. Then and only then. The slow walk into the bedroom.
The slow undressing. Until finally the bed where my tongue.
My dearly departed. Slips into the place a man takes for granted.
A husband thinks he owns. She never liked you very much.
Your wife.

THE PUBLISHER: Goodbye old friend. I read some of your
words yesterday. Last night. To get into the spirit of the
occasion. I read some of you while on my way here from your
memorial luncheon with the dreary likes of you-know-who.
She'll come to me. The one who never fails to think that it's all

about her. *For God's sake. You know the one.* The one in the end who will forget about you. *The poet.* I hear it will be cremation. Beware old friend. It's against the natural order. Going up in flames. The safer route is to slowly drift away. Unnoticed. Into the organic order of Nature's poetry. I hear the grinding of the presses. I smell the ink. You wouldn't let me edit a word of your primordial poetry. Every word had a price. But you paid. You paid dearly for the privilege. Did you know it was a privilege? You stopped a few moments in time. I'll give you that. Your poetry seemed to ignite the best. The worst. *Something else.* You began to sound like your poetry. You became your poetry. You took extremes in such a way and bent them till they were conjoined. Neither could exist without the other. You and your poetry. What had first seemed linear and distant now spun and wove its mystery into sonnets and quatrains. All that distance in a flash. A heartbeat. *What black art is this?*

THE LAWYER: Hello my friend. Thought you'd like to know I'm finally retiring. It's time. You look good. For a man who's dead. When my time comes I hope I look half as good. Well. Maybe three quarters as good. You were a funny man. I don't think most saw that side of you. You were so busy being the poet you rarely showed yourself as the man you were. They may not remember the man quite so well. Just the poet. My friend. Much of the man you were and the good you did remained unseen. To most. But I held your hand through so many tears.

Didn't I? It was a rough road sometimes. Wasn't it? The divorce of your first wife. I don't mind telling you I thought that was a mistake. It was an easy settlement. Amicable. A rare divorce. She wanted to give you everything and you wanted to give her everything. I think it was a mistake. The divorce. Any regrets? She's here. Standing by the guest book. Writing something. I wonder if she ever remarried. She was definitely my cup of tea. Maybe I'll stroll on over after awhile. Give my condolences. The student at NYU who accused you of rape. She said it was right after your lecture. That you had asked her to your room at the Algonquin where you raped her. I've no doubt it was a horrible seven months for you. Waiting for the trial. Being shunned. The vicious news accounts. You thought you'd never recover. I thought you were going to kill yourself then. Brown and Regis cancelled your lectures. No bookings came in. When we finally did go to trial we showed her for the liar she was. She thought she could make an easy buck. Maybe make herself famous. From a poet? .That's a laugh. So much to mend after you've been wrongly accused. I never would have completely gotten over it. Forgiven her. Did you? I see your son is out of prison. There was no way I could have won that case. Someone could have died in the fire. He seemed proud of setting it. He admitted it. Said he'd do it again. I never understood that boy. Good Catholic upbringing and all. I only took the case because he was your son. Not my cup of tea. Maybe now he'll get his life together. He's here too. Over there. Next to his mother and sister. Your poor daughter. Still in that home. I recall so much of your life as a man. I never read one of your poems. Not my cup of tea. I think I'll go over and say hello to the family. *Give my condolences.*

THE NAVAJO GIFT-BEARER: *Yá'át'ééh.* Hello. Nineteen hundred and twenty-four. Taos. New Mexico. A letter from David Herbert Lawrence to my great grandmother. Handwritten. It belongs to you. To take on your voyage. To take with you as your spirit rises upon the fiery blaze. I have been holding it for you. For generations we have been holding it for you. If anybody should have it. It is you. Not some airless archive. In this letter Mr. Lawrence thanked my great grandmother for the kindness she bestowed upon him while he was visiting her pueblo. I never knew what that kindness was. I don't think anybody did. It was her secret. He thanked her for sharing and ended with *"I will remember you with every gentle breeze and with every drop of rain."* I am told this letter was her most precious possession. And now it is yours. *Here.* Let it go up in flames with you. Our spirits have touched many times. I saw you once at the university in Albuquerque. You were reading from *Pueblo Poems.* Naturally I had to be there. You autographed my copy.

Weightless sparks of light/ soaring dreams through silent air/ night flight and prayers.

It is my greatest treasure. Perhaps one I shall take with me when it is time for my voyage into the sky.

Silently he sleeps/ dreaming of the moon and stars/ awake she sees clouds.

You spoke in great length about Mr. Lawrence. You said you had just come from visiting the place where his ashes are imprisoned in a block of cement in Taos. And you told us a story about your adventure in Sitting Bull Falls. Thank you for coming to the land of enchantment. And thank you for *Pueblo Poems.*

There is no god he cries/ into his midlife morning/ then prays for an answer.
I need to fly back to New Mexico tonight. I will remember you with every gentle breeze and with every drop of rain. I wish you a safe journey. *Héógoóne'.* Goodbye. *(He put the letter into the coffin.)*

THE SISTER: Earlier today I was trying to remember the last time I saw you. You came home after giving a reading at Vassar. I think. Maybe it was after that. So many flowers. There is nothing that smells more like death than flowers. Odd. Isn't it? Something so beautiful. So filled with life. When I walked in here and the scent caught me I became a child. I thought of mother. Lying there. White skin. Smooth. Cold. My lips on her cheek. Smelling like the flowers that surrounded her. I could not make out the scent of a single flower. Just the single scent of the combination. The odor of death. Sweet. Pungent.

Like now.   Once you've been there you never forget.   Pass a florist shop and for a moment you're back watching a loved one laid to rest.   Voiceless.   Never to be heard from again.   You captured it all so well in *The Age of Matricide* collection.   That won't be your fate.   You've all those books of poetry.   Speaking for you.   Whispering your presence for years to come.   I liked having you for a brother.   You were kind and considerate.   Not to everyone.   That's for sure.   But you were always kind to me.   Always.   I shall miss you.   I shall miss you reading me Proust.   Proust's cookie.   Remember?   We laughed way into the night thinking of things to touch.   To smell.   To hear.   To taste.   Like Proust's cookie.   Remember?   One bite and we were transported.   Like Proust.   Going on for a hundred pages triggered only by the taste of a madeleine.   When I walked in and smelled the flowers.   I half expected to see mother lying here.   Not you.   Not my brother.   I shall miss you reading me Proust.   I shall miss you.   I think it was when you came upstate to do a reading at Vassar.   When did I last see you?   I can't remember.

THE VOLUNTARY MOURNER: Asparagus.   Broccoli.   Mushrooms.   A poet.   A poet laureate.   Laureate.   Carrots.   What's a laureate?   Must be something big.   Salmon.   Look at the people here.   I go to two or three funerals a week.   And a few wakes a month.   Turkey.   Smoked and not smoked.   I like not-smoked better.   Salad and all kinds of little sandwiches.   So many choices.   One could die of starvation just trying to make a choice.   One can't eat everything.   Not at once.   Some try.   But it only leads to rejection by society and then to an early death. What's that? You were in the paper. Open house. Light refreshments. Open bar. Hot stuff. Poet laureate. La-de-da. Roast beef. Deviled eggs with caviar. Posh. I wonder if there's anybody famous here? Besides you. Check the guest book. Lots of old people. Lots of funerals and wakes. Beans. Green and Baked. Lettuce. Nice digs. Rolls. Cold cuts. Cake. Chocolate. Lemon. Hey. Nice chatting. Laureate. Catch you later. *Double fudge chocolate cake.*

THE AGENT: Oh, darling, look at yourself. I heard about it on my way to London. I read about it in *The Times.* Your death. So sad. I was devastated. *Totally.* Venice has a chill to the air this time of the year. Any time of the year really. But it remains *old world. Old world* has its charm they say. I say it is a necessary remedy for what ails.   One develops a sense for history. Becomes part of history. You already are. Aren't you? But one can't get good old fish and chips in Venice. Not for all the Euros on Earth. *Venice.* The whole damn place is sinking. Who cares? It's charming! It's History. Eventually history sinks. The canals with their arched bridges. Expensive rides in gondolas. Urban life deafens us to repetitive sounds. The hustle and the bustle of commerce. Even to the sounds of ourselves. Nobody has time anymore. Few know to reach out and take it. Time. *Boom. Boom. Boom.* Next thing you know it's the old ticker. Weak kidneys. Black lungs. Green liver. Or *ka-bam!* It's a bus. Sometimes my dear friend it's *suicide.* That's a cruel way to go.

Why? Why did you take that way out? How did the world fail you? You should have gone back to Venice. Darling.

THE MAN FROM THE BAR: Remember me? I was the man from the bar. In the shadows. A small table. Away from the glare. The afternoon. You walked in. Ordered a Margarita. Remember me? Hot day. Dark. Cool inside. I was also having a Margarita. Everyone else was drinking beer. That's what brought you to my attention. The Margarita. Our shared taste. Well. More than that. I thought you were the most gorgeous man I'd ever seen. I sent you a drink. You came to my table. We talked. I desired. *Oh God.* I was shivering with desire. The constant erection. What would you be like in bed? Did you know I was *that way?* Did you feel just a small bit of my longing? We talked and talked. I heard your magic. Your words lifted me into worlds I never knew existed. Your words became me. About me. You took me to Heaven and sex became trivial that afternoon in the shadows. Remember me? *The dark-eyed pagan. The savage in a godless world. Reckless. Beating his drum. Swimming against the current.* That's what you said. It was your way of saying you knew. Of saying it was all right. I told you how I preferred thinking myself a part of Nature's design. A part of the weave. The fabric. The garment itself. Years later I would read my words in one of your poems. "The Man from the Bar." I knew it was about me. What was that funny business about trinities? Something about everything coming in threes. Not the seasons I said. Yes you said. Summer is life you

said. Winter is death you said. And the space between the two
makes three. The anticipation of life or the anticipation of death
share the same space. We drank and laughed the afternoon into
sunset. Talking of *what?* I will remember you. The joy. The
laughter. The honeyed taste of Heaven. The poem you wrote for
me. The stranger. Remember me. *Please.* Remember me. *The
man from the bar.*

THE FIRST WIFE: Hello love. I've missed you. All these
years. I've thought about you. Often. What actually happened?
I thought you were. Well. You know. I never thought. I mean
you were a poet. That didn't seem manly. At the time. 'Though
you were great sex. The best. Uninhibited. Wild. God how I
miss it. You. Your love. The feeling of being in love. Love
stops time. Doesn't it? Yes. We are suspended in it. By it. I
wonder. Did you ever think of me? Through all these years?
Ever? I'm so sorry. I was young. Forgive me. I've gone
through two more after you. Can you imagine that? Of course
you can. You warned me. I just stayed too young. Too long.
The last one. I'm still with the last one. Nowhere to go. Where
does an old woman go when there's nowhere to go? Where?
The truth is I love my husband. I don't know why. He's seldom
there. I don't want anything bad for him. I just want something
good for me. He drinks his vodka and I watch him disappear
with the unwinding of the day. There. In his chair
watching the early news he begins to nod off and I am.

Alone. That's no way to be when you're married. That's no way to be. Alone. Week to week to week and life passes like untouchable scenery outside a train's window. Why did you shoot yourself? Were you alone too? Did you cry yourself to sleep? Did you spend year after year waiting for someone to love you? For someone to love. Someone in your life who remains in your life and doesn't disappear during the six o'clock news. All that waiting. Too late now. The woman in the mirror can only wait for it all to be over. Was it like that for you? God! You were great sex. I'm so sorry. I was young. Forgive me. I don't want to wait anymore. Alone. I'm so tired. I need. I need to get my hands on a gun.

THE DAUGHTER: Daddy. I miss you. They told me you were dead. *Yes.* I know what dead means. There was a spider in the bathtub this morning. *Yes.* A very little spider. *Yes.* I took my medication. I haven't gone crazy in a long time. Listen to me. *Please.* There was a spider in the bathtub. I saw it. I did. The nurse doesn't always believe me but it was a spider all right. I watched it float down along its thread. Unseen. Not invisible. I knew it had to be there. Nothing is invisible. You taught me that. *Yes.* There are the things we see and the things we do not see. You know where it landed? It landed right on my sponge and then it ran right back up. Gathering the unseen with it. It kept an eye on me. *Yes.* It did. I could see its two little black eyes looking at me. *Me.* The crazy woman. That's what they call me there. In that place. The home. Stinks of urine. *Yes.* It does. Ever so carefully the spider lowered himself again and stood there on the sponge watching me. I washed myself very carefully with only my hands. *Yes.* I did. Slowly I stepped out of the tub and pulled the plug while keeping an eye on my friend. *Yes.* He was my friend and I didn't want him to drown. *Yes.* I didn't want my friend to go down the drain. And drown. Like me. *Yes.* So I kept an eye on my tiny friend and watched. Just watched. *Yes.* Just watched. Daddy. I wonder if my friend felt as pleased as me? I wish I could have shared my joy with him. With you. *Yes.* It was joy. I know it was. Joy from knowing I was doing my best. You always told me to do my best. *Yes.* The *best* you said. You'll know it when you do it. You said. The best is having the right response to the situation. You said. *Yes.* I had the right response. Didn't I? *Daddy. Didn't I?* .You know what? My friend trusted me and that scared me. I gave him good reason to trust me. Daddy. He really trusted me and it scared me. *Yes.* You know what else you used to say? You used to say *with trust comes terrible responsibility. Yes.* Yes you did. I'm afraid. *Afraid.* I miss you. Daddy. I know you're dead. Daddy. I know what dead means.

THE STUDENT: You ruined my life you smug son of a bitch. You laughed at me when I read my poem. *Me.* In front of *everyone.* I was an "A" student. Everyone knew I was the best. I had a future. But right there in the lecture hall you laughed at me. Humiliated me. Murdered me. Did you know it was me who arranged your visit? Not everyone wanted you. They said you were too traditional. A throwback. Ancient history. I had to deal with that crazy agent of yours. She didn't make it easy but I wanted you. *Poet Laureate.* You laughed at me and said my poem lacked intent. Said it reminded you of Frankenstein. Too many parts exhumed from other poets. *Exhumed.* You ruined my life right there in front of *everyone* and I never wrote another poem since. Not one. Do you know what I do now? *Huh?* Do you care what I do now because of you? I teach middle school English. Reduced to middle school English. I wish it had been me. I wish it had been *my* finger on that trigger. Pulling it. Watching the bullet enter your head. Watching you die. I would have loved that. It would have given me *pleasure.* Maybe then I could have *exhumed* the life you took.

THE PETRIFIED FLORIST: Oh my!   What horticultural nightmare have we here? I did my best to mix my magnificent flower arrangements in with this god-awful mish mash. Mercy. The taste of a Puerto Rican drag queen. Who in their right mind mixes tulips with snapdragons and baby's breath? The nerve of some people. They look more like sympathy flowers from an Ukrainian wedding. And they call themselves florists. Florists my ass! Butchers and piñata makers! Oh my nerves. Lilies. Tulips.   Gladiolus.   And sun flowers.   Is that mad queen demented or what? The lavender standing spray is nice. The bitch ripped me off. That standing lavender is one of my signature sympathy arrangements. Though it does work well at commitment ceremonies. Some florists have no shame. *I know.* They'll rob you blind. Oh my god! Take a gander at that standing cross with red and white roses. How *passé* is that? Let me get out my tambourine and love beads. Compare it to my lily and eucalyptus standing spray. Now that pops. Be still my heart. Or my full flower wreath. How fabulous is that? *Hmmm.* Alstroemerias. Delphiniums. Hydrangeas. Ferns. Daisies and bamboo penis-looking things. Leftovers from a Chinese lesbian orgy if you ask me. How about that bleeding open heart standing spray? Or that white rose topiary sympathy basket? *Oh my nerves.* Give this girl a break! Was somebody inspired by dog shit? It petrifies me to think how little talent there is in the flower biz. Well. Thank God there's me. Oh look there. Carnations and pansies. Who'd have thunk it? All these people in mourning. All these dying flowers. They look embalmed. And I don't mean just the flowers. You've got some real tight ass friends sweetie. This party needs a little life! Potted plants would do the trick. Potted carnivorous plants. *Mon Dieu!* Carnivores would be just too perfect. An arrangement for every occasion. Pitcher plants with their pool of digestive juices mixed in with ferns and snapdragons. Baby showers. Or bachelor parties. Flypaper traps that force their prey to stick to them till they are slowly devoured. Oh my nerves. Definitely a wedding arrangement. Bladder plants that suck their prey into a deadly vacuum. Sounds like my first lover. I think I should add a bit of plumage to that. Peacock feathers maybe. The Venus Flytrap. My favorite. It lies in wait till the victim brushes up against it. Then. Snap! Like a drag queen in heat it snatches its prey. *Yup.* The death pot. How divine is that? Top that you uninspired horticultural bitches. Happy trails. Darling.

THE EMPATHETIC MOURNER: You were supposed to read at The Poetry Center at the Y from your new collection. *The Age of Matricide.* It was your best. Painful. Honest. I came into the city just to see you. Hear you read. I took the train. All the way from Albany to uptown Manhattan. I'd planned it for months. You didn't show. Your capriciousness preceded you. But still I was surprised. Disappointed. How could you do such a thing? Later I learned you had a temper tantrum at the Algonquin. With the desk clerk. And you couldn't see yourself clear to attend. We waited. And waited. I was devastated. I cried all the way back to Albany. Years later I read somewhere that you were bi-polar. *The American Poetry Review* or maybe it was *The Yale Review.* I can't remember. But I read that you were bi-polar. Suddenly I understood your tantrum. The depressions. The undermining of the Self. The sudden outbursts. The violence. The quick withdrawal. The passionate hating. The passionate loving. The overwhelming tenderness. The vicious uncaring. The beautiful outpouring of the soul. The endless hours in bed. The reaching out to others. The withdrawal. The heart-stopping beauty of your poetry. Your art.

And now that alone explains the suicide. Look at you. Finally I see you in person. I shall take your image back to Albany. For all time. I would not have missed this for all the world. We're so much alike. You and me. We are bound by our disease.

THE INFREQUENT LOVER: I don't know what to say. I thought I would be the first to go. You would come round every so often. Never often enough. Walk into my life as though you'd never been gone. Months. Sometimes years between visits. Walk into my room. Erect. Wordlessly. Enter me. Make love. And then we'd talk. And then we'd touch. Really touch. And the words would flow. I know when words ring true. And I know when words come from the heart. And I know how it feels to be touched by another soul. You touched me. And I know how you felt. How it feels. Everything changes after the moment we take a good hard look at our lives. After we've seen it. Our lives. In the very next moment everything is changed. The light is a little brighter and the load is a little lighter. And once we've shared that moment a greater good begins to flow between souls no longer burdened with a sense of isolation. That is how you felt. My infrequent lover. You touched me with your beauty and I became more beautiful. I became more Human from the bit of Humanity you left within. I don't know what to say. I thought I would be the first to go. I thought I would see you again. And here you are.

THE CONSTANT INITIATE: What in hell is all this? The

working toward? The dreaming of? The wishing for? The desires? The shaking of hands? The "how do you dos?" and the "I love yous?" You think of those. You think you've been a liar all your life. Whose thoughts are you thinking now? *Liar.* All your life. Sorry but I seem to be thinking of me. You're dead and I'm here and as usual I'm thinking of me. Whose words are these? That's where it starts you know. When it starts. It starts with words drummed into our skulls until we learn to say "da-da" and "ma-ma." Not long before we say "screw you!" and we move out of the house and onto the streets. Where you found me and treated me to dinner. To some comfort. And a copy of your poems. *Ways to Hear.* Tell me something I haven't heard before. I bet you can't. Let me tell you something. Did you know that bodies litter the streets where they rot and die because of words? Did you know that all the wars that ever were began with words? Did you know that all the pain in all the world began with words? They define us. Confine us. Kill us. Imagine a mute planet. A silent planet. Who spoke the first words? The first expression? Why do we repeat them? Over and over. They aren't our words or our thoughts. They're hand-me-downs from generation to generation. *Thief.* You're a thief just like me. So don't lie there dead pretending you don't understand. You feel its truth. We are connected. You and me. I can't get you out of my brain. Your poetry taught me to think. Oh well. It doesn't really matter. *Does it?* Thinking is highly overrated.

THE INTENTIONAL WRITER: *"At the moment I am trying*

to write something. Finish something. I can't seem to muster the passion and I'm not the biggest fan of my writing right now. Nor of myself. I'm filled with doubt and questions concerning a need for honesty. What seems honest one day seems pretense the next. It is a confusion of great distraction. I am between two worlds and without footing in either. Perhaps this is where it ends. Without Knowledge. Without Truth. Only the intentional decisions we make from word to word. From moment to moment." You wrote me those words on a postcard from Mexico shortly before. Before. Where's the euphemism when you need one? Before. *Demise?* No. That's not it. I might as well say *before you blew your fucking head off!* As a fellow writer I understand how those doubts can lead to. Well. You know. Your transitioning. Your *euphemism.* I want to believe. I want to believe there's more. Something beyond here. Beyond now. If there isn't something more then what's the use? What's the sense of it all? Why care? Why not join the rabble? Forget the concept of responsibility. Become the anti-existentialist. Live with reckless abandon without regard to consequences. Has spending the better part of a life to create literature been a fool's occupation? Trying to create immortality. To leave a piece of the soul in one's work. A piece that will come to life in another's mind after you're long gone. Just in case. Just in case there's nothing beyond what we create here in life. Is that the closest one can get to immortality? Perhaps we do move from moment to moment without knowledge. Only the illusion of knowledge. The acceptance of it. Without truth. Only the lies we convince

ourselves to believe through the ignorance of faith.   From
moment to moment with only words to verify an existence.
When the words stop does the intentional writer?   Have you
gone to another plane?   Have you transitioned?   Or is it all just
another euphemism for non-existence?   For no longer being.

THE NOT SO VERY REVEREND: We were here in town for
a meeting with the Cardinal when the news of your death
reached us.   Nothing left to say after you've been
excommunicated.   What did you think you were doing?   You
came to Rome and you attacked the Church.   Deliberate and
premeditated.   Not only with your blasphemous poetry.   But with
the venom you spewed in the evil agenda of your lecture.
Paganism.   Hedonism.   The philosophy of D. H. Lawrence.
Henry David Thoreau.   Vile Humanism.   It has no place in the
Church.   You have no place.   You were warned.   And suicide.
We take pity on your soul.   But we cannot save it.   God is not
simply an animating spirit.   Although He is within every human
being He is not merely the sum total of every human being.
Your ideas are the devil's ideas.   Your poetry may be popular in
certain academic circles.   But it is corrupting our youth.
Damning them for all eternity.   It is fitting that the death you
chose was delivered by your own hands.   Perhaps that one last
act will put a damper on your influence.   Just one last look upon
the evil that is you before returning to Rome.   It is saddening to
know your soul will suffer the pains of Hell for all eternity.   To
know there is no redemption.   No absolution.   No prayers that

will save you.   Was your poetry worth the price you paid?   *In Nomine Patris, et Filii, et Spiritus Sancti. Amen.*

THE DISENCHANTED PRIOR NUN: I did it. You told me I would and I did. No longer a bride of Jesus. Not so much a divorce as it was an annulment. Well. After all those years of conditioning one never really walks away without some lingering residue. One can never really shake oneself free of it. But I did leave the convent. And the Church. You told me I would. You knew I was trapped in a lie. I became a nun because it was what everybody expected of me. My parents. Mother Rosa. All the nuns who taught at our school. So I began to expect it of myself. I didn't want to disappoint anybody. I needed their approval. I needed everybody's approval. I never heard voices. Got the call or anything like that. It just seemed the next logical step. But I knew I was lying. From the day I entered the convent. I knew. And you knew. You knew back in high school when you begged me not to go. I didn't listen. I'm sorry. Those are the most dreaded lies of all. The lies we tell ourselves. And the guilt. All those years of guilt. For what? Approval? Someone to tell me I was. *What? Who?* Anyway. Here I am. You'd be proud of me.   One more disenchanted Catholic.

THE SON: Hello. Dad. Mother made me come. It wasn't my idea. I said I didn't ever want to see you again. Not for as long as you lived. It worked out that way. Didn't it? So here I am. I thought about this day. Often. I thought about how much I hated you. Often. But I don't. Not anymore. I don't hate you. I'm tired of all the hate. I was only hating myself. Any day now. I am older now than you were the last time I saw you. Any day now I will forgive myself. Any day. God says very little nowadays. Not so judgmental. That's for sure. God moves with the Self that moves through us all. I understand that now. I guess you would approve of that. My understanding. I'm sorry. I'm tired of all the hate. Sometimes when I think I am hearing God, I am hearing the best within me. Sometimes I think it is you. Mother made me come. It wasn't my idea. But then you know that. After I left the seminary I lived with my sister for awhile. Before she had her breakdown. Before she. I haven't seen her in many years. Until today. She didn't recognize me. Mother said she's doing better. That she'll be home for a couple days. Any day now. She didn't recognize me. I don't suppose I would have either. She seems to have gotten worse. Mother has her for a couple days. But you already know that. And then she'll need to go back. She'll die there. In that home. I read some of your books. Your poems. I realized I never knew you. When I got out of prison I thought of coming to visit you. I did. I truly did. But I couldn't. Do you know to this day I'm not allowed within five-hundred feet of an abortion clinic? Did you know that? Did mother tell you? God says very little nowadays. Hell is the distance between father and son. I was in Hell. Were you?

THE POET'S ANGEL: You were eleven.   The age of matricide. You said. Or so you thought. I tried to change your mind. To tell you it wasn't your fault. But you would have none of it. You believed it was. Right up till the other day. When you pulled the trigger. You believed. *Do you see the light?* Your mother. I know you wanted her out of your life. Those times you were rescued by a neighbor from having her hold your head along with her own in the oven with all the gas jets open. I was that neighbor. Or the time when she held you in a death grip in her arms while the two of you lay on the railroad tracks for the next oncoming train. You broke free and called upon a stranger's kindness to help drag her from the tracks. I was that stranger. *Do you see the light?* That day you sensed something different. The day of matricide. Everything went quiet and you felt the silence. Yes. This time it was different. This time the urgency of the drama was calmed by carefully calculated intent. You knew. You knew before she fully realized that this would be her time. I knew because I am your angel. This would be the time that she would succeed in causing her own death. This time you would not be going with her. This time you would not try to save her. Enough was enough. *Matricide? Do you see the light?* Your mother's bedroom was dark. She was under the cover of a pink chenille bedspread. The shades had been lowered to keep the bright Indian summer day from slipping into her bedroom and reminding her that life was worth living. That death was worth re-thinking. That depression was transitory. Shafts of sunlight were abuzz with those fine bits of dust and creation that float in the light of the heated air. They bent over the dresser with the clear crystal perfume bottles setting on an oval mirrored tray. The shafts of sunlight spread over bookshelves that were crowded with books she always initialed in green ink and dated after reading. Sunlight bent into the corners of the pink painted walls and bounced from off Jesus crucified. You were eleven. The age of matricide. *Do you see the light?* You crawled into bed next to her and went to sleep. When you awoke the shaft of light had moved several more feet away from Jesus crucified. You got out of bed and noticed that while you were sleeping she had written several pages and had placed them on the nightstand next to empty containers of sleeping pills. You didn't need to read what she had written to know what she had done. You knew. You knew because you had been there many times before. But this time you would let her will be done. It was I who watched as her will was done. *Do you see the light?*

THE PLAYWRIGHT: My play is almost complete. It's about you. All about you. You invented and re-invented and became your own creation. Yet in the end you came full circle and you became who you always were. Who you were meant to be. Who your already were when you first entered this world. Nothing changes but points of view and the words we use to describe what we are seeing. Perhaps I've taken some artistic liberties here and there. It never was intended to be the story of your life. It was the spirit of you I was trying to record. The soul of you I sought to capture. All else is history. All else dies with the man. My play is almost complete. I followed your life very carefully. Sometimes not understanding you. Sometimes believing I did. Who am I kidding? Most times not understanding you. I don't think you did either. Of course not. Who does? But with you it is in your poetry. Your spirit. Your soul. Your life. All that searching. Always the searching. Seeking to understand. So much more important than seeking to be understood. You could never be understood. Least of all to yourself. My play is almost complete. Did you find any wisdom along the way? I think you did. Did you apply it? I don't know. Did you? In writing your life as a play I found myself writing my own. I found myself looking for me while searching for you. When I started out on the road to chronicle the life and times of the poet I found the road leading right back to me. Back to something essential. Back to a shared sense of being. A commonality. A universality. My play is almost complete. Your poetry goes on. That was your life's struggle. Wasn't it? To create something in life that would live beyond your life. Will my play live beyond my own? Is that the only immortality? The best one can hope for? Oh well. A few more finishing touches and my play will be complete. I will be complete. And I will go on. Will you? Will anyone ever know why you did it? Why you picked up the and shot yourself. Maybe we'll never know why. Did you?

THE CORPSE: At last. Out of this coffin. Beyond the wall. The mortar and bricks of life. Unbound. At last. Where is it? I don't see it. The life. The man. The poet. Who died here? At last. Was it really suicide? Or was a murder committed here? What have I done? We're caretakers of sorts. Aren't we? Our body. Our planet. Have I betrayed a sacred trust? At last.

THE BEST FRIEND: So much sadness.   So much pain.   I heard it in your voice.

THE WIDOW: I never liked you very much.   No.   Not as much as you led yourself to believe.   Who am I kidding?   You never believed. *Never.*

THE CORPSE: *I believed.*   But there's really not much left to say when you're dead.   Is there?   I've spent my life living in words.   In poetry.   I think I ceased to exist long before the main event.   The bullet that ended my so-called life.   Right into the skull.   Right here.   I didn't feel a thing.   Except remorse.   At last. And that came too late.   The bullet had already begun its journey. Although one could argue that the bullet was triggered more than half a century ago.

THE STUDENT: I wish it had been *my* finger on that trigger. Pulling it.   Watching the bullet enter your head.   Watching you die.   I would have loved that.   It would have given me *pleasure.* Maybe then I could have *exhumed* the life you took.

THE FIRST WIFE: Week to week to week and life passes by like untouchable scenery outside a train's window.

THE OTHER POET: We're all at sea. Closer to some sort of perfection? Or farther away? Adrift? Too soon we begin to slow and grind to a halt on unseen shoals. At some point. Still in life. We stop.

THE CORPSE: Somewhere I stopped. I became a spectator. I wanted to know. I wanted to be in control. But I was afraid of the responsibility. I was afraid that I might have discovered that I *was* God. *Oh God.* I just wanted to touch the soul of another. I wanted to know. *God.* I wanted to know God.

THE WOMAN IN THE BLACK-RIMMED HAT: All the elements gathered in celebration to a life few knew. Fewer understood. How carefully they wear their masks.

THE WIDOW'S LOVER: You'll go up in flames and as quick as that you'll be forgotten. Who in Hell was he?

THE VOLUNTARY MOURNER: So many choices. One could die of starvation just trying to make a choice.

THE BORROWER: Those who didn't want to be with you wanted to be you. But you were bigger than life. A force of nature big. *What happened?*

THE CORPSE: I was a spectator for the most part. Perhaps in youth there were a few moments when I actually did "live." Before the self-consciousness came. When I was unconsciously a part of the natural order. When I was not preoccupied with Self. Not myself. *The* Self. The realm of the poet. I could never get anyone to understand that. I really cared about the world outside myself. I cared! I cared about the people in the world outside myself. But I was a poet. I had to go within to find the Human thread that held us all together. The universal thread of Self. The collective spirit of Humanity. That Self that is all selves. Where we are One. And the One is God.

THE NOT SO VERY REVEREND: *In Nomine Patris, et Filii, et Spiritus Sancti.*

THE CONSTANT INITIATE: So don't lie there dead pretending you don't understand. You feel its truth. We are connected. You and me. I can't get you out of my brain. Your poetry taught me to think.

THE PUBLISHER: The safer route is to slowly drift away. Unnoticed. Into the organic order of Nature's poetry.

THE EMPATHETIC MOURNER: Look at you. Finally I see you in person. I shall take your image back to Albany. For all time. I would not have missed this for all the world. We're so much alike. You and me. We are bound by our disease.

THE AGENT: One develops a sense for history. Becomes part of history. You already are. Aren't you?

THE CABBIE: *From poems.* What a world.

THE REMORSEFUL CRITIC: Sometimes we need others to show us the way. Others to tell us what to like and what not to like.

THE DAUGHTER: You used to say with *trust comes terrible responsibility. Yes.* Yes you did. I'm afraid. *Afraid.* I miss you. Daddy. I know you're dead. Daddy. I know what dead is.

THE CORPSE: I loved! I loved deeply. I loved within myself. The best kind of self-love embraces all Humanity. *Please.* Tell me it's not a delusion. Tell me I didn't waste a life. Tell me I did something worthwhile. Something. *Anything.* Don't let it be for naught. Suicide? I didn't take my life. I took the life of the poet. Not me. .I didn't want to die. I never wanted to die. The poet had taken my life long ago. I didn't enjoy life after that. How could I? I didn't have a life to enjoy. I lived in words. Words. Just words. I was on paper. I was in books. I was on the tongues of others. It wasn't my life I took. I murdered the thing that robbed me of life long before the bullet that ended the poet.

THE MAN FROM THE BAR: Your words lifted me into worlds I never knew existed. Your words became me. About me. You took me to Heaven and sex became trivial that afternoon in the shadows.

THE YOUNG FAN: Sometimes they take control of you. The muses. Don't they? They must. Isn't that genius?

THE PETRIFIED FLORIST: All these people in mourning. All these dying flowers.

THE WOMAN WITH A PAST: How quickly the senses embrace the next revelation. We're like flies. You and I. Buzzing and flitting about. Waiting for the next sensation. The next time we touch.

THE OTHER WOMAN: I heard new sounds that day. They came from you. You were beautiful that day. In the middle of the road. In the middle of the night. In the middle of the world. *Trembling.*

THE INTENTIONAL WRITER: *Perhaps this is where it ends. Without Knowledge. Without Truth. Only the intentional decisions we make from word to word. From moment to moment.*

THE SISTER: I shall miss you reading me Proust.

THE LAWYER: I recall so much of your life as a man. I never read one of your poems. Not my cup of tea.

THE CORPSE: A man is more than what he does. He is also why he does what he does. What he thinks. What he feels. I await a revelation. Wisdom comes through revelation. *Revelation.* I thought how exquisite it would be to live in a world of my own making. To be my own creation. To create hand in hand with God. To really have free will. Free choice. To exercise it. To build upon what God had already created. But then I did. Didn't I? I know now that I could have chosen to live a fuller life. I know now that I could have mustered the strength of my convictions. The advice I gave others. The songs I sang through my poetry. I know that I should have. *Could.* Had I another chance. *Revelation.* There's small salvation there. At last. Ironic. Isn't it?

THE INFREQUENT LOVER: You touched me with your beauty and I became more beautiful.

THE SON: God says very little nowadays.

THE NAVAJO GIFT-BEARER: I will remember you with every gentle breeze and with every drop of rain. I wish you a safe journey. *Héógoóne'.*

THE PLAYWRIGHT: Nothing changes but points of view and the words we use to describe them.

THE POET'S ANGEL: It was written long ago. The light. *Do you see the light?*

THE CORPSE: There must be something better. But I don't see it. Where is the light? God. I dedicated my poetry and my life to you.

THE UNDERTAKER: The terrible pain of Being diminishes the dreadful anxiety of death. All knew they would cease to be. But nobody believed it.

THE CORPSE: I don't see the light. Oh God. Help me. I don't know why I did it. It just seemed the right time to do it. To pull the trigger. I don't see any light. *Do you?*

END OF PLAY

6 FULL-LENGTH PLAYS
VOLUME TWO   Edward Crosby Wells

E. C. W. 2020
Denver Colorado

edwardcrosbywells@yahoo.com

Printed in Great Britain
by Amazon